Other Books by Lesley Krueger

Short Stories

Hard Travel

Novels

Poor Player

Drink the Sky

Non-fiction

Foreign Correspondences: A Traveller's Tales

THE CORNER GARDEN

LESLEY KRUEGER

PENGUIN
CANADA

PENGUIN CANADA

Published by the Penguin Group

Penguin Books, a division of Pearson Canada, 10 Alcorn Avenue, Toronto, Ontario,
Canada M4V 3B2

Penguin Books Ltd, 80 Strand, London WC2R 0RL, England

Penguin Putnam Inc., 375 Hudson Street, New York, New York 10014, U.S.A.

Penguin Books Australia Ltd, 250 Camberwell Road, Camberwell, Victoria 3124, Australia

Penguin Books India (P) Ltd, 11, Community Centre, Panchsheel Park,
New Delhi – 110 017, India

Penguin Books (NZ) Ltd, cnr Rosedale and Airborne Roads, Albany, Auckland 1310,
New Zealand

Penguin Books (South Africa) (Pty) Ltd, 24 Sturdee Avenue, Rosebank 2196, South Africa

Penguin Books Ltd, Registered Offices: 80 Strand, London WC2R 0RL, England

First published 2003

1 3 5 7 9 10 8 6 4 2

Author representation: Westwood Creative Artists
94 Harbord Street, Toronto, Ontario M5S 1G6

Manufactured in Canada.

NATIONAL LIBRARY OF CANADA CATALOGUING IN PUBLICATION

Krueger, Lesley
The corner garden / Lesley Krueger.

ISBN 0-14-301273-8

I. Title.

PS8571.R786C67 2003   C813'.54   C2003-900006-0
PR9199.3.K76C67 2003

Visit Penguin Books' website at **www.penguin.ca**

In memory of Sharon Stevenson

You must live with your knowledge.
Way back, beyond, outside of you are others,
In moonless absences you never heard of,
    Who have certainly heard of you,
Beings of unknown number and gender:
    And they do not like you.

    What have you done to them?
Nothing? Nothing is not an answer:
You will come to believe—how can you help it?—
    That you did, you did do something . . .
    There will be no peace.

                        —*W.H. Auden*

JULY.

ONE

The girl will not leave. I am left to grasp the handle, digging the spade into the earth to push myself upright, refusing to kneel before the adolescent. It is true she is a fair girl with good strong bones. But I can see now that the bust is half bared above my climbing roses. Such frail clothes they use, it is disgusting. My roses once blocked out nosy persons in the laneway, climbing over the arbour until four years ago when winterkill took half my garden. The unforgiving nature of this cold and shabby country. This girl is its product, a yield.

I have not seen your cat, I tell her. They invent chemicals which discourage animals from soiling private property. I have the privilege to use them.

He's an indoor cat, the girl insists. I'm the person, a person who moved in next door, and he got out when a friend who was helping us move . . .

The prisoner escapes. It is a case for congratulations, in fact. Just so long as he doesn't soil your private property.

Exactly. We understand each other.

He's black and white. All his paws are white; he's got this black freckle on his nose, and this white patch . . .

If the cat doesn't come back to your door, it is gone. Get another, if you like. There will be no problem. They breed.

———————

Sunday, July 2

I've moved in next door to a total witch. She's the best thing about this mismatched street. One scattered house after another and then there's her, right on the corner, behind masses of fruit trees and roses, like the witch with the candy house luring in Hansel and Gretel.

I think I'll call myself Gretel in this book. It's not really my name. My name is really Jessie Barfoot, which is a perfectly respectable name, I guess, except that there's nothing respectable about me. That's one of the reasons we moved to Toronto. I've reached the age of fifteen and a half, and we're going to get a New Start.

I don't know what to say about Toronto except that it's bigger than you might expect. I mean, Canada, right? It's a secondary place. But Toronto turns out to be like Amoeba City, spreading for maybe 300 kilometres along the shore of Great Lake Ontario. It changes its name en route the way that bigger streets do, but I recently discovered how you can drive for hours and the development just pushes along beside you, starting from downtown Toronto with its lofty glass skyline and needling CN Tower and the huge vinyl pincushion of a sports dome. It's true the downtown falls off suddenly after the Dome, which appears to be the geographic signal for all the skyscrapers to shrink like dinosaurs into birds, but you still get all these low-rise offices and warehouses and newbie condos rolling by until you've blended into the western suburb of Mississauga, which is named after the former Indian tribe it enveloped, then the suburb of Oakville, which is not. You keep waiting for it to end, but all you get are more suburbs that soon become ex-urbs of the so-called separate city of Hamilton, which scrolls out next in this unending band of urbanity that stretches right to the US border and Niagara Falls, where you finally encounter the famous Disappointment (Oscar Wilde) cascading below these wide stone walls, a mint-coloured flow of water thundering boisterously north.

Seven or eight million people live inside the Amoeba, all of them in perpetual motion. I don't mean just that people drive from their suburbs to work or from work to their suburbs, although if you pictured the Amoeba at night from space, it would be this throbbing electrified splat of humanity with lines of sparkling traffic blinking on and off inside its wavy boundaries.

No, what I mean is how I've learned that most people moved to Toronto from someplace else, usually somewhere more crucial than mundane little Kingston, which is where I spent Time Immemorable myself. On the shopping streets nearby this house, I have already found bakeries from Afghanistan and Scotland, a pro-Serbian Butcher, Home decorating stores from the pages of expensive magazines, bookstores made in Canada and restaurants hailing down from Greece, Japan, Ethiopia, Italy, Cuba, Mexico, India and the US, i.e. a McDonald's. The Amoeba is digesting people from all over, making this quote, The Most Multicultural City in the World, although as far as I can figure out, that just means people arrive from different countries in order to work in the same jobs as other people from the same country and live with them in the same neigh-bourhoods until they can move en masse to the mundane suburbs, where they finally grow absorbed in leading Canadian lives, with dietary distinctions.

I noticed when we drove down from Kingston over the past year, for instance, that almost all the ladies working in parking-lot booths were pretty, tinted and foreign-speaking. I was informed they had recently arrived from Africa, i.e. Somalia, which made me wonder about the moment they decided to pack up and leave their war behind. They couldn't have said to themselves, I think I'll go be a parking-lot attendant in Toronto. In order to better my life, I'll subject myself to Racist and Sexist comments from the car ahead of the one driven by the sympathetic doofus from Kingston, who doesn't know that you don't have to apologize for slurs made by other white people. (Or do you?) I'm sure the Somali ladies were far more Hopeful than that. Looking around, I get the feeling that the expansive Amoeba City is throbbing with Hope, as around me millions of people from all over the world struggle to get their personal New Start.

Or maybe not. Maybe that's just my Mom's outlook, not to mention her vocabulary. My Mom tends to speak in subject headings. I figure that's because she was a part-time University student back in Kingston, where I personally find it notable that the two main industries are Education and the Penitentiary. I also find it notable that the main downtown buildings, if Kingston can claim to have a downtown, are square bulky nineteenth-century structures made of lime-stone, i.e. the fossilized bodies of tiny sea creatures. When you think about it, Kingston is a small hard fossil, Toronto a huge living Amoeba. Maybe my Mom is right.

That's a weird thought, considering that my Mom is the type of person who keeps a Wish List stuck to the fridge with inspirational fridge magnets. Whenever we moved into a new apartment back in Kingston, practically the first thing she did was decorate the fridge, displaying my school pictures inside these magnetized frames or putting up sticky plastic affirmations, "You Are a Special Somebody," when the Wish List was already the saddest thing in the world, considering that nothing good ever got crossed off, like "Car," even though she wrote "(Used)" after it, but only the most mundane things, like "Toilet Brush." The worst thing was when she bought something at a Flea Market and then wrote it down on the Wish List so she could turn around and cross it off.

I caught this weird glimpse of Mom just before we left Kingston, the first time I didn't see her as familiar old Mom. Not that she's old, being the somewhat embarrassing age of thirty-one, but I mean that I didn't recognize her at first as she walked toward me down the sidewalk between some real students from the University. I just saw her as a certain type of person you get in school, i.e. a member of the Yearbook Committee or the UN Club, the type who's only ever technically young, with that kind of thick, wavy light-brown hair you can't cut short and pale powdery skin, her sweater stretched over those huge zooms so it was too loose at the waist. The thing is, she's not fat. She's just kind of medium-sized and wide, as if some big hand laid itself flat on the top of her head and squashed her down so she popped out in selected places: pop pop zooms, POP butt.

That was my Mom? That person who was shorter than I am? That *student?* It was totally weird. Except that it also wasn't, since Mom has been in school ever since I can remember. Or at least in University. We moved down to Kingston when I was just a little kid so Mom could go to Queen's and the fact is, she's never really stopped. Unless she's stopping now, I guess. I'm not sure what happens now that we've moved up in the world, whether things will change or what.

I don't see how they can. I mean, she's always worked at mundane jobs like waitress, cab driver etc., this being what my crippled Family does, so it's probably genetic, plus she's very proud of the fact she's also always taken courses, even though it took her nine years to finish her BA, at which point she found it didn't get her anywhere so she had to start in on her Master's. I don't see her quitting her Master's, my Mom being so unidirectional. It takes her more or less a Geological Age to make up her mind, which can be exacerbating, but get her started down the track and she just keeps going, which can be even more exacerbating, although it's also not her fault. My Mom is really a nice person. That's just what she's like.

I didn't glimpse her on the street for very long. As usual, she was slower and I don't know, more *careful* than other people, so she sort of disappeared behind the real students, but I kept standing there on the sidewalk until she literally walked right into me. There was this powdery whumpf and there was my Mom, her brown eyes blinking up at me in this kind of scary uninhabited fashion, especially considering that when you looked down, all you saw was the big gross scar across her neck.

"Oh, baby, are you here? I'm sorry, I guess I was somewhere else."

Now we're all somewhere else, my Mom having finally got married last month, lucking out, in the opinion of the world, by landing Pudge. That's my name for him, not that he minds it. I haven't found anything that Pudge minds, at least not yet, even though he and Mom were together long-distance for about a year before we moved down here. Pudge is pretty easy-going. When he gets old and his beard goes white, he can play Santa at the local Mall. I don't mean that he's fat, but he's one of those people who looks fat even when he isn't, with those twinkly blue eyes and the round ho-ho cheeks and all that curly brown hair and this little bowlful of jelly inside his checked flannel shirts. His appearance is somewhat deceiving, however, since Pudge is a lawyer. Mom is stunned jawless. She married a Toronto lawyer! Who works for Worthy Causes! Personally I figure that if you're doing lawyers, why not go for the suit? I consider myself far too young to have learned the meaning of *pro bono,* much less feel its impact upon my so-called innocent life.

Like I say, I'm exactly fifteen and a half, my Mom being almost thirty-two. Do the arithmetic, everyone else does. But maybe that's what we're leaving behind by moving here. Maybe we're finally getting away from all the people who know the real story behind my so-called father. Not that I'm supposed to know the truth about my quote, father either, except that I do. Anyone who thinks you can keep a Family Secret never had cousins. But I have cousins up the nostril, more and more of them every year, especially Janelle Pigott. I mean that there's more of Janelle Piglet every time you see her, and I see her every summer. Not that I'm going to see her this year, I refused. This year, I'm planning to spend the summer working in Toronto.

But until now, Mom always shipped me off to visit the cousins up in Campbellton as soon as school got out, Campbellton being this little town where I was born, and Mom was born, and where we lived until Mom graduated high school when she was, I don't know, twenty? It's this little tourist town in Northern Ontario where my so-called cousin Janelle Piglet lays her head, not to mention half the boys at school. It's also where the Piglet chose an otherwise sunny day last summer to tell me the truth about my quote, father, not to mention the disgusting story of how I was supposed to be conceived, even though I don't believe a word she says. Being a person with some degree of standards, I refuse.

I'm trying not to think about Campbellton at all, actually. I got Paws, my cat, in Campbellton last summer, and yesterday Paws ran away. He took a hike while we were moving in, although to look on the bright side, that's how I met the witch next door. This didn't exactly impress me as a gripping neighbourhood until then, even though Pudge says that Amoeba City is famous for its neighbourhoods, i.e. the way people huddle together into packed little nuclei so they can feel At Home.

The thing is, Mom and Pudge seem to have gone out of their way to choose a mismatched street in an unfocused part of town known as the East End. You can tell from just the restaurants that no particular group of people lives here, and on even your brief morning walk, you end up seeing neighbourhood ladies in head scarves who are both religiously Middle Eastern and black-widowed Greek, as well as Chinese-speaking neighbours, people with Caribbean accents, a notable Homeless contingent and born-here Canadians of many hews. The houses are just the same, I mean in being different. You get a big house next to a bungalow, attached, detached, cared-for and not. Nothing fits together, which gives you the confused sensation that even the houses have wandered in from other developments, sadly settling their foundations down beside each other when they realized they were lost. If I don't watch myself, I can get a Lost sensation on this mismatched street. What really belongs here? Nothing seems to belong here, which makes you wonder about me.

I felt pretty bad this morning, actually, when I was out in the laneway behind the houses searching for little cat bodies or whatever. Then I saw this fountain of pink roses right next door, this total spree of pink foaming in the breeze, flowers moving back and forth like the splash of happy water. I began to cheer up, being such a crip for flowers. I'm especially crippled by roses, so I guess I went over to smell them, walking inside that rosy smell before I looked across and saw this old lady kneeling on a Golf Course-style lawn. The fence between our houses is really high, and she's got trees and bushes where there isn't any fence down on the corner, so I hadn't noticed her before. I probably wouldn't have noticed her at all if I hadn't been searching. But there she was, right by clumps of lilies in colours I didn't know that lilies came in, these ripe peach-coloured ones and buttery ones and deeply bloody Sacred Heart flowers bigger than your hand, all these lilies and so many roses the wind smelled like incense and the fruit trees danced in total stoned ecstasy above.

She didn't see me. But I got this optimistic feeling that she probably had at least eight cats herself. I was probably calling out to the neighbourhood cat lady when I cried Hello, scaring her into dropping her clippers. First she glared at me in an Evil manner and then she tried to ignore me, but I just stood there smiling like a Down's Syndrome until she had to get up. It was weird, she turned out to be every bit as tall as I am, even though I have a general impression that tall people don't live very long. She seemed stiff, though, and thin, so maybe she was sick. Maybe she has cancer or something, I don't know, although I think she must have been as naturally blonde as I am once upon a time, her hair being inadequate now and tied back in a bun. I wondered if this was what would happen to me: stiff, thin, pale, half bald and totally crabby, saying it was my quote, privilege, to use sprays to keep cats and dogs out of my garden.

"He's an indoor cat," I told her.

"Congratulations. He made his escape."

Which is true, when you think about it. My Mom was the one who wanted Paws to stay indoors, having read an article where experts from the Humane Society advised against letting cats outside to get squashed by cars. Not that Paws had anything to do with the Humane Society. Like I say, he was a

Campbellton cat, a barn kitten we got almost precisely a year ago when I was visiting Gramps, and when you think about it, Paws probably inherited the Campbellton gene that programs you to Get The Fuck Out. Not that I remember much about moving away from Campbellton, I was too little, although I'm so glad to leave lousy old Kingston that it hurts. And the thought of Paws on the loose in the big city is kind of appealing, how he'll be able to act the way he wants to for a change, hanging out with members of his own species, choking up hairballs wherever he feels like it, maybe landing a bowl of milk at someone's back door before dropping home for the occasional scratch. When the old witch predicted that I wouldn't find Paws, that he'll have to come back on his own, I kind of accepted that, and felt much better from then on.

I've been sitting here thinking about that for a while, and decided it really is true. Because the thing about Campbellton is, you really have to get out. Like I say, it's this tiny little tourist town up in the Lakes, where it clings to the rocky pink granite of the Canadian Shield, the Shield being so old it's pre-fossilized, pre-Cambrian, and so hard that even if it wasn't so far outside the Amoeba's reach and grasp, it would probably be indigestible anyway. If you don't get out of there, you end up being bent by your hard environment, my cousin Janelle Pigott being Exhibit A. I had to beat the crap out of Janelle Piglet last summer after she told me the so-called truth about my quote, father. She's the kind of person who inspires you to beat her up, not to mention use both her names, especially given how she uses both of mine. *Jessie Barfoot, Jessie Barfoot.* Or sometimes only, *Baaaar-foot.* I'm supposed to feel ashamed I've got my mother's last name? Which is also my Gramps's last name? He's her Gramps, too. All the little Piglets are my mother's older sister's kids and they live in Campbellton. Aunt Sis never managed to leave Campbellton, even after Uncle Gord got killed the winter before.

He was drunk, it was his own fault, he should never have been driving. Everybody knows that. But I never said a word about Uncle Gord, not even to piggy Janelle, who has the family stature package, hand squashed down on head, pop pop, and in her case the family features too, which luckily my Mom escaped. Mom looks like Gramps, she has Fine Features. I look like myself, my Mom always says, which had me fooled forever. But the Piglet looks like someone took one of her cheeks in each hand and pulled them apart, so her eyes are spaced wide apart, her piggy mouth is wide, even her snout is wide and thick as a pig-pig-piglet's, which is what I was screaming last summer on Gramps's lawn when I landed on her for saying all that fucking crap about how I was conceived.

"You take that back, you fucking pig."

"Getta fuck offa me!"

I made pig noises, pushing her down, kneeling on her fat pig gut so she made a squealing wee-wee sound. It felt so good to finally smash her, to feel her wide piggy face get all teary snotty wet. I hated that fucking bitch, she never let me alone. Anybody's back was turned, I got *Bar-foot, Bar-foot.* Now she says *this.*

"You're a fucking liar. It never fucking happened like that. People never get born like that. That's totally disgusting. You admit you're a piggy fucking liar!"

"Lee me lone. Lee meeeeee . . ."

Until I felt my arm pulled back sharply and there was Gram hollering behind me, strong old crap, Janelle her sweet widdle pig-pig-pigwet, both of them wide as fucking barns, fingers digging into me, pulling me back, she's going to break my fucking arm.

"Get off!" Gram hollers. "Get off, you filthy little fucker!"

So I did, I gave in, she was old. Kneeling there panting, both of us, Janelle still squealing like a pig but lower now, wee wee wee. The thing is, Gram never asked, she just looked at me.

"The apple never falls too far from the tree," she said, and heaved herself upright and left.

Later, I was in Gramps's workshop. Gram and Gramps live on the back side of Campbellton, i.e. the opposite side from the highway, their big old house squatting on this sloping property that Gram likes to garden and mow. Gramps tends to be found in his basement workshop, and he's fixed it up like a ship's cabin the way I imagine one. It's got this nice clean sawdust smell and everything's handy to reach, the screws and nails in jars you spin around and the tools hung up on a pegboard, and my Gramps is always bent over his workbench, fixing whatever.

I must have got my height from Gramps, just like my Mom got her Fine Features. He and Gram are like, *Jack Sprat could eat no fat, his wife could eat no lean,* especially in how he doesn't talk hardly at all, having been changed by the war. It was almost over when he signed up, aged merely eighteen. But from what I hear, he got caught up in the last traumatic battles in Europe, then drifted for years before he came back to Campbellton and married Gram. It all changed him, like I say, making him a crip for Lost Souls, i.e. Losers, giving them a bite to eat whenever they wandered into town, even letting them bunk down in the shed, *trusting* them, at least if you believed what Janelle Piglet said, all that fucking garbage about a Loser raping Mom and getting her pregnant, i.e. with *me*. I especially refuse to believe what the Piglet said about the Loser trying to slit Mom's throat. Gramps just isn't strong enough to overpower someone from doing that. Even if he ran in and caught somebody trying, I fail to see how Gramps could overpower him, especially with such fatal results. I mean, you should see my Gramps. He's old.

The problem is, you never knew how to talk to Gramps, and you had to talk when you got ordered down to the basement. Also, you couldn't say what the Piglet said without sounding just as ignorant. You've got to be careful how you sound, coming from my Family. That's the one thing I've learned in life. Most people don't listen to what you say, they listen to how you say it. Educated persons tend to disregard the opinion of my Family because their grammar is incorrect, even though for most of my Family, incorrect doesn't mean ignorant, with certain piggy exceptions.

Gramps was fixing up some old clock radio. He took the back off, biting his tongue between his teeth the way that half my cousins do. Everything's genetic in a Family like mine.

"Gramps, you never really had to kill anyone, did you?" I asked.

He picked up his soldering iron to fix a broken wire, setting off bright fizzy sparks that caused a bitter smell like alum, the alum stick he used to seal the nicks when he cut himself shaving. When he just kept soldering, I knew Janelle was wrong, no rape, no killed Loser, that big gross scar across Mom's neck coming via somewhere else, someone else, which meant that I did, too.

It was weird that Gramps wouldn't answer me, though.

"I mean, like in the War," I said. "Maybe you had to kill someone, like in defence of your Family and your country? So the person you killed, he was the one being violent, he was the one who started it. He was the one who attacked, right? You fought him off during an attack. Like the Nazis invaded England, right? So you fought them off, right?" Gramps put the soldering iron back in its stand. "That's not murder, I don't think. No one's gone and turned you into a murderer, no matter what anyone says."

Gramps was looking down at his workbench. "No one can turn you into anything you're not."

"But if you killed someone, like to stop the War or this attack or whatever, you're a hero, right? You're not a murderer, right? The proof is, you never got sent to jail. You did the right thing, not the wrong one. You had to do it, you didn't have a choice. Because if you hadn't killed him, he would have killed someone else, right? You're stopping him from killing somebody else. And because he started it, it's totally his fault. It's not anybody else's fault. That's why he gets punished and not you. I mean, by being dead."

"You feel punished," he said. "Happy, now?"

You never knew how to answer Gramps, the things he came back with.

"The Nazis invaded Poland," he said. "And France. And Belgium. And Holland. They bombed England, but they never set foot. You remember that."

Which meant that I could go upstairs, no punishment at all.

I've been thinking about how my Mom took me out to get Paws the next afternoon, once she'd been called up from Kingston. It was all pretty backward, beating up a Piglet and then getting the pet you'd been wanting forever. I guess Gramps decided it was the Piglet's fault, which it was, lying like that, although I don't think he told my Mom the particular way in which the Piglet lied. Of course he didn't. Mom would have been upset which *a)* you don't want and *b)* would have set her off after Janelle, or at least against Janelle's Ma, Aunt Sis, which you *really* don't want. So it turns out that I got to beat the crap out of Janelle Piglet, ha ha. Then one day later I was pulling up at the Arnott place, this back-country farm of former hippies who are now as respectable as anyone else around Campbellton, which isn't saying much.

"Dad says you've got some kittens?" Mom asked.

We had to climb right up into the hayloft, where the light flooded in like golden sunset. Christy Arnott took them out of a cardboard box, four of the cutest little kittens, two ginger ones, a tortoiseshell, and this little black-and-white one. I could tell Mom wanted the tortoiseshell, they're guaranteed female. When the aunts were talking Female one day, I heard Mom say, "I wanted a girl," and this silence descended, as if she had no right. But the thing is, the black-and-white kitten kept trying to get away, scattering across the hay. The other ones just sort of rolled around, lolling their heads like Stunned Monkeys, but the black-and-white kitten kept making a beeline to get out of there. Time and again, you'd pick him up, weighing like dandelion fluff, but as soon as you put him down again, off he went, the cutest little white paws sort of pattering like cartoon feet at the end of these scrawny-chicken black legs. The fact he kept trying to escape struck me as intelligent.

"You choose the one you want," my Mom said. "It's your kitten."

Christy Arnott picked him up and looked underneath his tail in a rude fashion. "Male," she said.

But the thing is, it's mundane to say that Paws left now because he tried to leave then. You can't blame a Campbellton gene, not really. Things aren't that logical in real life. If you take one example, there's rape. In Family Studies class, when they taught us about rape, they said it had nothing to do with sex. You'd think it was totally about sex. I mean, what happens, right? But they taught us that rape is really an exercise of Power. It's one person proving he has Power over another person, and therefore over persons in general, which in a way means it isn't personal at all. So when you think of it, if someone really *was* born like that, that person wouldn't be the result of a dirty personal sexual act, which in fact most people are. That person would be the end result of Power, and all sorts of Power could reside within that person, right?

Except that I recently read in the newspaper about some new scientists saying that rape is really the way that Loser males who can't pass on their genes any other way, i.e. by actually mating with a female, try to pass on their Loser genes to create Loser offspring. The thing I notice about newspapers is they always sound as if they're writing about somebody else. It's like they're not expecting anyone actually involved in what they write to read their crippled paper. You get these sad old ferries sinking in the Philippines and these melancholy famines in Africa, and of course you feel awful, at least for a moment, but since it didn't happen to you, for the most part you get to feel superior. I think people read newspapers so they can feel superior to the rest of the world. I'm addicted to reading them but I really ought to stop. It's crippled.

It's also very late. I've been sitting here writing all evening, for hours upon hours. What else is there to do? The TV isn't even unpacked, or the VCR, and they haven't hooked up Cable yet, anyway. From the peaceful look Pudge gets on his face around the subject of Cable, I'm not even sure that he's even planning to get it. It's probably unecological somehow, or otherwise beneath us, like Wal-Mart. You keep getting all these signals that Pudge expects us to live differently. Like, Pudge is the one who gave me this Notebook for my housewarming present last night.

"Now you can write down the case against your Wicked Stepfather."

"Oh, Murray," Mom said. "I'm sure Jessie doesn't see you in that light."

My Mom never gets anything ironical. When someone is ironical, her face kind of blows open. In my opinion, Pudge has to cut back on the verbal quotation marks, it makes my Mom too anxious. But you can see him trying, so you get these ironical sentences, then he looks at Mom and his shoulders sort of melt and his voice turns total butterscotch.

"Jessie and I understand each other very well."

But the thing is, I'm going to keep this Notebook anyway. I have a particular reason: in my Family, this is the Crucial Year. Something always happens to us the year we turn sixteen. That's how old Gramps was when his brother got killed Overseas, i.e. when he decided to be a soldier, too. It's also the age my Mom had me. So this book will be a record of something earth-shaking that's going to happen, something Powerful. We get this genetic promise that it will.

But I take it back, what I said about Down's Syndrome. That was mean. The only nice Pigott is Bradley and he has Down's. Bradley loves fireflies. When they come out, which is like every summer, he bursts into Gramps's house going, *"Fireflies!"* as if they're some new creation emanating directly from God. And I always run outside with him, and he's chasing them down the lawn toward the creek, and he's non-stop giggling and chortling and waving his arms, and you get back into being a little kid with him again, when things are simple and unknown. You giggle and run and wave your arms, going, *"Fireflies!"* in this ecstatic voice, feeling totally unharmed.

If I put a bowl of food outside the back door, I bet Paws will smell it and come home.

TWO

I have not seen your cat.

It's just that maybe he's unhappy. He's probably frightened. It isn't like in Kingston when he got out. Then we had friends everywhere looking. One of our neighbours found him underneath her rhubarb. He was *crouching*. And he ate so much when he got home. I just know he's so scared and so sad.

This is an animal. It does not feel the same emotion you do.

We're animals.

This is true but irrelevant. What is your name?

. . .

You are wise not to give your name to a stranger.

Gretel.

So! You do not wish to be wise.

Yes, but other things too.

That is an interesting answer. Still, *liebe* Gretel, I have not seen your cat.

You're speaking ironically.

Do you think so?

I like your garden, anyway. It makes me think of something I read. This writer, Katherine Mansfield. *Flowers respond wonderfully, but they don't sympathize.*

That is true precisely.

But you still haven't seen my cat.

I have not seen your cat.

My very dear Father,

Slugs remain a problem. Slug bait has proven inadequate; June was far too damp. I have had recourse to a jar of salt each morning this week, picking slugs off like berries to place inside the jar. However, I must apologize. This morning I discovered that two of your tuberous dahlias suffered badly overnight, vars. "Wooten impact" and "Pearl of Heemstede." I subsequently ate an omelette for breakfast and placed the crushed eggshells around the plants, a folk remedy which is said to repulse the attack. You can't make an omelette without breaking eggs!

Otherwise, I am pleased to report that we seem to be past the disruptive heat of early May. Flowers now open at the expected time. The *Lilium* are particularly fine this year, *L. speciosum rubrum* currently coming into bloom. My lavender border is past its prime; I speak of *Lavandula officinalis*. This week it attracted two species of butterflies, the Cabbage and Red Admiral.

Inquiry was made two days ago about a lost cat. You will be piqued to learn that a German family has moved into the house to the north, the girl who lost her cat being a splendid specimen of Aryan youth by the name of Gretel. "You speak ironically," she tells me. My dear Father will not suspect me of irony when I say that I hope that this family will thoroughly repair both house and garage. It is true that the north fence blocks off view of this ruined establishment, but I know that it is there.

No doubt it is because of the Germans that I had my dream again last night.

"Ah yes, Maaike van der Velde. Miss Maaike van der Velde. My Gertrud speaks of you often. She speaks of you highly.

Such an example to the other girls. Such an example to all the boys and girls."

You perceive that it was not precisely a dream, Father. His Berlin accent was as clear as if we had spoken yesterday, not above fifty-five years before. More than fifty-five years, Father. I did not understand at the time how adults could be afraid of adolescents, but I sensed his fear well enough. An officer of the powerful *Wehrmacht* was made nervous by a mere Dutch girl. It disgusted me. He disgusted me, and that is how the dream came to me last night, bathed in disgust. So I awoke bathed in perspiration! The plague of slugs no doubt contributes to this mood, the way their flesh bubbles and shrivels when placed in salt. Disgust disgust disgust

My Father will forgive me. For so many years, I have tried to forget the war. Now I look at the girl next door and remember. She is the age that I was then. I believe she must be the age I was when our group took its bicycling holiday to the national park, when everything started. Everything followed from that holiday, I believe. It was not a straight line, but it led here. Lying awake, after my dream, I found myself thinking of the diary that I kept throughout the war and wishing to reread it. What sort of girl was I then? Having become a gardener, I thought I might identify the seeds of the woman who writes to you now.

I cannot bear to look at it. However, I shall consider rereading some of the later diaries that I have retained, even though it is probably useless to look backwards like Lot's wife. One does not wish to become a pillar of salt—even though salt is a powerful weapon against slugs!

I have little else to report, Father. When it does not rain, the air is fine and dry. We have not had significant humidity since the first week of May. The house remains in excellent repair, and I have bicycled twice this week to the boardwalk, where the breeze is pleasant but there are too many dogs.

I can only hope that you are sleeping well.

Your loving,

Daughter

THREE

Thursday, July 6

My report card arrived in the mail this morning, so the other shoe hit the fan. Luckily, Pudge had already set up his tent in the backyard to air it out, so I was able to move right in with a foamie and a sleeping bag and everything comfortably arranged. You wouldn't hear them say it, but I think this proves how considerate I am at heart.

The thing is, this dilapidating house demands a lot of work, like half the houses in this neighbourhood. It's a detached three-storey, what Pudge calls a typical Toronto bowling-alley house, long and narrow, the rooms lined up one after the other on every conceivable floor. The Inspector said that the wiring and so on were acceptable, but the old people who owned the house before suffered from declining eyesight, pack-rat tendencies, poor taste, etc., and everything needs cleaning out and painting. Making myself a temporary Home in the tent means that the Newlyweds can take the only half-decent bedroom, which seems to have been the second spare room and unused for half a century, no seven layers of dusty carpet on the floor, the window unpainted for years and years, but also not painted shut. It's really best for me to stay out here at night and help with cleanup during the day. I'm good at cleaning. I can clean one room while my Mom does another, which should take at least a couple of weeks. After work, Pudge is going to throw stuff out of the cluttered garage and basement, but he doesn't have much time off at the moment, so when we're finished cleaning, I can probably sort things out for him during the day, especially since they won't throw anything out. They'll Recycle.

My Mom doesn't understand about school, that's the problem. She's spent too much time in University, where they treat you like an adult. At places like Sacred Nostril Academy, they just want you to be a statistical average. I speak as a three-year survivor of Sacred Elbow, the smallest and oldest Catholic High School in Kingston, where the limestone towers and carved impediments made the place seem like a shrunken castle. With a few rare exceptions, the teachers at Sacred Windpipe never cared if you knew anything, they merely pressured you to be respectfully ignorant. Like in Mr. (Weepy) Willow's geography class, I remember him asking Emma Bundt the reasons behind the reunification of East and West Germany, and the Bundt Cake said, "Berlin is the capital of reunified Germany, sir, and the reasons behind it were political?"

We didn't call him Weepy just because of his name. He also suffered from a tear-duct problem and had to keep wiping his eyes with a handkerchief, turning to face the maps at the front of the class to weep and wipe, as if the Fallen state of the world was enough to make him despair. The whole spectacle was hard to look at, actually. His eyes were always red and damp, and his presumptuously negative world view wasn't exactly encouraging. But I guess that it wasn't really his fault, and you probably wouldn't have noticed it at all if he was nicer.

"Halfway there, Emma," he told the Bundt Cake, giving her this damp smile. "Miss Barfoot?" he asked. "Miss Barfoot, can we tear you away from your reveries for long enough to hazard a guess?"

"Fall of Communism," I said. It really *was* hard to look at. You probably would have noticed it anyway.

"Fall of Communism what?" he asked.

"Fall of Communism, sir, and the subsequent dismantling of the Berlin Wall, allowing for the joining of East and West Germany into one political and economic unit."

Weepy wiped his eyes. "Thank you, Miss Barfoot. If your level of emotional maturity ever catches up to your degree of intellectual attainment, you might be able to make some use of your extensive reading. Now, class . . ."

I put up my hand. "Is reading supposed to be useful, sir?" I asked. "Or is Knowledge an end in itself? I'm just curious, sir, if you believe there's really any use in me knowing, for example, that Berlin is the capital of reunified Germany? I mean, sir, other than for the sheer increase in my Knowledge. Since I'm unlikely to go there in the near future, sir."

Geography, 52 per cent. Math, 54 per cent. Biology, 51 per cent, Ancient Civ., 55 per cent, French, 51 per cent, English, 88 per cent, Art, 52 per cent, Phys. Ed., 61 per cent. Grade 11: Pass.

I'd been trying to get the mail before my Mom, but I slipped up on the Crucial day. I heard the screen door snap open and the envelopes whap on the floor. But when I tiptoed into the back hallway, Mom was already up front, tearing open this big brown paper envelope that made me feel sick just to glimpse it. She shuffled through the printouts inside, then ran upstairs calling, "Murray?" which offended me. Whose report card was it, anyway? I think it was *my* report card. I felt totally offended, and sort of scrounched way far down in my chair when the time came to face The Talk.

"The thing that really disappoints me, Jessica," Mom said, "is the way I kept asking if you were doing your homework, and the way you kept saying yes. And you always seemed to have your nose in a book." Major Project Incomplete, Homework Not Handed In, Major Project Incomplete. The teachers' comments were all computer generated. They must have moved the cursor down some report-card program and selected off these stock comments. These are people who never would have recognized if I'd generated stock essays off the Net. I could have easily generated stock essays off the Net but had honourably chosen not to. And they had the nerve to criticize me?

"I'm really sorry, Mom," I said. "I'll do better next year. Next year, the University looks at your marks. But this year doesn't count, so it was kind of hard to get up for it. I'm sorry, though. I really am."

"That's what you told me after your first-term report. And I really thought the second term showed an improvement. It *did* show an improvement. Which means that in some of these courses, you must have failed third term to get such dismal final marks."

"But I passed the year. I'm really sorry about everything, but I passed the year."

"And what does that say, Jessica?"

"That I can pass without doing any work?"

Pudge made this sound behind Mom. We were in the dining room, with Mom and me at opposite sides of the table and Pudge leaning against the wall. I chose to ignore him.

"Jessica, you're *very intelligent*," Mom said. "Many people would kill for your brains. But look at how you use them. I've seen it far too often in my family, people who only use their brains to invent excuses for failing. They're very inventive excuses, but they still fail. It never fails to pain me, knowing they could use all that energy to succeed."

Mom was wiping her eyes with the back of her hand, a sight far worse than Weepy Willow.

"You're making me anxious," I told her.

"I want you to promise me to stop this. I don't know what you're trying to prove, but I want it to stop. You've been completely impossible all year. Yes, you have. Let me finish. It's been going on for a full year. That phone call from Gram—it was August long weekend. You think I like getting phone calls saying that you've beaten up your cousin? Girls your age don't do that, Jess. And it's been downhill ever since. Your mouth this year. Your marks on a skid. Hanging out with that Matthew Cavanaugh. You take a good long look at him, girl. He's failure on a stick. Take a good long look at what you've been doing with your life. What do you think you've been doing with your life? Until this year, you got straight A's."

"I said I'd do better," I replied. "I already said. Can we finish now? I said I'd do better. I said I was sorry. I *said.*"

"But what's the problem, Jess?" Pudge asked, launching himself away from the wall. "What's bothering you? Wouldn't you like to talk?"

"You fuck off, Pudge. This is none of your business."

"Jessica!" my Mom said. Like he's going to dump her because of *me?*

"It just *isn't.*"

"I would argue that it is," Pudge said. "But also that it's no big deal. I flamed out of Grade 10 myself and somehow I got by. You're always allowed one bad year. Now you've had yours and it's no big deal. Right?"

I totally ignored him.

"So I spoke my piece and it's not so bad." Pudge gave this fake little laugh.

"Eighty-eight in English," Mom said. "When you've never got less than ninety. Major Assignment Incomplete."

"I'm supposed to waste precious seconds of my life writing a paper about *I Heard the Owl Call My Name?*"

"I liked that book," Mom said.

The problem is, I've never really enjoyed school. There was the friends situation, for one thing. I almost always had friends, one or two at any given time, but they had a sad tendency to go away. For instance, my most recent friend was Kate Armstrong, but she moved out West last October when her dad got a job at Stony Mountain Penitentiary. Karen Whitlock was my friend for most of Grade 9, but then she got popular and ignored me. Before her it was Melissa Duffy back in middle school, who left for religious reasons. Melissa's whole family had previously been home-schooled from kindergarten onward in the Magisterial Teachings of the Holy Mother Church, but then Mrs. Duffy got sick and they had to send the kids off to regular school, which is where Melissa and I met. I guess she and I were friends for about six months before she had to leave again, her Mom having got stabilized, medically speaking.

Still, I was always proud of my friends. For one thing, their diverse natures meant they knew different things. Kate had undeniable mechanical proclivities, being able to tell you how a carburetor worked even if you didn't ask. Meanwhile, Melissa Duffy was a girly-girl who had memorized all the dirtier parts of the Bible, including the lady's verses from the Song of Songs that were the most aching smut imaginable:

A bundle of myrrh is my well-beloved unto me; he shall lie all night betwixt my breasts.

And the King says,

Thy two breasts are like two young roes that are twins,
which feed among the lilies.
Until the day break, and the shadows flee away, I will get me
to the mountain of myrrh, and to the hill of frankincense.

Melissa had a smut mouth, in a coded sort of way. We knew
each other in Grade 7, back at Holy Shame, when most girls
had developed roes but some still hadn't. She had to wear these
dresses with white collars, long frilly things with crippled little
flowers basically designed for a roe-less chest, but she packed a
couple of grown deer there herself. Total zooms, so the boys
sort of barked around her like little dogs turning in circles,
their claws scratching the hardwood floor. We chose not to let
them bother us, which Melissa managed better than me. Her
chin had this naturally upward bent, and her big movie-star
lips fell into this chronically amused and superior smile. She
was my prettiest friend ever, although the other girls didn't
treat her that way, never inviting her to their parties, even when
they invited me. I guess her eyes popped out a little, and she
had to keep her hair in a bun, although it's true that Tendrils
escaped in the course of a day, especially when she had to go to
the washroom.

"Melissa, your hair is untidy," her father would say.

"Is it? I don't pay any attention to my hair," she would answer,
patting it absent-mindedly, which you could tell was the correct
response from the way her father nodded. Her Mom was something else. Melissa sometimes caught her Mom's eye and they
exchanged a Look, which I noticed my friends often did with
their Moms re: their fathers. That was probably the reason it took
my Mom so long to get married. She didn't do Underhanded any
more than she did Irony. My Mom seems biologically restricted
to Sincere, although in this case it doesn't seem to be genetic.

"Jessica, if you have something to say, I wish you'd just say it." The plaintive cry of the Unwed Mom.

But if they'd known what Melissa was saying at Holy Name (Shame, Pain, Stained) they would have shit nuns. Some of the Grade 8 boys claimed that they'd whiffed frankincense already. They'd whiffed it with Ashley, the school slut. So we'd be walking down the hallway and Melissa would go, "He's never climbed so much as a mountain of myrrh," which would set us off.

"And the hill of frankincense?" I'd ask.

"His rod and his staff they comfort him."

It was kind of fetid, actually. Melissa liked it more than I did. When she got going, I felt carried along on her amused superiority, which was a different feeling for me, but also made me anxious. I didn't actually mind it so much when her parents pulled her out of Holy Lame, to be honest. I guess some friends are a Phase. That sounds cruel, and I know it was Immature to stop answering her phone calls, but I guess I outgrew frankincense and myrrh, on top of which I never could stand what she claimed about me liking Matthew Cavanaugh, which was totally untrue even back then. I guess Melissa was just the kind of person with a limited range of interests, although that was probably her parents' fault, home-schooling and all that. She showed me one of the home-schooling workbooks once and they were all multiple-choice questions with four possible answers. So there are only four possible answers in life? I'm sorry, but that's *too* scary. I think there's more to learn than that, otherwise what's the point?

That's probably the real reason I've never liked school: I like learning things too much. It's always been a weird fascination of mine, but for a long time, I could also play the game. I could eke out a small portion of Knowledge for their tests and assignments, keeping my Mom happy with her straight A's. Lately I can't be bothered any more. I just can't. Don't ask me why, but I can't.

Matthew Cavanaugh, though. He was a grade ahead of me in school from kindergarten onward, and I guess it was flattering that he periodically noticed my existence, especially since he was so smart. But Melissa got it wrong, just like my Mom. I never actually liked Matthew Cavanaugh *per se*. It's just that he didn't have any friends, being too smart for the Bad Boys and too bad for the smart ones. So at times when I didn't have any friends either, we tended to hang out, like we did for most of last year after Kate Armstrong moved out West.

Not that Matthew cared about friends, popularity, etc. His father was a notably mean guard at the Penitentiary, and with him as a dad, Matthew was hard to perturb, even after his parents got divorced. I mean, what could you do in comparison? He stuck pretty much to his own rules, handing in assignments when the subject interested him, or if he liked the teacher (Mr. C.), or maybe if he wanted to infuriate the vice prinicipal by getting a string of A's. He also had an interesting fashion sense, which tended toward the black. Matthew was a Military Buff, which is something he got off his father, so he'd show up in these black-and-grey camouflage fatigues with big black boots laced up to his knees. Sometimes he wore a beret, sometimes this Nazi Iron Cross he bought on-line. He even wore mascara for a while, not exactly to bug people, although he succeeded. Matthew was kind of deep that way, not caring what people thought but doing it anyway.

I remember once when we were skipping, hanging out on some old log in the woods. I was in Grade 7, which would put him in Grade 8.

"Did you ever see this?" he asked. He opened up his coat and pants, and there it was, standing up the way I'd always heard, the Chubby Flagpole.

"Not really," I answered.

"People are sometimes interested," Matthew said.

"I'm not," I answered, after which he thought for a minute and put it back. I don't think he was offended, since we went on as if nothing had happened, and it didn't. But you didn't exactly *like* that sort of person, did you, Melissa Duffy? You didn't exactly miss him, did you? You didn't have a *crush* on that sort of person. Just to clear things up.

It's really dark out here. Also a bit spooky. When the people shut and locked their sliding door across the laneway, it sounded like a stifled explosion. The vinyl siding on the house to the north is creak-creak-*snapping*, I guess as it cools down. But there's one more thing I want to write, something that I learned this evening, speaking of learning. My Mom was talking over the fence to the neighbour with the siding, a mundane neighbour who has the smell of a future Mom's Friend. Francie looks all perky and healthy and she's got this little baby boy who's just a few months old, this really cute little butter baby she carries around on her hip. And what Francie said was, the witch-like garden neighbour on the other side of us is Dutch. She's another ingredient in the Multicultural stew, although an older one, since she's lived there since anyone can remember, probably since the Fifties. She used to live there with her father, Francie said, but two years ago, he died.

"He must have been well into his nineties. *Well* into his nineties, and an absolute grinch! Seldom was heard an encouraging word." Francie leaned over the fence and whispered loudly, "She's not much better than he was, frankly."

Pudge leaned over, too. "One of the partners in the firm where I articled came from a Dutch family," he said. "And he told me that an interesting percentage of the Dutch immigration to Canada, the post-war immigration, came from members of the Armed Resistance. They couldn't settle back into normal life after the war. He said that one of the guys who hid Anne Frank's family immigrated here. And apparently that wasn't all he did. Those people were members of a Resistance cell. Real heroes. And one of them ended up in boring old Toronto. Imagine that."

Pudge gives this annoying chuck-chuck-chuckle when he finishes up some gossip. It takes me the wrong way, to be honest, although I know that Pudge really isn't so bad. He tries, you know? He gives it the old college try. And that was really crippled, what he said about the Dutch, even though it was also incomplete. For a moment, I felt like the city wasn't an Amoeba so much as a Puzzle. Or maybe an Amoeba cut up into a Jigsaw Puzzle, all these differing streets and neighbourhoods and people you've got to try to put together to make some sense of your New Start, even though they don't give you much of a clue. Like, what did this guy's father *do* during the War? It makes you wonder.

It makes you wonder and makes you tired, thinking and writing as much as this, although at least I'm finished with July 6th. It's nearly midnight, so I guess July 6th is also finished with me. I wish this foamie was more comfortable, but if I continue to work exhaustively during the day, I should be able to get to sleep at night, despite the creakings and cracklings and unexplainable Sounds drifting down the alleyway. Time to get to sleep!

Good night, friendly moon.

Good night, Loony-Tunes.

Good night, poor old Paws, wherever you are, and Gretel, whoever you may be.

FOUR

Near Arnhem,
April, 1942

I thrill to the discipline of wartime. Is it dreadful to admit it?
To be a girl of fifteen is usually no great fate. I correct myself:
there is a grand discipline in submitting oneself to the
humdrum, the homely, the everyday. A nation rests upon its
mothers' laps. But how much grander it is to take a part,
however small, in the great storm of history!

This morning before ten we left the Arnhem train station
with our bicycles and knapsacks, taking grateful advantage of
a kind invitation from the uncle and aunt of Elisabeth van N.
to visit their farm near the De Hoge Veluwe National Park.
Our small group shall use these few days off from our lyceum
in Amsterdam to breathe freely in the good green lungs of
our country. Healthful exercise, fresh country food, excellent
Dutch folk: all shall be as it seems and as it should be. I am not
a sophisticated girl. I prefer the straightforward, the straight
and narrow. Yet that, too, is an advantage of wartime. There are
two sides, right and wrong, and it does not require any degree
of sophistication to tell the difference between them.

From the Arnhem station, we followed pleasantly curving
streets through the ancient centre of town, respectable buildings with their clean, white-curtained windows rising on either
side of us, looking not unlike the canal houses in my own dear
Amsterdam, although, it must be said, more provincial. Our

caps bobbed in unison as we pedalled into the suburbs, the gardens just coming into bloom beneath trees not yet in leaf. It's true that the cap of Elisabeth van N. bobbed farther and farther behind us. She claims asthma and has a sad tendency to whine, and if not for the hospitable uncle and aunt, as group leader I would certainly not have brought her. In fact, she is not asthmatic (as I am) but spoiled and rather fat. If her father were not my own dear Father's colleague, I would suspect him of providing her with some of the "extra" ration coupons which I happen to know he distributes.

But that is dreadfully indiscreet! I should say merely that the cap of Elisabeth van N. bobbed farther behind us, but the poor girl suffers from asthma, the inconveniences of which I know too well, and one must, in all charity, make allowances.

I will not write down our exact route out of town, since this is wartime and lips must stay closed. I know it is a sad fault of mine to speak too fully. Only last week at the lyceum, the worthy Mr. B. chided me, "Maaike, Maaike, Maaike. I asked for an answer, not a speech." I saw my error right away and felt very downcast, especially when the other students laughed, not all of them in a friendly manner. I longed to be more popular, even though my dear Father has warned me repeatedly that many at the lyceum cannot be trusted. Indeed, even the worthy Mr. B. sometimes strikes me as rather heavy and mocking. However, his grandfather played an important part in our national history, as he never tires of telling us, so I'm sure that I must have been mistaken.

As we left the suburbs of Arnhem, we entered pleasantly rolling wooded country, the trees still bare of branch, the fall's brown leaves still covering the ground. The temperature was acceptable, the rain light. I took the lead in our little group of eight, with the others spaced behind me down the winding road. Before too long, I fell into a fine rhythm, and the rhythm soon brought rapture. The great beauty of our country! The coastal dunes, the inland dikes, the brilliant springtime tulip fields! That morning, on the train, we'd passed rich green pastures frisky with lambs. We'd passed flocks of ducks and swans nesting in the woven reeds of the canals. And now these green hills all around us. Nature, water, and man's ingenuity: everything combined in our dear country to bless us.

"Maaike, you'd better slow down. Half the others can't keep up. This isn't a race. We're supposed to be having fun."

Jannie didn't wait for an answer. She just dropped rather pointedly behind me, and when I looked back, I saw her dismounted by the side of the road. She was in a hollow, standing at the base of a hill while I was halfway up the slope. Both were impractical places to stop, so I pedalled to the top of the hill before dismounting.

"Up here!" I cried, challenging the others to speed down dale and up hill, joining me at the summit. But as each cyclist reached the hollow, she dismounted to join Jannie. They took their time, drinking from their water flasks, then walking their bicycles up the hill, gossiping as if they hadn't seen each other for years. Jannie S. is a very pretty girl, sometimes shockingly casual, yet dependable too, calm and athletic, so you can't really blame them for their preference.

I know that it's a fault of mine to be too intense. I wish I knew the secret of not caring about things. I wish that I was more like Jannie, who is so breezy and matter-of-fact. I'd give anything not to be so self-conscious, so stupidly frightened of making a mistake. I think you need to be very brave to risk failure, and I seem to be far from brave. It's so much easier for me to do things properly, step by careful step. By "easier," I mean "safer." I wish that people understood. They think I'm trying to show them up. They call me Miss Priss, Teacher's Pet, Miss Perfect. But they should really call me Miss Scaredy Cat. Why don't they understand that I'm terrified of making a mistake?

Oh, I wish that I were a better, braver person! I long to meet my dearest Father's standards, but so often I fall short. I wish my face were softer, my cheeks redder, my eyes bigger, my nose more snub (although I have excellent teeth). My Father is kind enough to tell me, "One day you'll show them. You'll still have your face when they've all gone to fat." But these days, there isn't any "one day." There's only "today." That's why I want so very, very much to improve.

"Ready?" I asked, forcing myself to be cheerful when they joined me.

Elisabeth gave a mocking salute that she thought I wouldn't see. They never think I see them, but I always do. Yet I think I made an excellent show of ignoring her as I kicked off, leading the way down the hill. It's true that we arrived much later than we should have at the entrance to the national park. I'd planned to organize a leisurely lunch beneath the pines, and felt rattled at first that we would have to rush. Yet the park was so lovely and peaceful that in a very few minutes, I forgot all of my recent bad humour.

What words can convey the great beauty of our national park? How can I capture the majesty of its lofty pines, the ancient branching oaks? Not far inside the gate, we saw a sweet fawn standing on new legs, and bicycled past to eat our picnic on the inland dunes, relaxing under a clearing sky. Afterwards, we cycled back to the farm, where we were greeted by good Mr. and Mrs. N., the brother and sister-in-law of Elisabeth's notably jolly (fat!) mother.

We were to sleep in the barn, with the exception of Elisabeth, taken into her youngest cousin's bed. What can be more healthful than a barn! After profusely thanking our very kind hosts, I flew around like a barn swallow, urging the oldest to unroll their bedrolls and helping the youngest make their nests in the bales of clean-smelling hay. How much better to finish the day's work before taking a rest! I honestly fail to understand how people—Florrie B., for example— can lie around complaining about work instead of getting it over with.

"Maaike, don't you ever stop?" Florrie asked.

"Of course I stop. I stop when everything's finished. There wouldn't be any point in keeping on when things are finished, would there?"

One tries to inject cheerful common sense into the most everyday conversations in order to set an example as leader. Yet Florrie still lay on the bales of hay like an Oriental pasha, or perhaps like a member of his harem, her cap askew and chin cupped idly in her hand. Once again, I failed to see why Jannie and Florrie were such close friends; indeed, why the others paid so much attention to Florrie. Maybe it was simply because she and Jannie were both a year older than me, even though I'd skipped a grade and we were in the same class at school. Despite my happy optimism, Florrie seemed to set a tone, so that when we came to eat our dinner in this pleasant farm- house kitchen, Mrs. N.'s kind hospitality and warm milk were greeted with yawns and complaints.

"The hills around here are so beautiful," I said. "Such a stimulating change from the scenery at home."

"And a change in the muscles you use to bike it," Florrie said. "I think I had muscles I've never met come up and introduce themselves. 'Hello, I live behind your knee and I *ache*.'"

"Whenever we visit," Elisabeth said, snuggling under her aunt's arm, "I can't walk for the first few days because I'm so stiff. Then I can't walk for the next few days because I'm so full of my aunt's good cooking!"

She took another slice of meat.

"You must think we're dreadfully spoiled city children," I told Mrs. N.

"Oh, my dear, we're all used to what we're used to. When we go into town, the cobbles hurt my poor feet powerfully."

"I love the birds here," Jannie said. "Listen to the birds. So peaceful, hearing birds in the evening."

"And not air raid sirens," Florrie said.

"Don't!" the youngest girl cried.

"We're away from those," Elisabeth said.

"Is it bad, then?" Mrs. N. asked. "Poor children."

"We're at war," I said. "Naturally there are sirens. Would you rather not hear sirens? Where would any of us be if we *didn't* hear sirens? Barring victory, of course."

"It's the machine guns I hate," one girl put in. "Last week, I was visiting my father's shop, and when we left, we actually *saw*. There was this, there was this, there was this . . ."

"Hush, child," said kindly Mrs. N.

"He'd worked next door to my father. Someone we'd, we used to, I don't know what he'd done . . ."

"Hush, now."

"But he fell, he fell, he was *jerking*."

"Guns don't sound like they do in the movies," Florrie said. "They go pop. *Pop*."

"Don't do that, Florrie," I said. "Honestly."

"It's the silences that frighten me," Jannie put in. "After the sirens go off and before the guns start, there's that silence when you know that no one in the city breathes. You can hear everyone in the city not breathing. And I'm always afraid it will go on like that, everyone not breathing forever."

"That's morbid, Jannie," I told her. "Although very well put."

"Doesn't anything frighten you, Maaike?" Jannie asked.

"If I thought we might lose the war, that would be frightening," I said. "But of course we're not going to."

"We can't," Florrie said.

"Very true," I answered, giving her some credit.

"First they'd shoot our parents and then they'd shoot us. They'd find us, then they'd shoot us down in the streets like they shot Jannie's poor Uncle Bertus."

"We don't talk about that," I said.

"And we don't stop thinking about it," Florrie said. "I don't, anyway."

"Maaike's right," Jannie said. "This is very morbid. We're on holidays, we should be enjoying ourselves. Listen to the birds."

"Why do you have holidays?" good Farmer N. asked, taking his pipe out of his mouth. "I didn't get that."

"Water problems in the building," Jannie said.

"A piece of good luck," Florrie put in, making jolly Mrs. N. chuckle. It must be said that Mrs. N.'s rough speech showed that she hadn't had much schooling herself, although she was very generous to take us in and feed us so amply.

"My dear Father suggested we use the long weekend for a trip," I told Mr. N. "And then your sister, Mrs. van N., made the kind suggestion . . ."

"So your father's got some clout," Mr. N. said. His voice was somewhat too casual, I thought. With a chill, I wondered if he could be trusted.

I can't write that either! I shouldn't write any of this! If the enemy ever got his hands

I know what I'll do. I'll tear out these last few pages, as if I'm dissatisfied with my writing, then casually stroll over to the stove and burn them. That way, I can finish our conversation properly on the next clean page.

"I love the birds here," Jannie said. "Listen to the birds. Aren't they peaceful? Birds in the evening."

As Jannie suggested, we listened to the birds, idly discussing our most wonderful day, while kindly Mr. N. smoked his pipe by the fire. Before sunset fell and the light dimmed, I reminded those in our group who kept diaries that the time had come to record the day's news, and brought out this harmless little volume myself. It was slightly troubling to see Florrie B. open another small book. I mean, that she was the only one to do so. I wonder what she writes about? No doubt the same things I do, the great beauty of our country . . . although I write so poorly, I've had to tear out several pages, as must be obvious to anyone who might chance upon this innocent and useless scribble.

"Feeding the fire, young Maaike?" Mr. N. asked, when I returned from the stove.

"I seem to be having trouble expressing myself," I told him. "I'd like to be better at so many things than I am."

"You're young. I imagine there's still hope."

Of course, Mr. N. was right. I took heart from his words, although I must admit that the rather heavy and indecipherable look on his face made me think of Mr. B. at the lyceum, and for one cynical moment, I wondered if our kind host really meant what he said.

But I am not a cynical girl. I am not sophisticated. Oh! Why can't other people be as straightforward and sincere as I am? A dark suspicion entered my mind that our host was too satirical for a farmer.

But I shouldn't say that either. What am I allowed to say?

Tomorrow we plan to return to the national park.

But does one write down plans? Itineraries? Should one be writing anything, really? What indiscretions is Florrie putting on paper?

I don't know how to end this, how it's all going to

Today has been a most satisfactory beginning to what doubtless will prove a highly memorable journey.

FIVE

Saturday, July 15

Today is my day off, so I went to get a library card. Such lurid excitement in my new little life, I'm not sure I'll be able to stand it. But at least I've graduated from the slavery of cleaning to paid employment in terms of painting the house, which is going to be my Summer Job, since Mom is helping Pudge at his office.

We finished clearing the place out on Monday, the last layers of carpet off, every cranny washed, including the windows, which now actually open. I mean that Mom and I finished our part of the Job. Pudge is totally crippled in the way he quote, de-acquisitions items from his area of responsibility. He starts out by moving bits and pieces of old wood around the basement, then he can't make a pile where he wants to because there's this flimsy particleboard wall in the way dividing nothing from nothing. So he starts wrecking out the particleboard, at which junction he decides the old crowbar he found isn't sufficient and goes off to Canadian Tire for maybe six hours, coming back with everything except a new crowbar and then it's dinnertime anyway. Mom calls this style of operating a Male Trait and admits that Males aren't the most efficient, but she still acts as if Pudge has discovered a cure for drug-resistant tuberculosis every time he reveals his haul. "Oh, Murray! Imagine! Non-toxic grout cleaner!" I find it totally exacerbating.

The thing is, I can see how you could get completely side-tracked down in the basement if you were a certain type of person, since the old people left it jumbled full of potentially interesting items. I go down there sometimes, or into the garage, and I've already compiled a boxful of abandoned Collectibles. The box itself is an antique butter box of a type I recognize from Gramps's workshop. It has tongue-and-groove edges and you can just vaguely read the word Quality on one side, which is a type of affirmation, in my opinion. I keep it in my tent filled with other stuff I've saved or found, including this little tiny mouse skull and these old carved wooden picture frames that I'll use to feature my black-and-white photographs, seeing as how I'm going to be a photographer one day. You can imagine totally customizing your Home with photographs and Collectibles like that. I mean, once you finally get a Home of your own.

Mom and the Pudge aren't like that. They don't want to paint their own Home in noticeable colours and furnish it with items they customize themselves. Having cleaned the place down to its visible bones, their debate is now about which shade of white to paint everything, and they plan to go from room to room acquiring Good Pieces as they, or at least Pudge, can afford them. Mom clamped their Priorities List on the fridge with an ironic Elvis fridge magnet that was one of the few things Pudge saved from his apartment, his furniture being otherwise sent to Goodwill for someone else's New Start. Apparently our stuff will do for now, although I don't give it very long, beginning with my favourite old sofa, the first piece on the acquisitions list being a Divan. All this is Pudge's approach, but Mom is painfully grateful to go along, seeing as how she's a repressed Shopping Addict. One thing I've noticed is that the world is divided into people who like to buy stuff and those who prefer to make and/or customize it. The first type of person likes *having* things nice. The second type of person enjoys *making* them nice and is prepared to put up with the confusion while doing so. I believe that there's an overlap, but also an essential distinction.

My Mom, for instance, never complains, but the whole time we were cleaning the house, you could tell how much she hated it. Of course, she's over thirty now and I guess that after a certain point your body lets you down. But it was gruesome to see how often she'd make a face and arch her back with her hands on her hips exactly like Gram does. She had to wear rubber gloves when she cleaned and sometimes this useless white fume mask, unable to bear human contact with dirt and/or disinfectants, which she said made her gag.

No exaggeration. When I showed her this little mouse skull I found, she looked like she was going to york and yelled at me to *get that thing away* from her. She *yelled* at me, even though it was the most delicate little ghostly remembrance. But what really made me anxious was how tired Mom looked at night. I didn't like it. In fact, it got a little scary, and you could see Pudge grow more and more concerned like in time-lapse photography. I guess that's why he came up with this scheme for her to work in his office, filling in for the receptionist while she's on disability and I'm hired to paint the house.

I don't mind, especially after I went to the library this morning and ran into the witch from the garden next door. She gave me an idea for spending Part One of my money, which works for me on several levels. When you think about it, you can't just sit back and wait for your Crucial Year to unfold. You've got to put yourself out there, formulate Plans and accede to Movement the way the old witch does. Not that I ought to call the poor old lady a witch after learning her name, which is Miss Martha van Tellingen.

I admit that I wasn't in the best possible mood when I walked into the local library, which is this fake Elizabethan-style timbered structure on one of the main streets nearby, a false advertisement if ever I saw one, since the modern interior was bustling with men reading foreign newspapers on the main floor, and banks of computers amid the shelves of books, and mothers taking their Tots to the storytelling program upstairs. It was lively and Hopeful, which should also have been the case with someone who had managed to acquire a Summer Job the way she'd wanted, except that I had just been informed as to how there won't be any Cable even after the house is painted. It turns out that this isn't a question of Ecology or some new level of Acculturation we're supposed to aspire to, which would at least be consistent, if somewhat mundane. No, it's just that Pudge was a TV addict and now he's quitting cold turkey. So we have to? I didn't ask for a New Life, thank you. There was nothing wrong with my old life, if you don't mind. At least then I had my *cat*.

That was why I didn't talk to Miss van Tellingen when I first saw her in the library, she always mentions Paws. "No, I have not seen your cat." I am very well aware that nobody has seen my cat. I've looked for him every day, queried neighbours, put up notices on lampposts etc., and nobody has seen him, including me. Who needs to be reminded? So instead of lining up at the front desk re: my library card, I edged behind Miss van Tellingen into the bookshelves, keeping an eye on her since there's something so totally slant about an old lady wearing an old-lady dress typing commands into a gleaming new computer.

Tell all the Truth but tell it slant—
Success in Circuit lies

Too bright for our infirm Delight
The Truth's superb surprise.

Emily Dickinson. For some reason that flew into my head while I stood there watching. The old lady was at a slant, all right. Off-kilter, which I like. When she got up to go into the bookshelves, I decided to trade places, sitting down to find out what she'd been searching the computer for. She'd cleared the screen, but you just had to press B for Back and it came up Katherine Mansfield. She was searching for books by Katherine Mansfield. When I'd told her about Katherine Mansfield!

Usually no one listens to what I say, they're too caught up in how I say it.

Too Brightly, they think. Most people think I'm a little Too Bright.

Dear Diary: I know myself far better than anybody thinks. I know exactly how I come across, i.e. what people think of me. I just can't be bothered to change, that's all. Don't ask me why, but I can't be bothered, I just can't. Why should I?

And here's someone who listens to me the way I am?

She makes me drop the book, coming up behind me like her lost cat. I do not like cats. They're sneaky.

You are always making me drop things! I say.

She stoops to pick it up.

Katherine Mansfield, she reads, handing it back. *In a German Pension.*

That is what it is, yes.

I'm sure you're going to like it.

That is not inevitable.

I guess not. But what is?

I have lost the trick of sending people away. The girl will not leave. She wants something from me, I know. What do young girls want? A pat on the head, I think. They want to be told that they're a good cat, yes, they're a good cat with their pretty coat and delicate ears and yes, they will one day catch a mouse. Oh yes, they deserve to catch a mouse. In this case, however, I feel like a mouse myself, and am disinclined to pat.

You might have noticed that I'm living in a tent, she says. I'm going to be painting the whole house this summer. It's like my summer job. And so I'm making the tent my temporary home to escape the fumes, at least for part of the day. Fumes are a real concern on our side of the fence. But in the evening I can totally smell your garden wafting over. It's lovely. Thank you.

I nod and try to leave, but they make these aisles too narrow.

My Mom is going to help out in her husband's office while I'm painting, so they both escape the fumes during the day. That's her new husband. They just got married last month, then we moved into the house. We lived in Kingston before that. He lived here. They just used to visit, for like a year. I mean, almost a year. It was totally respectable. You've got very normal, respectable neighbours.

And I'm sure your father is very normal and respectable, as well, and you will have very normal and respectable visits on modern alternate weekends.

Oh, my father is dead.

I'm terribly sorry!

Oh, that's OK. I never met him. He died before I was born. I guess it was a family tragedy.

I'm very sorry. You grew up without a father, that is very sad. I am very sorry to both you and your mother.

The girl is looking at me, but I cannot help the feeling. The final illness of my own dear Father is still too painfully before me, so dreadful was his struggle not to give up his life at last.

It's really OK, the girl insists. We've got lots of family tragedies. You get used to them, more or less.

That is true, I reply, taking a breath. Eventually you do. More or less.

What should I read? she asks suddenly. I read a lot. It's like a hobby of mine. Maybe there's something you think I should read?

I thought modern young people watched the television.

I think people *should* watch television, she says. It's part of living in the modern world. The thing is, you maintain a balance. You watch some TV, you read some books, maybe some newspapers, and you're on the Net to a respectable extent. All of these are information sources. They're tools. You use them to learn things, which is a respectable avocation.

Avocation! I cannot help smiling.

I like to have a vocabulary. That's a tool, too. To rise above yourself, I mean. Above your lowly animal origins.

You are a very strange girl.

I know. What do strange people read?

The girl keeps looking at me.

I think you are at precisely the age to read *The Sorrows of Young Werther*, I say, succeeding to leave the aisle. Goethe, I say, over my shoulder.

Will you sign my library card if I have to get adult permission? she calls.

Fortunately, the young man at the desk informs that she may get the card herself.

Gretel Bundt, she is called. She shows him a student card from Kingston that has been through the washing machine and inked over to bring out her name. She has also brought some ownership documents to the house which I am surprised her step-father has allowed, proving their local residence. I am also surprised that these documents are sufficient to permit her a library card, especially since the names on the documents are very different from her own. There is social erosion; I do not like it. But then, it has been a very long time since I've been asked what I like.

It is a pleasant feeling, however, when it occurs.

———————

It's true, she really *does* listen. After I saw that about Katherine Mansfield, I went over to talk to her, although of course all I did at first was to chatter in a totally embarrassing fashion. I'm such a Loser, I really am. I hate myself. Part of me stands there listening to myself chatter and thinks, What a total hemorrhoid. No wonder she backs off. Who can blame her? I mean, she's being verbally attacked by the type of hemorrhoid who asks her to recommend something to read, then does her the disservice of thinking she'd come up with a kiddie book by a lady called Gerda?

That's the problem with trying to expand your vocabulary in private. You never know how things are pronounced, and sometimes what they mean. You have to sit down at the library computer, feeling kind of hurt before you realize that she's done you the honour of recommending a foreign book that in fact you've got to order from a big central branch of the library.

I can't get over this. I'd totally harassed that poor old lady and she was actually *listening* to me. She listened and assessed the fact that I was capable of digesting an advanced foreign book. But by the time I finally realized this, she was on her way out the door. She'd put together a towering pile of books and was heading outside, so I practically had to chase her into the street.

"Excuse me? Excuse me?"

That hemorrhoid again. She didn't even look at me.

"I just ordered *The Sorrows of Young Werther* from the Northern District Library. They're going to ship it over."

"They do that, of course," she said, stopping by a bike that was locked to the library rail.

"My name's Gretel. I already said that, how totally stupid. My Mom's name is Michelle. Can I ask what I should call you?"

"Yes, your name is Gretel Bundt, and your mother's name is Michelle Barfoot, and your stepfather seems to be called Murray Zimmerman, and you are a very modern mixed young family. I, however, am not very modern. I am a senior citizen, and you may call me Miss van Tellingen."

"Could you repeat that?"

"I am Miss Martha van Tellingen. Why do you ask twice?"

"I'm sorry, I guess I've got to clean out my ears. Which is what my Gram says, I mean inside the Family, so it's probably vulgar. I'm really sorry. But you sure have everyone else down. The ownership papers, right? They bought the place outright, cash. My mother's husband doesn't believe in accruing debt. He's kind of un-modern in that way, actually. But his Family has some money, I guess, and he's also socked away every penny he's ever earned, and he's been a lawyer for like eight years. So that's your bike?"

"That's why I put my books in the carrier. It is mine, yes."

"I'm going to get a bike with my painting money."

It spewed out, but as soon as I said it, I knew it was correct. I could *a)* broaden the search for Paws and *b)* cycle around looking for photographs I could take one day when I've reached the point of taking photographs, not to mention *c)* put myself out there on a collision course with the Crucial. In my opinion, people do too many things on a whim without sufficient preparation, e.g. putting their crippled poetry in the high school annual or, I don't know, getting married? Think first, Do later, that's my own philosophy, not to mention my Plan.

Without even nodding at me further, Miss V unlocked her bike and left. I was totally harassing the poor lady, which is such a stupid thing to do that I'm going to have to go over to her house and apologize, maybe once I've read the *Sorrows* and have a good excuse.

Later

It's early evening by now and I'm sitting outside my tent. On the one hand, I've said what I planned to say. On the other, I feel like writing today, so maybe I should describe my quote, New Start here at my quote, New Home in Toronto. Mostly the weather has been sunny and warm since I arrived, but yesterday there were two thunderstorms with thick rain, one in the morning and one in the afternoon, and now it's sort of hazy and feels like it's going to rain again. My tent dries out pretty quickly, though. I'm dry inside, especially since I pulled out the old lawn mower last week and mowed the lengthening grass so it wouldn't drip moisture onto the fly.

This is what it looks like here behind the bowling-alley house: There's a high fence on the south side of the property next to Miss V's house and a not-so-high fence on the north side between us and Francie, the future Mom's Friend. At the bottom of the yard, facing east, there's this peeling old wooden garage that opens onto the laneway. The house looms on the west side of the yard, which is just a mundane lawn of grass without any garden, although there's a bent old lilac tree up against the garage. Once I finish painting, I plan to plant a garden of roses. I've always been a crip for roses. Meanwhile my tent is a solitary bubble in the shadow of the house. Inside, I'm getting used to the foamie and sleeping bag, and I've got my butter box filled with CDs now as well as my Collectibles, a camping lantern placed on top even though I don't use it for long. I fall asleep early, blocking out the scary nighttime Sounds by listening hard to my CDs.

Mom doesn't like me living outside, being even more scared than I am of Sounds, Rabies, Vampires etc. surging up the laneway. But to me, it's a beneficent life. It's mine, anyway. You go to bed early and wake up early with the birds singing, the pretty calls of robins from the neighbouring roofs and the funny old starlings rattling a song in the back of their throats. A pair of cardinals lives around here, pewing at each other and cheering. Unlike humans, they mate for life. Otherwise, it's quiet except for garbage day, when the trucks bear down first thing in the morning like encroaching war.

That's how I woke up the first morning, to the squeal of air brakes, the grump and rattle of cans. I was stiff from the foamie and crawled outside to stretch. I'd slept in my clothes, so I did leg stretches like in Phys. Ed. Afterward, since I'd done the stretches, I thought I might as well run out into the laneway, heading north on the pavement until it turned to dirt and ruts, passing a dogwalker with a prancing little dog wearing a red-and-white neckerchief and, on either side of the ruts, the kind of tall weeds people let grow outside their back fences even when their property is groomed. The laneway was kind of slant, actually, part of this whole network of laneways surging like the Collective Subconscious through the Amoeba, its sides littered with crushed cans and sun-seeking weeds and broken bits of toys and cigarettes. I liked running too, even though I've never bothered being athletic despite having the build, which is the exact opposite of Mom, who's in perpetual danger of getting fat and signs up for every new exercise course she hears about, tai chi and Pilates and women's soccer league, without ever finding anything she likes.

Here's the thing: I liked the feeling of running so much that I decided to do it every morning. Also to go back to being Vegetarian. My Mom didn't go Veg last time I did, which was almost two years ago now, when she made me prepare my own dinners while she quote, cooked her own. Finally, I got annoyed at how bad a cook she was, at which point I gave up Veg and started cooking for both of us. I've been what Gram calls the chief cook and bottle washer ever since, and now that I've decided to go back to Veg, Mom will just have to get used to it. So will Pudge, even though he's a big meat-eater, his first purchase post the house itself being this big gas barbecue covered with black plastic that huddles outside the back door like Darth Vader. But the thing is, it's so much more convenient for me to have dinner waiting when they get back from work that I doubt they'll complain for long, and ha ha, I'll get my way.

I've also got my way in terms of personal hygiene, i.e. I'm using the little basement bathroom, showering there after my run, having scrubbed it to the point of grout cleaning. But if I went into the upstairs bathroom too early, I'd probably wake the Newlyweds. Either that or hear another kind of Sound, which is fetid enough to ruin your life. No, thank you. No thanks to them, I'm set up fine, with my tent, my bath, my Veg and running, a Summer Job and planned bike. Even if somebody else has got my cat.

Gretel Bundt, the Vegetarian runner. She even has ID, a library card. You can see her slowly coming into focus like a photograph you'll take one day. Developing, but not in any dirty sense. Maybe that's what life will be like here, a development, a surge toward the Crucial. It's nice to think so, anyway, when you consider the alternative.

The End.

SIX

I hear murmurs. The modern mixed young couple has come outside to sit on their front porch, hidden by my forsythia. The weather is unsettled today. This morning there was sun but thunderclouds now push their way in. I refuse to be pushed off my porch by the sound of these voices, although the murmur annoys me. Young people think that they must talk, as if everything has not already been said.

Feeling worse than you say . . . off your feet . . . wish you'd ask the doctor . . .

There is a tone of nagging in the male voice that I do not like.

You know that you're allowed to complain . . .

So unmanly, this little dog nipping at her heels.

It's never struck me that complaining helps, she says.

It is the female voice that carries, a slow and placid voice, but stubborn like the daughter. Barfoot must be the maiden name, kept according to the modern practice. Bundt would have been the real father, poor young man.

A passing car covers the sound of the male. It is instructive to hear a voice and not the words. This Zimmerman likes the sound of his own voice. The girl said he is a lawyer. Of course.

What I would like is for things to be normal, the Barfoot replies. A normal home. I'm not complaining when I say it's never been like that. And this business of the tent . . .

But that's the most normal thing in the world, the Zimmerman says, coming to stand near the forsythia. I spent

my summers in a tent, exiled to camp. I'm joking, I loved it.
Old Dan, he owned it, Dan was an old conservationist. He was
like the Jesuits, he got me early. They get you early and you're
warped for life. I'm joking, don't worry. It doesn't seem to
have hurt, spending my summers in tents and canoes. He even
got us composting. Growing an organic garden, identifying
species of maple and basswood. Asswood, we called it. You
used it as toilet paper out on the trail. There was also this
story about Windy's tree, this tree where one lone nerdy
camper was found dead one morning, having been chased
from his tent the night before. It was the only tree to survive
a big forest fire, left as a cosmic warning to be nice to nerds.
Which was just as well for me.

He laughs.

I loved that place, I really did. The sky at night—we had a
telescope—singing around the campfire. It was the sort of
place where you sang Dylan, *Ballad of a Thin Man. Desolation
Row.*

I wish she could have had some music lessons. In junior
high school, she wanted so badly to play the violin. I wish I
could have managed.

She sure loves that CD player you got her.

It's so much cheaper to buy entertainment these days than
to nurture talent. When I was growing up, I had two, three
great-uncles who were fiddlers, but there's no one even in my
generation who can play. People just go out now and buy a
big TV.

So we've decided there won't be any TV. And now that she's
set up her own personal camp . . .

He moves away from the railing.

Novelty wears off . . . she just needs a bit more time to get
used to the new . . .

I know she'll get what she needs, the Barfoot says. She always has. I'm proud of myself for that, compared to the way many, many people cope, and I'm honestly not complaining.

I cannot hear what he says. He has gone to the other end of the porch, a restless man.

The problem lies in getting what you want, Barfoot answers. If you never get what you want, you lose track of your preferences, and your tastes. You grow more limited and envious of other people. Believe me, I grew up with that, too, and I know.

. . .

I know.

. . .

I know.

. . .

You're right, I know.

It rains. The sky opens up; it is greenish-grey. On the radio, they warn about tornadoes north of the city. Here, lightning branches, thunder shakes the porch; the storm is almost overhead.

I *hate* the way she's out in this, the Barfoot says. I hope at least she's had enough sense to go inside the garage.

Their door shuts as I remain outside. We do not have tornadoes here, but last year lightning struck a Norway maple three doors to the north. I could not sleep so I saw this and felt the electrical charge travel through the air. The hairs on my arms rose and sparked like embers. Excitement! It is something I would like to feel again.

My very dear Father,

There is a storm as I write. The blue door across the street appears grey. A similar storm passed through here on Friday and weather conditions remained variable Saturday, Sunday and today (July 17). For this reason, the garden has been damp. Thursday morning, brown spot was observed on a lower branch of my white Schneezwerg rose and affected leaves removed. All of the roses were subsequently sprayed.

I must also report a betrayal. A *lilium* purchased as the pink variety Mr. Sam came up blatant orange. Father, it was too great a reminder of our lost country. I disposed of it in the garbage can, preferring not to compost the bulb in case it survived the winter. As I believe I reported, this happened last year with one of your discarded dahlia tubers. Of course, the winter was mild.

I fear there have been numerous reminders of the Old Country lately. The modern mixed young family which has moved in next door proves to be clean. The widowed mother was observed up a ladder washing her windows like a proper housewife. People in this country do not wash their windows; they hire roving criminals with pickup trucks to move dirty water from one side of the glass to the other. You will remember that we have discussed these men when they have knocked at the door. I continue to believe they are briefly released from prison, like roofers, and will wash my own windows in preference to becoming the victim of their next crime.

The house next door, however, grows increasingly clean. The Aryan daughter, Gretel Bundt, paints it inside while the husband, Zimmerman, works as a lawyer and the widowed mother assists in his office. The mother has the look of a Walloon, although the name must be English. Barfoot. A very modern mixed young family, I told the girl, and I am happy to say that she agreed.

The girl reminds me of Jannie from the old group, Father. It is not an obvious resemblance. I suspect that children of her own age do not find the girl pretty. Her features are larger than is liked at that age—as, you will remember, were mine. Yet there is Jannie's bloom of health and the same flaxen colouring. Dear Jannie was such a pretty girl, so athletic and reliable, and so very well liked. I am certain that she would not have gone to fat if she had survived.

Perhaps you are right; she was Catholic. After five or six children, the figure is gone. I'm sure you are right, Father.

I saw Jannie again in a dream. This is what I mean to tell you, Father, that I have suffered dreams lately. I am afraid that young Gretel brings it all back. I am afraid of what memories the girl will bring back, even though the dream was very lovely at first, as I admired Jannie's blooming youth without the childish envy. She was in the lyceum, which I knew to be the lyceum although it was very large and empty like a warehouse. She stood at the centre of the empty room in the light cast by a line of high windows. I can only describe this as a dingy light, and she was wearing her uniform and looking away. I was old in the dream, Father. I could not see myself, but was conscious of being myself as I have become.

Yet Jannie turned around and smiled at me so brilliantly! I could see her face, I could see it so clearly, the smooth flushed skin and very blue eyes brightening, the lovely smile and blonde hair curling out beneath her cap.

"Maaike!" she cried, in a tone of delight. "Here's Maaike van der Velde!"

"Ah yes, Maaike van der Velde. Miss Maaike van der Velde," came the cultured Berlin accent. Suddenly I was young again and speaking on the telephone. Both the warehouse and Jannie were gone.

"My Gertrud speaks of you often," the German said. "She speaks of you highly. Such an example to the other girls. Such an example to all the boys and girls."

"I'm glad to hear you say so, sir. I always like to be of help."

"No doubt, no doubt. It is the wish of all good Dutch citizens to be of help to the Reich. I have noticed this. Yes."

The unsettled weather brings on these dreams. Heavy weather, heavy humour, remembered so clearly. It comes back to me unchanged, as if this is not a dream but a tape recording. It comes back repeatedly, as if the recording runs on a loop. Over and over, I hear the Gestapo officer speaking. I hear the undertone of fear in his voice. He doesn't know why I have telephoned him at his office. Why have I telephoned him? What do I want? Whatever it is, it might mean trouble. He does not wish for any more trouble. The war is ending badly for him and he fears that I will make it worse. Here is another mystery: whether I did or not.

It thunders, Father. The green sky cracks with light. I must go inside now and mail this letter. It is late. I have no other news to add, and can only hope that the night's rain does not disturb your sleep.

Your loving,

Daughter

Light the match, burn the paper over the sink. Paper burning, browning at the edges. Heat grows towards fingers. Drop. Burning ashes float on a current of air.

Repeat:

My name is Martha van Tellingen. My father's name is Gerrit van Tellingen. We are Dutch citizens from Amsterdam who were arrested and sent to a transit camp not long before the end of the war. The reason was that my father had evaded his work notice from the Nazi occupation. He had been called up to work on a factory in Germany but clearly he did not wish to go. Instead, he hid in the countryside for more than a year. You must understand that thousands of men did this.

In fact, there were several farms; my father moved often. I was with him at the last farm when the Germans raided. No, I was living in Amsterdam. No, my mother was dead. I was on my own and very hungry. I went to the farm to look for food. My father always tried to let me know where he was. When we heard motors coming, the farmer locked us into a hidden room. However, we were discovered. No, I don't believe that the farmer was arrested. He was not taken away when we were. Perhaps he was shot.

A few days later, we were put on board a transport train. No, we weren't told where it was going. However, the train was bombed inside Germany and we escaped. This was very near the end of the war; you must understand the confusion. It is ironic, but we passed as Dutch labourers who had been bombed out of our jobs in a German factory. We ended up in Berlin during the air raids, which is where our papers were so badly damaged, as you can see. When the Red Army came in, life grew confused in a different way. However, we were able to leave Berlin and find work on a German farm. That is where we have been working until now. No, I have nothing to prove this, aside from the fact that I am alive.

I assure you, these papers are correct. My name is Martha van Tellingen. My father is Gerrit van Tellingen and my mother was Juultje, born de Graaf, who was killed at the beginning of the war. She had been visiting our family in Rotterdam. All of them were killed there. Yes, they all died in the bombing: my grandmother de Graaf, my uncle and aunt and their five children. They all lived in the same house. No, I do not wish to go back to the Netherlands. There is nothing to go back to.

That is why my father and I wish to emigrate to Canada. Thank you very much for considering our application.

Ashes in the sink. Turn on the tap, wash the residue away. Smoke hangs in the air like names, like lies. Names are lies. You think that they tell you something crucial about someone, but you don't know anything at all.

No, you don't.

You don't.

You don't.

SEVEN

I can't stop thinking about that poor little boy who died in the Tornado. Not the Tornado on Monday on the outer edge of the Amoeba where a few people's roofs were lifted off. No, I mean the Evil Tornado last Friday at the campground out in Alberta. Eleven people were killed, including this little red-headed boy who was torn from his father's arms. He was only two years old and he got torn away by the sucking Wind, spiralling up into the air until the Wind lost interest, so he fell to the earth and died.

I thought I was keeping myself together. I was keeping busy and keeping myself together, which is precisely why I wanted a Job. But I've been reading in the newspaper all week how people were pulled upward by the Tornado until they were flying like birds. They flew out over the campground so they could see it all below: the lake foaming like an angry ocean, the somersaulting picnic tables, the house trailers tossed around like oblong dice. Nearby cars twirled up into the sky, the people still strapped in their seat belts as they rode a three-dimensional highway. I keep seeing those people, the birds and the cars all twirling and jiving and spinning in space, all of them watching the destruction from every sick angle before the Tornado finally dropped them back on the hard wet ground. The cars dropped farthest away, exploding when they landed so people flew out from under their belts to

64

lie alone in the soggy fields, wondering if anyone else in the world was alive.

The little boy wasn't. He'd been alive, and then he wasn't. At first, when the Wind turned weird, his parents rushed him inside the nearest available shelter. His whole Family huddled there, his mother holding a baby girl, the boy clutched in his father's arms. His father held on for his very dear life as the shelter buckled and swayed, the boards groaning as they fought to stay planted into their concrete roots, the Tornado swearing at them and shrieking. It got so loud you couldn't hear a human thing, just the Wind howling and metal gnashing and crashing outside. Cans and plates went swirling through the shelter before they were sucked through the open door. The boy was sucked through the open door, pulled from his father's arms so he flew upward in the funnel of Wind. He must have laughed to find himself flying. "Daddy! Look at me, Daddy!" It took just seconds, everybody said. But after those few brief seconds of stupendous Flight, the little boy died forever.

The poor little thing was a Minister's son. He was a two-year-old red-headed Minister's son and you can't get any more innocent than that. It's all so crippled and sad. What had he ever done wrong in his life, that poor little two-year-old boy? He never got a chance to do anything, and his father, the Minister, couldn't protect him, no matter how hard he tried.

I can't stop thinking about that, the total lack of protection in this life. This whole overpopulated world is becoming like a series of giant Amoebas growing closer and closer together, strangling the Environment, sucking in Disease and Violence from all the threatened jungles outside. Growth and decay are swirling in a huge vortex around you. Read any newspaper and you'll see that you're caught in a worldwide Tornado, this swirl of Events that picks you up and throws you down regardless of whether you deserve it or not. I even wonder if "deserve" exists in the real world or if it's just a word that adults use to frighten children. "You deserve a good spanking." Whether you get it or not depends on their mood, not on what you did.

Is that what life is really like? On the one hand, random punishment. On the other, unearned rewards. Like getting Paws after whaling on Janelle Piglet? I end up asking myself what it all means. If modern life is just a swirl, if a doesn't logically lead to b, then nothing you might try to do is going to make your own crippled life better, Crucial Year or not.

I take that back. Life is even worse than crippled. Why did Pudge have to start that newspaper subscription, anyway? Why not get Cable instead? With Cable, you can change the channel, while a newspaper shoves bad news in your face, especially Global Warming. They've been putting stories about Global Warming beside pictures of the campground, scientists saying how all the emanations from cars and factories and everything we thought of as quote, progress are making the weather turn more unpredictable and punitive, so that when you do a hoping to get b, you don't just fail, you end up with q instead.

Weather used to follow its own rules. It never used to be humans' fault. When little two-year-old boys died in Tornadoes, you'd feel sad and broken, but you never had to feel guilty. Yet by bringing on Global Warming, humanity is responsible for all of the fierce Tornadoes we've been getting lately, and that awful ice storm we suffered through in Kingston, and all the wrinkly old droughts that poor people in Africa die from every day. No a b c d like in a happy nursery rhyme. Just b q r j p b squared. We're taking up so much of the Globe that it's turned as crippled as we are, which is *totally* frightening when you think about War and Genocide and

Terrorism (which I can't stand to think about at all), i.e. when you consider how truly crippled humans can be.

Then last night I read *The Sorrows of Young Werther,* which made me feel even worse. I got the automated message yesterday morning from the little local library (There is *one* library book available for the library customer with the initials *G B*) and I was planning to distract myself by reading it after my Job. It's pretty short, and when I first started, I thought it was going to be some eighteenth-century version of the Harlequin Romances my Mom used to sneak when her University friends weren't looking.

I felt amused, actually, if also shocked. Here was Mom feeling guilty about sneaking her Harlequins when all her University friends were off reading Goethe, but the secret is, they amount to the same thing. Young Werther yearns to whiff some frankincense with his best friend's girlfriend, and the girlfriend is a flirt, and the best friend is suitably absent-minded and embroiled in his job, but the girl rejects Werther to stand by her fiancé. Of course, that only sets it up so I expect the girlfriend's big Change of Heart, how she rushes into the manly arms of Young Werther, happy ending for all but the fiancé, who's so absent-minded he probably won't notice, anyway.

Then Werther goes and kills himself. I can't believe it. First the girlfriend marries the absent-minded fiancé, which is bad enough when you consider that back then they had no chance of divorce to extirpate themselves from an ill-advised Marriage. So already it's depressing, and then Young Werther goes and kills himself? I can't understand what Miss V was doing, recommending a book like that. Was she trying to send me a Subliminal Message?

Tell all the Truth but tell it slant. Except that there's nothing slant or Subliminal about it. Her message is pretty clear: Go kill

yourself, Jessie. Or Gretel, whatever your name is. Go kill yourself, you're in the fucking way. You're in the fucking way, Loser.
No one wants you, no one ever wanted you. They never wanted
you in the first place and they certainly don't want you now.
Look at them. They want to make their own little Home. You're
extraneous, Jessie. Go play in the Tornado and die.

Oh god. Oh god. I can't stop thinking about that evil
sucking Tornado. You're tossed around, no question of deserving or Progress so what's the point? What's the fucking point?
I know the point. I'm supposed to be painting this fucking
house. It's like my Job. So I've scraped and puttied and sanded
the middle bedroom, and now it's just painting white on green,
white on green, brush around the door, around the Window,
around the corners of the room, roller on the three full coats in
soothing soothing rhythm. That's what a Job does, it numbs
your mind so you don't think, you don't do, you don't do
anything do anything do anything.

I'm going next door to ask the old witch what the fuck she was
thinking to give me a book like that.

———————

She comes right into my garden this time. Only now do I
notice that the cloud of morning has given way to an over-
bright sun. There is much to do in a cool and damp summer to
fight an encroachment of slugs, earwigs, brown spot and
mildew, although aphids have not been a significant concern,
and my flowers do not fade as quickly as is usual in the spiteful
summers of this country.

I do not remember issuing an invitation onto private property,
I tell her, standing up with greater stiffness than I would prefer.

I have a question for you, she says. What do you mean by recommending a book that promotes suicide? I wonder what people would think if they knew you went around recommending books that promote suicide to teenage girls.

The dizziness hits, the vertigo.

What's your problem, that's what I want to know.

I have stood up too quickly, I manage to reply, and stumble over to my chair. She crosses her arms, however. The girl is as stubborn as I was.

I am sorry, I did not hear the question. Something about a book.

The Sorrows of Young Werther, she says.

Ah yes, that is a famous book *against* suicide. I make the hopeful emphasis.

So who mentioned suicide? What's your point? You think I should go out and kill myself or something? You think I'm like this complete unnecessary loser, is that it?

Vertigo and confusion. I do not know why this has happened to me when I live so inoffensively. She threatens me with the authorities. I make one mistake and she threatens me with authorities after all these years. She wants from me— what? This well-fed cat bristling in my garden.

I thought that you were bright enough to read a book that the clever students read when I was young, I say. It was a popular book when I was young. Perhaps tastes have changed. Certainly tastes have changed.

That's really insincere, she says. Excuse me, but it is.

I thought it was irony you accuse me of.

She is silent, though wary and watching me. I gather my courage and rise. You will come into my house for tea, I say, looking around for nosy neighbours. Thankfully, there are none nearby, but I still prefer the safety of my kitchen.

I am in need of a cup of tea, I say. If you prefer coffee, I have instant.

. . .

Perhaps you are not yet old enough to take either coffee or tea.

Tea, she says, and walks into my kitchen behind me.

It was a joke, that book, I tell her, going to the cupboard, my back to her now. That book was a joke when I was young, a novel loved by very old and stuffy schoolteachers. I was making a joke on myself, that I am now old and stuffy, and therefore recommend this book. It is a fault of the young, I say, turning to look at her, that they think they are at the centre of everyone else's regard, as well as their own. I was not thinking of you at all.

But of yourself, she says belligerently.

Of course. That is what people are like.

I realize that since I have come into the kitchen, every word I have spoken is the truth. She knows this and cannot think how to respond. I put on the kettle and run hot water into the teapot. The truth is difficult to answer. We are unaccustomed, meeting it so seldom in this life.

Later

I'm just back from Miss V's house, which is very spare and slant. It's as white as what Mom and Pudge are doing in their so-called Home, so I refrained from rude comments re: my Summer Job. But the noticeable difference, at least to me, is what a new condition she keeps it in, the walls as papery smooth as they must have been when these old houses were built. This neighbourhood is made of World War One houses, according to Pudge, and *his* walls look as if the War was fought there, the plasterwork all buckled and scarred and cracked, like bombs exploded just outside. I mean, they used to. I've been doing a lot of repair work in my Job, and if you ask me, Pudge is getting a Deal, since Gramps taught me how to repair the walls properly before you paint, gouging out cracks and filling them in with drywall mud you let dry between layers.

But the thing is, I can't do much about the ropy bulges that form in the walls where there's stress. There seem to be a couple of stress points in their quote, Home where there's maybe a weakness in the Foundation and therefore some settling. Pudge needs to drywall the front stairway, for example, and until he does, all I can do is give the old plaster a coat or three of his precious Sun and Star white interior latex.

Actually, Sun and Star was my Mom's choice, to be fair. She got her way on the paint, which I predict will be a Trend. By not saying much, she beat down Pudge's compromise of Wild Phlox white, and wouldn't even hear of his original Papineau. Not that I think she's wrong. Papineau isn't white. It's grey.

But if it were my Home, I wouldn't be so restrained. I'd paint the plaster bulges like brightly coloured snakes slithering up the walls. There's one thick ropy bulge right in that front stairway that I'd paint like a deadly coral snake, stripes of scarlet, black and yellow hissing toward the front door to warn Evil away. The rest of the wall you'd paint lemon yellow, and you could use different yellows and red on Focal Points throughout the house. I'm now thinking of Focal Points, since Miss V's house convinced me that for the most part, new drywall painted white would be a slant background for some real New Start that I might eventually have. Also for my future photographs.

Not that she hangs anything on the walls to speak of. Her house is bigger and wider than Pudge's, being on the corner lot and built according to a different Plan. The hall and stairs are at the centre of the house, which means the rooms on either side present her with Wall Space, although she chooses not to take advantage. In fact, her interior is notably austere, this whitewashed white with brightly shining floors and furniture from the Fifties or Sixties that's come back in style, although it looks as if she bought it new and kept it loyally while it was Out. Miss V doesn't do clutter, either. I had a quiet laugh to myself when I discovered no Wicked Witch fussy gingerbread decor or child-baking oven. She has normal gas, and the only Touches, as Mom would say, are a gold metal starburst clock on the kitchen wall and one small framed painting that I think I might have seen before. It's a reproduction painting of a huge wave cresting way out in the ocean. I think it might be Japanese, this huge wave cresting over the ocean as if it's about to crash down on itself with massive self-defacing power.

Which I guess sums up my condition when I barged into Miss V's garden.

I'm such a hemorrhoid, I really am. I barged into her garden and accused this poor old lady of advising me to commit Suicide. But why would anyone want to do that? Certainly not anyone who's never really met me. It was all a product of my own crippled mind and nobody else's. At least, that's what Miss V practically told me, and I could see she had a point.

"I was making a joke," she explained. This was in her kitchen. She'd invited me inside from her garden, and while she made us both some tea, she explained that she and her friends used to joke about *Werther* when they were my age. All of their teachers used to love it. Now that she was as quote, old and stuffy as her teachers, she was making fun of herself by recommending a book they loved.

"Young people always assume that they're the centre of attention," she said. "But actually they're not. I wasn't thinking about you at all."

"You were thinking about yourself," I said.

"That's what people are like."

So she's saying that's what I'm acting like? I digested her implication while she poured two cups of tea. I don't really drink tea, and I had to water mine down with milk and sugar. That's the way a Child drinks tea, and by that time I guess I felt pretty childish. I felt more and more ashamed of myself, to the point of almost cringing. I cringed over my baby's cup of milky tea, hating my fetid self. I longed to get out of there. I longed to *flee*.

But I was also curious. I admit to being nosy. Having made it into Miss V's house, I didn't have any intention of leaving before I got a good look around.

"It's not a very deep book," I told her, after what must have been a long pause. *"The Sorrows of Young Werther."*

"You're criticizing Goethe?"

"I'm sorry."

"It was written when he was only twenty-three years old."

"By the time I'm twenty-three, I'm going to be a photographer," I said.

"Then you'll be trying to see the world as it is. That's a good thing, not to let other people tell you how to see things. I will let you in on a big secret. Other people are often wrong, even though they claim very loudly otherwise."

This struck me deeply.

"So how do you do that?" I asked. "See the world as it really is?"

"By looking, I would think," she replied.

I thought about that, too. It was probably a hint that I should adopt, a route toward the Crucial. I decided right then that Miss V was worth adhering to. I should probably practise what she preached, starting right now.

"Excuse me," I asked. "But can I please use your bathroom?"

You will say that I was feeling too pleased with myself, Father, and you are right. The truth is very powerful. It is slippery and dangerous; it is a shark. And it surfaces so often lately, I am afraid. I am afraid that all I hear in my dreams these days are the damning tape-recorded loops.

Ah yes, Maaike van der Velde. Miss Maaike van der Velde. Such an example to the other girls. Such an example to all the boys and girls!

Maaike! Jannie cries. Here's Maaike van der Velde!

My name is Martha van Tellingen. My father's name is Gerrit van Tellingen. We are Dutch citizens from Amsterdam who were arrested and sent to a transit camp not long before the end of the war.

Could you repeat that? the girl asks.

I am a senior citizen, and you may call me Miss van Tellingen.

I must avoid this girl in the future, Father. She upsets me, and I do not wish to be upset.

She reminds me, Father. Oh! We had such fun! We were so young and innocent! But in truth, in the brutal truth, I cannot stand to be reminded. I cannot stand to be reminded of what I did during the war.

Who am I, Father? What have I done?

I am Miss Martha van Tellingen. Why do you ask twice?

EIGHT

Thursday, July 20

What you see when you see clearly: Tornadoes aren't so bad. I saw the aftermath of a Tornado once when we were driving up to Campbellton. We usually took the bus, but this was when Mom was driving Cab, and the owner let her have it a couple of times when she wanted to go up for the day.

So she's sitting there on her cushion, peering over the steering wheel. The cushion is designed to make her look taller, ensuring that people will treat her with respect. But mainly she looks like some carpool Mom plucked out of the driver's seat of her suv and set down at the wheel of a Cab. People are respectful toward her Momness, and maybe to the story they can visualize behind her misplacement. The cushion is not a factor, except to make them feel even more sorry for her if they notice, which they probably do.

Of course they do. Seeing clearly turns out to be easy. You just have to look through the wrong end of a mental telescope, trying for Distance to gain Perspective. Distance + Perspective = one very strange girl, as Miss V would say.

But the drive. The drive is a few years ago now, and I'm sitting up front beside my Mom. I'm twelve and it's July. I want to sit in back, wondering what it's like to be a fare, but Mom refuses.

"I'm not your chauffeur, Jessica."

Looking out the window, I can see the sun shining on farmland. Corn is growing on the flat sunny fields. We're almost at

75

the Canadian Shield and I'm waiting for it, those ancient rocks where Campbellton resides. But after turning a corner, we drive beside this long tilled field with telephone poles lined up along the ground near the road, their antlers pointing away from us. At first I assume that Bell is about to plant a new line of poles, setting them out yesterday at the proscribed intervals so they can dig them in later today. Then I notice the pole stumps. They *were* planted, but they've been broken off maybe a metre up, all of them snapped off at the same height and laid down neatly on the soil perhaps a metre distant, their crippled bottoms beige.

"Will you look," Mom says, slowing down. "I hope those wires aren't electrical."

"It's like a giant came along and broke them," I say. "Fee fi fo fum."

"There were Severe Weather Warnings yesterday. A Tornado must have touched down here. Look—it didn't touch the farmhouse. Thank heavens."

She slows down again as we turn another corner, almost at this little town. We've got the windows open, and when we hit the outskirts, we hear this buzzing like small planes. On either side, we start to see fallen trees, this gnarled old oak, a red maple, then a roof crushed down V-shaped on a house, a big tree at the bottom of the V. Now you see men with buzzing chainsaws straddling over branches on lawns and driveways, buzzing men dotted along the residential street with kids running back and forth, ragging as they watch. And what you smell is sawdust, this promising smell. It's like Gramps's workshop when he's making things. It's like the smell of Creation.

Mom is slowing down to a crawl. "Need any help?" she asks a woman out the window.

"We're fine," the woman says, smiling through the sawdust smell as if they're setting up a church bake sale. I mean that

she's got this totally superior smile, the Chosen smile. Smug?
This is probably the most excitement they'd had in years.

"I hope no one was hurt," Mom says.

The woman shakes her head and laughs. "The Insurance will
cover *everything*."

But even if someone had been hurt, you could see how
Destruction brought Reconstruction and therefore Creation.
The Tornado freed you up to start something new. So what I
think now is, say I *do* get caught up in the Tornado. There
would be moments of searing joy, riding there aloft, and after
I'm dead or whatever Mom really could start over. She and
Pudge could have their own kid, for example. Destruction =
ReCreation. You could live with that. I mean, if you survived.

I don't know whether I'll survive my Crucial Year, but
Miss V has started to give me hope, now that I've spent some
quality time with her. It's not just that *a)* she's survived being
tall well into her decrepitude, since she's now more than
seventy years of age, but *b)* I have an idea that she's going to be
the Teacher I've subliminally been looking for all along.
Teachers at school are such Losers. Those who can, Do. Those
who can't, Teach School. Miss V must have some background
in Education, she's so good at ordering you around. But I can
see that her real bent lies toward independent learning, which
is an approach I've always intended to try.

Now I've got the chance. I should *Carpe Diem*, stop
carping and just do it. Seek out Miss V and follow her advice.
When I thought about our visit yesterday, I could see how
she'd already given me hints to go down certain paths. First,
I should read. Second, I should try to see life clearly, which
involves testing it out for the truth. I think my Mom's wrong
in saying that I do enough testing already. I should probably
do even more.

Seeing, snooping, testing, testing. Watch out, Mom! Watch out, Pudge!

I shouldn't call Miss V a Teacher, though. She's really an Instigator. Dictionary definition: agitator, fomenter, mover and shaker, which is to say a Tornado unto herself.

Why not go for a ride?

NINE

Wednesday, July 26

For once I'm feeling pleased with myself. I've started to incite this new routine, going to Miss V's house for tea and paying attention to what she says. It casts the rest of life in a whole new light. A searchlight, actually.

Miss V mentioned how she pays attention to dreams, and I had a bad dream last night myself. The weather is getting so hot and humid that I haven't been sleeping very well, even in my tent. Inside the house, they're complaining. Well, Pudge is complaining. Mom just looks as if she wants to. Her health—what's the matter with her, anyway?

Maybe you don't want to shine the searchlight too Brightly. You can get anxious if you notice too much. But it's true, ever since we got here, Mom has been acting overtired. I mean, she's never totally bouncy like her new friend Francie the Home Birther next door, but she's usually like some big slow ship that just keeps plowing on ahead. Now she looks badly drawn when she gets in from work, this lousy picture of herself. She dumps her purse and throws herself down in her chair, only picking at whatever I cook and half listening to yet another mundane Baseball game on the radio, as if anyone cared about the so-called Toronto Blue Jays except Pudge.

It can't be anything serious, can it? I mean, you'd think she'd tell me if it was anything serious. I think she should tell me, I have a Right. Not that I'm going to ask. Prying visually is one thing, but you can't pry verbally. "Excuse me, but this disease, if you have a disease, does it look fatal?" You can't do that. All you can do is count on the fact she'll make a slip and then you'll know. She always does. Someone does, anyhow.

And in the meantime? Concentrate on the fact I had this dream, even though all I can remember is that I had untold quantities of nasty hair growing out of my legs. Could that be Significant? I'm not sure if it was, although I can see how some dreams about hair would be slant. You might want to be covered with fur. (Paws!) But this was nasty long crinkled hair sprouting out of my skin, each hair a pubic wire. Pubes on your legs?

I ran inside as soon as I woke up, not even waiting till after my exercise run, but showering and shaving myself so harshly that I opened up a long bleeding cut on the front of my right leg. It bled a lot, actually, but the cut wasn't that deep, so it's no real Issue. In fact, I sort of felt I deserved it, I mean, if you deserve anything, either for having such nasty hair or such nasty dreams, one or the other.

Maybe that's what my dream was saying. Nature may be Powerful, but people are small and nasty and mean. I don't know if Miss V intended to teach such a cynical lesson, but I think it's innately true. When I was going out to buy some paint the other day, I heard these little kids playing out in their backyard. These chiming little voices floated out into the laneway, and I thought they sounded so darn cute until I heard what they were saying.

"You're the cousin everyone hates," the first one said.

"I am not."

"You are. Just listen. If you had to hate any cousin in the family, who would it be?"

A little voice answered, "Dilip."

"You?"

"Dilip."

"You?"

"Dilip."

"You see? Every family has a cousin everyone hates, and in our family it's you."

I felt so sick for that poor little Dilip. People make me sick. If you start to pay attention, people make you sick all over the place. Like in the video store today at lunch, it looked all bright and happy with posters and movies playing on overhead TVs. I was in a concentrated mood, checking out the New Releases to stay on top of quote, Popular Culture in the faint hope that I might someday meet another person my own age. But a fat Biker-looking couple grazed the shelves beside me, and they liberally turned my stomach by talking about *spooks* in movies, too many *spooks* in movies these days, all those *spicks* and *spooks* in movies, *sss-sss-sss.*

Biker sees me and goes, "Too many spooky movies these days." Who did he think he was fooling? Coming from Campbellton, you know people like that. And Toronto, I guess. And Kingston. Not to mention everywhere else in this crippled old World.

I ended up feeling Blue by the time I knocked on Miss V's door after work. Also worried, not having seen her in her garden all day. She's old. Things happen. It's probably just as well I'm dropping over. Someone has to check up on her, and she doesn't seem to have anyone else.

But it turned out I'd made a mistake. She said she did her usual chores, I must just have missed seeing her. I can be such a Loser sometimes. And her reaction to my Biker story conflicted me.

"If this is what he believes, he must have the courage of his convictions," she said.

"You mean he should be like, I'm Racist and I'm proud of it?" I asked. "I really don't think that's right."

"You disagree with him, or you think that he must hide his beliefs? These are two different things."

She certainly gives you lots to mull over, anyway. Like, my Mom. Where's the courage of *her* convictions? She's lapsed from the Church, but she still sent me to Separate Schools. She says women are equal, but she debases herself before Pudge. She supports Freedom of Choice, but she says she'd never have an Abortion, period. Where's the logic in that?

"If she will not have an Abortion, she must think it's wrong, which means that it's wrong for everybody," Miss V said. "Wrong is wrong. She must therefore stand at a busy intersection and hold up her sign, *Abortion Kills Babies.*"

It made me feel weird to hear someone criticize my Mom, even if I asked for it. I also found it hard to tell what Miss V meant when she got Ironic.

"I don't know what to believe," I said. "But that's what you told me, isn't it? I have to see the World like it really is. If I do, then maybe I'll finally figure things out."

Miss V liked hearing me say that, you could tell from the way she sat back in her chair. I've always been pretty talented at saying things that people like to hear. I haven't been saying them lately, I guess. I can't be bothered lately, I don't know why. But I made a mental note that I can still do it if I want to.

And the thing is, I meant it this time. I really did. This searchlight business is hard to keep up, but I think it's true that Miss V brings out the best in me. I think I've made the right decision in adhering to her, and someday I'll even get her to admit it.

Right now, she doesn't admit to much. She won't answer any questions about herself, saying merely that she's Dutch

Canadian and prefers to live a quiet life. To me, this hints at Drama, a Tornado in her past. Why would you prefer to live a quiet life if you hadn't experienced the alternative? You'd want to test out the alternative, at least. Give it a ride. I know that I do. Maybe she'll show me how.

"Katherine Mansfield is an acceptable writer," Miss V said, out of the blue. "It is a correct picture of pre-War decadence."

"I'm glad you liked it," I said, cheering up.

"But I have not seen your cat, I'm afraid."

"I guess I've accepted that," I replied.

TEN

Saturday, July 29
The Worst Day of My Life

I'd wanted everything to go so well. I finished my Summer Job last night, phoning Mom at work and telling her to eat out so I could do the final Touches unmolested. Actually, I finished my painting before lunch, but I planned to surprise her by going over the house, not just scrubbing the kitchen floor and putting out clean towels etc., but rearranging the furniture and her Touches to make the rooms appear less boxy and pedantic.

I acted out her intentions, no clutter. But especially in cases of simplicity like this, you want to make sure the scant furniture appears Delightful in the room. Like in the spare bedroom, where she's got my former furniture, you don't need to push the bed up against the wall when it's got a headboard. You can set it out in the room with a stand-up lamp behind it. So I did arrangements like that, which some people couldn't do on account of their parents' quote, taste. In my case, however, I'm supposed to have an Eye.

It was depressing, though. When I was finished, I walked through the whole long house, *seeing clearly* by means of all the fresh white paint and shining wooden floors, and our crippled old furniture looked so scabby and sad. You could comprehend why Mom wanted to get new Pieces, but the way my whole past has been rendered shoddy and unwanted, all of it as a result of my own labour . . . I think that anyone would be depressed.

Our old sofa, where she used to lean against one arm and me against the other, and we'd watch TV with our legs lazing around each other, well, that's not going to happen any more, anyway. But that poor old sofa, the fabric screamed Nasty in this light, and Paws had made inroads on the arms I hadn't noticed before, despite yelling, *Paws! No scratching!* approximately 652 million times.

When Mom arrived, she raced around the house faster than she's moved in Glacial Ages, totally enraptured and exclaiming, "Jessie, this is brilliant. It's such a treat. You've got such an Eye. Look what Jessie's done in her own room, Murray."

She meant the spare room. Next door was the spare spare room, which being empty was verging on the acceptable. The Master Bedroom I wouldn't touch, but Mom cleaned it all the time, anyway. For the record, Pudge is a slob.

"What's the matter, baby? You look down. You must be exhausted, all your hard work. That's what Gramps says, we work hard in this family. Why don't you go to bed? You've made your room so cozy. Have you eaten?"

"I think so. I really am tired. Maybe I'd better go to bed."

I made for the stairs.

"But in your own room, baby. There aren't any more fumes."

She doesn't get it, does she? But what made me recoil was seeing Pudge put his hand on her arm to restrain her. From me?

"I'm like the dirtiest thing in this house," I told her. "Look at me. Have I had time for a shower? No, I haven't had time for a shower. I've been too busy working, haven't I?"

"Don't get upset, Jessie. You've done such a fine job. Don't get upset. Tomorrow it's my turn for a surprise, OK? You get a good night's sleep, and then we'll have a nice surprise."

Pudge waggled his head like one of those smiling china Noddy dolls. I wanted to break him into ceramic pieces, jagged little pieces you could grind under your heel, cutting perfection out of the floor. What did she mean, a nice surprise? She knew how much I hated surprises.

And that was only Friday night.

This morning, after my ritualistic run and a shower, I couldn't postpone it any longer. But when I walked into the kitchen, Mom stood up, leaving Pudge nodding away behind the paper.

"May I buy you breakfast, Madam?"

She used such a fake jolly voice that it grated badly on the ears. So badly, in fact, that I felt almost panicked. Like, her health?

But mainly I was thinking: Don't argue, let's just get this over with. It was funny, when I shrugged, Pudge shot me a sympathizing glance as if we were both being bossed around by a bigger kid. I guess that's one way to look at Pudge. I mean, maybe he's a professional who gets his name in the paper (Mom cut it out) but he hasn't yet embraced adulthood to the full extent of the law.

The thing is, Pudge gambles. We had to give up Cable because he was addicted, and I was exposed to this lurid verbal picture of the way Pudge had been spending his weekends channel surfing in the same temporary one-bedroom high-rise apartment where he'd been living since University. And in fact I could totally picture raccoon-eyed Pudge on his sofa-futon surrounded by fetid laundry, dead Chinese food and furniture that wasn't even as stop-gap as ours, which makes you think.

OK, so I stopped whining about Cable and he still gets to gamble? I mean, tell me who's crippled and how. Last Friday night, when he left for what turns out to be his monthly poker game, Mom explained in this prudent voice how it was high-stakes poker. Pudge might well lose more money than she and I could even hypothesize in one game, but he'd kept track over time, and most years he came out roughly even, or at least not too far behind, and sometimes he won pretty nicely, which helped explain this house.

"Murray is a good person," Mom said, which deranged me somewhat at the time, although I have to admit that it's probably true. He tries, which is more than most people bother. He doesn't totally succeed. He does *pro bono* work and resembles a future Mall Santa, but I guess you can't hold that against him. Before we left the kitchen, I gave Pudge a Look in return. Is it going to be all right? This time he avoided my eyes.

Looking back, I can say that the restaurant was acceptable, to use Miss V's word. It reminded me of one of the places Mom worked in Kingston, out near the highway but cheerier than a truck stop, with ruffled white curtains and geraniums in the windows. Mom seemed to want me to order French Toast so I did, and afterward she pulled out my final pay envelope. I'd asked her to pay me in cash, since it turned out the Bank wouldn't let me open a chequing account without parental signature. That meant I couldn't use my real name (Gretel) so I ended up banking with a loose brick in the basement wall. It didn't pay interest, but it didn't insult me with regulations about quote, children under sixteen, either.

"So we're really getting a New Start in our lovely new Home," Mom said. "You did such an amazing job."

"I still have lots to do," I told her. "Pudge is never going to clean out the basement and garage. That's not a criticism, he's busy. I figure you'd better let me handle it. Afterward, I can dig in a garden."

Mom got this reminiscent smile. "Jess and her flowers."

I told her to shut up, but she insisted on telling about the sweet peas. How I'd planted these sweet peas one year back in Kingston, and how we got evicted before they could bloom. Against all rules, I kept toddling back to the duplex, cutting these bouquets of sweet peas from the new people's garden. They were nice people, she said. It wasn't their fault we got evicted. That was a landlord-and-tenant dispute, as if she was going to put up with *that*. So I'd ring the bell and they'd find me there with my little red bucket and those blunt-ended scissors and they always let me in the yard. Afterward, they called her to say where I was. I was seven. No, eight.

It was one of those stories your parent tells so often that you think you remember it when you don't. The thing is, whenever she tells it, I seem to be looking down on this little innocent girl clutching her red bucket on some anonymous doorstep. But even if you discount the hovering perspective, I don't believe children go around feeling innocent. They only feel innocent when they've been accused of something, especially if they did it. So I must have known that I wasn't allowed to go back to the duplex and probably stood at the door feeling a combination of gleeful, guilty and stubborn, i.e. naughty, which is a feeling I remember very well.

But as I explained this, Mom's attention began to wane and I gave up. We both picked at our breakfast, then she put down her fork and said, "Baby, Paws is gone."

"So you've noticed?" I asked, and when she looked confused, "That was a joke."

"But here's your surprise. After breakfast, we're going down to the Humane Society to choose another kitten. I'll take care of the fee."

Totally no! I didn't want a replacement Paws. He was himself, veritably Paws, *le vrai Pattes*. How could you replace him? The whole proposal was insulting, both to Paws and to me.

"I know you don't like new and sudden ideas," she said, "but let's just think this one through."

Well excuse me, but she's the one who doesn't like new and sudden ideas. I'd mentioned my proposed new Plan, which was extensively well thought out. Yet did I hear a single word of inquiry? Not one single, solitary word.

I could have told her how once I got my bicycle *this afternoon*, I planned not only to widen my search for Paws. I could also use it to sell unwanted Collectibles from the basement and garage to nearby second-hand stores which, if she'd bothered to ask, I could have told her I'd already scouted after work. I could have outlined my methodology: how I'd put out utter garbage piece by piece, week by week, the way Miss V recommended, meanwhile piling up usable wood etc. to be driven (Rent-All Trailer) up to Gramps's place some weekend. I mean, Recycling, Creation, i.e. Gramps's carpentry projects? I'd covered all the bases. In payment, all I asked was those Collectibles I wished to retain. Plus, of course, the proceeds from my second-hand store sales, the exception being if I uncovered a true Antique, in which case I would turn it over to Pudge for consignment, being an Honest Person.

The thing is, I'd never noticed before how Dishonest my quote, mother was. First she says I dislike the new and the sudden, then she keeps claiming that I want a new kitten. Who really wanted a new kitten? It wasn't me.

But maybe that's just what people are like. They think you're longing for the same things they want. If they want something, it must be desirable, right? Yet being a different person, you've got your individual wants, needs, Plans etc.

That was even more depressing. My quote, mother wasn't insightful or to any degree perceptive. She was just as mundane as everybody else.

"Look, here's my Plan," I said, and told her.

"Lord, Jessie, you've been busy thinking," she said, glancing quickly at my eyes. Like she was frightened?

"That's what I do, I think. I'm the Bright one, right?"

"Then maybe you've already thought about the main thing we've got to discuss," she said, looking squarely into my face. "You might have noticed . . ."

"That you're pregnant."

I didn't know she was pregnant until I blurted it out. But you can't tell someone about Cancer at a restaurant, can you? A restaurant is for quote, happy occasions. Celebrations?

Right.

She confirmed that she was three months pregnant. Three months! So that's why they got married. I couldn't believe it. She'd trapped him! Even though she claimed he was happy, he liked children, they'd been planning to get married anyway— the fact is, she'd pulled a fast one in a sleazy, embarrassing fashion, trapping herself a husband. It was particularly embarrassing since I'd assured Miss V that she had totally respectable neighbours, and soon it would be crystal clear that she did not.

Or would it? I glanced at my quote, mother's waistline and realized that nothing showed. She was wide enough that you could hope it wouldn't show for a couple more months, and maybe when the little bastard was born you could pass it off as premature. I hadn't weighed that much myself. Maybe she'd have a small baby?

It offended me, however, that she was replacing me before I'd so much as left. She claimed it wasn't a replacement. "Jessie, it's not a replacement!" But then it turned out to be something worse than a replacement: another New Start.

"Jesus, Michelle," I said, feeling tired. "How many New Starts am I supposed to live through? How many this year? After how many last year? It gets a little nerve-racking after a while."

What could she say to that? I had her there, didn't I? Not that I felt victorious.

"I never asked for any of this," I told her. "None of it was my choice."

"I know, baby, and I'm sorry," she replied. "But sometimes you get what you ask for and sometimes other people do." For a moment, we were like two women looking at each other across an intervening man.

Dear Diary, how did I know that? I'm too young to know that. I didn't want to know that. I didn't want to know any of this. Who asked Janelle Piglet to lie about my so-called father? Who asked my quote, mother to date some *pro bono* lawyer? Before you know it, she's trying to impose a stepfather on me. I'm not the one who wanted to move to Toronto. I didn't ask to be threatened with a sibling. I didn't ask for any of this. It's like I said.

"We'll go get the kitten now," she said, paying the bill.

"I don't want any fucking kitten."

"Jessie! Language!" Then, "You'll get used to it, baby. I'm sorry it's a shock. It comes as a shock, and there isn't any way around it. But you'll get used to it, and then we'll all be fine. A little baby brother?"

"A live-in babysitter. How convenient."

Not that my existence was convenient at all.

Michelle drove straight to the Humane Society, heading west to a weedy neighbourhood on the fringes of downtown. She had

Pudge's car. Their car, I guess. It was a normal enough drive, but the building in question proved to be a squat concrete jail with a driveway leading behind it. Michelle pulled to stop in this isolated parking lot trapped between a muddy construction site and rusting railway tracks and some looming concrete bridge. There was no way I was going to wait in the car. But one step inside the glass doors proved that the Inhumane Society bunker was permeated with this stifling catty-doggy odour, like medicine combined with hair, and I didn't need that, either. All I wanted was to howl and keen: Don't do this! Get me out of here! I never asked for any of this! But that was undignified, so I just shuffled through the lobby unhappily and took my place in the lineup behind Michelle, fidgeting and slouching like a stupid hemorrhoid.

Then I started getting into Stupid, don't ask me why. It piqued my sense of humour, I guess. I began working up this total Down's Syndrome behind Michelle's back, pumping up my shuffle and releasing this slack-bellied, slack-armed look, my face hovering above it, all sunny and empty and flat. Good Morning, Toronto, meet Jessie, the human Vacant Lot.

Michelle doesn't notice things very speedily, but everybody else did. I mean, with Bradley Pigott as a cousin, I can do Down's. My face isn't Down's, but there isn't always that big a difference. Bradley doesn't look so different from Janelle Piglet and all his Piglet brothers and sisters. Why should he? All he has is one broken chromosome. If I had a Down's brother, he would only be one broken chromosome away from me. It's a pretty simple chromosome, too, so far as I can see, controlling muscle laxness and brain laxness. Once I slouched and went lax, even though my face wasn't Down's, I could see from my reflection in the lobby doors that I was doing a believable retard. Brain Damage? Maybe Oxygen Deprivation at birth. Weird, anyhow.

That's certainly the way people reacted. Walking past, they gave me a wide berth, as if Damage could be catching.

They were the retarded ones. I have increasingly concluded that people are totally retarded and mean. But as I did my Down's, I also grew more curious. How did Bradley Pigott see the world? He probably didn't see it very clearly. When you thought of it, he seemed to live within this unfocused, watery place where Delightful objects could swim across his field of vision, getting hooked on his attention like fish.

Step two: unfocus the eyes. I can do that, it's a Talent of mine. And what I saw when I unfocused was a dim fuzzy flattened place with all these distracting human elements rattling through. The human elements were darker. They absorbed light. They were dull at the centre, exuded noise and rattled distractingly all the time. I liked the walls better, the contented way they stayed put. Reflections were best, the shiny edges of the counter and the open doors. They're what looked happy.

You had to blink a lot to see this way, and before too long, your eyes got watery. It seemed best to stare straight in front and move your head to see what was peripherally envisioned. And when you wanted to see something properly, you got in close and peered. Like the man's hands behind the counter. Michelle had reached the front of the line and was talking to a man who had these pale loose hands reaching out of his sleeves like fish. They flopped like fish on the counter, and when you peered in behind Michelle's shoulder, you saw the pale fish had lines of neat black hair growing down the outer edges, these parallel hairs that looked like a cat had licked them flat. Cat licking fish, the salty ocean taste. I rolled my tongue out my mouth like a straw and bit to keep it round.

The man appeared from behind the counter and led Michelle through an open gap of door. On heavy feet, I trotted behind, but she dispersed through another gap ahead. Flopping around, I butted up against the wall, my forehead stubbing the concrete blocks. Up close, they looked like margarine. Their cool reliability was a comfort to my skin and I rolled one cheek against the blocks and then the other. Afterward I licked them, tasting the cool margarine walls.

The man was beside me.

"Wall," I said.

"Yes, that's a wall," he replied in a kindergarten voice. When I peered up, his face looked as pale as tapioca pudding. Michelle wasn't anywhere. I checked, turning in circles and flopping my heavy arms, raising and letting them drop.

"It's OK, she's through here. We're going through here. You'll find her here." Of course the hairy fish-pudding man would know where Michelle had gone. Taken a good look at her zooms, hadn't he?

In the next opening were cages of rats and rabbits and ferrets. I bent and peered, unfocusing hard, swimming after the watery feel. A ferret . . . a living rat-tail swished through the cage, a scarf you could draw through your half-open hand. I joined my thumb and forefinger and balanced so I could squint through them. Now I saw the fur whipping back and forth, curving, swishing side to side. Empty black eyes glanced through my joined fingers, empty black pinhead eyes stuck in a mean and pointed little face. I laughed in exalted horror.

"We're not getting a ferret," Michelle said behind me.

"Oh no, a ferret isn't appropriate," the man agreed. I knew how much he bewildered Michelle with that kindergarten tone of voice and fought the urge to shout out loud. Absolutely shout and scream with laughter, exploding apart the margarine walls in this atomic blast of hilarity.

"In any case, I think we've settled on a kitten," Michelle said.

"Kittens can be rambunctious," the man replied. "You think she could manage?"

I felt Michelle's perplexity through my spine. "Jessie is very good with animals," she said. Atomic amusement, nuclear howls built up inside me as they conducted this totally swollen conversation about rabbits being very calm pets (him) but we were thinking of a kitten (her) as Michelle faltered and hedged and didn't totally get what was going on (as usual).

But what almost set me off in howls was the way their conversation sustained itself above my head. I seemed to be crouching beneath the frame of their conversation, which was freshly painted on the air above. Damp words floated within the frame and I reached up to grasp one. Kitten: a sharp little prancing word that dug its claws into my knuckles. I flopped my hand to free it, so the fish-pudding man took my fingers in his, squeezing them gently and lowering my arm without breaking the ebb and flow of speech.

"There's quite a few kittens around the corner," he said.

I didn't make it around the corner, flopping on heavy feet into the adjoining room. More human elements fidgeted past me, absorbing the overhead light. It was hard to keep seeing this way. Unfocus, I told myself. Arms hang, jaw hanging, mouth gaping at the flattened sight.

Cages. Metal Cages. But you don't know that they're Cages. You see metal. You see lines, cross-hatching lines catching the light, sparkling at the cheerful corners with light. You chuckle, turning in slow circles to see the metal sparkling, flashing, glowing with delight. Happy, reaching, stretching your arms.

"Mommy, what's the matter with her?"

Murmurs. Mews, mews. Noisy place of sparkling light. Then a dart, a soft white dart between the metal lines. Startling. It upsets me. It happens again. A white soft paw darts out of the cage. Turning, I see they're everywhere around me. White paw, black fur rubbing against the sparkling grid. Animal eyes seek contact with mine. They're seeking, beseeching human contact: cats' eyes that are yellow and slitted and watching. They're watching and mew, mew, mew, throwing themselves at the sparkling mesh. They're pacing, they're pawing, they're trapped, trapped, trapped. Trapped and unwanted. Trapped and unwanted. Trapped and

Paws isn't in any of the cages. "Paws!" I cry.

"Mommy, what's the *matter* with her?" Frightened now as I'm turning in circles, hugging myself and turning in circles, turning in circles and sinking slowly onto the floor.

"She doesn't like Cages," an older child says.

"I don't like Cages, either," the fish-pudding man answers, bending down beside me as I rock on my knees. His hairy hands hover above me. Did I really want to lick them?

I recoil into powdery Michelle.

"Jess?" she asks.

"She's freaked by all the Cages," the fish-pudding man says. "She's right, too. It's awful to have to keep animals caged."

"She's always been sensitive," Michelle says, sounding so embarrassed that I totally lose it and howl.

"Paws!"

"That's our cat," Michelle says, crouching down beside me. "The one who went missing? It's been a month. I'm sorry, I really didn't expect . . ."

"Of course she's sensitive," the fish-pudding man says. "Up, now," he tells me, his hairy hands grasping under my arms. "Come on now, Jessie. We've got a real nice chair waiting outside."

Sitting in the chair, rocking and keening, tears snot spit running down my face. I don't care. I don't care.

"So much for that idea," Michelle says, and somehow it happens that I catch her eye.

"Well, in cases like this," the fish-pudding man says.

"Cases?" Michelle turns around sharply.

"I'm sorry. Of course she's not a case. She's just a little . . . If you saw her casually, you'd never . . . I'm putting my foot in it, aren't I? There's a reason I work with animals, I guess."

But Michelle is slowly putting two and two together. She's glancing down at my floppy feet, how they're rubbing circles on each other the way that Bradley Pigott's do. Comprehension blooms on her face. For one scant second Michelle looks amused. She totally gets it. Then she's so disgusted she could spit.

"Jessie, that's enough of a performance. You can stop right now."

The fish-pudding man shuffles.

"Jessie!"

"Well, now," the man objects.

"It's the way we treat cases like this," Michelle tells him. And to me, "Here. Blow your nose. You can stop this right now. I've had more than enough for one day."

I stay in character. I do a bad job of snuffling out my nose, snot spattering across my face. Michelle grabs another tissue and wipes me off, muttering how if I'm going to act like a baby . . . Acting like a big baby, she tells me, and she's precisely half right. It's correct that I'm acting. But this is also how I truly feel, and how I now know Bradley Pigott must feel, trapped outside life, extraneous and lost.

"Paws," I whimper, meaning it, but also not. I'm over it and also not.

"I give up," Michelle tells me. "You win. OK? You win. We won't get a kitten. Now wind up your performance, roll the freaking credits and I'll meet you outside." She strides down the corridor and out the door, leaving the poor fish-pudding man totally perplexed, his hands flopping out his sleeves now for real. In another moment, I cease to weep, wiping my face and standing up with dignity.

"I'm sorry," I tell him. "It's a recessive gene." Then I follow Michelle to the car.

She floored it out of the parking lot and drove rapidly away, not talking through a busy left turn and blocks of angling north and east. Once she said something about hoping I was satisfied, which was not the right word. I stayed silent in my dignity, and when we reached the corner nearest the local bicycle store, I hopped out on a red light and told Michelle that my future bicycle and I would see her around.

But like I said, this was the worst day of my life. The store proved to be closed for the weekend, and when I retreated to Miss V's house, she was out. I sat in her garden for the longest time, wondering where to go and what to do. It had rained a little early in the morning but the day had turned out sunny and heated, a humid blanketing day that didn't give you any ideas. After a while, I got totally bored and unfocused on the cascade of roses nearby. White petals ran together into fuzzy unformed flowers, a swaying fall of unformed flowers like

A bad painting, that's what it was like. I suddenly saw it as one of those paintings by an Amateur where they couldn't get the petals right, or the shadows, or the subject's hands, so they claimed that it was abstract. Impressionistic? Right. They could claim what they wanted, but one look at the clumsy canvas and you knew they were a Fraud. They nailed their Fraud to a public wall and acted as if you ought to believe it. It was total conceit and enormous self-delusion. Fraud. Fraud. Fraud.

I hated myself. This feeling washed over me: I totally and utterly hated myself. What had I been thinking, behaving like that? I didn't know what I'd been thinking and felt a total wash of shame, shame so flaming and profound that I wanted to bash my head against a concrete wall. What had I been thinking, scaring poor little children like that?

Mommy, what's the matter with her?

I didn't know where to start so I started running, my feet hitting the alley in this rat-a-tat pattern. I hate my-self, I hate my-self, I hate my-self, chanted loudly in my head. Running north, I passed discarded fast-food wrappers all piss-yellow and ratty empty Coke cans and lawn cuttings thrown nastily over the fence. I hate myself, I hate myself, and hate this fucking city, too. Look at that hairy undershirt working on his car. Who asked for this? Who asked for him? Who asked for *me?* Turning right and looking at that *fucking* garage, illegal workshop polluting the air, bristly thistles growing like Cancer. I hate myself and hate this place and hate and hate and hate . . .

The smell of weed is wafting by. Thistles scrape my aching legs, burrs bristle on my socks. I run so long my knees are weak, run too close to growling dogs and slinking well-fed cats. Paws! No pause. I hate myself, I hate myself, I hate my stinking lonely self as rancid sweat runs down my pits and ankles bend and hot lungs groan. I have to lean on someone's fence and gasp and grasp for cleaner air.

Here? There's just Pollution here, there's only Global Warming. Global warning: Amoebic dysentery envelopes you here. Out of control. This city is expanding out of control, swallowing people and places and me.

Breathing hard, I limp back slowly to the yard, finding my way to the basement shower and turning the water on hot. I scrub myself with stinging soap, letting it run into my eyes before scrubbing hard between my legs. Then I shave, cutting the scab off my shin so the soapy red water runs down the drain. I shave every vestige of hair from my stupid aching legs and tear into my pits, remembering that sorrowful Dream of pube-like hair and shaving every fetid wire, scraping out the hidden roots until my pits are bleeding and deserving every nick of it.

Bleeding and aching, I remember those hands, fish-pudding hands, hair licked as straight as my fetid pubes beneath the streaming shower. I hate myself and shave my pubes, shaving them so totally that I nick the fetid skin, totally disgusting and disgusted with my totally crippled self.

What's the *matter* with her, Mommy?

She's retarded. She's hateful. She's bleeding.

Later

I hurt so much. I hurt everywhere. My legs are sore from running and my hand is cramped from writing and my skin is raw from shaving and between my legs from scrubbing. The one thing is, I'm no longer hungry. Pudge came out a while ago with a plate of couscous salad. He chuckled sadly but didn't bother me much, so when the salad was lukewarm and arguably Toxic I did him a favour and ate it. Afterward I wrote some more, although now I'm finished. I suppose that I'm finished, I'm finished off.

With the result? That I totally and implacably hate my Damaged self.

I hate myself. I hate myself. I hate. I hate. I hate hate hate hate hate

Miss V: Why weren't you home?

ELEVEN

Near Arnhem,
April, 1942

I don't know how to make sense of what happened today. I don't know what to write, or even whether I should write. Perhaps I shouldn't write anything because it's suspicious to write too much and then burn it in the stove. I would be suspicious of someone who filled pages with writing and then burned what she'd written. In fact, I wouldn't even think of writing, except that my dear Father isn't here to explain what happened, and I must present him with a clear account when we return so he can explain everything.

I should do this: write it all down clearly to prepare for speaking. Afterwards, I can keep the diary in my underclothing as I sleep; also tomorrow in case there is another dreadful incident. It would be unfortunate if my diary were discovered, but also painful to present my Father with an unclear account. I find it so painful to fail. I dislike the cruel laughter that greets failure, the public chiding. Not from my dear Father! He is kind enough to refrain from punishing me in public. I mean from quarters that a more sophisticated person would ignore. Clearly I am not a sophisticated girl.

However, if I am to write, I should say that the day began well. Kindly Mrs. N. packed us a generous lunch for our second trip to the national park. I must describe Mrs. N. as an ample, well-meaning lady of such casual country manners that she

101

forgets to take her apron off at table, or perhaps doesn't know that she should.

That's not good enough. Mrs. N. is better described as the salt of our salty earth, a jovial provincial of the type pictured in the early work of our dear Frans Hals. Privately, of course, she reminds me of a potato-eating peasant from the work of the decadent van Gogh, far from the sort of jolly housewife one admires. But of course I can't say that; she is the sister of my dear Father's colleague. Hals will do. I must try to remember the name of an appropriate painting to show my Father that I have paid attention in class.

Our picnic: fresh bread and a good wedge of cheese. Mrs. N. believes us to be "poor skinny waifs," although I have assured her that our excellent parents provide us with the best rations. Still, the bread and cheese smelled so delicious as she wrapped it up that the others insisted I carry it in my pack, making sure that no crusts or crumbs would disappear before we shared out equal portions at noon. I felt uplifted by their trust, although I'm sure that Jannie was worthy as well, and even Florrie B., who can be fervent beneath her laziness and cynicism. Indeed, carrying the lunch soon became less an honour than a punishment, for despite our filling breakfast, the burden grew more and more tempting as we cycled for hours through cool and sometimes hilly country. I admit that my stomach began to growl. It has been a long time since I've smelled such fat, buttery cheese!

But that comes a little close to complaining and I am not a person who ever complains. All I really mean to say is that we packed up our lunch, or I did, and then cycled towards our country's new national park on a cool but pretty morning. The spring sun shone and fleecy, windblown clouds scudded across the blue sky. Indeed, the wind blew unusually hard, making my eyes water and sting. Well, there's a reason we developed wind-mills in our country! As Florrie B. pointed out, cycling uphill against the wind was excellent exercise for the calves and thighs. And after the labour of pedalling up some pleasantly rolling hills, we enjoyed the great pleasure of gliding back down, the younger girls kicking their legs straight out in the rushing air, squealing with delight at their freedom and speed. I think we must have made a lovely picture, a line of young girls in our identical blouses, skirts and ties, coats open as the day grew warmer, caps tucked in our pockets, hair flying, laughing into the breeze.

When I think back, however, it reveals something of Florrie's mixed character that she mentioned the slimming part of the exercise. That is the business of movie stars, not of ordinary girls. Yet while she could be lazy and even sulky at times, Florrie took the lead this morning, urging the rest of us onwards, pedalling quickly and calling back over her shoulder, "Come on! We're going to have fun if it kills us!"

Once we'd turned into the forest, she led us forward heed-lessly on a maze of identical paths. It was beautiful, of course. This was a national park. The brown of the leafless oak forest and the blue of the spring sky formed a restful contrast. Such strength in the brave upthrust branches. Such hope in the new spring buds of bursting green.

Et cetera, et cetera. As a matter of fact, I had to concentrate on where we were going to make sure that we didn't get lost. Florrie would probably have got us lost if I hadn't kept an eye on the signposts. Without the signposts, we would certainly have been lost. As it was, I sometimes felt confused—even doubting the truth of the posts!—and when we hadn't passed a post for too long, I grew afraid that we had veered out of the park completely onto wild or private land.

When I dismounted to get my bearings, I was surprised to find Jannie coming to a stop beside me.

"As long as we turn west soon, we're fine," she said.

"That would be wonderful if we knew where west was," I answered, and she pointed.

"The sun," she said.

"Of course." I felt like a foolish city girl, but said briskly, "Then we'd better catch up to Florrie and turn her in the right direction. We should be stopping for lunch before too long."

"I have to stop right now, I'm afraid. I've got to fix myself up. I'm on the rag. Can you just watch out for a minute while I duck behind a bush?"

"We should get going," I said, disliking myself for sounding shrill. Yet what if Florrie and the others got too far ahead?

"I don't have any choice," she answered, calling out as she disappeared, "You'll find out soon enough. Then you'll wish you hadn't."

I blush far too often. But Jannie is so shockingly casual that she can sometimes seem vulgar. How could I even come close to repeating words like that to my dearest Father? But it is understandable that she and I might have stopped to speak about our route. She is a practical person. Perhaps that's the best way to put it: Jannie is practical-minded. Athletes are like that, and Jannie is a famous athlete. Her speciality is the discus, although with those strong arms, she wins prizes at archery, too. Also hurdles, where she set a city-wide record last fall, but that's her legs. It's co-ordination, that's the proper word. Jannie is a person who shows admirable co-ordination and balance. How I wish that I was like her!

Not that I'm unathletic. My event is the dash, where willpower can often take me the distance. Asthma keeps me from competing in events of endurance, which I would otherwise prefer; they prove more. If not for the asthma, I think I would be quite athletic, much like my dear Father in his golden youth. Then I would truly make him proud, an athletic daughter—almost a son! Unfortunately, I can change neither my sex nor my medical condition, and while I would like to ignore it, the asthma refuses to ignore me. In fact, while Jannie arranged herself behind the bush, moving just at the edge of my vision, I realized that my chest was growing tight as I grew more and more anxious. Was anybody coming? Would anybody see?

Nobody was coming. We hadn't seen many others in the park that day. Yet my chest grew painfully tight. I knew I had to be careful and crouched down, wheezing a little and trying to relax, keeping watch yet breathing, watching—relaxing—breathing, watching—trying to relax—until Jannie came out, straightening her coat. By then, I was foolishly nervous of having an attack in the middle of the park. Perhaps not so foolishly. Two days of cycling seemed to be catching up with me all at once.

Of course I couldn't rest. I had to get back on my bike. Jannie thanked me casually and kicked off, leaving me to labour behind her. It seemed best to try to match my pedalling with hers: one leg, two leg, one leg, two leg, breathe, breathe, breathe, but all this effort against a tight chest and the steady wind soon had me seeing stars.

They were not stars. People say "seeing stars" but I saw blotches, white and black and red against the wintry landscape; wintry, now, since everything seemed far away and I couldn't see signs of spring. I seemed to be looking through the wrong end of a telescope, the high blue sky and thin brown branches sharp and distant, with ugly red blotches swimming in front of them. Jannie's legs were columns ahead of me, beige columns and low socks, until soon even they half disappeared, splotchy with explosions of black and red. I felt half choked and half blind, almost ready to fall off my bike by the time I saw some distant forms ahead. The others! I felt so grateful, even for Elisabeth's cry, "Here comes lunch!"

I don't remember exactly what happened next. Even though I am not a person to complain and would never have said anything about my problem, I believe that as I reached them and stepped down, I drew a long and ghastly breath. I do remember that Florrie looked exasperated, which struck me as unfair. Then I think that Florrie lifted my pack off my back and Jannie led me to a red-blotched tree, sitting me down and repeating with admirable calm and concentration, "Now breathe. Now breathe. Now breathe."

Florrie must have divided up the lunch, no doubt evenly, and I'm sure the others ate. It is certainly true that the band around my chest slowly loosened. I began to breathe more easily, feeling the pain go away and the perspiration on my forehead evaporate in the cool breeze. The world moved towards me. It had been at the wrong end of a telescope but it moved back, and my foolish anxiety decreased.

Perhaps it had not been so foolish.

"I'm fine now," I told Jannie, starting to get up.

"Don't you dare," Jannie said. "Giving us a scare like that. Sit down and eat your lunch."

Grateful for her consideration, I sat back down, although I had little appetite and the food felt bulky as it moved down my throat. Now that the attack had passed, I felt drained and nervous, unable to forget the black and red blotches between the landscape and my eyes. Luckily the others ignored me, either gossiping beneath the trees or, like Florrie and Jannie, strolling up and down the road chatting. Florrie had decided to stop near the main road out of the forest. Yet that was lucky too: a quick route out. When I finished my lunch, we were ready to leave.

"Time to go," I said, leaping up with a show of energy.

"Where do we have to go, and by what time?" Florrie answered, so the others giggled and resumed their endless chatter.

It was late afternoon when we finally got back on our bikes, and I can't help noting that if we'd left when I'd suggested, nothing would have happened. I would have wrapped up my account by now, and Mrs. N. would not just have said, "My goodness, you're writing so much! I was never much for writing, myself."

Jannie didn't need to give me a warning glance. "Our national park is truly one of the wonders of the world," I said. "Such great beauty."

"Fair number of trees," agreed good Mr. N. with typical Dutch understatement. Either that or sarcasm, it was hard to decide.

I must cover my page as I write what happened next; I have promised. Yet the incident began with only a mild surprise. Turning a corner just inside the park, we saw a black car stopped on the road ahead of us, blocking the way. It was a *Wehrmacht* car, or at least, one requisitioned by the army. The hood was open and a man bent under it. Two German officers stood talking beside the passenger door, perhaps even arguing. Luckily, I was in the lead, having insisted on setting a wise pace at the head of our group (although I hadn't liked to hear Jannie tell Florrie, "Let her").

I brought our little group to a stop and led the regulation salute. The officers saluted back and the mechanic—I imagine he was actually the driver—glanced out from under the hood before resuming his work.

"Can we be of any help?" I asked politely. German is one of my best subjects in school, yet neither officer seemed to be impressed. Perhaps they were out of sorts about the car, or had indeed been arguing. Now that we were close, I saw that both were young lieutenants, probably about the age of Elisabeth's older brothers.

"Garber, here's a band of mobile female mechanics offering to help," the first officer said, and the driver glanced up again briefly. "The Dutch are such practical little trolls. How can one fail to distrust them?"

"But we're members of the Youth Storm," I replied. When none of the Germans reacted, I understood that they were new to the country. "You would call us members of the Hitler Youth."

"Congratulations," the first officer said. The second one had noticed Jannie, whose colour was good in the country air. "I mean that sincerely," the first one added. "Congratulations."

"Thank you," I said, feeling somewhat confused. "I only meant, could we go for help?"

"I think we can take care of ourselves," he replied. "Can't we, Garber?"

"Sir," the driver agreed.

I took in a welter of impressions. The officers both looked splendid in their uniforms, although the first one was far more splendid than the second. He thought so too, keeping an eye on his reflection in the car window. I disliked myself for noticing this. From what I'd heard, it was common for people to feel disappointed when they met movie stars, who often proved to be short. I did not wish to be common. Yet I also couldn't help noticing that the second officer resembled one of Elisabeth's brothers, which was probably why I'd thought of them in the first place. With such a broad snub nose, he looked girlish but also coarse, and one suspected he came from the country.

That is dreadfully common! These young men had volunteered their youth for the Reich, prepared to die for the cause! What would my dear Father say to hear such unworthy reflections? I'd deserve a beating for that!

"You like bicycling?" the second officer asked Jannie.

"It's a convenient way to get around," she replied.

"Get around, do you?" he asked.

Jannie's smile suggested that she didn't understand much German. Well, you don't expect scholarship from an athlete.

"Jannie is one of our best athletes," I said. "She holds an all-Amsterdam record for hurdles."

For some reason, the second officer found this funny and began to laugh, while the first one raised his eyebrows. "For all of Amsterdam?"

"Back off, Maaike," Florrie whispered, coming up behind me. "Let's just get out of here."

I didn't understand and turned to look at her. But then I heard confusion behind me, and turned back to find the second officer taking Jannie's bike. The first one looked disgusted at first, then brightened as he observed that his friend probably needed to go for a ride.

"Been a while since you were in the saddle, hasn't it, Krull? Probably more than a while." His friend wobbled off down the road, waving one arm behind him, the gesture rude but vigorous, common to arguing boys.

Of course: they were boys! They were two splendid boys, teasing each other—and teasing us—just as Elisabeth's older brothers did. We were perhaps eight or ten years younger than they were, no doubt the age of their little sisters at home! Just as our country was a dear little sister to theirs!

I turned to the handsome lieutenant. "Our parents are all members of the NSB," I told him. "We were National Socialists in my family well before the war."

"Congratulations," he said, laughing quietly as he watched the second officer, who wobbled back towards us.

"My father has a very responsible position on the leader's security staff," I said. "The SS? We're just on holiday here. We're all from the capital. I think you'll find your allies in the NSB ready to welcome you to your new post with every . . ."

"Krull, you're a sorry sight," the officer called. "You're a disgrace to the uniform, so long out of the saddle. How long since you've been for a ride, you sorry bastard?" Turning back to me, he said in a kind voice, "The NSB couldn't run an ice-cream parlour."

I didn't know how to answer, but in any case, he turned away again.

"Krull," he called. "Krull? I said the NSB couldn't run a bloody ice-cream parlour. We have to show them how to do it."

"Almost finished, sir," the mechanic told him.

"That's why we're here, running ice-cream parlours for the NSB. You up to it, Krull? Or can you only run cars into the ground? Do you specialize in killing cars, Krull? Not that he was driving," the officer told me. "Of course he wasn't driving. It's Garber's job to drive, isn't it Garber?"

"I do what I'm told, sir."

What was going on? I didn't know how to answer the officer, I felt so confused. I was also distracted by Lieut. Krull, who had reached our little group again and wanted Jannie to ride on the handlebars, looking almost angry as he grabbed her by the arms.

"She can't do that," Florrie said loudly. "She's not in any state."

I didn't know how she could even allude to something like that. What if they understood her implication? I couldn't have blushed any harder.

"Overawed by your abilities," Florrie said, and hopped onto the handlebars herself. "You'd better watch out for my elbows," she told the lieutenant. "I'd love to take a quick trip down to the corner and back. Then we'll leave you to your repairs."

They wobbled off again and I heard myself wheeze. The first officer once more disputed the riding abilities of his friend so crudely that I wanted to set him straight, despite my embarrassment. Instead, I felt Jannie's hand on my arm.

"Don't provoke him any further," she whispered, pulling me back. "We've got to get out of here."

"I'm not provoking him. Look what Florrie's doing."

"Florrie's helping," answered Jannie. "Florrie's my friend."

"What's the problem with them?" I asked, wheezing. "They're impostors. They're not real *Wehrmacht*. What's going on here?"

"They're drunk, Maaike. They've been drinking. They've had a picnic and an accident, and this one is afraid they're going to get into trouble. As soon as Florrie gets back, we're leaving them to fight it out."

"But they're not supposed to . . ."

"Stop thinking about what's supposed to be and start thinking about what is."

It was agony. I don't know how I can even begin to describe the scene to my dearest Father. I was in utter agony as one lieutenant wobbled away with Florrie on his handlebars, looking comical as enemy propaganda as he disappeared down a path. The other seemed distracted by the sight of his reflection in the car window, raising his chin and stroking it, checking one side, then the other, smirking all the while.

"You should be ashamed of yourself," I burst out. "Drinking while in uniform."

"Please excuse her mistake," Jannie said, confusing me by switching to fluent German. "She had an asthma attack earlier today and I'm afraid it's made her light-headed. I'm very sorry. She's young for her age and often gets hysterical."

The officer turned around slowly, looking from me to Jannie. "I recognize the type," he said mildly. He and Jannie exchanged a smile; I could see it quite clearly in the car window. Laughing at me in public! My agony grew.

"Of course we haven't been drinking," he added.

"I know that you wouldn't," Jannie answered.

"We have prigs like her in the enlisted ranks," the officer went on. "They often rise to the position of sergeant. Did you hear that, Garber?"

The driver looked out from under the hood as I felt my chest constrict. Jannie smiled at the driver, then back at the officer. I heard myself wheeze loudly.

"You see? She's having an asthma attack. Excuse me while I deal with it. You will please excuse me?"

"Could you look at the motor, sir?" I met the driver's sharp eyes, wondering what was going on as Jannie pulled me away.

"Breathe now, you stupid idiot. Breathe now, you total imbecile. Breathe now. If you say another word I'll break your stupid neck."

What did I do to deserve this? Jannie berated me while the other girls huddled nearby. Florrie and the officer eventually returned, apparently having had a fall. It didn't seem to bother the officer, at least at first. He was very jolly, laughing in a superior fashion until his friend began to chide him about soiling his uniform.

"You're in for it now, Krull," the handsome officer said. "I take no responsibility. I've been trying to warn you."

What was going on here? Lieut. Krull began to sulk and Florrie cried. Her clothes were even more muddy than the officer's and she seemed stiff, as if she were in pain. I didn't understand why her face was so dirty that you could see the marks of tears down her cheeks. Had she fallen on her face? I could only assume that she'd fallen on her face in the mud at the side of the road. She'd also ripped her uniform badly. Staring at the torn fabric, I concluded the fall had been nasty. So how could Florrie jump so quickly on her bicycle and lead us so rapidly away?

Outside the park, very close to the farm, Jannie brought us to a halt.

"Nothing happened today," she told us. "We met no one and saw nothing. Two deer and the groundskeeper, that's all we saw. Florrie had a fall."

"Are you all right, Florrie?" one of the younger girls asked.

"I hope so," she replied, but wept anew. Watching her, I felt growing sympathy, understanding that she'd been very brave to cycle away so quickly from the unspeakable scene. The poor girl was in real pain. Reaching over awkwardly, I gave her a tender pat on the shoulder.

"Don't touch me," she shrieked, hitting my hand away. I felt shocked at her violence, and even more shocked as she started bawling. I'm afraid there's no other word for it. She bawled like a baby, and I could only stand there watching as tears dripped from her mouth and nose. Silly girl, I thought, to make such a fuss over a stupid fall. Over nothing! My sympathy gave way to disgust as we remounted our bicycles and slowly rode back to the farm.

On reflection, I believe that the men must have been enemy infiltrators disguised in Axis uniforms. I hope that my dear Father agrees, and feels that I acquitted myself properly as leader of the group. I hope that he won't have to beat me for making a mistake. I probably made some kind of mistake, but I don't think it was all that bad, since I frankly can't see what it was despite writing here for hours. When I make a mistake, I usually know it.

Perhaps it was Florrie who made the mistake. Florrie went to bed long ago, pleading stiffness from her fall. But didn't that serve her right? Florrie shouldn't have tried to take over our expedition when I had been named as leader. She didn't deserve to be leader. If she did, she would have been chosen. Florrie usually arrived late for Youth Storm gatherings, refused to compete athletically and was an inconsistent student. She could get good marks if she bothered, but she only bothered in bursts. What did that say about her character?

That's unkind. I have no wish to be unkind, and I'm too foolish to try to sort out blame. I'm too inexperienced. My job is to get the other girls to bed—it's late—and then to hide this diary close to my body until we complete our holiday tomorrow. Afterwards, my dearest Father will be able to relieve my mind by telling me what really happened.

"Promise, Maaike?" Jannie insisted. "We won't say a word."
Except to you, Father. She couldn't have meant you.

AUGUST

TWELVE

The girl is coming into my garden again. I believe these visits to be innocent. She speaks of me as an old lady who does not have anyone to watch over her. The mother has taught her not to say old lady but that is clearly what she means. Why not? It is true.

So, you have come for your tea, I say.

The girl has started to wear more clothing, T-shirts that somewhat cover the arms and slacks to cover the legs. These slacks are called khakis. I see from the billboards that this is the summer uniform: khaki slacks and grey T-shirts with modest sleeves. Sometimes the fashion is acceptable. Unfortunately, there is also a fashion for children to use wheeled playthings on the sidewalk that threaten the balance of pedestrians. These children are like unleashed dogs and should be restrained.

Did you answer?

I said thank you, she replies in a louder voice. She has been attentive for several days, but also quiet. Do you like my new haircut? she asks.

You have cut it yourself.

I know it looks crooked, she says. I'll do better next time.

It is the fashion to wear the hair short, I tell her, coming into my kitchen. An improvement, I think.

. . .

You are speaking far too quietly.

I said thank you. I'm trying to be different.

By being the same as all the other young people. Yes, it is the way.

I meant different than I was. I've always been different than everybody else.

And now you are the same. It is probably for the best.

To go around in disguise.

The girl knows what I am thinking. She mumbles, but I know what she says. It is what I am thinking, and uncanny. I busy myself with the tea. A disguise, I say.

Not really a disguise, an improvement. That's what you said.

But perhaps I am wrong, I tell her. Perhaps a butterfly is merely a caterpillar wearing disguise.

Please don't say that. If you can't improve, what's the point? Improvement is crucial.

I am surprised by her emotion. Young girls are too emotional; it is the hormones. I refrain from telling her that there is no point.

Here is your tea. You may try it with lemon and sugar. With milk, it is far too sweet.

She spoons excessive sugar into her cup. I'm reading Goethe's *Selected Poems,* she says. It was in the library.

So.

I read his poem about the Erlkönig.

Pronounce it properly: Earl-kerr-nig. King of the Alders.

I thought it meant King of the Elves.

They live in the alderwoods where there is mist.

Mein Sohn, was birgst du so bang dein Gesicht?—
Siehst, Vater, du den Erlkönig nicht?
Der Erlenkönig mit Kron und Schweif—
Mein Sohn, es ist ein Nebelstreif.—

You understand? They are riding through a forest; we know this. Now the father asks why the son hides his face. You do not see him, Father? the boy asks. It is the King of the Alders with his crown and his robe. Ah, my son, it is only the mist.

I read it in English but I guess it's the same. The little boy's in danger and his father can't even see it.

That is correct. Goethe says that children are still close enough to nature to sense what adults can no longer understand. Danger.

You see, Goethe believes that danger is female. It is seductive. And so the child can see the Erlkönig's mother and daughters when his father cannot.

Mein Vater, mein Vater, und siehst du nicht dort
Erlkönigs Töchter am düstern Ort?

The boy asks his father if he sees how the daughters wave to him, then the father tells him it is just some old willows. His father only sees the truth when it is already too late. Schubert has set the poem to music. Here, I will play you the recording.

Story of the Elvenking
By Gretel von Bundt

Once upon a time, a Father drove through the northern woods, his Son on the seat beside him, wrapped in a fleecy lambskin.

"What are you hiding from?" the Father asked merrily, as the Son shrank into the fleece.

"Right alongside us!" the Son cried. "He's gliding along in his chariot, dressed in his crown and his mantle. It's the King of the Elves, come to take me away!"

"Nonsense," his Father told him. "It's a windy, rainy after-noon. That's just a slipstream of mist through the headlights. There's an explanation for everything."

Come my child and play with me
We'll ride a Tornado out to sea
Daisies and marigolds bloom on the strand
My Mother's embroidery stitched into sand.

"Father! He sang to me! He's calling me to join him!"
"Don't be silly. It's just the sound of the traffic. It's a busy afternoon. People are rushing to get home before the rain really hits."
"I want to go Home, Father."
"We'll be there soon. Don't worry."

Come with me, sweet red-headed mite,
My horses ride currents up to the light
Let my daughters beguile you with music and dance
Whirling and spinning a lullaby trance.

"Father, can't you see them? The Elvenking's daughters. They're so pale and thin and reaching, just like in the movies! Over there! By the side of the road."
"Those are just birches. It's a weird light, almost green. The storm is getting nasty. But they look pretty, don't they? Caught in the light?"
"I don't like them. How long before we get Home?"
"Ten minutes sooner than the last time you asked."

Oh my beauty, oh my child
Your innocence will drive me wild

If you won't come along with me
I'll take you, twist you, tug you free.

"Daddy, he's got me! Daddy!"

"Oh my God, it's a Tornado!"

The car flew into the sky, spinning and whirling with the fierce draw of the Elvenking's desire. His pale daughters flew by them, and his mother in her marigold robes the colour of stormy sunset. The King's laughter was like moaning and thunder, a deep growl with an undertow of Power. The poor mortal Father clutched his Son to his chest, covering his ears against the Elvish song that drives all children mad.

You are not your Mother's child
You are mine and you are wild
I'm your Father, King of Sin,
Come dance with me on vicious Winds

The Tornado abated slowly, almost gently, laying the car to rest on an exposed hump of Canadian Shield that was far harder than any human road.

"Thank God!" the Father cried.

But the Father's jubilation quickly turned to horror. In the circle of his sheltering arms, the innocent Child lay dead.

———————

That's a beautiful song. But it's sad.

These things go together, I tell her.

Flowers are beautiful without being sad. It's like that quotation from Katherine Mansfield. They respond wonderfully but they don't sympathize. They have needs, not feelings. Like half the human race these days.

Flowers don't have feelings, it is true. But do they have beauty either without people to judge them? And if their beauty comes from people, can it be extricable from the sadness people also feel, looking at their beauty and knowing that it does not last?

You're being philosophical. That's the wrong expression. "Being philosophical" means you're pretending things are better than they really are. I mean you're being epistemological. Is that the right word?

I find myself laughing.

That's not the right word?

Epistemology is a study of the way we know things. It is the theory of knowledge.

I know lots of words and names. I just don't always understand what they mean.

But I am afraid that names mean nothing, really. They are labels, like *Gap* on your clothing. Does the label cover a gap on your clothing? I hope that it does not. I hope that it covers fabric. So you see, the name Gap covers a non-gap in the fabric. It is misleading, and perhaps also a joke.

You must be a professor. A retired professor?

I laugh again and tell her, Once I professed many things and now I do not. So in a way, yes, I am a retired professor. And you are a girl who tries to lift herself above her lowly animal origins.

She does not seem to remember saying that, but I am enjoying this conversation.

You must read philosophy, I tell her. Nietzsche. He will help you understand so-called meaning. Also to be philosophical about it. Do not put so much sugar into your tea.

A question of identity, she mumbles.

I question your identity.

Which does she say? I do not hear her.

I do not hear you, I tell her sharply. You mumble.

I like it sweet, she answers, looking surprised.

My very dear Father,

Weather has been more seasonal since the beginning of the month (August). Humid periods have repeatedly been followed by thundershowers, although the temperature continues below the normal average. For these reasons, pests remain abundant. Earwigs pursue their annual assault upon your tuberous dahlias, but I assure you, Father, they have met their match.

Horticulturally, my phlox *(P. paniculata)* is fragrant when evenings are cool, having spread so that its scent fills the garden. Therefore the planting retains its place. I continue to find the blooms sufficiently undistinguished that I would otherwise replace it, perhaps for an untried variety of platy-codon that I have my eye on, *P. grandiflorus* "Shell Pink." Meanwhile, the *Hibiscus syriacus* (Rose of Sharon) has begun to flower. You will no doubt remark that this is somewhat earlier than usual.

Nearby, other gardens have begun their yearly decline as amateur gardeners run out of steam. Either that, or these gardens are given over to lurid annuals, many of them clashing orange and red. These are further mixed with pastels, Father. Petunias, coleus and marigolds: the palette could scarcely be more painful. Bicycling past, one averts the eyes.

I can also report that the girl, Gretel, has been a frequent visitor. She is neglected by her mother and step-father, who abandon her for work each day. Not long after I last wrote, I

provided the girl with tea. This has become a regular occurrence, and has led to a decision: I will do what I can for the
child. She is a clever girl, Father, but confused. In this, she is
the opposite of Jannie, who was unwavering but lacked
intellect. The only real resemblance between the two lies in
the bloom (so pink!) and the similar athletic physique.
However, this is a good start. *Mens sana in corpore sano*. My
young neighbour has disciplined herself to run daily. I will
improve the mind.

You have heard me remark that she is clever. She is also
studious and earnest. In this (if I may say so) our young neighbour resembles the girl that I once was. Indeed, I have lately
amused myself by thinking that she is an amalgam of Jannie
and myself. I confess that the thought gives me pleasure. "If
you can't improve, what's the point?" she asks. Of course, there
is no point, but she is right, one must improve; the race must
improve. I mean to say "species." Perhaps she is already an
improvement in the way she joins Jannie's athleticism to my
quick mind. Yet I have recommended Nietzsche to pull her up
further. Let us see if she can start to understand what my good
Nietzsche teaches. I said "start," Father.

I must report, as well, that there are dreams. These are often
acceptable, and more. I can feel such lightness. Last night, I
dreamed I was here in your house but it was huge and I was a
child. I was ill in bed, as I so often was, but this time I threw
back the covers and flew through the house. I was not in the
least bit frightened, but glided through the halls at waist level,
turning corners with joy, passing deep wainscotting that was
not ours and gliding down an aristocratic staircase. In the
sitting room, I flew past cabinets and bevelled glass windows,
sailing over Turkish rugs we have never owned and an ante-
room of antique Delftware tiles. Always I felt supported,

although the support was merely air. I had such freedom, Father. How long has it been since I've known such freedom?

I was happy when I woke up, and wondered if I had finally become one of Nietzsche's *über-Menschen*. Do you not see the connection, Father? In this shabby continent, the *über-Mensch* has been vulgarized into the comic book Superman, so it is perhaps a joke of the jokey subconscious that an *über-Mensch* could fly. Supported by the herd, no doubt. As Nietzsche says,

> *Main consideration: not to see the task of the higher species in leading the lower . . . but the lower as a base upon which the higher species performs its own tasks—upon which alone it can stand.*

Or fly?

I take liberties, Father. One must recollect the position of woman. Woman cannot be *über*-man; it is a contradiction. Of course I know that, Father, and understand very well what I deserve. Speaking of this, you will be pleased to hear that the other dream comes often too, the dream of the Gestapo officer repeating through the night like multiplication tables chanted in school, one time after another, sometimes more of the telephone call and sometimes less, its words staccato and unvarying.

"This is Maaike van der Velde speaking," I tell him. "I know your daughter Gertrud from the Hitler Youth, do you remember? I've been a member since we called it the Youth Storm."

"Ah yes, Maaike van der Velde," he says. "Miss Maaike van der Velde. My Gertrud speaks of you often. She speaks of you highly. Such an example to the other girls. Such an example to all the boys and girls."

"I'm glad to hear you say so, sir. I always like to be of help."

"No doubt, no doubt. It is the wish of all good Dutch citizens to be of help to the Reich. I have noticed this. Yes."

"But I have something to tell you, sir," I say. "Do you have time for me to tell you something important? Or should we meet in person?"

Of course it is Gretel who brings this back. I know you are right, Father. If I don't wish to remember what happened, I should not allow her to visit. Nor should I let her tempt me into rereading my diaries, especially the one you gave me for my thirtieth birthday. In fact, I should probably burn that volume shortly. The incendiary volume, Father!

Perhaps burning it will do no good; I will remember anyway. The floodgates have opened, Father. I find that I am able to picture events from my youth with surprising clarity. As I reflect upon our trip to the national park, I can see again a fawn we passed standing in a dappled glade. I can see his spotted coat and spindly legs. I can see his nostrils quivering and knees shaking, his innocence and weakness and terror.

Or do I merely see myself in him?

I have been thinking a great deal about that trip, Father. I now wonder if I would have told you about the *Wehrmacht* officers if I had been less of an innocent and understood the true nature of Florrie's fall. Would I have spoken if I'd realized that by speaking out I would disgrace her? Yet if I'd kept quiet, as Jannie wished, I am not certain that this, by itself, would have been enough to halt everything that followed, all the U-turns and disenchantment and betrayals, everything that led me to make that dangerous call to the Gestapo two years later; everything that led us to Berlin, and here.

Gretel would accuse me of practising epistemology. Here are the facts: If I had been less of an innocent, I would not have been myself. If I had not been myself, I would not have acted precisely as I did. But being myself, I described to you what had happened in the forest, and our lives unwound.

You have no idea what I'm talking about, do you, Father? A little beyond your understanding, I think.

Excuse me, dear. That was unfair. I would do better to close. Rereading this, I see that I have nothing to add. I have nothing to say. It is a letter truly worthy of burning. You will say I am ironical. That is to say, my little friend Gretel would find me ironical.

I will continue to see her, however.

Your loving

Daughter.

(2nd draft)

The Tornado abated slowly, almost gently, laying the car to rest beside their newly purchased Home.

"Thank God!" the Father cried.

But the Father's jubilation quickly turned to horror. In the circle of his smothering arms, the innocent Child lay dead.

THIRTEEN

Friday, August 4

I haven't written here all week, I don't know why. I'm ready today, though, and intend to press forward on Plan B. It's a breezy, sunny summer day like those fine days we had in July. The week has been mainly sweaty and nasty to work in, but yesterday the humidity blew over, and today things really are fine in the sense Gramps uses: a fine day.

I'm fine, you're fine, we're all going to be fine. What makes things especially fine is that Pudge and Michelle are working late again tonight. I'm luxuriously permitted to be alone, writing down Plan B, meanwhile updating my Dear Diary one missing day at a time.

We won't refer to Saturday again, but I should note that I spent all day Sunday reading in my tent. Sunday being the day of rest, how normal can you get? Monday was all right, too. I started work on the basement even though I was going to take a break between jobs, since I didn't deserve a break, i.e. because no one ever deserves anything.

It's kind of sad, though. The reason Pudge could move into the house right after buying is that the old people had already been placed in a Home, which is a word with an ambiguous entomology when you think about it. A niece was behind the sale, and I believe that's why only the upstairs part of the house was cleared out. A daughter would have insisted on going through everything to find what she'd lost. Instead, on Monday morning, I was left to survey the basement-centred Subconscious of the old people's life: Lumber, junk, Collectibles all chaotically mingled together.

I decided to start by wrecking out the rest of the particle-board walls, clearing myself a level playing field. The old nails screeched and groaned, pulling Pudge downstairs to investigate, still in his dressing gown. He offered to help, scratching his beard since I'd woken him up (at 7:30?) but I pointed out that space was limited, demonstrating by taking a swing behind me with my crowbar.

Pudge jumped back, agreeing that I knew what I was talking about and padding back upstairs, although it irked to hear through the hot-air register how he talked to Michelle in the kitchen.

". . . let her work it all out of her system, crashing and banging as much as she . . ."

I yanked this particleboard wall down with a total snap. Snap! Crash! Screech!

Female voice: ". . . long as she doesn't hurt herself . . ."

What do you care, Michelle? Who cares? It was satisfying to reduce the partitioned-off basement to one big room plus bathroom plus laundry, pieces of the past everywhere around me. I tied the particleboard into bundles to go out with the garbage, sweeping up so indefatigably that I tired myself out, feeling proud of how much you can accomplish in one hard-working day.

I also realized that if I kept this up, I'd be out of a Job by the end of the week. That's when I decided to undertake Plan B, scheduling each day as a healthful fusion of exercise and work, sorting the Subconscious into categories each morning but also running, cycling, reading, writing and having tea with Miss V next door.

Is it true that if you exercise too much your period stops? That would be a bonus. And if there's any truth to the theory that Bleeding purges you of Evil Humours, then I'm covered on that front, too. I seem to cut myself shaving lately, tsk tsk, no wonder I had to buy those cover-up clothes on Tuesday. Evil Humours bled out of you without having to have your period: that's almost as good as a Plan in itself.

But I'm getting ahead of myself. I bought the clothes Tuesday afternoon. Tuesday morning I got my bike. It's a Kona, black like my future, a mountain bike with hybrid tires for city riding. I also got this black Bell helmet to match and a Kryptonite U-bolt lock, then rode downtown to shop.

I rode along Bloor Street, the big east-west artery as they say, flowing like a corpuscle of blood between the rounded corpuscular cars, pausing at the regular traffic lights as if the cosmic heart was pumping me from light (beat) to light (beat). At first, I felt scared and little, cars brushing past me even though I kept to the bike lane. I've never paid so much attention to side-view mirrors in my life, how they could slip a hand under your elbow and pull you Underneath.

Then things changed. Danger is seductive, as Miss V says, and I began to feel its power as I sped across the Viaduct: this psychic tunnel that bathes you in invitations from dead Jumpers, tempting you to join them. I leaned across my handlebars, that taste of salt scouring the back of my throat, afraid that I would Suicide but also starting to get off on being scared. The feeling inhabited my knees the way it did when I joined Matthew Cavanaugh's plans, shoplifting, vandalism etc., riding this fuck-you high. I pedalled harder, daring myself to skim even closer to cars than they did to me, wheeling between them, swerving over from lane to lane. Look at me! Grabbing the back of this dirty white truck, then letting go to stream through traffic like a courier.

"You're going to get yourself killed!" one lady yelled, sticking her head out the driver's-side window. When I looked back, she was just sitting in her car at the intersection, even though the light had turned green and people were honking at her like geese. Their cars were, I mean. They were honking their horns. People were honking their horns. Let's get this straight.

That's how you turn people into murderers, when you think of it. Janelle Piglet accused Michelle of turning Gramps into a murderer by making a Big Mistake, i.e. by allowing herself to be trapped alone in the house with a Drifter, or at least by not giving into him when he wanted it. But creating a murder isn't any big deal. Michelle isn't any big deal when murder is actually such a mundane occurrence. People can become murderers as a result of the most paltry events, and don't try to tell me any different, because merely by riding my bike through traffic *I just proved it.*

At least, I almost did. I don't know, I feel like acting Stupid lately, even though *a)* it really is acting, at least partly, and *b)* I don't feel that way all the time. On Wednesday, for example, I kept to the Plan and nothing abnormal happened. I'm not a Loser all the time.

Yet I don't have much luck in my so-called life. I have to admit, something made me sad again on Thursday, and now I'm forced to write about it. I don't want to, but it happened, so I'm impaled by necessity. Overall, it's been a week.

On Thursday afternoon, I was checking out the price of a couple of Collectibles in one of the Queen Street second-hand stores. It's the one neighbourhood I like in this city, a strip of stores to the South where the owners visibly revel in their Taste. You get angled Art Deco or kidney-shaped Fifties or endearing Discards that the owners don't really want to sell, although if you stumble onto something they like, i.e. in the basement, they're usually fervid to buy it off you. Tramping up and down the street, you enter these huge stores totally crammed with rooms of furniture, many so deep and dim you can hardly see the back wall. Beside them are tiny little cubbyholes full of teapots and Depressed glass and piles of old *Life* magazines to the extent that you soon lose sight of the door. You find hip places, scanty and disdainful, and sad dusty jumbles of Lost Hope, all of them tucked between truck-stop cafés and brioche sellers and Convenience Stores rife with potted plants and lottery signs.

I don't know. Maybe I just like second-hand stores because I'm such a piece of junk myself. In any case, I was in this cavernous store when it happened, a huge place lined with what the owner calls self-referential mirrors, the smallest of which represented my first sale from the old people's basement. The owner also stocked Fifties furniture, and I was checking out her telephone tables when I saw this familiar-looking back.

"Cooper!" I cried.

A stranger turned around. A seedy-looking individual, as Gram would say, tall with pumped biceps like Cooper and a billiard-bald head, but otherwise a smudged copy. I mumbled some apology, wondering how I could make such a stupid mistake, especially in a Hall of Mirrors. I'm such a hemor-rhoid, I really am. I mean, one month out of Kingston and I'd forgotten Cooper's back?

What I'd forgotten was the finality of his mood as Cooper moved me and Michelle down to Toronto. Pudge had to work so they didn't get to meet, which I thought would finally happen. I mean, you'd think Pudge would have been the one to move us, the new husband instead of the old boyfriend. Or at least help out? But Pudge was tied up so it fell to Cooper, and frankly I don't understand why he agreed to do all that work and then merely left.

Yes, I do. Michelle asked. End of story.

Except it doesn't feel like the end. After writing all that, I put down my pen, hoping it was over. But Cooper kept coming vividly to mind, the past Bleeding into Toronto. I'm going to have to write some more, Bleeding Cooper out of my head, down my arm and onto the paper, where he can dry like ink. I've got to shed this vision of Blood, which holds me enthralled even though Cooper isn't Blood-related and is certainly not my father: Michelle told me so unswervingly.

Still, we felt this affinity, and it's making me so sad. The thing is, despite the Truth or whatever, Cooper happens to look like me. They call him the Gentle Giant, meaning that he's tall, athletic (pumped) and blond. At least, he used to be blond until he shaved his head. So what if his goatee grew in red? Cooper's eyes are exactly the same deep and unfathomable blue as mine, at least almost, even though Michelle started to claim last year that he's just unfocused. Plus he liked me, you know?

He always did, right from the start. It started the year I was in Grade 1, when Cooper found me all alone in the apartment after Mrs. Hoskins had left. Mrs. Hoskins was the babysitter, and one night when Michelle stayed out later than she'd promised, Mrs. Hoskins woke me up to say that she was leaving. To teach Michelle a lesson?

That Hoskins bitch, I can still see her face, that crippled old face looming in on me, the red cheeks and smelly false teeth and fingerprints smudged on her glasses.

"You stay in that bed now, you listenin to me? There's a Bogeyman waitin out your door. You get outta bed and that Bogeyman gonna getcha."

Then she left. I must have been six years old and didn't deign to believe in Bogeymen, except I also did. You can't be sure of anything in this world, so I hung back in the corner of my bed waiting till Michelle got back from the party. It was winter, November-December, and the best way to keep myself awake was to get cold outside the covers, except that getting cold made me want to pee. I could hold it at first, but before too long I really needed to go. I really *really* needed to go, more and more when Michelle didn't show, didn't show, I really *really* gotta go.

You can't pee the bed and you can't get out and finally you can't hold it any longer, jumping down on your ice-cube feet, knocking over the bedside lamp and making a run for the bathroom. The Bogeyman is gonna getcha gonna getcha but whatcha gonna do? You pee and pee, oh no, he's gonna reach right up the terlet, cross yourself, cross yourself, run shaking shaking back to bed, sitting there in the corner in the dark, lamp broken, light from passing cars like ghosts until finally you fall asleep because it's morning and you can't find Michelle anywhere, no Michelle in the apartment but feet on the stairs and it's her and you're running and the door opens and

A man! Screaming and hugging your pillow in front

"You know me. It's only me."

Cooper. I'd seen him around, he was at Michelle's parties. So were lots of people. Michelle was a party animal back then. But everyone knew Cooper, he was the Gentle Giant, everybody called him that.

"Where's your mother? She didn't show up at work."

I could only shake my

"You got no one here with you?"

Shake my

"It's ok, I'm here now. We're ok, little chick."

And it was OK, like he said. I felt something unfamiliar, which I think of now as being safe. It must have been the end of the month because there wasn't much food in the house. But Cooper found some oatmeal, and after making a face at the milk, he got me to stand by the window where I could see him go to the Convenience Store across the street. We were on top of the Laundromat so it was me looking down, him waving at me from in front of the store and later from inside when he was paying, coming back out carrying all these frail white plastic bags, waving again and dropping one right in the middle of the crosswalk, milk spattering like white rain.

It's OK, Cooper made it feel OK. All that food! Not just the milky oatmeal but the golden brown sugar he crumbled on top when I was so *hungry,* cheese bread for toast, chunks of cold butter, orange juice, this tub of strawberry yoghurt. He cooked himself an omelette brunch with green and red peppers, Cooper being a Healthful cook, giving me a corner to taste before saying he'd have to call about Michelle, which didn't alarm me by then.

"Your Mom had to stay the night in the country," he said, after hanging up. "It's OK. She'll be back pretty soon."

"Don't go away," I told him.

He looked like he was thinking, then nodded and cleaned out the fridge, picking out a cucumber so dead it left a trail of slime behind it like a snail. Cooper scrubbed out the cupboards to put in more new groceries, then we swept the floors and vacuumed the rugs before watching TV. I already liked him when the doorbell rang and it was my Grade 1 teacher, Ms. Pembroke. I could hear her voice saying not in school again, you're the father? And Cooper saying no, no, babysitter, little girl feeling under the weather. You're supposed to call the school and let us know. Oh, Cooper says, Michelle hadn't called? Mixed signals, he thought she'd called and probably she'd thought he'd called, sorry about that, except Ms. Pembroke told him they'd called the Plant and Michelle hadn't shown. The Plant was way casual, Cooper told her, they commonly made mistakes, which Ms. Pembroke had to admit. But there's still the fact Jessica's been coming to school with open-toed sandals, inappropriate clothes, this being winter can I see the Child?

Ms. Pembroke is looming over me now, but I've crawled under the afghan looking pathetic on a cleaned-up sofa. Tummy, I tell her, and Ms. Pembroke leaves.

He lied for me, and he got Michelle back. I remember Michelle running in afterward looking so scared that she scared me and I started to cry.

"Oh baby, I'm sorry. I'm so sorry. I'll never, ever do that again, I promise."

And she didn't, not too often and not for much longer, although Cooper stayed around anyway. Michelle began to joke that she couldn't get rid of him, even though he left all the time. Cooper liked driving down to Mexico every winter in his camper, but Michelle didn't enjoy travelling so we never went along. Plus he was a long-distance trucker, at least when his licence wasn't suspended, and there was that time in Guelph Correctional after his experiment in hydroponics, i.e. the herbaceous crop, and all their fights when they didn't speak, even when they were living together. Especially when they were living together, I guess.

We lived all over the place, actually. Cooper preferred to make his Home in the country, and when I was little, Michelle was game to try. I remember how the first property was full of streams and tadpoles, your hands all silver and golden under the water. That place was like an Eden to me. But despite its

Edenic propensities, I kept hearing Michelle talk about Transportation, Isolation, problems with Trans/Isol/ation. I think it was my fault. School buses? In any case, she and I moved back into Kingston.

Then, I don't know, maybe it was a landlord-and-tenant dispute. We moved back out to the country again, this time to a place that Cooper had bought. He'd got his hands on a Ski-Doo that he trusted me to drive, all this Power under my control as I banked and flung along the trails. It made up for the jazz I got at school about life in the sticks, being a hick, show me your tricks, little mama. But Cooper's Saturday Nights were a growing problem, Michelle having started to lose interest in parties, plus there was his infatuation with smokable herbs, even after the Correctional. Especially after the Correctional, I believe. We finally left Cooper and his predilection out in the country, although he was still the official boyfriend and hung out with us in Kingston all the time, at least when Michelle's University friends weren't around. Cooper was proud of Michelle wanting to improve herself, but he never liked the real students, referring to himself through their eyes as The Specimen, which I never got. A Specimen of what?

I'm making it sound so negative when we had so much fun. Cooper and I liked cooking and Michelle was always an appreciative eater. He taught me how to shoot pool. Michelle taught us Monopoly and Scrabble, Cooper's vocabulary being larger than you'd think. We'd go camping, rent videos. We even shot some Home Videos, at least before Cooper tripped and broke the Videocam. But at the same time, I don't know why, things kept going wrong.

The fall before last was the worst. Michelle and I had been living in our final apartment in Kingston for a couple of years by then, and we wanted to move some accumulated boxes into Cooper's garage for the winter. As we pulled into the driveway, the automatic door would only open halfway. It had been sticking all fall, so Cooper got out of his vehicle to take a look, leaving Michelle to manipulate the opener. She pushed a button, saying, "Cooper, what . . ."

The door fell down hard, cutting off half Cooper's index finger. He gave this deep moan which made my arm hairs stand on end. At the same time, Michelle hooted like an owl. It was so weird, I couldn't even cry.

Cooper swivelled to face us. Crouching, cupping one hand in the other, he told me, "Jess, you go get that plastic bag of ice out the freezer."

When I got back, he plunged his bloody hand in the ice. Michelle drove fast to Emergency and they took him straight in. She and I expected to wait while they reattached his finger. Michelle said that's what they'd do, microsurgery techniques being improved and this being a University Hospital. But it wasn't long before Cooper rejoined us in the waiting room, his bandaged hand held up in this grey foam sling.

"You ready?" he asked.

"But the surgery? Aren't they going to . . ."

"They cut off the gristle and sewed it up. Nothing else they could do."

In the truck, on the way back to our place, Cooper finally said, "It wasn't your fault."

"I know," Michelle answered. After a long pause, she asked, "Cooper, tell me how it always happens with us, that I end up feeling guilty for things I'm not responsible for?"

"Creature of habit," Cooper said.

Neither liked the other's answer, you could tell.

That winter, it felt as if Cooper would never get back from Mexico.

"I can do better," Michelle kept saying. But she'd totally lost her taste for parties by then, and I don't think she knew where else to look. We ended up waiting for Cooper, me especially, and just about the time I thought he'd gone for good, he finally arrived home. Cooper looked good, cleaned up and relaxed with his new goatee. I thought things were going to get better after that, Cooper and Michelle were both so relieved to see each other. But then we had to get our boxes out of the garage, and when we went to open the door, the rest of Cooper's finger fell onto the driveway, fingernail and all.

Michelle screamed, then sucked in a long breath. "What goes on in your head, Cooper? I'm afraid I just don't get it."

"Just got mad and left it there," Cooper said, picking it up. "Mummified. Or freeze-dried all winter." He threw it into the bushes nearby.

Afterward, Michelle talked to her University friends about Cooper, which she never had before. She used words like unfocused and luckless and especially feckless, which I had to look up in the dictionary. She even said the L word. "It's too true. Cooper is a Loser." I heard this and saw this and knew what it meant, although I guess I was In Denial. When I went up to Campbellton that summer, last summer, I told myself that their time without the burden of me would get them back together, and it's true that Michelle sounded happy when she phoned, and if I called Cooper, he was just the same.

When I had my alternation with Janelle Piglet, I knew they would call Michelle and tell her to come up to Campbellton. I expected her to show up with Cooper, although that wasn't why I did it. It's not. It really isn't. I just assumed that Cooper would come up too, since he always did, and when an unfamiliar hatchback pulled up, I merely thought, Cooper's new car?

Pudge was driving. Cooper really was the Loser, there's no question of that.

I saw Cooper numerous times over the succeeding year, dropping in for visits. But nothing I said or did could get him and Michelle back together. How could it? Peerless girl: both her sperm and pretend fathers are Losers. No wonder she's Lost so much in her life. Look at her. She keeps Losing friends, she Loses the entire city of Kingston, she even manages to Lose her own fucking mother. Which makes her into what?

I am Jessie Barfoot, that's all I am. Gretel von Bundt is a fantasy. She even writes fantasies. She took Goethe's *Selected Poems* out of the Library and wrote some crippled modern fairy tale.

But maybe she should do more of that. Maybe she should even write a book of modernistic fairy tales while I make photographs for them. I'll take black-and-white pictures on a digital camera, then manipulate the images through a computer, unfocusing some and running swaths of colour through the others, portraying the Surreal.

When you think about it, that's a good idea. I'll save Collectibles money to buy myself a digital camera. She'll use her library card to get more books. I'll observe, she'll create. I'll get a computer, guilting Pudge for a Back-to-School present. She'll spend her evenings writing, as I have today.

She/I. I/She.

Eye/I. She/See.

I can't see what's going to become of me. The Suicide Bridge exerts its pull. You need to Plan your escape from the Suicide Bridge. Plan B, that's your escape. Eye see Plan B. You see Plan B. We all see Plan B. What's going to become of me?

I am indeed a strange little chick, as someone used to say.

It was Cooper who let Paws out when we moved. That was an accident and I know he felt pretty bad. Except that now I think of it, it probably wasn't an accident. Paws probably hitched a ride back Home in Cooper's truck. Cooper's revenge. Not that you can blame him.

FOURTEEN

Florrie Brouwer—Her Book
Day One of Her Visit to the Sticks

Dearest Piet,

What did I do to deserve this? To be given the old heave-ho out of the city—and your divine presence—to visit a *farm*. And in company like this! Half a dozen babies led by a prig. Plus Jannie Schippers, of course. Thank God for Jannie Schippers! I couldn't make it without Jannie to talk to, confide in—confide about us, about *you*.

How else would I get through three punk days? By watching the everlasting grass grow? Or observing Mrs. Farmer Noort dribble cream down her chin?

Stop it, Florrie. She's a kind old cow. And Pieter Verhoef doesn't even know you're alive. If he did and stopped to think about it, he'd call you a lucky girl to get three days on a farm after half starving all winter. Pieter is a sensible boy. Unlike you . . .

Who can't helping laughing at the picture of Mrs. Farmer Cow slowly chewing her cud behind a groaning table, where magic bowls spill delectable food onto your plate and pitchers pour floods of cream. It's a fairy-tale farmhouse, with bottomless pots and talking cows and quests that pit our plucky young heroine against great loss and absolute crushing agony.

Like not being able to go to the cinema on Saturday and sleeping in a *barn*.

141

I think you might survive it, Florrie, especially if you try to have fun with what you find on hand. Here you sit with a spotted cow and her husband, Farmer Toad. Look at the Toad's fat sausage fingers spread across his corporation and the wide Toad mouth that burps out sarcastic remarks at the prig, otherwise Maaike van der Velde, who doesn't get what he says for a minute.

I'm laughing already. I'm laughing inside at Farmer Toad, Mrs. Cow and their yappy little dog Maaike. That's Maaike, all right—one of those spoiled white nippy floor mops exactly like Mrs. Mannheim's Pouffie. Not that I was supposed to know Mrs. Mannheim all that well, but I did. Yes, I did. Snuck off to visit her *long* after she couldn't pay Granny to clean any more even though Daddy said *Juden Viertel*—not that she looked like a Jewess, a rich German Jewess fleeing to our soggy shores . . .

But she read to me from Schiller, Stendhal, the divine Robert Louis Stevenson, her Dutch accent awful, of course, but her voice so lovely—deep—theatrical. She said I was her teacher, teaching her a new language, a new *accent,* then she fed me marzipan and cakes which the *help* once baked, my dear, although *she* had to now . . .

It was so breathlessly daring to go there. If stupid Pouffie bit me, if Daddy found out—one leading to the other to a beating. He'd beat me within an inch of my life. So Daddy said. He *promised*.

"Down, Pouffie. Down!"

"I must apologize, my dear. I've always had them. The breed is good. But you must understand—the individual cannot be predicted. Individuals are most unpredictable. I'd like you to remember that. *Count on no one*."

Where did she go? Switzerland? Vanished off the face of the earth one morning last December, her furniture abandoned,

Pouffie quivering under the table. A note pleading for someone to take care of him. No one did.

But it's true—you've got to take care not *of* but *with* Maaike van der Velde—watch every word you say—bite your tongue—and at the same time tell yourself that it's not her fault. The poor thing, really. How would *you* turn out if you'd found your mother hanged in the attic? Before the war, when you hadn't got used to any of this, more or less.

I'm a year older than Maaike so she would have been . . . ten? Little ten-year-old Maaike finally discovered in the attic, having pushed the kitchen chair back up on its legs. Sitting in the kitchen chair holding onto her dead mother's knee, Mrs. van der Velde's face hideously purple, they said, her tongue bulging out, eyes all popping and jutting (her pants filled—they whispered that the *smell* . . .)

They also said she was part Jewess—there was a grand-mother or great-grandmother—but when they had to, the papers turned out clean. They must have done for Maaike to shine like Orion's saintly Belt in the Youth Storm. Of course, a few people said the papers turned *up* clean. My Granny was boiling mad at the whole sorry business. Maaike's *brutal* father was perfectly capable of kicking that chair . . .

Cleansed, that's the word my Granny used. I remember now. I hadn't heard it before.

Cuckoo word. It's a cuckoo evening, banished to the sticks. Maaike and I have both been scribbling in our dear, dear diaries half the sainted evening, except that she just got up to toss some torn-out pages in the fire.

Cleansed by blood, my Granny said. Cleansed by fire.

"Feeding the flames, young Maaike?" Farmer Toad burps.

"I seem to be having trouble saying what I mean," she yaps. "I wish I was a better person."

"You're young. There's hope," Toad burps, when in her case, *clearly* there is none.

Cow, toad, pug—who else can I picture? The younger girls are newly hatched chicks, staggering on their pins now, half asleep standing up. And Jannie? Look at her watching over the children from her place near the fire. She's like a glorious racehorse resting in her stall. Our thoroughbred to beat all thoroughbreds.

That's not right. Thoroughbreds are bundles of nerves when Jannie is famously calm. She's a unicorn, majestic, lordly, flying high above us all. Nothing touches Jannie.

No matter how much the boys *long* to . . .

And *moi?* A lost princess—ready, to be honest, to kiss them all right *off.*

Dearest Piet, would you laugh to see us pictured this way? What if I wrote up our silly little trip as a fable? I know I'd have to make it much more gentle and far less satiric—more feminine—instructive—the tale of our sweet helpless female band off to look for . . .

What am I searching for, dearest Piet, but the key to your heart?

As if he doesn't have better things to do, Florrie, than read your drivel. Informing to the ss for a start.

Hush. Hush! You overheard. You eavesdropped. And who else was talking to the ss man? Jannie's Uncle Bertus. Darling Piet was in cahoots with poor Bertus van Dijk, informing on the opening forays of the Resistance. And what happened the next day to poor Uncle Bertus?

Bang bang bang bang bang

Except that's not what guns sound like. We were talking about it earlier this evening. They go pop. Pop!

You don't want the Resistance to do that to Piet, do you, Florrie? Clearly not. Piet should stop playing stupid games and put his true allegiance out into the open. The average man in the street may not like it when you're a member of the Youth Storm but they'll accept it. They know your parents are NSB and absolutely *force* you to join. They know it isn't your fault. Piet ought to join Youth Storm and let them know where he stands so there aren't any more—Pop!—surprises.

Actually, he should probably join the *Wehrmacht* a year early and get his carcass out of here before he joins Uncle Bertus in becoming another . . .

Join the army and leave a girl behind. Silently cherish her snapshot, press it to his manly heart. I'm going to get a studio portrait taken when we get home. Borrow cousin Johanna's angora sweater, wear it with my box-pleated skirt. Wave my hair so it swoops down daringly over one eye.

He'd cherish it, I know he would. He watches me the way that I watch him, I know he does. He just can't say it openly because of the stupid games he plays.

When we're together, there's never enough oxygen in the room.

If he watches you, Florrie—and I'm not convinced that he does—then he knows that you're not really interested in sweetly feminine fairy tales. It's the darker stories that you adore—the princess cutting off her little finger to make a bony key, freeing her handsome Swan Prince brothers . . .

And the movies—darling movies—especially the ones they won't let us see anymore. Dearest, dearest Hollywood. As far as I'm concerned, they can give the Yanks the whole of Belgium to get my *adored* Garbo back. The woman of mystery—just like me! I'd do anything to see my dearest Garbo again. More than anything to *be* Garbo . . .

Or Vivien Leigh. *Gone with the Wind*. One day, that will be me.

What would you make of that one, Piet? Florrie's secret nature. Florrie's *divided* nature, pulled in two competing directions.

Oh yes, she is. I am. Just last week my Granny said that I couldn't visit her any more unless I quit the Youth Storm. To which Daddy replied that he'd lock me in the attic for the duration if I did—absolutely *forcing* me into the countryside to remember which side my bread is buttered on.

Buttered thickly—thank you, dear old Mrs. Cow.

Even though I have a suspicion that Mr. Toad would butter it even more thickly if we came to him from the other side.

What do you think, Piet? What would you make of Farmer Toad? Or let me secretly ask you this—What would you make of the way my cousins disappear from Granny's house at all hours of the day and night? Breaking curfew—probably breaking far more than that. It's amazing how often Resistance actions follow hard on the heels of my cousins' disappearance. It makes a girl a little suspicious. And you? What would *you* do, Piet, if you suspected my cousins of everything that I suspect?

What would they do to you, my darling, if they knew all that I know about you?

Will we ever talk, dearest Piet? Will we ever go beyond glances in the hallway—math class—ice-cream parlour? Will you ever learn that I live and breathe a drama in which you play a starring role? You're the Rhett to my Scarlett, the Prince in my secret fairy tale. Would you like that, dearest boy?

I have a pretty good idea that you would. I think you secretly *love* drama every bit as much as I do—that we'd understand each other—that we *do* understand each other. We could pour out our hearts to each other, I know we could—if we could ever stop blushing for long enough to get the words out.

Thank God for Jannie. Tomorrow we're off to the national park. I plan to confide in her, telling all to my dearest and most sensible Jannie . . .

I don't mean *all*. I'm not stupid. People may say that Florrie Brouwer is dreamy—that she's lazy—moody—that she never lives up to her potential—but no one ever claimed that she was stupid. I wouldn't *dream* of putting Jannie at risk. Or you, Piet, you can rest assured. Or my Granny, or my cousins . . .

Myself? Some things I'm prepared for. You have to be prepared to be a heroine—and what's the point being anything else? I'm prepared to be a heroine, Piet. I'm *ready*—just like you.

Once upon a time . . . it was time for bed.

In a *barn*.

Amsterdam

I'm going to get Maaike van der Velde for opening her big mouth. I'm going to get her sneering, sanctimonious father. My father's going to be pretty damn sorry that he threw me out. And as for all of those sniggering brats in the Youth Storm . . .

It isn't as if it was my fault. How can they say that I asked for it? How can they say that?

Let it here be indelibly recorded that I'm going to *get them all*.

FIFTEEN

Waking up in the middle of the night, I thought the search-lights were on me. I must have been having a dream. My feeling was that somebody was looking and looking. But as I began to wake up, I understood there was actual light going on, and unzipped my tent to check outside.

Northern Lights! Northern Lights lit up the sky from one horizon to the other, colourless, almost green, almost red, this friction of zipping light, snapping and unreeling like a fishing line casting movement across the sky. It rippled and heaved, and I heaved my sleeping bag out of my tent to lie down on Gramps's lawn, staring up at the best Display I have ever seen, electric currents shocking the night.

I like Northern Lights, they're so unhindered. I felt happy and unhindered myself, everyone else sleeping, no one else seeing. I loved my private Display, especially when a star hurtled to earth behind the curtain of ghostly light, an arc of falling star so bright that I made a wish upon it. I felt vehement and special. All this Power, just for me.

Another star fell, and another and another, more and brighter than I had ever seen, all these stars flinging themselves under the Northern Lights in a spree of burning ecstasy. There were so many of them. There were too many. It was scary to see so many falling stars, which I understood included me. I'd been

148

progressing forward in my new life, instituting Plan B. But as I lay on the rocky lawn, my cold eyes pelted by falling stars, I realized that coming to Campbellton was a step backward. I'd made a mistake, heading backward to such an extent that the heavens were pelting light at me and

Gram calling breakfast. That's one thing I always forget about this place. You can never get a moment's peace.

Later

Like I was saying, I made a wrong turn in Plan B. I should just have sent Pudge and Michelle up with the Recyclables yesterday without coming along myself. I thought it would be OK. I'd have my privacy, setting up my tent outside the house. I could show Gramps what I'd brought and ignore everyone else.

Big mistake. But it occurs to me now that if I retain my concentration, this only has to be a detour—at least so long as Pudge and Michelle don't try to leave me up here, dumping me for a quote, vacation. I'll have to watch out for that. But otherwise, I'll hide away, running and hiking, reading and writing, *meanwhile avoiding my Family at all costs.*

I was reminded of that fact a couple of hours ago, when I had to run inside again as Gram hollered supper. You truly can't get a moment to yourself in this place. I just wanted to sit by myself at the bottom of the garden, but instead I had to run inside, fuming like a bus.

"I'm here, OK?" I told them. "Jeez Louise."

"Jessica, don't talk to your grandmother that way."

"Certainly, Michelle," I replied.

Michelle pinched my arm and whispered, "Who wanted to come up here?"

"They're your Family," I whispered back.

"Yours, too," she replied.

"And whose fault is that?"

I had her there. But that's what I mean to write about. Why do you always forget what your Family is really like? I mean, look at my Family: Uncle Bob Barfoot and Auntie Gail stumping into the dining room followed by a passel of wide-mouthed Pigotts. Look at the Chief Piglet, Janelle, strutting in behind. Janelle has quote, matured since last summer. She's starved herself skinny and finally got the Drummond looks, lips bigger than her slit blue eyes, pointy chin and illustrious complexion. As Michelle puts it, she's blooming like a peony. But don't they also say that scum blooms on a pond? Which is appropriate, since as far as I can see, Janelle remains a Piglet in her piggy little heart. She remains Family. I wonder if you can ever escape.

Not that Janelle *per se* bothers me any more, since argumentatively I have overtaken her. I mean, with six library books checked out each week, not to mention the increasing guidance of Miss i.e. Professor V, I can profess intellectual growth in myself, when the Piglet has merely aged. Let it be recorded here that I can endure her for a weekend, having already put up with her for Saturday, more or less.

Thank heavens for small mercies. Her male equivalents, Uncle Bob's two sons, the Neanderthal Twins, didn't grace us with their company at supper.

"Saturday night," Uncle Bob explained, taking his usual chair midway down the table.

"Off getting pissed," said Janelle Piglet, sitting down beside him.

"Boys being animals," Uncle Bob agreed. "Except our Drummond, he don't drink. Designated driver."

"Drummond don't drink like a puppy don't poo," Janelle told him. Then, seeing that Pudge was sitting down across from her, "Doesn't."

That's what made me see my Family so clearly. Pudge. Sitting beside him on a sucking vinyl-covered chair, passing the potato salad, I realized that his Family in Montreal don't have supper, they have dinner two hours later. They have Persian carpets, not domestic wall-to-wall. Their silverware is silver, the glasses are glass. And if Pudge has an Uncle Robert, he doesn't work on a county road crew like Uncle Bob Barfoot, or dominate the conversation with his opinions on the subject of effen jerk-off kids these days, effen Ford vehicles, effen fucken oil pans, until he is finally through his recurrent complaints and can turn to Pudge, whom he has been watching like a hungry hawk, so that everyone at the table except poor Pudge knows that Uncle Bob has been winding up to jive him.

"So," he said. "Hear you brung some junk up for Dad."

"Brought," the Piglet and Auntie Gail Barfoot both said at once. They linked little fingers and made a wish.

"Clearing out the basement, eh? Shovelling off the excess at the local dump. That whatcha think?"

I couldn't help blushing at Uncle Bob's implication. His imprecation? I'd never thought of the Recyclables like that. I thought I was doing a good job.

"Jessie did a really good job on the basement," Pudge said. "She thought her Granddad might have some use for all that lumber and stuff. It's good solid wood. A friend of mine, cabinetmaker up near Bowmanville, he wanted to take it off my hands, especially those planks of oak. But Jessie wanted her Granddad to have it, and this being a case of Family . . ."

So Pudge thought it was all my fault. I'd forced him to visit my Family, feeding him like Jiminy Cricket to a terrarium full of lizards. I blushed even harder, even though I also began to suspect that Pudge was a snob. He sounded like a snob, Subliminally complaining about my Family. He had some nerve. They were my Family! And if he felt snobbishly superior to my Family, what did he feel about me?

The reason you can never remember what your Family are like: You keep on changing your mind.

"The local dump," Uncle Bob repeated.

"I appreciate that oak," Gramps said, and everybody turned. "Jessie done real good with that oak. Good eye."

Gramps gave Uncle Bob the eye. End of discussion.

"Great chicken," Pudge observed, chuckling as he cleaned his plate. I couldn't believe that he didn't understand what had just gone on. A creature so ignorant, you couldn't help picking off its wings.

"Pudge is taking a break from my cooking," I said. "He prefers Gram's chicken and jellied marshmallow salad."

"Pudge?" Uncle Bob asked.

"If the bottom falls out of law, he can always be a mall Santa."

"Jessica!" Michelle said.

"The world's only Santa Jew," Pudge said, chuckling again, wiping his chin. My Family looked as if he'd farted. Jew! How could they? How could he? I failed to understand how so-called adults could embarrass themselves so utterly while remaining oblivious to the imprecations.

"Jessie, you haven't touched your chicken," Aunt Sis said.

"You shouldn't have given her none," Janelle answered. "She's a vegetarian, Ma."

"Vegetarian, is she?"

"It's a diet, Ma. Leave her alone."

"It's an ethic," I said.

My Family paused.

"How's the weather down there in Toronto?" Auntie Gail Barfoot asked. "Hot?"

"We're having a very pleasant summer," Michelle replied.

Sunday, August 13

> *Exam Question: How is life in a Small Town different than life in the Big City? Get through the rest of the weekend by a) noting as many examples as possible and b) writing them down in essay form. (10 marks)*

Picture a typical Small Town. The Highway swoops toward Campbellton, Ontario, along the western shore of Campbell's Lake, home in summer to the rich and year-round to the poor in spirit. Where it crosses the Concession Road, one sign warns drivers to reduce speed, which they ignore, and another that they have arrived in Campbellton, ditto. The town's main stores are placed along the Highway across from the Lake, including McNeeth's Grocery and Convenience, the Cozy Times Café, Lil's Video's (sic), two empty storefronts that were once Moberley Antiques[1] and Dirk's Autobody, along with the Black Point Motel, the bar of which is open all winter.[2]

Running up the sloping hill behind the stores are streets embracing old houses on big lots you could buy for a song, just ask, along with a Catholic Church near the bottom and a

---

1. Before being Moberley Antiques, they were Lils Bar and Grill. Let it be noted that Lil had trouble with apostrophes even before she moved.

2. The above paragraph is rendered from both Personal Observation, currently being recorded in this Diary, Sunday, August 13, along with indelible memories.

United near the top. The soil isn't deep this way. The Canadian Shield runs just a few feet underneath, elbowing its way through the lawn sometimes, creating a Focal Point in gardens that are usually planted with orange lilies and gnomes. When the land levels out on the flatlands up top, there is a small and formerly modern development, infested with Cousins, which passes for suburbia in a Small Town like this. There you will find several satellite dishes and, farther back toward the Swamp, several yards strewn with car parts that might come in handy, said parts still contained within rusted-out cars.

Clearly, the Big City is in great contrast to this small, rock-hard town, which is balled up like a fist. The City is more like the Amoeba-shaped Lake beside it, liquid and fluent and difficult to grasp, containing communities within its depths, but also threatening to drown you.

Given their lack of similarity, life in a Small Town must be different from life in the Big City for many reasons. One of these reasons is the different means of speech. In the Big City, truth is also liquid, which is a polite way of saying that the inhabitants use speech to lie all the time. Examples of this can commonly be found as one walks down a teeming street accidentally overhearing cellphone conversations. It is quite common, for instance, for someone walking past to say into their cell, "Sorry I'm late. I'm caught in the worst traffic jam you ever saw. Yeah, on the Parkway. I'll be at least half an hour."[3] It has also been observed that in a coffee shop, i.e. The Fresh Pot, someone at a table cherishing a solitary cup of Latte will pass off a cellphone caller by saying, "Look, I'm in the middle of an important meeting. Check you later."[4]

---

3. Personal Observation, recorded in Diary, Wednesday, August 9.

4. Personal Observation, recorded in Diary, Tuesday, July 11. It must be noted, however, there is a possibility that the speaker was consumed in a meeting with herself.

In a Small Town, however, speech is thin as the soil, and it is most often used to avoid saying anything at all. It is the experience of this writer that lies are not uttered to the same extent because you always get caught.[5] However, saying the truth is even more dangerous because then you're stuck with it.[6] Therefore, the most usual form of speech is non-communication. An example of this is the favourite use of the word "different" by Aunt Gail Barfoot, e.g. in describing the wedding of her niece Dyan (not on the Barfoot side).[7]

"Dyan's wedding was different,"[8] she said. "Her dress was pretty different too, I'll say that.[9] And Al, you know, he's really different."[10]

Because she does not say "different" from what, the lack of comparison renders her statement meaningless.[11]

Another way in which Small Town life is different is that you never get a moment's peace. In the Big City, during six weeks' residence, I have made one friend,[12] and spent most of my days in solitary communion with myself. The busy, rushing City turns out to be a lonely place, subdivided into neighbourhoods and streets and individuals who swim past each other like silent fish. Since arriving in a Small Town on Friday night, however, I haven't been able to escape the inhabitants any more than gardeners are able to ignore the Shield, examples being:

---

5. Personal examples too numerous to mention.

6. Ibid.

7. Personal Communication, currently being recorded in Diary, Sunday, August 13. Made in the presence of the writer after supper the previous evening.

8. It was held at The Good News Tabernacle.

9. Ecru leather with a dropped Empire waist.

10. A Biker.

11. Although this writer knows exactly what she means.

12. Dr. van Tellingen, a retired Professor from the University.

a) setting up my tent on Friday night with the assistance of my Cousin Bradley Pigott,[13] who was very helpful at pounding in the tent pegs with a flat rock, saying, "Hit. Hit. Hit," even though he wouldn't get out of the tent afterward until I told him there were fireflies outside[14];

b) overhearing my so-called mother telling my so-called grandmother nearby, "She's on a health kick. Leave her alone. She'll get over it"[15];

c) unloading the U-Haul the whole of Saturday morning with the assistance of my Gramps, Pudge, Bradley ("heavy, heavy") and his older brother Casey Piglet, who spent the whole time yapping about employment prospects down at Kingston Pen, how you can jump to the head of the lineup by putting down on the application form that you're Métis and they can't check because of Discrimination, he'll be in like a dirty shirt[16];

d) eating Lunch with all of the above[17];

e) spending the afternoon unsuccessfully avoiding contact with Janelle Piglet, who wants to yap as much as her brother lately;

f) eating Supper with the whole Family.[18]

---

13. Down's Syndrome.

14. Thus proving that Civic Lies are catching.

15. No, I won't.

16. Except that Uncle Bob Barfoot said after supper last night, when Casey was yapping on again, "You stupid arsehole, what you think folks mean when they talk about Pigotts having people down on the Reserve? If you're not a breed, who is?" (In reference to the thesis of this essay, i.e. people not saying anything in Small Towns: a) Auntie Sis began to speak at once about the price of gas and b) Uncle Bob Barfoot is the exception that proves the rule. He can be counted on to say what everyone else is merely thinking.)

17. Cold roast beef sandwiches without the roast beef.

18. A non-chicken repast consisting of potato salad.

This goes to prove that in a Small Town, it is impossible to be alone, except if you pretend to be asleep when they call you for Mass this morning and your Gramps says, "Leave her be. Kids that age, they need their sleep." This has the disadvantage of causing your writer to miss her breakfast, but since she is quote, on a health kick, she is presumptuously strong enough to survive until Sunday Dinner. Also, she would not have had time to write in her Diary otherwise and might have gone Stark Raving Mad, to which she has skated close enough already, or at least bicycled.

One final difference: in the Big City, they do not have Sunday Dinner, they have Sunday Brunch.

The End.

Topics for further investigation:

Whether the cellphone is causing a decline of Morals in the Big City owing to the increase in certifiable but unpunished public lying;

Whether lying was more or less shameful when it wasn't in public, i.e. only in front of your secretary.

Whether the use of devices such as cellphones, pagers, Palm Pilots etc. renders the whole world into your office, and turns everyone else into your secretary. (Look up origin of the word secret-ary.)

B—

Your conclusion is weak, Miss von B. I suspect that you are growing bored of the Subject, and perhaps of life itself. Now please continue with your assigned reading, which will help. Yours sincerely, Dr. V

This afternoon's conversation with Janelle Piglet, recorded for posterity:[19]

"What's that book?"

"The Will to Power."

"Self-help?"

"Nietzsche."

Janelle sat down beside me, trying to read over my shoulder.

"You taking a summer-school course?" she asked.

"A course of personal improvement."

"So it *is* self-help."

"Well aren't you the cat licking cream," I told her.

Janelle lay back on the grass, her arms behind her head. "Lesbo? I don't think so. I know a pair at school, though. Might let them show me."

I ignored her boasts and read Nietzsche.

"I might. I think it's kind of cute, actually. Girls. So what's the problem? Especially if it's three of you. Pyjama party or what?"

You can ignore her, I told myself.

"No way I'm pregnant at grad like Lauren was. Already got my dress picked out. It's sky blue with . . ."

"No lace, Mrs. Bennet. No lace."

"Pardon?"

"That's a quotation from *Pride and Prejudice,*" I told her. "The TV series, not the book. Michelle's got the boxed videos, which she's seen like five hundred times. If you wanted, I could probably recite if off by heart. Seeing as how we don't have a VCR any more."

"You should of brought it up. Gramps could fix it."

"If it ain't broke, can't fix it."

---

19. Also because I'm bored.

"OK, so I don't get half what you come out with."

"Pudge disapproves of television. We're not allowed to have one."

"Pain," she said.

"Pain," I repeated, closing my book.

"At least you can get away with calling him Pudge. And Michelle? Ma would have my ass."

"It's actually a form of payback," I told her. "They disrupt your entire life, you get to give them shit. They expect you to. They want you to. Beat me, beat me."

I briefly contemplated the cloudless sky.

"I heard you had a boyfriend down there in Kingston," the Piglet said. "Matthew Cavanaugh? His cousin Evie works in the . . ."

"His cousin Evie is a liar," I said.

"Just as well. Skinhead, from what Evie says."

"Maybe he has his own sense of personal style," I told her.

"So he *is* your boyfriend."

"Matthew Cavanaugh was a grade above me in school. How many boys a grade above are your boyfriend, Janelle Pigott?"

"So far, Jessie Barfoot?"

I turned back to my book.

"You let him have any?" she asked.

"Will you stop with Matthew Cavanaugh? You don't know when to stop, do you?"

"Unfortunately not," Janelle said, scratching her nose. "And so I don't condemn. You never got that, did you? Who am I in particular? I'm not like Ma and Gram, thinking they're so much better. The way they're off after your Mom. So what if she didn't get married in the Church? Nobody cares any more. He's a Jewish person. So what? At least he's white. And if he wasn't? Those little brown babies are the cutest thing. You like a little brown brother?"

"You're Métis. Uncle Bob said."

"Uncle Bob talks out of his twisted ass. There happen to be lots of white men living down on the reserve. They're living with their wives, who cares? That's what Uncle Bob means by so-called people in the family. Some of Dad's people living down on the reserve with their wives and kids. Big deal, anyway. I'm not one of your racist skinheads. I was defending your Mom, in case you're interested."

"I'm trying to remember the last time you said the faintest thing that interested me."

"Lots of room for self-help," Janelle said, standing up. "Just as well you're off that Matthew Cavanaugh. Bad seed, from what I hear. Heading straight to Kingston Pen."

"Just like your brother."

"Yeah, but Case will be the one holding the key."

"I wouldn't guarantee it," I said, standing up to face her.

"Fuck you," Janelle told me, head on.

"Fuck you," I said.

"Girls!"

Michelle was standing nearby. How long had she been skulking there? Eavesdropping? My privacy having been infringed, I sat back down with my book, turning its spine on both of them.

"I won't have another cat fight," Michelle said.

"She's just," Janelle started, then stopped. "My Cousin is so impossible."

"Listen to that, Jessie," Michelle told me. "Janelle is right, you're Cousins. Why not try . . ."

I read Nietzsche. Sometimes there's little alternative.

"Spoiled rotten," Janelle said. "By Gramps I mean, Auntie Michelle."

"Who told you that?" Michelle asked.

Gram's voice came out the kitchen door. "Nobody around here wants to eat?"

Michelle let out a big sigh. "You heard your Gram," she said. "Soup's on."

"What a treat," we both said at once.

"Link fingers and make a wish," Michelle told us. I refused to comply. "Link fingers and make a wish," she insisted, and we linked unhappily, our wishes no doubt disparate as night and day.

Monday, August 14
TORONTO

> *Everything on our way is slippery and dangerous, and the ice that still supports us has become thin: all of us feel the warm, uncanny breath of the thawing wind; where we still walk, soon no one will be able to walk.*
>
> Friedrich Nietzsche

More than a hundred years ago, Nietzsche predicted Global Warming. That tells you to pay attention to what he wrote and what Dr. V recommends. They know what they're talking about.

For instance, when I went for our usual tea this afternoon, Dr. V told me that what I saw up in Campbellton was called the Perseid Meteor Shower. She saw it herself, having gone to visit a hotel outside the city limits the way she does every year. Imagine: both of us were watching the Perseid Meteor Shower at the same time. Although it's kind of sad that both of us had to see it alone, when you think about it.

As we sipped our iced tea, the doctor brought out a book about the Shower. I read how it occurs every year around the night of August 11, when the Earth passes through a cosmic conveyor belt of rocky Debris that circles the sun at a skewed angle to the orbit of the Earth. August 11 is about when the two orbits (i.e. Debris and Earth) collide, and some of the Debris is captured by the Earth's gravity. As it falls through the atmosphere, this Debris is frictioned by the air and burns up, creating the streaks of light I saw in the sky. "Falling Star" is a misnomer. The correct term is meteor.

Dr. V says that it is possible for a large-scale meteor or asteroid to one day strike the planet with great Power. She says the asteroid will not only destroy the place it lands, it will probably cause Mass Extinction. Tornadoes and firestorms will fly out of the crater, and a cloud of ash will smother all higher life from Earth. She approved of me reading *The Will to Power*, and quoted Nietzsche:

Many species of animals have already vanished; if man too should vanish, nothing would be lacking in the world.

"So you see, there is nothing to fear in this," she said. "At least, not for me. You are allowed to be frightened, however. Fear is pardonable in youth, but a vanity in age. There, you see! I have made an aphorism!"

"I'm not frightened," I answered. "You've got to leave yourself open to experience, it's like you said. And you can't do that if you let yourself be frightened."

Dr. V approved again and poured me another glass of iced tea. I prefer my tea to be iced if I have to take lemon and sugar.

"Here is something, however," she said. "If Nietzsche proves too difficult, you may start with an entertainment. There is a lady called Ayn Rand, a Russian lady who lived in the United States. She took the ideas of Nietzsche and wrote them as a novel. It is called *The Fountainhead* and is very much fun to read."

"I don't need a novelization," I said. "I can handle the original."

"Well," she replied, and I wasn't sure whether that was agreement or instruction, although I think it was probably both.

On the other hand, there's Campbellton. How could you handle what happened in Campbellton? I mean after Sunday Dinner. My predisposition was to ignore Sunday when I got back, but I think that's probably cowardice, i.e. being frightened, and also another detour from Plan B. The thing is, I'm supposed to fill this Diary to perfect my literary skills before writing The Illustrated Fables of Modern Life.

At least, Greta is. That's her new name, courtesy of Gram.

"Can't anyone get a moment's peace around here?" I ended up yelling.

"Who you think you are? Greta Garbo? *I vant to be alone,*" Gram said.

It piqued me. Apparently, GG was a Movie Star starting from the days of Silent Screen. Silent Screams, that's what I emitted the whole weekend, at least until I got loud.

"Call me Greta," I told Pudge afterward.

"Me too," he whispered, looking around to make sure that no one heard.

You couldn't blame him. I couldn't, anyway, since the Fight was totally my fault. Observe the hemorrhoid at work: When most of them are out at Mass that morning, she decides to take a shower. In the bathroom, she finds that she's forgotten her razor and has to borrow Gramps's. My goodness, it's sharp! She can't help but cut herself, after which she uses his alum stick to staunch the heavy Bleeding. The stick hurts worse than alcohol, being stronger, not to mention deadly. Alum = aluminum = cause of Alzheimer's Disease, at least according to the newspaper. Therefore she decides that Gramps better not use the stick any more and takes it for herself, at least most of it, leaving a small stub so he'll think he's used it up (at least if he's in the early stages of Alzheimer's, bad joke). Afterward, she cleans the Blood off the bathroom floor. What a hemorrhoid. She believes that no one will notice.

But Gramps wondered how his razor got Bloody, and Gram blamed Pudge, who stayed behind from Mass, as well. Not to his face, she wouldn't do that. Instead, she accused Michelle when we were cleaning up the kitchen after Dinner.

After stumping around, Gram finally came out with it. "You might ask your husband not to use Dad's razor," she accused.

"For heaven's sake," Michelle replied. "Murray has a beard. Why would he use Dad's razor?"

"As if they don't shave around the edges," Gram said.

Aunt Sis rattled the dishes loudly as she put them away and Gram glowered. Things can go badly when Gram starts glowering, so before she turned too red in the face, I stepped in to confess.

"I'm the one who used it," I said. "I forgot mine and used his. He never used to mind before, seeing as how we're all the same Blood."

I think I acted like a true *Mensch,* which is a word both Pudge and Nietzsche use. I'm trying to progress, to prepare myself for the Crucial, and I'd like to record that on this one occasion at least, I succeeded.

And look what it got me. A pat on the back? Thanks for your Maturity: is that what I got? No, it isn't. All I got was a letter from Janelle Piglet, which she slipped me before we left.

A letter from Janelle Piglet: Talk about wasted paper. What does the Piglet know about writing letters? This is probably the first non-school composition she's ever perpetrated in her life. You need practice to write properly, just like in running. You can travel faster and go farther if you run every day. If you write every day, like in a Diary, *ibid* and ditto. Slowly, your self-hood acquires the ability to come out on the page.

That's what's been happening to me. I've been writing myself deeper as I've been writing myself down. Janelle Piglet wouldn't be able to do that, would she? Janelle Piglet doesn't come out with anything, on paper or anywhere else. She's the type who merely *gives* it out, i.e. a case of arresting development. After reading her letter, I chucked it in a roadside bin, never to be mentioned again.

Ditto Campbellton. Like Greta Garbo, I'll leave it alone. Now if only Campbellton would do me the same favour.

At least I'm back in Toronto, aren't I? Like I said, this afternoon I got back to tea with Dr. V, who went so far as to show me that library book about the Perseid Meteor Shower. Sometimes you're able to stumble onto something that makes some sense of your life. Dr. V and Nietzsche, they've got it down. Which I can say after reading Nietzsche all morning:

Man a little, eccentric species of animal, which—fortu-
nately—has its day; all on earth a mere moment, an
incident, an exception without consequences, something of
no importance to the general character of the earth; the earth
itself, like every star, a hiatus between two nothingnesses, an
event without plan, reason, will, self-consciousness, the worst
kind of necessity, stupid necessity—

Ibid.

Very late at night

It piques me, though, the Sunday Fight. I can't seem to get out of Campbellton, after all. Words keep rattling around in my head, words from all the women in the kitchen after Dinner. Women washing dishes, drying dishes, stacking plates. The Fight was filled with words as hard as plates. A day like plates. The Family Circle closing in. No wonder you can't get out of it.

I keep hearing them speak:

"You might ask your husband not to use Dad's razor."

"For Heaven's sake, Murray has a beard. Why would he use Dad's razor?"

"As if they don't shave around the edges."

"He trims it," Michelle said. "With scissors. Being very considerate to clean up when he's done."

"Don't take that tone with me, Michelle Barfoot. Bad as that daughter of yours. See where she gets it from."

As usual, they'd forgotten I was there. Which is crippled, given the way I can never forget about them. The Piglet and I were scraping pots in the corner, working industriously, keeping our heads down. I admit, you didn't want to miss a thing when the Family fought. But not missing a thing some-times meant that you caught it.

"Michelle *Zimmerman*," she said, pulling her hands out of the dishwater. "I'm sorry, Mother, but enough is sufficient. You've been after Murray and Jessie all weekend. I thought this would be a happy occasion. I imagined that you would welcome the baby. You're always happy for everyone else. But nothing I do is ever going to be good enough, is it?"

"Zimmerman," Aunt Sis said. "How you could come to Mass this morning."

"We're decent people," Michelle told her. "We're trying to live decent lives. Murray would never dream of using Dad's razor."

"A Catholic named Zimmerman. Now I've heard everything," Aunt Sis said.

"I'm agnostic. I only came to be polite."

"Agnostic," Gram said. "Confirmed in the Church, as I recall. Some people learn to leave well enough alone. Some people realize who knows better."

"This isn't what other Families are like," Michelle said. "People are given a break sometimes. Everyone doesn't pick on everyone else, all the way down the line. It's no fun being the youngest, I can tell you."

"Agnostic," Gram said.

"And I'm vegetarian," I told her.

Michelle looked surprised that I was still there. "You might want to pack up your tent, Jess," she said, before plunging her hands back into the water and frowning at Aunt Sis. "For your information, the weekend we went to Montreal, Murray's family was uniformly kind."

"Kind, were they?" Aunt Sis replied. "I suppose he's gone agnostic, too. Or can his type be agnostic?"

"That's it," Michelle said, backing quickly away from the sink. "We're leaving right now. Jessie, pack."

"Uncle Murray is nice," Janelle said, making everyone look at her. "He tells jokes all the time. He wants everyone to be happy. I call that a refreshing change."

You don't want to be outclassed by Janelle Piglet. Outclassed by a Piglet? I admit, I wasn't being totally noble when I confessed.

"I'm the one who used Gramps's razor," I said. "I forgot mine, and I needed to shave. He never minded when I used it before. We're all the same Blood. I mean, if you nick yourself."

I wasn't totally noble, but it still felt good, switching off the fight. Janelle and I were the centre of attention, filling a vacuum of indrawn breath.

"Legs or pits?" Janelle asked, scraping out another pot. "Don't you hate it when you nick your pits? I would of loaned you my razor. It's electric, so it don't nick. Nicked pits, I hate 'em."

"Fetid," I agreed, as Michelle stood drying her hands.

"Nicked pubes, they're even worse," Janelle said. "Mind you, not as bad as waxing. But what is?"

"You watch your mouth," Gram told her.

"I waxed this little heart down there on Valentine's Day."

"Janelle Pigott!"

"It wasn't as if anyone was going to see it, Gram. It's just, you know you got it and you feel . . ."

"Pleasantly fetid," I said.

"That sounds about right."

"I think I was exchanged at birth," Michelle said.

"You girls," Aunt Gail told us. "You go take your combined vocabularies outside. Go on, go look after Bradley. He's been out there waiting."

It wasn't fair, getting turfed out when you'd been noble, more or less.

"Why do I have to do anything?" I asked. "Can't I sit down with a cup of tea? Can't anyone get a moment's peace around here? What do you have to do around here to get left alone?"

"You think you're Greta Garbo?" Gram asked. "*I vant to be alone.*"

Now, there was a word to hold onto. "Greta," I repeated. "I like that. Thanks, Gram. I should probably change my name. Greta. I like that."

"But Jessica is a name Shakespeare made up," Michelle said, drying her hands over and over. "The baby book said the

Biblical root means God Beholds. He looks after you. He *recog-nizes* you. I chose it with such care."

"What you naming this one?" Aunt Gail asked.

"If it's a boy, Daniel."

"In the lion's den," Aunt Gail said.

"Subliminal," I told them.

"It's her vocabulary that's the problem," Janelle said. "Not mine."

This afternoon, back home, I told Dr. V that I was changing my name to Greta. "Gretel has braids. Greta has Attitude."

"What is Attitude?"

"A cosmic joke," I told her.

I'll tell you a real joke. Janelle Piglet's letter.

Who does she think she is?

Family, that's who. Coming or going, they get you every time.

SIXTEEN

Excuse me? Excuse me? I'm from next door.

You are Greta's mother, I say, rising from my knees at the lavender border. I wish to be rid of the woman, but walk to the gate. She smiles.

She told you the name change, did she? I guess we should take it seriously, then.

I wonder why she therefore smiles. Sternly I tell her, Things are important to young people which are not to their elders. One must respect this.

Of course, she says. I brought you some lemon pound cake. I'm not much of a cook, but there's no beating my lemon pound cake.

She holds it over the gate. I accept, but will not let her in.

To say thank you for your kindness to to . . . Greta, she says. She's out at the library before they close. A book she ordered just came in. I wanted to take the opportunity to thank you for all your help.

. . .

That's your influence, I think. That she's at the library.

I have no influence over the girl.

Of course, she's always been a reader. But we were worried that she'd feel lost, moving here. You seem to have helped her grow a few roots. Your garden is so lovely, she says, craning over my shoulder.

It is midsummer, I tell her, turning in preparation to leave. No doubt I will enjoy your lemon pound cake. I thank you.

But there's something I wanted to ask.

Reluctantly, I turn back.

We can't get her to sleep inside. She's out in that tent in all weather.

It is midsummer, I repeat. The girl blooms. What is the problem?

I'm worried about types in the alley. I haven't got a full night's sleep since we moved in. Waking up at all hours to check out the window, trying to see if she's all right.

So it is your own health which concerns you, I say. She flushes, but does not respond. I am sorry, I tell her. But if you feel better, I will say this: Old ladies do not sleep heavily at night. If there is a problem, I will hear it.

But she was telling her cousin last weekend that she means to stay out there all winter. And with the windows closed . . .

My window is open a crack all winter. This is healthful. Also, types do not come outside in winter. They rob garages only in summer, and even that is rare. You need not concern yourself of this.

I'm her mother. I can't help but feel concerned, and I was frankly hoping . . .

She will no doubt move inside during the rains of November. They are relentless, and her tent will smell.

November!

Of course, I say, smiling slightly to myself, if you were to buy her this computer, I think she would stay more inside.

. . .

She has not spoken of this computer? I wonder if the mother is slow-witted. The expression is confused.

She hasn't, the mother says finally. But of course she'd want a computer. She's so very intelligent. I know it's a funny thing to say, but I feel like her custodian sometimes instead of her mother. It's my privilege to look after her, as if she's a monument or a natural glory. I'll speak to my husband about the computer. Did she mention what kind?

Mac, I say.

Thank you so much, the mother replies, with a pretty smile. I was hoping you'd have more of an idea than we do. The parents are usually the last to know.

Now she is the one who turns to leave.

Do not tell that I have informed you, I am forced to say, although I do not like it.

Again the Barfoot woman looks puzzled. Clearly, the girl's intelligence comes from the dead father. Slowly she understands that I have betrayed a confidence. Having worked this out, she smiles again. Of course, she says. I've never even met you!

Finally she leaves my gate. Enjoy the pound cake! she cries.

Indeed, it smells very good, yet I return to my garden feeling displeased. Am I to know the whole family? No, I will not. If the step-father comes, I will send him away. Indeed, I will enjoy sending him away.

Do you know what I have discovered, Father, thinking so much about the past? I don't like men. They can be as sneaky as cats. This Zimmerman pads around his property like a fat neutered tom. He hums snatches of songs in a self-satisfied purr. Yet blessed silence doesn't mean that he has finally gone inside. He will startle me by appearing at my gate, like a cat stealing in through the fence.

"Well, doesn't your garden look lovely?" he says, as if anybody asked him.

You are also impertinent, Father. Yes, you are; you are my prime study of the male. And when I remember the way you behaved, I grow angry at you, Father. Furious! I am furious at what you did to my life. Yes, I told you about Florrie's fall, but you were not required to take me to Florrie's house uninvited and surprise her father with my naïve recitation. You could have hushed it up the way that Jannie wanted. You had no need to disgrace Florrie and set all of the other dominoes falling. And as for what you did on my thirtieth birthday! No, I have not burned the diary yet. I have again reread it, feeling so bitter. You are to blame for my solitary life, Father—not just because of what you have done to me over the years, but because of the way you died and left me alone.

Yes, you are dead, Father. Have I not mentioned this fact? Your memory lives on only in me. I am the one who still lives in the world . . . holding a lemon pound cake!

It smells delicious. Oh, you would like it, Father. You would enjoy a slice.

Perhaps I will eat just a slice before dinner. After all, I can still enjoy it!

Lemon. Poppy seeds. It is good.

SEVENTEEN

Today is my birthday and the girls asked to go out after work in celebration. It is now more than two years in this job at the Beneficial Life Insurance Corporation which my dear Father approved, for it is one large and respectable organization in which quiet girl (mouse) like me may not be bothered or noticed. Indeed, it was big surprise to receive this invitation when I had mentioned with no more than five passing words that it was my special day. It was certainly the most congenial surprise. And so I have the privilege to open with this congenial story the new diary which my dear Father has given for my birthday (thirty!) along with one fine Dutch-English dictionary. With regular use of both, I may perfect my English and disappear from notice completely.

I do not wish to disappear. I wish to be like this: You are on the crowded street of persons in winter overcoats and hats walking past on edge of vision. You have your head down, which is how you pass one girl and do not quite see her. Later, you have the niggling sensation that you saw something different today. What did you see? You picture again the crowded street, beginning to rise above it until you succeed to look down. And what do you discover? You are one little part of the crowd and not its centre. Around you are unknown persons which are as important to themselves as you are to you. They contain beliefs and knowledge which you do not understand. You are merely one atomic particle. You know nothing.

I would like to give people this feeling that others are different and unknown. I would like to be nothing more than one niggling memory to strangers of someone they did not thoroughly see. There is colloquial expression here: nothing you can put your finger on. I wish that to be me.

The Beneficial Life Insurance Corporation is the most impressive structure, however, and I am pleased every day to see how thoroughly it is untouched by war. By this I intend the concrete building; inside are many former soldiers. I have noticed that Canada is the opposite of Germany, where cities were much damaged when the war ended, but as our three years there passed, one met fewer and fewer men who had fought in the *Wehrmacht*.

I had never thought to work at the Beneficial Life Insurance Corporation when my dear Father felt time came to leave the store. I had been employed in the Select Paint and Wallpaper almost three years as bookkeeper, which is one very strange word when I write it down with repeated double letters. But that is something bookkeepers do: make double entries! My dear Father perceived one of the men in the warehouse was showing me too much interest. I did not like this man, it is true. But corporations normally do not hire DPs (Displaced Persons) and I would not have responded the advertisement if my Father did not point out we would already be dust in Europe without pushing against closed doors.

I was surprised to be called to interview and made the excuse of some doctor's visit to leave Select Paint and Wallpaper. Yes, I was nervous. Outside the office, I was asked to wait with other girls and we did not speak, although one girl licked her eyebrows straight using her vulgar compact which united the rest of us in the belief that she was unsuitable; also that she would be hired. However, Mr. Warnicke's secretary called me into his office where he was friendly. He informed that he was among the Canadian Army that occupied the Netherlands after the war, beginning quickly to reminisce and to make himself smile.

"We marched into Utrecht behind a pipe and drum corps. I don't think they'd ever heard anything like it. But they danced as best they could."

"I would think so, sir."

"And you, Miss van Tellingen," he said, looking to my application. "Where did you end the war?"

"Not in Utrecht, sir. I am from Amsterdam." Often this answer will suffice the job, but he continued to look at me. "My story is difficult." Still it was not enough, and I was forced to speak it again.

"You understand, sir, that during the war, when Germans came into my country, they wished Dutch men to work in their factories. The men did not wish this, including my Father. He had been called up to work for the factory in Germany but clearly he did not wish to go. Instead, he hid in our countryside for more than one year. You must understand that thousands of men did this."

Mr. Warnicke had one intelligent face, and very fair. He nodded

"It is true there were several farms; my Father moved often. I was with him at the last farm when Germans raided. I was living in Amsterdam, but I was on my own and very hungry. I went to this farm to look for food. My Father always tried to let me know where he was. When we heard motors coming, the farmer locked us into the hidden room. However, we were discovered, and some few days later, put on board the transport train. But this train was bombed inside Germany and we escaped. This was very near the end of the war; you must understand the confusion."

Again he nodded. I discover since that Mr. Warnicke is indeed one fair man.

"It is ironic, I think. We passed as Dutch labourers who had been bombed out of jobs in German factories, and soon we were in Berlin during these air raids." I took a breath, stopping myself. "So you see, that is where we ended the war."

"I'm sorry," he said.

Here is where I told him, "Officers of the Canadian army do not need to apologize to former Dutch citizens, sir."

"I was not an officer," he said, and I did not know what to answer.

"Why do you wish to leave your present employment?" he asked most abruptly.

"I have been glad to work there, sir," I said. "But this position is of more responsibility, and I wish to improve myself."

He studied my application. "You weren't nineteen when the war ended," he said. "I wasn't quite twenty."

I knew this must be why he spoke about the war. He had not seen much, so for him it had ended as he said. Those who find that it has not ended fail to speak with such open heart (hope).

"People deserve their chance," Mr. Warnicke said, looking at my application but not my eyes. Therefore I did not understand what he said, and was surprised to receive this job despite even the pretty girl with her eyebrows.

I have been very thankful, however, for the Beneficial Life Insurance Corporation is the most congenial place to work. The atmosphere I find polite and the premises, clean. Quiet girls are not teased, nor is the work difficult. I mean to say it is not difficult for me. Mathematics and algebra were my good subjects at the lyceum, at least until my education became interrupted, which is to say my schooling, when the lyceum was closed because of war. Also I scored top marks in my course of evening study at the Toronto School of Business in the double-letter (duplicitous!) subject of bookkeeping (that is joke!). So I received quickly my reputation for being prompt and dependable girl, and Mr. Warnicke, who is boss of my department, made it soon clear he believed in his decision to hire me.

"Give it to Miss van Tellingen," he said within six months. "It has to be done right."

"Well, aren't you the blue-eyed girl," Miss Watson (Bertha) whispered. "Too bad he's married."

Certainly it proved unfortunate that Mr. Warnicke had married Mrs. Warnicke. Once, when I had been there nine months, she came into the office. The door opened with a crash, which stopped the typists (silence), and one dark-haired lady walked down the corridor between the desks with empty expression on her face, although her suit was correct and her lipstick applied with talent. When she reached to the door at the opposite end, she merely turned to walk back, then back again, making it seem as if she would continue forever, like Dante's circle of hell.

"Mrs. Warnicke?" asked Miss Watson (Bertha), who had met her before. She then took this lady by her arm to Mr. Warnicke's office.

It was Mr. Warnicke's confidential secretary, Miss Carcross, who told the story of Mrs. Warnicke after her sad visit. This was inexcusable of Miss Carcross, but one listened. She told that when I arrived at Beneficial Life, the couple was expecting third child; the elder daughters were four years old and two. Soon another girl was born; as my dear Father would say, poor luck. Miss Carcross whispered that even worse was the mother's behaviour, which resulted in electrical shock.

Now, said Miss Carcross, Mr. Warnicke's mother was coming to live with him, for his wife had gone to live in the hospital (funny farm). After hearing this story, the girls in the office also provided for Mr. Warnicke the understanding of mothers, which however he did not need, for Mr. Warnicke did not begin to use his voice irritably, and certainly did not complain, but merely drooped his shoulders, gained weight and became more bald.

The unimaginable followed. His wife stepped off the Viaduct, which is the famous place for the sin of suicide in this city. It is big disgrace! To leave behind three little children! Daughters! And a husband like Mr. Warnicke, who is intelligent, fair and of disposition hopeful. One wishes indeed to mother for him.

It was amusing, however, to watch the speed with which many girls afterwards grew less like mothers and more attractive in their appearance (sirens). I mean the speed which each girl considered this proper. I do not wear make-up, myself. Yet I walk across the Viaduct each morning and evening, and therefore the fact of the deceased wife is also much before me. I write her death to start my new diary, and often when I walk, I think I hear the moans of dead sinners mocking me from hell, for one day I shall join them.

Enough. I have no belief in hell. It is merely the conventional way to speak, just as the Viaduct is merely some bridge, and I walk across it on all but the inclement days with honest reason to exercise my cramped limbs and save the streetcar fare.

Here is one true fact: My dear Father has succeeded to buy on twenty-five year mortgage this most comfortable house merely three miles east from the Beneficial Life Insurance Corporation. It is one big achievement, when first we arrived in this country with no possessions (1948) and were required to work two years for the farm in Niagara Peninsula. Even then my dear Father saved our hard-earned wages, the meaning of which expression I know very well. It is one year now we have lived in my Father's dear house, and today is also a special day because of his announcement, which agitates me—I intend in some pleasant manner. I am, as my dictionary says: anticipatory, in earnest hope, agreeable, accommodating, compliant (resigned).

But I get ahead of my story in agitation. Remembering the suicide has agitated me, not my dear Father's announcement indeed, which announcement from my dear Father naturally came after my congenial invitation from the girls, so I am out of order and it is true this silly writing makes no sense.

Now I have composed myself to write in proper fashion. This noon hour I received my most congenial invitation in the lunchroom, where there is bantering at which I (mouse) have begun to nibble. When first I arrived at Beneficial Life, I passed unnoticed for many months, sitting at one table near to Miss Watson's (Bertha's) group of friends to understand their English. I noticed other girl sitting alone nearby and could see that she (Miss Hall) also noticed me. However, it was many more months before I began to sit with this Miss Hall, which came before my invitation, and which happened in one disturbing manner, like this:

There began to be famous the play performed in New York called The Diary of Anne Frank. Soon in Toronto it was heard about and the book read, and one day Miss Watson's (Bertha's) friends mentioned it at the table behind me.

I am afraid Miss Bertha Watson must be considered some sort of unattractive girl. She has big bones in her body with fleshy face and uses much red lipstick, which makes her mouth look wide and her eyes like a monkey. I am sorry, but it is true. Also she has the loud voice and stays unmarried at her age approaching mine. I think she is kind, however. I am certain she did not mean to be unkind when she said to me, "You're Dutch."

"That is my old country," I agreed, feeling merely startled.

"And you must be about her age," she said with calculation, being a bookkeeper also. "Anne Frank, the diary of. She would have been about your age, if you don't mind my saying."

I have read about Anne Frank in the newspaper, although I do not like to read the book.

"I think you are right," I said.

"You're not from that Amsterdam, are you?"

"You see, I am."

"Well, there you go," she replied. "So what do you hear? The inside poop?"

I did not know what this expression intended and felt some confusion.

"Amsterdam is a big city," Mr. Warnicke said behind me. "There were lots of people hiding out from old Adolf during the war. The Dutch were famous for hiding people like Anne Frank. Some of them even survived."

I smiled up at him, perhaps nervous still. I would not have expected him to remember our conversation.

"*Onderduikers*," he said, with bad pronunciation. "They said when people went into hiding, they 'dove under.' That's what it means. Because in Holland it's so wet they didn't go underground, they went underwater. Am I correct, Miss van Tellingen?"

"Yes, sir, that is very correct."

Mr. Warnicke nodded, and told long story about how he marched into Amsterdam in 1945 with his army, seeing people so pale they were like ghosts in the crowd. He was told these people had been hiding from Germans and had not been outside for two, three years. They had been hiding in attics, in basements: this is surely true. Mr. Warnicke shook his head. "They were like pillars of salt in the crowds, I thought. I don't know why I thought that."

"Because so many are looking back on what has happened," I said. "They have lost ability to look forward. They do not look forward to anything now. I think that has happened to many people who have survived this war."

"That's the most words I've ever heard you put together," said Miss Bertha Watson. Mr. Warnicke smiled, however, and the girl (Miss Hall) who normally sat on the other side of Miss Bertha Watson's girlfriends sat down beside me the next day.

"I liked what you said yesterday," Miss Hall told me with nervous laugh, and thankfully did not speak more.

Here is why this effected my invitation: not only has Miss Hall continued to sit beside me, I have also achieved better identity at Beneficial Life Insurance Corporation, for now I am "the Dutch girl" and not (whispers) "the DP."

As well, it is true that Mr. Warnicke began afterwards to watch me at times, which is different story and thrills me with nervousness, especially since his wife is dead.

"The boss has his eye on you," Miss Bertha Watson said. "Or did I mean" (singing) "he only has eyes for you."

She will whisper, "Here comes your beau."

"A bit of lipstick wouldn't hurt. With that skin, you don't need much. I'd kill for your skin. There's not much you can do with your hair, I agree."

"What's the matter with her hair?" asked Miss Hall, with this laugh.

"Honey, her hair's so thin, it's got beriberi. Maybe one of the new short cuts?" She made one expression at herself in the washroom mirror which I did not understand. "I'd be a good mother to pretty daughters," she said.

Perhaps it is my position surrounded by female voices which causes the dream. I began to have this dream soon after the conversation (Anne Frank). Now it comes often, one nightmare that encroaches upon my sleep as chorus of female voices calling for Maaike van der Velde, which is one mysterious thing.

"Maaike van der Velde. Maaike van der Velde!"

Who is this Maaike van der Velde? I ask this of my diary, just as I would ask of whoever might say it, and ask indeed of all these female voices:

"Who is Maaike van der Velde? Is she one dead girl from the war? I do not know this Maaike van der Velde. I am Miss van Tellingen, Miss Martha van Tellingen, and I do not know any girl named Maaike van der Velde."

"Maaike van der Velde, Maaike van der Velde."

"Ah yes, Maaike van der Velde. Miss Maaike van der Velde," comes the voice of some male person. "My Gertrud speaks of you often. She speaks of you highly! Such an example to the other girls. Such an example to the boys and girls!"

"I'm glad to hear you say so, sir," says the female voice. This dream is a telephone call; I cannot see her face. However, it must be Maaike van der Velde who tells this man, "I always like to be of help."

"No doubt, no doubt," says the man in his German voice. "It is the wish of all good Dutch citizens to be of help to the Reich. I have noticed this. Yes."

"But I have something to tell you, sir," I say. "Do you have time for me to tell you something important? Or should we meet in person?"

"You have something to tell me?" the man asks.

"I have learned about activities, sir. If I make myself clear, there is something hidden that must be brought to light. Will you see me, sir?"

It is garbage dream. It is what I dislike, the way DPs to this country imply stories of the war. From what they say, all of them are innocent now, and indeed many have become heroes. Yes, they finally joined the resistance, they will tell you, as if resistance were not also killers. They will even tell about the time they lured *Wehrmacht* officers to their death with girlish telephone calls. "Or should we meet in person?" they asked, setting diabolic trap. What is more, people here (suckers) rush to believe them.

I think that with this famous Anne Frank play, the total of New York and Canada will believe soon how sterling, brave and murderous are all the Dutch. But the truth is not exactly like that. Here is the truth: the resistance was small and the armed resistance not merely smaller but also rough characters (thugs). Most people had not to do with either, although it is the case that they would not tattle-tale if they did. You see, they wished to survive the war.

Before the war, it was Depression in my country with much unemployment and the National Socialism grew popular. A percentage of people welcomed the *Wehrmacht*, not because of Jewish Question (Anne Frank) but because they believed German Reich would put the end to unemployment. Afterwards, most persons worked naturally at their jobs. To eat, one worked; to work, one worked under German occupations.

Adults went to offices with photographs of *Der Führer* above. Signs in the street told *Joden Niet Gewenscht,* they are not welcome, and these were obeyed. Children could play sports only in approved youth organizations, which is how they played sports if their parents wished them to remain healthy.

It is true that such normal work (collaboration) became unpopular in the last year or two of the war, and some persons who were once supporters for National Socialism and the NSB no longer believed. Indeed, some became one hundred per cent against former beliefs, not trusted by other Dutch it is true, but acting still in defiant fashion: for instance, hiding the male persons in their families which joined the popular idea to evade work in German factories, like every other Dutch. Of course they did, these factories being bombarded nightly by the Royal Air Force and daily by the Americans.

And so: I am not sure how it is possible to judge persons either on basis of first or last years of war, or even both together. I am not sure war can be made so little complicated, or how it is possible to remain innocent while war carries on. I dream garbage about one Maaike van der Velde because Canadians do not understand what I know and who I am. The "Dutch girl" is (I am) one big simplification. However, it is also not their poor fault. I do not recognize myself by now, so why indeed should they?

Martha van Tellingen. I am Miss Martha van Tellingen. My Father's name is Mr. Gerrit van Tellingen, and now we live in Toronto in one comfortable house with twenty-five-year mortgage and no history. Today is my birthday, by the way.

"Today is my birthday," I informed Miss Hall in the lunchroom.
   "Happy birthday," she said.

"It's your birthday?" said Miss Bertha Watson, whom I did not expect to hear. Standing up beside her table of friends, she began to conduct them in singing, "Happy Birthday to You, Happy Birthday to You, Happy Birthday Miss van Tellingen, Happy Birthday to You."

It was most congenial and I laughed. I am not used to hear myself laughing in the Beneficial Life Insurance Corporation, or indeed outside movies (Saturday matinee). I stood up also and made little curtsy to the chorus, which was to thank them before sitting back down.

"Why don't you come out with us tonight?" Miss Bertha Watson went on. "We're going out for our regular Friday-night bite. Why not add some cake for your celebration?"

I was unable to know how to answer, and looked in some confusion at Miss Hall.

"Your friend is welcome to come along," Miss Bertha Watson said.

"I have to get home to my mother," said Miss Hall rapidly, being a true mouse (shy). "Thank you," she said.

"Yes, thank you very much," I said. "It is also the case that my Father will expect me home for dinner. He will have planned some little celebration, such as we have each year."

"There's that," agreed Miss Bertha Watson. "So we'll make it next week. You can come along then."

Her congeniality made me feel most pleasantly warm. I did not know if my Father would give permission, but wished that he might. "Thank you. I will ask."

"Ask?"

I wondered if this was not the fashion here "My Father," I said.

Miss Bertha Watson's look was most piercing. I grew nervous, having perceived especially that Mr. Warnicke was listening nearby. I wondered how they should think of me. That I was pleasing in my obedience (which is to say consideration of my dear Father), or doormat (colloquial)?

"We come from this old-fashioned country," I said.

"So do we all," said Miss Bertha Watson. "My parents still live there, but I moved."

"You come from where?" I asked.

She swept her hand toward the window. "Six blocks south."

"Don't torment her," said Miss Hall, in her rapid voice and blushes. "Some people still respect their parents."

"I thank you very much for your congenial invitation," I interrupted to Miss Bertha Watson. "I would very much like to have bite on Friday night that is coming. I will make some necessary arrangements, that is all."

Afterwards, Mr. Warnicke found me out, standing close by to say, "Happy birthday."

I thanked him very much, feeling another warmth.

"If you're accepting invitations," he told me, "maybe you'd consider coming to my house for dinner sometime. My mother's heard so much about you, she'd be happy to cook dinner. Saturday week? If it proves convenient? Or maybe the week after, if two days in a row is too much."

Mr. Warnicke blushed like Miss Hall when he spoke, for he is very fair man in skin also: pale eyes and round, smooth, agreeable face that is soft and accepting. If you placed on it your finger, I believe his cheek would dimple like bread dough. I wished to do this, standing so close and warm beside him, to give him dimples on each cheek to complete his bashful smile.

Am I not droll? Also to keep secret until now that I received *two* invitations today. A double entry! That is what it is like to be the keeper: keeper of secrets as well as of books: which this

diary is! Oh, we have double meanings today! Am I not duplicitous? I assure you I am. I fear that I am.

"I hope it proves convenient," I replied to Mr. Warnicke,
blushing very bad indeed and wishing that it was.

I returned home at the usual time. Through the kitchen
window, I could see my Father kneeling in the garden, which is
harvest garden with vegetables most profuse. He is friendly
giant (colloquial expression), with big head even, massive brow
under which blue Dutch eyes watch out cleverly for angles.
These are quick eyes, far more smart than mine, and he is
massive also in the shoulders and chest from many years in
foreman or security position.

Now he wore soiled clothes from his also important job to
extend the Toronto subway line. It is excellent luck for the
Toronto Transit Commission that my Father (Dutch) is able to
assist with complications of water and drainage. I think soon
they must give him another title from construction worker to
honour his age and ability; also more pay. My dear Father is
now four years with the Toronto Transit Commission, which
is steady job.

On my kitchen counter was the cake I woke up early to bake.
Outside, my dear Father stood up from his bad knee, taking
one chicken and sharply wringing her neck. So: special chicken
dinner tonight. I turned on my oven as dear Father plucked the
chicken, which he knows I dislike to do.

"This," he said, placing plucked chicken on counter and
proceeding downstairs, where is the place to wash himself
and leave soiled clothes for me to wash, clean clothes hanging
on the hook for his change. It is good to have such steady
routine. It is good to have each day so much the same (peace)
that one is permitted routine. I placed out my dear Father's

packet of Matinees for his smoke, pleased that his cheeks looked red and healthy, for it is sad when he is pale.

As he washed, I began to cook. When we succeeded to our first apartment in this country, my Father found me as birthday present the modern *Cookbook for Beginners (Cookbook for Brides) Featuring Cooking for Two* by Miss Dorothy Malone. On the rear cover of my red-and-blue Bible (joke!) Miss Dixie Oliver from the newspaper *Houston Chronicle* writes, "Run down to your nearest bookstore and purchase this priceless volume." Of course it is impossible to purchase what is priceless. Oxymoron: my dictionary has taught me a good word. However, my dear Father prefers Miss Oliver's recipes for the first Sunday of month, especially Pork Chop Hodge-Podge Casserole, for we are provided in the garden with one Spy apple tree. Also Boiled Beef with Horseradish-Applesauce, while for lunchbucket: Sardine Triple-Decker Sandwiches.

"Tonight we have Exotic Hawaiian Chicken Casserole," I told dear Father, who came upstairs. "It adds one can of pineapple because it is my special day."

We speak English, you see. However, my Father does not speak much before his smoke, so merely he sat in his place at the kitchen table and watched me to cook. He is not a mobile man, except when he is required to be.

"Also we have glazed onions from garden, mashed potatoes, and tomato coleslaw," I told him. "Tomato coleslaw is the experimental recipe from my dear book."

"Does not sound good," my Father replied. "Coleslaw from tomatoes."

"Well, we will not know until we try it," I told him, aware how I spoke too much and too nervously. You see, feeling his eyes on me, I thought about Miss Bertha Wilson's kind invitation (also other) which it was difficult to mention. Perhaps I might ask: One time I could go? Perhaps I might say: It is unnatural if mice do not scurry sometimes from their holes. It is noticed! Persons asked: Why do they not? Are they dead mice which soon begin to stink?

It was good to make joke of serious business, I thought, cooking glazed onions. This was one great favourite of my Father's. Onions, not jokes. His Matinees were not true favourites of mine, however; it is the asthma from which I suffer. I left the door open a crack.

"You let out smell of cooking."

"I am sorry, Father," I told him, hastening to close. Not the good mood tonight, I thought. Something at work? He was not perhaps treated with dignity. This happens often to Displaced Persons (DPs), which is national disgrace, to accept people into this country in order to abuse them. I resolved to mention Miss Bertha Wilson's kind invitation only after dinner; also to cook sliced tomatoes with dill.

"So, no tomato coleslaw," he said.

"I think you are right, Father. It does not sound good. Simple is better, I believe."

He nodded at me, yet throughout dinner he was silent. One truly bad day, I thought, ~~watching my Father use his thumbs to shovel food, which is pig country habit he knows I despise~~ and resolved to mention Miss Bertha Wilson perhaps tomorrow. Perhaps later.

Perhaps not at all. My Father's face did not improve with dessert, and I began to worry that he had heard Miss Bertha Wilson's kind invitation; I did not know how. It is true I call out in my nightmares, so my Father tells me, and also perhaps that I speak out loud to myself sometimes inside walls like these, which are safe. But no night had passed since the invitation, and I disciplined myself in particular today not to speak while I was cooking, which is some bad habit and must be crushed.

He could not know about Miss Bertha Wilson. Yet I concluded that he did, and opened my dear presents with fluttering fingers and too many words, thanking my dear Father most humbly, for he thinks of everything, he thinks of everything for me . . . all while thinking, he knows, he knows, until my breathing grew tight, stupid asthma squeezing my stupid chest, and I resolved that I must say and get it over with.

"But I am naughty girl," I told him. "You give me such presents, yet now I am forced to ask for your help. In the lunchroom, you see, the girls at work pressed me for dinner to celebrate my special day."

"The girls," my Father said, with voice so deep and angry I could not succeed to answer. Now he was foreman and sergeant again forced to deal with some silly stupid mouse. I ducked my head in case he would strike me.

"The girls," I repeated anxiously.

"So this is your girl: one Boss Warnicke."

"Mr. Warnicke!"

"Who uses Emergency Telephone Number to ask your Father's permission for dinner, creating all confusion at work."

Oh no. On the Form we filled out Emergency Telephone Number and now I saw how this use by Mr. Warnicke caused my Father much worry, brought to the front office of Toronto Transit Commission by Emergency telephone call, all eyes singling him out. I deserved for him to strike me, and apologized most humbly for my dear Father's worry, which I did not suspect, explaining in many, many words my whole story (congenial) of birthday chorus, birthday wishes, invitations, girls indeed and how I wished to join them, although clearly not Mr. Warnicke with his invitation, which I did not understand.

"What is this invitation from Mr. Warnicke?" I asked him. "There are parties in the office which I don't take part. But when the invitation comes from some Boss, must it be accepted? Do you think it must, Father? I am sure you must know about this type of order. But I do not know how to manage these matters my own stupid self."

"What does your old Father know?" he replied.

"But I think you must know, Father. You always do."

"You go ask. You go ask: this old Dutchman, what does he know? Him, he don't know nothing, that's what they'll say. He don't know English, he's just one big knucklehead DP."

I tried to speak, but he would not let.

"This Boss Warnicke, you ask what he thinks. You go ask. Or maybe you know. You already decided. This old Dutchman, he's one stupid knucklehead to his own daughter—his own daughter he does everything for. You think your old Father is stupid DP. You think he don't understand nothing you say."

"No, Father!"

"No dinner with Boss. You hear me? Or are you too stupid to hear me? Stupid brain in stupid head. Stupid girl forgets, number one, she lives inside one big lie. She uses lying papers to come into this country. That's how she gets to damned stupid country. Damned stupid country, that's what it is. Number two, someone learns how she lied, then what?"

It was true. Duplicitous, double-entry me. However, I am one strange girl. This picture amused me, strange girl that I am. Let him strike me if he wished!

"Yes, I am liar," I told my Father, standing up. "For you see, here is truth: that I did intend to tell you Miss Bertha Wilson's invitation, and to get your permission to go for this bite. But I intended also to mention the wrong day. I would mention Saturday, so I could go to Mr. Warnicke's house instead. Here is your truth: that I wish to have my second chance. Now I am no liar at all. I was not nineteen when the war ended, and I intend to have my second chance."

"Second chance," my Father said, in his face a disgust. I knew what he thought: how he had wished to return to the Old Country after the war, how he did not care what Dutch people thought, what they did to himself etc., how I was the one who wished to escape some murderous past, who cried and cried not to see again the streets where Dutch people died, and *Wehrmacht,* pleading for this big demand, to make the move to Canada. Second chance was coming here.

Yes it was. But now we reach next possible step, disappearing into Canadian life. Colloquial expression: go the whole hog. I wished to go whole hog, disappearing into Canadian life, lock, stock and barrel!

"Disappearing from your old Father," he replied. "What happens to him? What does he do now, when he does everything for his own little girl?"

I knew it was true. I also knew it would always be true, no matter where and how I lived. And so, I laughed. I was so brave that I laughed until there came to me one bat out of hell: What did he say to Mr. Warnicke?

"What did you say to Mr. Warnicke, Father?" I asked, feeling the asthma choke on my chest, and hearing my poor words strangle.

My Father's smart eyes looked over my face, and he did not answer. Instead he lit another smoke, watching my poor breath fail.

"Clearly that you did not wish to eat his mother's dinner, but you are too shy to know how to refuse," he told me finally, and once he said this, his voice became kind. "Also, in fact, how you prefer to leave this job at Beneficial Life Insurance

Corporation, making quiet home now for your old Father."

"No!" I cried.

"Financial picture improves," he told me, enjoying his smoke. "You need not to work any more. You may stay home with your cooking and garden. Save money from the office clothes. Here it is good for you, little Maaike. Here it is safe."

I did not know this Maaike. My name is Martha van Tellingen. I did not know what my Father referred to, and did not wish to leave my job. My chest grew tight and I did not hear what he told: that two weeks' notice was required, that Mr. Warnicke had accepted my Father's notice, that on my last Friday, I had my Father's permission to join the girls for bite, but I must inform beforehand which café, so that he might pass outside once or twice, ensuring it was bite with girls and not Boss Warnicke, who spoke to him like he was old Dutch knucklehead, for which my Father set Boss straight.

"I set him straight," my Father told me, then added like a boy, "You need not to recognize me inside your café. I will be wearing the work clothes, and merely pass by, looking in the window."

"I do not wish to leave my job, Father," I said, beginning to laugh and cry. "I will go mad, too much time to think. I will be one big candidate for funny farm."

My Father smiled also. "It is a weakness of this Warnicke boss, for crazy little women," he teased. "Perhaps I share this weakness myself."

Here is when my asthma attacked, a long hard fight which frightens him every time.

"Will you survive, Maaike?" he pleaded.

"Martha," I corrected, with strangled breath.

What I write is so true that anyone may read this book. You too, Father. Isn't that why you gave it to me? You wish to read the truth of my life in these pages—which I have also scattered with lies. Yes, I have written here many lies. Which is which, Father, are you able to know? I wonder if you will permit yourself to remember what truly happened during the war. Can you separate the truth from lies? I think that is what books ask their reader to do.

And now, having filled many pages of this book, I am ready to lay down the pen. Excuse me: one final song. Happy Birthday to me. Happy Birthday to me. Happy Birthday Miss Funny Farm, Happy Birthday to me.

I will die if I see Mr. Warnicke again. For two more weeks, I shall die each day.

Hell comes after and I do not deserve it.

Yes I do.

EIGHTEEN

Monday, August 21

One thing after another. How much more can I take? People are required to take too much in this life, if you ask me. They just keep piling it on top of you. Who asked for any of this? I never asked for any of this. I don't know why anyone would.

Of course, Pudge and Michelle would claim they're not taking from me, they're giving, i.e. a new computer. But that's just a mask for their real purpose, which is to get whatever they want. They're so obvious they make me want to run in the opposing direction. You can totally see why people decide to take a run. Matthew Cavanaugh ran away to Toronto last summer, living with Homeless Persons on the street until the police shipped him back to Kingston. I mean, there comes a point. There truly does.

It started this evening, with Pudge and his wife sneaking in through the front door after work. Naturally, I was cooking in the kitchen, the lowly dentured servant going about her toil amid the steam and hiss of pots, slowly grasping that the Master and Mistress were tiptoeing up and down the front stairs like children who thought they had you fooled. I could see how in the veritable Age of Fairy Tales, servants must have thought their Masters were like children, caring about themselves instead of taking care of themselves, i.e. they couldn't boil an egg, which is true of Pudge today.

It's also true that I wasn't totally displeased to see the computer, at least not at first. After Michelle induced her head into the kitchen, calling me up to the spare room, I saw how they'd assembled an office chair and desk topped with this cartoon-style bubble monitor. Actually, that's pretty much what you want in a computer. You don't want to take them too seriously, right? They're a tool, right? Not a lifestyle unto themselves.

Propped against the pillows on the bed was a new Accent Cushion the same teal colour as the Mac, but that was a lapse I chose to ignore. I admit, my initial mood was good.

"Hey, thank you, guys," I said. "It's great."

"Nice little machine," Pudge told me, patting the monitor.

"Imagine having your own computer," Michelle said.

"We've already set you up on-line."

"Your first computer!"

"Ergonomic chair."

"All so cozy and snug."

I sat down in the ergonomic chair and quickly got onto the Net, which they thought was an act of Genius, although we had computers at Sacred Armpit, and I've been working in the Library to check out Collectible prices on-line. To be honest, their high self-approval rating was already starting to annoy me. I couldn't help but see it as underhanded in the sense that Dr. V had extricated for me earlier.

"Young people always assume that they're the centre of attention," she said. "But actually they're not. I wasn't thinking about you at all."

"You were thinking about yourself," I said.

"That's what people are like."[1]

---

1. As recorded in my Diary, Wednesday, July 19. It is useful to reread my Diary periodically in order to perceive what Dr. V really said to me, which I often don't understand at the time.

In fact, Dr. V allowed me to hear what Michelle and Pudge were really saying, as *per* the footnoted translation (attached).

Pudge: "It's an intuitive system."[2]

Michelle: "Jess, you're just so amazingly smart."[3]

P: "You can plug right in."[4]

M: "And get your marks back up at school."[5]

Annoying, right? For a while, however, I resolved to be Above It All, truly Nietszchean in my lofty condescension, i.e. not whine at them to shut up shut up this is *my* computer, go away and leave me alone.

"Thanks, guys," I said. "I really appreciate this. It's like you knew what I wanted. And Michelle can do her thesis on it, too."

Then Michelle glanced Significantly at Pudge, which is something that you don't want to see. I pretended not to see it, merely admitting that I'd never grasped whether Michelle was going to finish her master's long-distance at Queen's or whether she was transferring down to the University of Toronto. School started next month at the University, too. We could share the computer until the zygote was born.

"You can finish your thesis in six months," I told her, then realized my mistake. "Five."

"Jess, here's the thing," Michelle replied, sitting down across from me on the bed. I hate it when they do that. You know that something's up. You wish they'd leave well enough alone. But Michelle just had to lob her bomb, didn't she?

"I'm postponing my master's," she said, glancing back at Pudge. "That's not honest. The fact is, Jess, I'm letting it slide. I enjoy working in Murray's office, and he needs my help right

---

2. "I made a good choice."

3. "I'm so smart, figuring out what you wanted."

4. "I made a *really* good choice."

5. "You've got to show them how smart my daughter really is."

now. It's a relief. A rest, in a way, working in a place where we all have everything in common. Murray's assembled a lovely team, and I have my contribution to make, getting the office running more efficiently. Afterward, when the baby's born, I'll be staying at Home for a couple of years. For at least a couple of years, the way I did with you. Making a Home for everyone. After that?"

She shrugged. How could she do that? Shrug. I didn't know how she could do that.

"You could finish your master's afterward," I said.

"I could take a course for paralegals. That's one option."

"Go to law school," I told her, feeling panicked.

"Jess, listen," she said. "I've always pushed myself pretty hard. I've pushed myself and led an interesting life, and I don't regret one moment. Just a scant few moments, well in the past. But I also understand why it's a Chinese curse, May you live in interesting times. I want to gear down from that, and Murray's been good enough to give me the option. His mother worked all through his childhood, and he'd like it if I stayed at Home with you and the baby and, who knows? We're young. We're still young. I want to lead a quieter life. You be the one to get the degrees. You're the real scholar in the family. Look at all your reading! You'll go so far, baby. But for myself, I don't want to try to prove anything any more to anyone. Not a single thing."

I couldn't believe it. Michelle was giving up. At least I'd always been able to pride myself on having a mother who was somewhat different than other mothers. I mean, she tried, you know? Even if she never totally succeeded, Michelle tried. But now she was ceding Control to Pudge. I could see that clearly. Pudge was the one who really ruled the roost, ruled and tainted it at the same time. I'd almost started to like Pudge, or at least to tolerate his presence, but now he'd gone and tainted what Gram called Michelle's fabled independence. She'd always stood on her own two feet, but Pudge had got her leaning. He'd got her Retreating into the Past, attempting to correct his own unhappy childhood by becoming a Stay-at-Home Mom, giving up her ambitions for life as a Domestic Drudge.

A Pudge Drudge, what a fate. Mrs. Mall Santa. Would she find it quote, a rest and a relief to work in Santa's Village? Would she have everything in common with the plastic reindeer and ergonomic female Elves?

"I think I might have mentioned that I prefer the name Greta," I said.

"Fair enough," the Drudge replied. "But in that case, Greta, I think you might appreciate the fact that other people seek to change their identities, too."

"Thank you, Mrs. Zimmerman."

"Baby, I know it's another surprise. Another change and another surprise. I guess it's our final break with Kingston. One thing has kind of been following another this summer, hasn't it? But I promise this is the last change for a long while. Frankly, I don't like surprises much, either."

"Computers aside," Pudge said.

"Computers aside," came his echo.

Nietzsche speaks about the herd mentality. I'd never understood what he meant before. But now I could see that they were the ones who really acted like servants, toothless and dentured. They had no intention to rise above their Past, whether it came courtesy of a Loser family up in Campbellton or by Pudge's career mother in Montreal.

Well, they can go fuck themselves. I refuse to be as herd-like as they are. I refuse to be an Intellectual Suicide, no matter what ends up happening to me physically. I'm going to reach the Crucial, even if the only persons I can rely on any more are Dr. V and Nietzsche.

Also Matthew Cavanaugh. I think I saw Matthew Cavanaugh this morning, talking to a Homeless Person outside the big church. The one on the main shopping street? I ran across traffic, dodging cars, but when I got there, he was gone. The Homeless guy told me that he'd never met the Dude, who was inquiring about panhandling territories. That could have been Matthew, who'd panhandled when he'd run away to Toronto before. It's true that I only saw Dude's back, and I don't have a good record lately in identifying backs, but I'm pretty sure it was Matthew Cavanaugh. As Nietzsche says, trust your eyes.

Actually, the way Nietzsche puts it is pretty interesting, given the time frame in which he lived:

There are many kinds of eyes. Even the sphinx has eyes— and consequently there are many kinds of "truths," and consequently there is no truth.

The Internet, right? It's a Web of observation(s), both true and untrue. So Nietzsche predicted the Internet, too. It makes you think.

I already know I'm good at thinking, however. What comes next is acting, but I have a feeling we'll see about that before too long.

NINETEEN

Dear Jessy,

I wish to apologize for what I said the previous summer even if it was true. It was not my place to come out with it Jessy. I should learn to keep my big mouth shut. That is a fact and I know it Jessy. The fact that other people should also keep their own mouths shut is none of my business. Gramps says I owe you an apology for what I come out with last summer and since you wont give me the time of day in person this summer Jessy I write it here so you can tell Gramps I did and theres an end to it.

I also wish to say Jessy that you might be alot more happy if you stopped to smell the roses sometimes. What I notice about summer people up from the city and that includes you is how they cant keep their butt in a chair for two fucken seconds. Excuse my vocabulery as Auntie Gail says but facts are harsh in this fucken world and their harsh enough without making them worse by brooding on them Jessy instead of making the best of a bad lot.

You might not be the only person in the world without a father Jessy and you might pause to consider that being without a father sooner rather than later is not the worse fate in the world OK? So your father was a bad seed but I don't know what thats got to do with you when Gramps had to do him in before you ~~was~~ were born. It wasnt like he set a bad example for instance beating on your Ma or giving you the back of his hand which it turns out is child abuse. So I dont know what you got to complain about in terms of Aunt Michelle and now Uncle Murray who looks worth the wait no matter what Gram says and so what if he turns out to be a rich Jewish person so long as he is rich ha ha.

So this is my advice to you Jessy to stop and smell the roses and stop feeling so fucken sorry for yourself because what good does it do anyway.

Yours sincerely,

(Your cousin) Jan

TWENTY

This being the week to register for school, I set out yesterday for the local Collegiate. Education is an ally, and you have to seek the best. Also the framework least tied to the Past. I had expected some resistance when I stated my refusal to attend a Catholic school, which would represent not only a Retreat, but also be hypocritical based on my growing atheism. Atheism or pantheism, I haven't decided which.

No objections were raised. This must be Pudge's influence. Either that or they just don't care.

The Drudge: "I'm glad you've given so much thought to the matter. You're old enough now to choose your own school. You know where you'll be most happy."

Translation: I can't be bothered looking into it myself.

I decided to leave my bike in the garage and walk. The bicycle is a mode of transportation, while walking is a means of *seeing clearly,* maybe even seeing Matthew Cavanaugh en route. Given the opportunity, I thought I should try one final time to truly understand the neighbourhood, attempting to grasp its almost mythic Loneliness, all these people from all over (Iraq, the Netherlands, Kingston) living together in a peculiar corner of the Amoeba where no one truly Belongs. I say "one final time" since it had occurred to me that once I entered the Collegiate, I would also enter a community, and risk losing my summer's clarity of vision in a sudden influx of relief.

I left through the front door of the house, not wanting to start such a potentially Crucial errand via the scruffy laneway. It was a very hot day, but maple trees arched over the street out front, making a cool green tunnel. Sawflies called from the wires, if that's where they live. They sound like wires, anyway. Buzzing wires getting ready to explode, then slowly fading away.

A few steps into my journey, I was struck by the appearance of Dr. V's front garden. It looked calm under the maples. The lawn was a calm green mountain lake, the Rose of Sharon trees spaced around it like islands, pink and white islands surrounded by mounds of scented lavender blooming for the second time this year. The border gardens grew dahlias and daisies that were pink and white and lavender, too. You had to pause at Dr. V's garden. What it said was Peace.

Then off down the street, where no one else bothered with a garden, just tired August grass. Turn left onto the shopping street, where more people brushed against you on the sidewalk. There was no sign of Matthew Cavanaugh, but an old Chinese lady jostled by, holding her umbrella up against the glaring sun. Two other ladies in floor-length Muslim robes swept past. They had hoods on their heads with little grilles in front of their faces like portable confessionals. Did that mean the ladies always had to tell the truth? Being an atheist is probably easier, when you think about it.

People wore normal clothes as well, Western clothes, advertised clothes, I guess. Turn downhill at the traffic lights and a red-headed woman puffed up, her shorts cutting into her fat freckled thighs. Three Multi skaters whizzed past. I wondered if they knew Matthew Cavanaugh but decided to let it go. A few cars turned left in front of me, and a beaten pickup truck. A very black man came out of the Laundromat carrying a wicker basket of very white shirts.

On the way downhill, the few stores changed to houses with gardens no more than a metre deep. Some were spicy from annuals, some junked with bricks and stinkweed, some poured with cement. They all looked a little sad, frankly. Across the road it was even sadder, a high white plaster wall that Pudge said hid the old Jewish cemetery. The door and trim were painted black and a sign said where you found the key, but I decided: You're not going to get me yet.

An ambulance whizzed past, its siren shrieking. To my left, a Greek lady sat sewing in a glassed-in porch in front of a tiny garden that she couldn't see.

Schools now, a Catholic and a Public Elementary glaring at each other across the road. Train tracks ran on the lower side, crossing the road on an overpass that was painted with lousy murals underneath. One mural said "racism sucks" in letters you couldn't read up close. Then, after the underpass, the road turned up and down again, passing a bright blue house with a huge plant in a half-barrel outside, an itchy-looking specimen with big dark leaves like fingers spread out wide that grew these spiky reddish lychee nuts just like in the grocery store.

Funny when you bent down to smell them. All you got was baking bread: the bakery wasn't far away. Standing up, you saw a smokestack rising into the smoggy sky.

Finally the Collegiate. I'd picked it off the Net as the closest one with an Academic reputation. It also had a new building, even with a swimming pool, which showed they somewhat cared. Now I saw its long wall of windows and four caretakers sitting in the loading bay, perching on the back two legs of their chairs and enjoying a smoke. Four caretakers! When all we'd had at Sacred Nostril was Mumbling Montague, a Disability promoted to janitor in the Devonian Era. That's what people said, anyway. Maybe he'd been normal at first and just given up. You could see people do that, more than just the Pudge's wife: how they tried at first and then gave up.

It was true the narrow school garden looked weedy and the steps were strewn with paper garbage. Inside the glass door you found the usual high walls and the familiar school Smell: chalk, squashed sandwiches and nerd farts. But past The Office I could see an Atrium of three-storey glass, and when I walked in there, I went all hopeful again. You could imagine the Greeks disclaiming there, Aristotle in his tunic teaching Ancient Civ., Plato on the Modern side with his knowledge of Republicans.

That was a joke you could imagine people here might get, even though it was lame. *Because* it was lame. This was an Academic enclave, right? I could almost imagine finding Friends here. Finding a community here. Imagine for one brief shining instant how you might finally Belong.

They didn't want me. When I went into The Office, the lone unbusy secretary told me that this was a Closed School. You could only go here if you started in Grade 9, and only if you'd lived in the neighbourhood for untold months before that. If you moved in later, you had to go to another Collegiate, the one I'd rejected when I'd seen it on the Net. It looked like Sacred Nostril, impediments and all.

"I'm sorry, dear," the secretary said. "But so many people want to come here, the Board had to make a policy. It's nothing personal."

"But policies affect individuals," I said. "And what affects individuals is by definition personal."

"It's too bad," a man said behind me. "I'm sure you'd be an asset. But policy is policy."

You can tell a vice principal through the back of your neck. I hardly bothered to turn around before returning my transcripts to my backpack. "Yes, sir," I said.

He told me that Second Best Collegiate was quote, a fine school. "Why don't you buzz on up there right now? I'm sure they'd be happy to have you."

"Yes, sir," I answered, slinging on my backpack and retreating down the whole sorry route, slinking through the high bland halls, down paper-strewn steps, past windows and caretakers still on their break, past the lychee nut house and the lousy mural now reading "sucks racism," the tempting cemetery and the lady still sewing at her window. Then I turned right at the lights, drifting past the uncaring storefronts of fake English pubs and Arabic bakeries and dejected old Dollar Stores, finally depositing myself at the big brick entrance of the so-called Collegiate, formerly Tech.

The Office was about ten times the size of the one at the real Collegiate, which told you how many Disciplines they had to send down there every day. It was also busy and bustling. You had to line up forever, waiting behind people who would obviously have preferred to be elsewhere. But when you finally made the front of the line, all the secretary wanted to do was make an appointment with the vice principal for later in the week. "He'll take care of the registration," she said.

What was it with the schools in this City that they did nothing but throw roadblocks in the face of your desire for an education?

"When can your parents come in for an appointment, dear?"

And what was all this "dear" talk, anyway? They wanted you to be a dear and not cause them any problems? You were about as Powerful as a deer caught in the headlights? I decided that I'd had more than enough of that, more than enough of everything, in fact, and started smiling at the secretary like a happy Down's.

"Actually, it's just me and my Mom," I said. "She's really busy right now. We've just moved down here from Kingston. So she can do her Ph.D.? We only got our own place on the 15th of the month, and she's got total mountains to do. I mean, to settle in at the University. We're into the apartment already. So I said I'd do the registration myself, which would save her the trouble. If it's all right with you."

"We still need your mother, dear. Unless you're over eighteen."

She already knew the answer to that, so why did she ask? Not that she did me the courtesy of asking. I totally hated this degrading charade. I hated my babyfat face. Why had Janelle Piglet quote, matured and not me, who needed it far more? Standing there, I was deeply struck by the unfairness of life, although it was true that producing adult ID would have been a problem.

"She said she was going to try to wrap up early on Friday. So maybe later Friday afternoon?"

"Her name then, dear?"

"My name is Greta von Bundt." It wasn't enough. Nothing I did was ever enough. "Hers is Ilsa." The She-Wolf of the ss? It's a porno, I believe. It was also the only German name I could think of on such short notice, being a hemorrhoid and having temporarily forgotten the name of Young Werther's sweetheart, the one who married the wrong man.

"We're very proud of our Germanic heritage," I said. "If there's a space for ethnic on your form."

"Address and phone will do nicely," she said, so I doubled the number of the address and gave her the street name one road over in case she asked me to repeat. For the phone, I did the first three digits of the Toronto number and the last four from Kingston, which gave you a 666 in the middle. Warning, warning.

"Your appointment is at 3 p.m. Friday, dear. Your mother can call the school if she needs to reschedule."

"One thing," I said, before she turned. "If you could give me a package like that lady has? That way, I can look at the courses you offer. And my Mom can fill out the registration forms beforehand to save the vice principal some time."

She wasn't going to give it to me. She didn't like me. They didn't even want me at Loser High. The secretary probably suffered from anti-Germanic prejudice, thinking Hitler and not Goethe, even though Dr. V said the vast majority of Teutonic citizens embraced Hitler for normal patriotic reasons and not for any superstitious rejection of the Jewish race.

"For instance, what languages do you offer?" I asked. "At my old school, they only offered French. But in the postmodern world, I think it's to your advantage to speak as many languages as possible. Spanish is the fourth most spoken language in the world. And there was a bad decision taken some years ago to downgrade Latin in the public schools. At least, that's what my mother says."

The secretary gave me the package. As it turned out, they didn't offer Latin, but you could take German, Spanish or French. I mean, if you intended to play along.

That night, last night, I gave the forms to Pudge's wife after dinner, saying that if she filled them out, I could give them to the vice principal during my appointment at 10 a.m. the next morning. She filled them out at the kitchen table with her usual neat printing and meticulous manner, her husband leaning over her shoulder to look. Both were impressed by the size of the registration package and the multiplicity of information it purported to contain. Also by the way I said to put Pudge down on the masculine side of the form. It had a series of designations there for father, guardian etc. which the wife's pen hovered over until I suggested she check the box called "other," then leave the line blank beside it.

"You're just so outside the box, Pudge," I said, and he chuckled, rocking back on his heels. Naturally, his wife didn't get it.

"Maybe the vice principal can fill it in," she said. "He'll probably ask you why it's blank, and I want you to give him a straight answer. Then he can put in whatever he wants. Stepfather, guardian. It's only a form."

"I think you can trust me to handle this," I told her. "Or did you think I'm doing a bad job so far?"

"Not at all, baby. It's just . . . the vice principal. They're always scary. I'll go along to the appointment if you need support. Murray can probably do without me at that meeting."

"So you don't trust me," I said.

"Baby, you're doing a great job. It's just too bad about the other Collegiate."

"But it wasn't strong on languages. This one has languages. Who cares about a stupid swimming pool, anyway? They can keep their snobby swimming pool. What if I took Spanish on top of French?"

It was a thick course book, I'll give them that. Pre-engineering, a gifted program. Not that they'd probably let you take anything worthwhile unless you'd lived in the neighbourhood since you were a zygote.

Who cares? No one cared, and Pudge's happy little Family played poker half the night, spreading chips and cards across the kitchen table, the wife losing helplessly and cashing in early, but me having some luck for once and giving Pudge a run for his money, i.e. pennies, until my pile rivalled his.

"Look at the time," his wife finally shrieked. "When you've got to get up for your appointment."

For the record, my luck held this morning. They had to leave early for their precious work, so I had plenty of time to *a)* practise and *b)* fake an unreadable vice-principalian signature on the parents' copy of the registration form, afterward reducing the other copies to near-confetti which I placed in my backpack. I even had time to make out a plausible timetable according to the course guide, and when I left for the laneway promptly at 9:40 a.m., who should be out in her backyard but Francie, the wife's new Bosom Buddy next door. She was braving the rain to take out her morning compost.

"Off to see the vice principal, I hear," Francie called. "I'll tell you a secret. They're human. My Mom's a VP."

It figured. What else would a vice principal spawn but a Home Birther like Francie? She made me anxious, and it wasn't just that blinkless stare. She and the wife were becoming so close, you could picture how Francie might even trigger a Home Birth over here. They'd probably try to make me watch, and eat the placenta afterward. Francie struck me as a placenta-eater. That would explain her eyes.

"I hope my one glimpse of a vice principal this week is the last I'll ever have," I replied cheerfully.

My answer didn't satisfy Francie, but I doubt that anything ever does. Waving happily, I let myself into the laneway, striding off in the direction of the so-called Collegiate as Francie composted in the rain.

Yet before going far, I detoured south, making for the Dumpster behind the Italian Supermarket a couple of main intersections away. The Dumpster was in another laneway, normally deserted of prying eyes, although I had to pass by a couple of times before a scrounging Homeless Person had finished his business. Yet finally, without anybody seeing, I was able to download the near-confetti into the Dumpster and head off on my merry way. Free of all Collegiates, so-called and otherwise! Now I can self-educate, just like Dr. V did during the War.

There was one peculiar thing, however. I never did see Matthew Cavanaugh, but I think I saw Paws in the window of a house near the Dumpster. At least, it was a black-and-white cat with familiar markings, although I didn't get a very close look. Before I made it to the front window, the cat jumped down, and I couldn't see him anywhere inside. If it was really Paws, I thought he might have gone to the door, waiting for me to let him out. But when I knocked and rattled, both front and back doors proved firmly locked, and no Paws-like mew answered my calls.

It probably wasn't Paws. He never came back to the window, even though I waited for more than an hour. Paws would have been smart enough to come back where I could see him, while a non-Paws might have been scared and fled upstairs. I'm sure non-Paws would have been scared, seeing this unfamiliar hemorrhoid looming up at him from all reachable windows.

But that just makes it more Uncanny. Within three weeks, I've seen non-Cooper, non-Matthew Cavanaugh and now non-Paws (although I think it was really Matthew Cavanaugh). It's hard to believe that all these sightings have been mere coincidence. Coincidence doesn't happen that often in normal life.

They're Portents, that's what I think. Portents that the Crucial is almost here.

Let us throw confetti into the air to celebrate the Crucial!

Except that I mixed the confetti with mouldy eggplant in the Dumpster to make sure that it never got found.

Still, if it *was* Paws, I can understand why he's there. In his explorations, he must have made it across a couple of main, traffic-laden streets, then got too scared to cross back. It's also nice to know that he's found a good Home. It was a Tasteful place, with solid furniture and patterned rugs and what looked like real artwork on the walls. There was even a piano against one wall with Family photographs on top.

I think they were Family photographs. They usually put Family photographs on top of pianos, at least in magazines. Maybe I'll find out if they're Family photographs some other time. I should probably keep an eye on that place in case it really is Paws.

If it is, I'm not sure yet whether I'll steal him back. He might not want to come with me. Who would, if they'd found a Home at last?

SEPTEMBER

TWENTY-ONE

Friday, September 1

It turned hot this week, summer deciding to punish us all at once. This makes the days feel long and suspended, as if you were waiting. Of course I'm waiting. I've been waiting for school not to start, not for me. It feels jittery to set out on a real Plan, one that makes a difference. Everything up to now has been mere practice, a case of getting in shape. In my mental rear-view mirror, I can see how I knew that I could do whatever I tried. Cleaning, painting, reading, cycling: You can manage that. But not going to school? I'd never done that, not since before daycare, back in the Bronze Age.[1]

Skipping classes doesn't count. Skipping you do against school, which assumes that school is there in the first place. But school isn't there for me any more. It abandoned me. It didn't want me. I'm utterly on my own. At least, I will be next week. And waiting for that feels like someone has taken a giant Global breath and drawn all the air out of the atmosphere.

Global Warming. It's so hot, I'm stifled. The City traps you like the overheated hallways of an old folks' home, the Campbellton County Home where you had to visit discarded great-aunts. You can't flee any more than they could. You're trapped inside both this huge Amoeba and this small square of backyard, everything reeking of mouldy air-conditioning units

---

1. Bronzed Baby Shoes. Sorry.

and rotten breath and roiling sewers and boiling steam and greasy fast-food pollution. The sky looks like blinded eyes, the blue filming over.

Who knew Global Warming would come home like this, turning into the only Home you knew? With the Tropics moving north, I've ended up living in a defeated square of some swarming megalopolis like a Third World peon, drained by overwork. All week long, I've overworked to fend off the yawn of waiting. In a final quote, before-school push, I finished cleaning out the garage and basement, then scraped and painted the whole garage through the next heated days so Dr. V wouldn't have to live next door to a slum, which she couldn't see through the height of the fence but knew was there, anyway.

When I was finished painting yesterday, I had nothing left to do. Totally *nada*. Dr. V told me not to dig out a garden until the heat went away. I would dry out the soil and kill necessary Organisms. All I could do this morning after my run was put the sprinkler on in front, wandering inside in a bored fashion. They'd put up new Blinds in the living room, and with all that shadowed white, it looked as milky and blind as the cataract sky.

Blind, blind, blind. Pudge and the Drudge embarrassed me deeply, they were so eyeless. Hopeful yet eyeless. They'd got their new cinnamon-coloured Divan, and a pregnancy book with fetid illustrations lay open on the footstool. They'd also framed my school picture from last year and put it on the mantle. They had no idea what was going on. How could they be that ignorant? I grew so embarrassed that I had to leave the room.

My tent looked almost as mundane. I felt bored of everything, the same old Collectibles, the emptied-out picture frames, the crumbling old mouse skull and a Blue Jay's feather with an edge that no longer looked quote, blue as the evening

sky.[2] The picture of Paws propped up on the butter box was out
of focus, and the box itself held the same crippled collection of
CDs that I'd listened to incessantly, the writings and rewritings
of my so-called fairy tales and this endless maw of notebook. I
even disliked the Aphorisms on Post-it notes stuck up around
my tent.

> . . . like Goethe, one clings with ever-greater pleasure and
> warmth to the "things of this world":—for in this way he
> holds firmly to the great conception of man, that man
> becomes the transfigurer of existence when he learns to
> transfigure himself.
>
> F.N.

What did that mean? It sounded right, so I'd put it up, but
what did it mean? I tried to figure it out, but it grew so
phenomenally heated in the tent that I had to move outside,
searching for a frail patch of shade under the lilac tree. Even
there, I sweated so hard my shaving nicks began to sting.
Looking them over, I found that some were growing red and
blistered. I was Infecting, but here's the joke. Assuming Dr. V to
be a master of herbal lore, I went over to ask for a cure, and she
sent me to the drugstore for a tube of antibiotic cream.

Not that I bothered. It's too hot to bother with anything,
and Dr. V sympathized with my boredom, at least.

I think she sympathized. She also looked amused in a superior fashion, maybe because she thought I was whining, which
I probably was.

"Having work is better," she agreed, then laughed as she
taught me an old German saying, *Arbeit Macht Frei*. Work will

---

2. Diary entry, July 21. Puke.

set you free. "Certainly it is freer than what will happen if you don't work."

Afterward, she got more serious. "You must not tell your German teacher what I say," she instructed. "It is our secret that I will help with your homework. You don't wish to have it known that you have help when starting a new school. It will stand you apart from the other students, which you don't wish to happen. At first you must be quiet as a mouse. Slowly they will notice and accept you."

I feel bad pretending to Dr. V that I'm going to school. But she approves of schools, which is natural in a retired professor. One can make use of them, learning from even old and stuffy teachers. So I have to pretend, there's no way out. Plus she can really help me learn German. I've already looked at my quote, textbook. There's no way I could learn it on my own.

This is the Plan: to study my Subjects at the Library during the day using the quote, textbooks I found in the Second-hand Bookstore. I wasn't originally planning to study German. But last week, while making up my quote, timetable, I realized that I was a hemorrhoid.[3] For some unknown reason, I'd been talking about studying Spanish. Why not German? Especially when I'd had a Sign. Looking through the Bookstore, I'd already noticed a How-To *Sprechen* German book on one of the dusty chalk-full shelves. So I erased Spanish from my quote, timetable and wrote in German instead.

Core subjects: English, Math, Physics and Geography, plus Electives in German, Philosophy and French, along with a Spare. The Bookstore Guy has already put aside my quote, textbooks so I can pick them up after school starts. Some are even real textbooks, cast off when they changed the Curriculum. But

---

3. Not for the first time.

if other generations survived the Old Math, why can't I? It doesn't seem to have hampered, for instance, Bill Gates. And if it did to some degree, it's probably just as well.

The remaining texts are merely Volumes that would fool at a glance. I don't think Bookstore Guy is fooled, but I'm betting that he can't be bothered interfering. He acts amused by my Plan, or at least by me, which would be demeaning if he didn't also seem underhandedly Supportive. In my experience, that's what Bookstore Guys are like.

"So we're going to study German, too," Guy said the other day, his ironic eyes hidden in his cheeks and scraggly beard, a ho-ho belly carried out front. "*Mein Führer,*" he cried. "I can walk!"

That was from Dr. Strangelove. I rented the video with Cooper in Kingston. "My mother's new husband has cut off Cable and the vcr," I replied. "When you think of it, he's depriving us of filmic history."

"You could always take an afternoon course," Guy said. "The Revue matinee?"

Bookstore Guys are unsuccessful Pudges, when you think of it. You can see how close the unwed Pudge probably skated to working in a Book or possibly Video store, living alone in that one-bedroom apartment, addicted to takeout, irony and Cable. However, there's also an essential difference. Underneath it all, Pudge Cares. He's a Softie. Bookstore Guys aren't Softies, they're just soft.

Later

I had to cook dinner, but now I'm back. I'm back and feeling Gleeful. I've finally found something that gets up Pudge's nostril. After dinner tonight, I got a Lecture on German. Pudge isn't soft on Germans, that's for sure. Now I really have to study the language, climbing further up his nose even if German proves flagrantly hard.

I'd already noticed that Pudge wasn't happy last Thursday evening following my quote, interview with the vice principal. He seemed to be studying my so-called timetable for a long time. It made me nervous, frankly. There had been nothing to stop them from phoning the Collegiate to check up on me. I would have phoned if I were them.

"I thought you were going to study Spanish," Pudge said finally.

My fear deflated, and I explained how I'd been planning to, but the entry-level Spanish class conflicted with Philosophy. I really wanted to take Philosophy, so the vice principal suggested I take German instead. "There isn't any conflict between Philosophy and German."

"Depends on which Philosophy," Pudge replied. But that was Racist and I ignored him, so the subject was dropped.

Tonight his wife got up to clear the table, which is usually a signal that you're free.[4] But this time, I was requested to sit down again by my self-proclaimed Wicked Stepfather,[5] who proceeded to detail his Family History, his beard wagging solemnly, as Dr. V would say. Apparently the Zimmermans were originally German and proud of being so: Land of Goethe, Beethoven etc. Pudge's great-grandfather even served in the German Army during World War One, where he was injured in Battle, his leg uselessly shattered.

"What became the bone of contention," Pudge said, chuck chuck chuckling. After the War, when his great-grandfather

---

4. *Frei.*
5. Diary entry, Sunday, July 2.

tried to get a Pension, he was blocked by petty Officialdom for a pyramid of untold reasons. It was Kafkaesque. It was like some Spanish book: *No One Writes to the Colonel.*

It was a Reading List, so far as I could see, not a Family History. Trapped inside the airless house, I felt chafing and impatient. The kitchen was so stifling my legs puddled sweat onto the wooden chair. I wanted to get out of there, asking myself why adults felt compelled to burden you with the story of their life. I would never do that. Explanations are useless, like those sixth toes Matthew Cavanaugh had on the edges of his feet before they cut them off. What difference did they make? You know what a person is like, they don't need to tell you. You can discover without extra assistance that life is unfair. That's one of the things I respect about Dr. V. She doesn't make a Lesson out of her life story. She doesn't subject you to her life story at all, even when you ask.

I made a mental note to investigate the Authors mentioned in case they proved acceptable, having heard of Kafka, at least. At the same time, I yawned in exacerbated fashion, hoping that Pudge would get the hint. He didn't.

"For years after the War," he went on, "my great-grandfather fought for the type of Pension that was freely granted other veterans."

It was heart-rending, Pudge said. In his dogged search for justice, the great-grandfather wrote letters and paid visits to many Officials, finally stumbling on one Official who agreed to do everything in his Power. The great-grandfather only had to hand over his documents and (they suspected) a payment, which he did. He was a trusting man, Pudge said, just an ordinary Joe, a mild and somewhat nervous fellow with a small moustache and no peculiar talents. In a disorderly post-War economy, the Pension was his great Hope to advance his wife and two little children. Without its help, he could look forward to a life spent labouring as a waiter in his father-in-law's restaurant, dragging his leg across the floor.

Then one day in the 1920s, he was walking home from work when he chanced upon an early march of Fascist brownshirts, possibly led by Hitler himself. He would always say that leading the march was an unimpressive little man he was later sure he recognized in newsreels. They blocked the great-grandfather from crossing the street, making him sweat at the sight of their aggressive discipline, head turning one way, glaring at the crowd, then snapping back. There weren't so many, he would say, but they made their presence known. And there, near the end of the march, was the petty Official who had taken all his documents. His fat neck and wide mouth puffed out of his uniform like an adder.

Watching the Official marching past, *seeing* him, I suppose, the ordinary great-grandfather had the great prescience of mind to decide to quit Germany. He would pack up his Family and take them to America. He'd never thought of America before, Pudge said, but in that moment he Knew. Dogged as he was, he finally wore down his unhappy father-in-law, who advanced him the money for the trip. America, Canada, they didn't know the difference. A boat was going to Montreal and that's where the Family landed, after which the mild great-grandfather did nothing else out of the ordinary for the rest of his life, working for a furrier, going to the synagogue and educating his eventual Family of five children, three girls and two boys.

Pudge's grandfather was the oldest son, who got his father's revenge by fighting Hitler as a soldier in the Canadian Army during World War Two. This grandfather was famous within the Family for getting married, signing up and becoming a father all in the space of 1943. After the War, he studied psychiatry. A generation later, so did Pudge's father, who was the wartime son. The joke was, both decided to become psychiatrists in order to get the treatment they deserved. The grandfather needed it because he'd fought in the War, the son because his father was a psychiatrist.

Two points stood out for me at the end of Pudge's Family History.

One, I knew Pudge, Pudge had known his great-grandfather in Montreal, his great-grandfather had seen Hitler and Hitler had met all the historic leaders of the former world. That put only three or four degrees of separation between me and all the most Powerful figures of the Twentieth Century, which made you think.

Two, that Pudge's grandfather had fought in the Canadian Army during World War Two. My grandfather had fought in the Canadian Army during World War Two. That meant Pudge and I belonged to the same generation. He was a full generation younger than his wife. Fetid.

The point Pudge wished to make struck me as more obscure. I think he was saying that German History is hard, and in studying the language, I must not forget that it is brewed with History. That's not the right word. Imbued, according to the dictionary. I think that's what Pudge meant to say, at least when he followed his Family History by reminding me of the night we had dinner with his parents in Montreal. His sister was also there, the linguist.

"Remember what she said?" Pudge didn't seem to expect me to, but I'd been struck by the way she called German a hard language, a rigid and formal language, very complicated with all those grammatical building blocks called cases. It was an inward-looking language, she said, which was another style of being sophisticated. She even called it a labyrinth.

Which is all she said, but Pudge told me how he started to think about his great-grandfather, how they excluded him, and how they excluded him through language. That's what bureaucracy is, Pudge said. What law is, too.

"It's language," he told me. "Words on paper. That's all law is, really. It's words we've decided to put on paper and more or less enforce. Sometimes more, sometimes less. They used words against my great-grandfather, this labyrinth of bureaucracy. Didn't get so far as excluding him from the land of the living. That was only everyone else in my family. But they excluded him just the same."

His point being?

"I'm not sure what my point is, Jess. But if you're gonna study German—OK, you're going to study it—I want you to remember that it's a formal, hard, exclusionary language. It's imbued with a hard, exclusionary history. You're being pretty ambitious here, Jess. Excuse my mood, but it feels better at the moment to call you Jess. It's an ambitious timetable. Physics, German, Advanced Math. You're not exactly piling on the bird courses, are you? And with German, I don't want you to feel let down or defeated if it seems very hard. It's not your fault, OK? It's not your fault if any of this turns out to be more than you can handle.

"I'm probably underestimating you wildly, but you've had to face a lot of changes lately. If you end up feeling left behind or shut out in any manner, I can fully sympathize. You can talk to me about it. Just remember that none of this is your fault, OK?"

Much later

On reflection, I think that Pudge meant more than he said. He was being Subliminal, i.e. trying to talk me out of taking

German. He doesn't think I'm up to it, which really gets up *my* nostril. I wonder who he thinks he is, trying to downgrade my schooling, not to mention my self-confidence. Especially since Matthew Cavanaugh knows far more about Military History than Pudge ever will in his dreams.

Matthew isn't a Skinhead, you can stick that up your ass, Janelle Piglet. His father is the one who supports White Supremacy, and there's no reason why Matthew Cavanaugh should buy into what his father believes. After his parents split, he hardly saw his dad at all. But given his interest in Military History, he's kept abreast of Second World War developments on the Internet, and if he therefore visits Skinhead sites, that's merely research. You can be sure that Matthew forms his own opinions independent of those advocated by rioters. His interest is more epistemological, i.e., he mainly wants to know things, just like me.

Not that Matthew feels compelled to parade his knowledge. Actually, his main point is observational. He believes there's so much racism rampant in the world that we should stop trying to live together. We should declare Multiculturalism a failure and go back to where we came from, which in North America means giving the Aboriginal people back their land. The American Amoeba should explode, Black people thrust back to Africa, Europeans back to Europe, etc. This isn't a racist theory because it's advocated by certain African American leaders, and you can't be racist if you're African American, can you?

Matthew also says that men and women should live separately to avoid inherent problems. There would be visitation, of course. Not that Matthew believes any of this will happen, or cares if it does, but having thought about the problem, he has come to this solution. Which, when you think of it, would also take care of my expansive problems with Pudge.

That really was Matthew outside the church, by the way. I've gone back every day to talk to the Homeless Person who works the shady corner under the tree, this short, sleepy, virtually hairless guy in cut-offs who has a notably big head under his baseball cap and calls himself a Street Kid even though he looks at least twenty-one.

"How's it going, man?" he asks everyone, regardless of genderation. People seem to know him, since he's worked the locality for more than two years. That's what he says, anyway. He signalled me over this morning when I was en route to buy milk, even though I was planning to talk to him on the way back.

"Dude came by," he told me. "He says if you're Jessie he'll be seeing you. If you're not you can fuck off."

"My name used to be Jessie," I said.

"Cool," the Person said. "Mine used to be Demo. I'm Wheezer now on account of my chronic chest."

I sat down beside him just as Francie passed by across the street, craning her neck.

"He knows you're living in like a tent. He got your address, which is like how he found the neighbourhood? He'll come and visit you."

"Did he say when?"

"Can't remember."

I got up. You have to watch out for Francie, who is a potential hazard to the Plan.

"Like it costs, man," the Person said. "The chronic chest? I got lots of medication. I got to eat right, man. Maintain a roof. God bless," he said, when I clattered him some change into his empty Latte cup. "Dude's an asshole, man. He's like baneful in the Biblical sense. I belong to a group like? We give voice to Street Kids who suffered abuse? We're coming from a therapeutic Christian perspective, man. Agape, hear the Word. But Dude, he's out there. He's way out there, man. I would move my address if I was you."

· I have noted his speech down precisely. How can you take seriously someone who talks like that? Even though this used to be a much more heavily Greek neighbourhood than it is now and Demo stands for Demosthenes. It's ironic, when you think of it.

It also goes to prove that language isn't a labyrinth. It's plates, like I said back in Campbellton. Words are like plates that shatter into pieces, cutting you with their ironies.

"None of this is your fault," Pudge told me.

Actually, it is. What's going to happen is my fault, no one else's. And I can hardly wait.

TWENTY-TWO

Dear Father,

After a week of unnecessary warmth, a cool wind blew through last night and brought the end of summer. It is the Labour Day holiday, so I have not laboured! Instead, I have sat in your garden and read a book. Of course the day is not cool; I should be more precise, Father. The weather is pleasant. However, the wind is somewhat brisk and the sky a deeper shade of blue that suggests the coming fall.

I did not read my book. I reflected, instead, on the changes I have seen from this garden over forty-five years. Forty-five years, Father! And fifty in this city! Trapped for two years on that farm in Niagara, how I longed for the city, but I could not help my disappointment when we arrived. Despite its ambitious train station, Toronto seemed prudent, in spirit more like Arnhem than my Amsterdam. I saw little hustle and bustle outside, no buildings chockablock, built so hard against each other they had to strive upwards. No! Walking north to the rooming house, I saw wide modern buildings on ample lots. Or dusty little stores on finger lots. Or vacant lots and sleepy weeds nodding their heads. All were jumbled together. This sleepy provincial town had a skyline like a comb with many teeth missing.

This was the New World? It seemed to have so little ambition, Father, yet to be so smug. I saw this over many months in Toronto and felt much confusion. Where were the Mounties and the Indians, the French lumberjacks come into town and rum-running gangsters and great rail barons and artists in buckskins and plucky girls like Anne of Green Gables? This was supposed to be the other side of the rainbow, a hardy place on the northern frontier where you could finally feel free. You would grow as large and as healthy as a Canadian soldier from eating chocolate bars all day. You would grow rich and drive a Chevrolet and keep a washing machine in your basement. Canada, the land of milk and honey. Mink and money! I thought that Canada would be more homey than the United States, the Netherlands to their Germany. But also far emptier. An empty slate on which to write: this is what I wish to be.

Perhaps I came one hundred years too late. Or perhaps it is merely true that life for the immigrant is always harder and more frugal than they would wish. In the 1950s, Canada was not an exciting place. Over the previous one hundred years, the prudent Canadians had pushed the frontier far back from their cities. The books and movies did not show this. They did not show that most people lived in staid provincial cities surrounded by rings first of new suburbs, then of farmland, then of tourist cottages on lakes and finally the wilderness with its small towns and resources. They did not show that the cities were proud to be uninteresting. Civic fathers of Scottish origin ensured this. The laws on selling liquor were strict and there were very few restaurants. Travelling companies of second-rate English actors sometimes presented plays.

Of course we couldn't afford liquor and restaurants and plays, but these things set a mood for the city. They said: There is no wish for public life here. They said: We aspire to a private life in our homes. That is what we think worthwhile, our homes and our privacy. We are Nietzsche's herd: *modest, industrious, benevolent and temperate.*

As my dear Nietzsche asks:

Is that how you would have man? Good men? *But to me
that seems only the ideal slave, the slave of the future.*

So it seemed to me also. Where were the city's plazas, its
version—attempt—at my beloved Leidseplein? An open place
to stroll, to meet, to rally. Here they preferred a grid of roads
filled with cars. They did not leave their cars when they went
on Sunday drives. What could give rise to culture? Or a great
leader? Canada was proud of the calibre of its civil service;
need anything more be said?

Yet you knew, Father, what I came to recognize, that this
value for privacy would serve us well. We could use it. We would
become *Onderduikers* here, diving into the small pond that was
Toronto and disappearing into plain sight. Our European
accents meant that everyone knew who we were; we were DPs.
Yet "Displaced Persons" was a misnomer, for it did not signify
persons at all, but a category. We were not persons, we were a
category of post-war immigration. Few Canadians looked
beyond that. I soon noticed how they disliked to ask questions,
given their wish to mind their own business. You were clever in
choosing our neighbourhoods, Father, first for flats and then
for this house. In none did we find any Dutch, nor they us.

I kicked against it, didn't I? I wanted to be seen, at least
peripherally. I wanted to be noticed. Stupid girl, flaunting
herself in little jobs. Bookkeeper to Select Paint and Wallpaper,
to Beneficial Life Insurance Corporation. Thinking herself a
tragic heroine straight from one of Wagner's operas. Silly,
stupid girl, risking exposure. For what?

I have lately been reading in my diary about that awful time
in 1958, seven months after I finished my work at Beneficial

Life. We were on Yonge Street, although I didn't record the reason for this; I was too upset. For suddenly there came the voice from behind you. We recognized him instantly, didn't we, Father? The man from the armed resistance.

"So, they let scum in here, van der Velde," he said.

He was a dark man with that uneven face, one eyebrow slyly higher than the other.

"So I see," you answered, looking him straight in the eye. "They let in murderers like you."

The man did not notice me, so intent was your joined stare.

"Ach, you were small potatoes," the man said finally. "You were nothing. Whore to the whores. Latrine cleaner. Bum boy. Ass licker. Go live with your guilt."

"And you with yours," you replied. "You are welcome to yours."

Sweating, wheezing, terrified, I began to value privacy then. I began to fear that it would end. They would get to know us in our neighbourhood. They would grow familiar and start to ask questions. We would make a mistake. The knock at the door . . .

I always feared that it might happen, Father. Indeed, did I not turn into a true little mouse, hiding inside your house and garden? I hid for so many, many years. Yet, after all this time, it has finally occurred to me that a knock was most unlikely, for this is a country of displacement and immigration that does not end. You are never known here. Your neighbours do not stay long enough to know you. I have lately read the local history pamphlets in the filing cabinet at the library, learning that this neighbourhood was built around the time of the First World War for the settlement of clerks and labourers from the British Isles. Some of them were growing old when we arrived here, Father. Yet their children did not care to inherit their patrimony. They did not wish to stay in their parents' houses and be known as adults by their old school friends. Instead, these grown children wished to live in big houses in the suburbs, preferring to sell the older homes and move their parents into institutions; alternatively, their basements. I merely describe, Father; I do not condone. I find it distasteful that elders are often institutionalized here, while the insane are freed and left to beg on the streets.

Yet clearly this proved fortunate for us, Father, since these houses were available and cheap. I can also see how clever you were to choose a neighbourhood filled with Greek and Italian immigrants. We could scarcely exchange a word! And by the time they had learned English, they also wanted to buy bigger houses in the suburbs. Different suburbs, one gathers. After which, their Canadian children began moving to other suburbs; moving "up," as they put it. Perhaps some of them also moved "down." In any case, they refused to stay put. As meanwhile new immigrants moved in near us, their languages increasingly impenetrable. I learned some Greek in the stores. *Ne!* means yes. *Efharisto:* thank you. But now I see veiled women on the street, their language the sound of wind blowing across a desert. I won't learn it. I am too old.

At the same time, I am old enough to stand back and see what life is truly like here. I have finally come to understand that everyone in this country is a DP, even when they are born in Canada. They wander from house to house, city to city, as if they were not permitted to stay. Each is not a person but a category, although this is by preference now. They are a Greek who lives on the Danforth Avenue or a Greek Canadian in the suburb of Scarborough. They are the wandering Jew who hopes to move from Bathurst Street to the city of North York to the enclave of Forest Hill Village. They are a Ukrainian from Roncesvalles, a little lapsed

Catholic from Kingston. In a multicultural society, each speaks of his category before himself.

Yet it remains true that by hiding within their category, individuals may protect their privacy. Now that you know I am Dutch Canadian, what more need you ask? Privacy remains much valued here. In fact, it has probably become inescapable, so greatly has the city grown. How can one make one's mark on such a teeming place? My little friend Greta calls it Amoeba City. She made a joke, so I told her another. Despite all its growth, the city has still not developed a public space. It is a bad joke, Father. A city of this size with no centre. It has cultivated no style of architecture. It has produced no great sculptors, no grand composers, no enduring school of visual artists. Nor has it grown a single leader worthy of the name. It is a city, a province, a country led by small-town burghers and salesmen who are soon forgotten, leaving no monuments behind.

It is true that this country has recently become known for its writing. There are now famous authors walking these streets. I have seen one or two myself, wearing their scruffy black clothes. Yet what is writing but the most private of arts? This is a private country. A private city. What else could flourish here but writing? I rest my case.

You see that I have been reflecting, Father. I have been reflecting on all the changes I have seen. In the end, they amount to nothing. The city has grown bigger but it has not grown up. However, in the modern world, adolescence is valued. People are admired for not growing up. So Toronto is the city of the moment, hailed by the United Nations as the world's most multicultural city, among the best cities in which to live. Others must wish to be like it! Indeed, many cities have grown like it, with their populations of modern DPs. Many cities have grown physically, yet have not matured. My little Greta makes me dwell on this, Father. She has the adolescent wish to discover who she is, just as a city like Toronto does. Greta searches for her identity. Yet how can she find an identity when she has nothing with which she may identify?

This adolescent society has let down its children. It does not protect them. The city has no centre because its people are self-centred, and leave their children too often alone. We know what my little Greta needs, dear. She needs a Father, just as this city and country require a true leader. Enough of the dull burghers! Before I die, I would like to see a great man step forward, a man of vision and discipline ready to impose coherence on this watery stew. This Amoeba! Challenge its flabby mediocrity with soaring public works! Give it a centre that will hold! No more mealy-mouthed temporizing that all is equal, all is good. No! Nietzsche knows about this vaunted equality:

The terrible consequence of "equality"—finally, everyone believes he has a right to every problem.

That is modern sickness in a nutshell.

Yet my Nietzsche's great man is surely our cure:

"He is colder, harder, less hesitating and without fear of 'opinion;' he lacks the virtues that accompany respect and 'respectability'," "he may snarl at some things he meets on his way," "he wants no 'sympathetic' heart, but servants, tools; in his intercourse with men, he is always intent on making something out of them . . . he finds it tasteless to be familiar. . . . When not speaking to himself, he wears a mask. . . ."

I have had such a Father, but the city has had none. Poor Greta has had none. I feel sorry for the child. Her life has been lacking. Sometimes I rebelled against you, Father, but I always came back. I rebel even these days, but I still come back. I have you, Father, yet the poor girl has nowhere. She lacks a centre to her life, and cannot therefore revolve home. What will become of her, Father?

I don't know. I know nothing. I am nothing; none of us is. That is the answer to the riddle of modern identity. We cannot find it because nothing is there. First task, to understand this. Second task, to feel relief.

I am relieved you are not here, Father.

I am, nevertheless,

Your loving daughter

TWENTY–THREE

Friday, September 8

I'm not sure I can do this. It's much harder than you'd think to pretend. Now I know why actors earn all that money. Successful ones, I mean.

Tuesday wasn't bad for the first day of non-school. I took off on my bike toward Reject Collegiate, then just kept riding East. I don't know why people turn up their noses at whatever lies to the East, but it's probably to my benefit, i.e. Francie ignores the cheaper stores nearby and walks West every morning with her baby and twig basket to shop at the Ecological boutiques of Carrot Common, the name of which I'm not making up.

Anyway, I felt safe cruising this unfashionably Eastern neighbourhood of bungalows, little cookie-cutter Homes in red brick with hexagonal windows beside the front door and very green lawns with *Warning: Pesticide!* signs and periodic gnomes and plantations of Busy Lizzy. Impatiens, as Dr. V would say. But the morning was so sunny that I hadn't worn a jacket, and it turned out to be chilly. I had to keep pedalling to stay warm, which got exhaustive after a while. First day is always a shortened day at school, but I still had to spend a couple of frigid hours cruising before I could drop by the Bookstore, pick up some of my quote, textbooks and finally bike back.

Francie pounced on me when I'd barely unlatched the gate. "So how was it?"

"It was refreshing," I replied. "I prefer to be optimistic. It was refreshing to go somewhere new."

The thing is, you don't want to turn into a liar just because you're doing something fictitious. My Grade 10 English Teacher, Mr. Bowker, taught us the secret of novels, saying that they had to adhere to some Greater Truth even though they were totally made up. I had therefore set this as a goal, to explore Truth through autodidacticism, i.e. self-learning. This would have the beneficent side effect of enlarging my vocabulary even further, enabling me to use such big words that no one would know what the fuck I was talking about.

Francie's going to be a problem, though. She's always out in her back garden being Healthful with the baby. It never bothered me before, at least not much, but now you can see how she's going to spy on my schedule with those bugged-out placenta eyes. I won't be able to sneak back and hide in the tent. Once I leave in the mornings, I'll have to stay out all day, not even coming back for lunch in case she raises a worry that I'm not making any Friends. Pudge's wife used to worry about Friends back in Kingston, and sometimes even embarrass me by making appointments with the School Counsellor, which you clearly wish to avoid.

"I'm sure you're going to have a blast there," Francie said. "Like Michelle says, it's a New Start, and that's always exciting."

"I've heard her say that," I replied. "Now, if you'll excuse me, I'm starving for lunch. They're sort of hunger-inducing in my experience. New Starts."

The next day was worse. I wore heavier clothes because it looked like another sunny, chilly day. When it warmed up, I nearly evaporated. Plus I decided to spend the second half-day in the little red-brick Library branch to the East of here, plotting out how fast to cover the Units in the quote, textbooks while drawing up some additional reading lists along with probable Homework assignments.

But I'm not a Teacher. Teachers go to University, where they presumptuously learn how to create Homework on top of how to stifle students, which are not always the same thing. I had no idea how fast you were supposed to cover a Unit in a textbook. On the one hand, you'd think you should cover it as fast as you could. But Teachers were so hyped about Review, there was obviously some concern about how hard you had to pound Knowledge into the brain before it lodged there sufficiently not to pop back out. I had the impression that when I read in a concentrated fashion, Knowledge got thoroughly lodged. But how did I know that *I hadn't forgotten that I'd forgotten something?* Maybe the point of being as annoying as Teachers like Weepy Willow was that students grew subliminally determined to retain Knowledge from your class so they could use it to harass you.

I also began to notice that one of the Librarians was watching me. I was being harmless, but I could feel her eyes on the back of my head. She might pretend to reshelf books, but she was clearly wondering if I was Truant and whether she should call the School Board. If she'd asked, I could have told her that I was sixteen and being home-schooled. Librarians don't have the right to demand your ID except when you check out a book. At least, I don't think they do. I think Citizen's Arrest is fictitious. But she made me so anxious that I had to force myself not to leave abruptly, which would have looked even more suspicious. Instead, I waited until the dot of Lunch, allowing her to conclude that an adult had exiled me there for the full morning, not a moment less.

But if you couldn't go to the Library, where could you go? Yesterday morning, I tried the local Mall, built beside the railroad tracks and so far downscale that if anyone Pudge knew saw me there, they'd never be able to admit it. But I liked it, especially when I noticed that many of the patrons seated in the Food Court were elderly people of Chinese heritage who were apparently unable to speak much English, or at least preferred to play checkers. Mothers shopping with small children were so busy talking to their friends while wiping chins they clearly had no time to think about me. But the janitor who was swabbing down tables with his bucket and this folded grey cloth said something accusing to me in Chinese, picking up my books in one hand and scrubbing the table furiously with the other. I could tell he saw through me, and I had to slink out. Afterward, when I tried studying at McDonald's, this jolly manager-type person felt restrained to point out the *No Loitering* sign.

"If you stay much longer, we're going to have to ask you to buy something more. Either that or give you a job."

He didn't have to make threats. I'd already been traumatized by two beefy Policemen strolling in wearing bulletproof vests. Why bulletproof vests? It wasn't like I was going to give them any trouble. Of course, if Dr. V was right, they were only thinking about themselves. Maybe they were just protecting their beefy selves in case one of the McSlaves behind the counter tried to grill and bag them. But wasn't it a Policeman's job to keep you in order? They had to know I wasn't supposed to be there. At least, they would have known if they paid attention to anything besides consuming their coffee and salads. (Salads?) I was actually glad that the manager turfed me out before they noticed anything amiss. Miss Amiss, that's me. Not that I had anywhere left to go, except this deserted little Works Yard I found built against the railway embankment, with a *No Trespassing* sign at the entrance and trains whizzing above.

Forgive us those who Trespass against us. I didn't notice anyone forgiving me. On the other hand, nobody saw me, either. It was a warm enough day, so I sat in a scrubby growth of trees and started to read some English curriculum, i.e. *Great Expectations,* before assigning myself some Homework.

That turned out to be the worst so far. *How I Spent My Summer Vacation.* I'm not sure anyone really assigns that, but when I sat down at the computer last night after dinner, I totally got into it, writing things like:

This summer, I took a vacation from vacationing and went to work.

I spent myself this summer vacation.

Instead of vacationing this summer, I spent my time creating a Home. It wasn't any Home I was planning to inhabit. Instead, it was a Project I undertook on behalf of other persons. It was as if I was paid to create a full-sized Doll's House they could play in, i.e. a Playhouse, which is a word with many meanings, including Theatric. In fact, you could say that I built a Theatric Set this summer for a story that was being played out within it. I designed the setting for a Work of fiction, working up my fictitious role as Dutiful Daughter moving into a New Home.

Actually, that's better than what I wrote last night. I should write another version this evening. But the problem is, last night I wrote so many versions that my eyes grew cloudy and I had to lie down on the bed for a while to rest from the computer.

Pudge and his wife woke me up there this morning. A knock on the door, two faces peering in. They were already getting to resemble each other, like owners and their dogs. I bleakly noted two round moon faces, one of them furred with beard. Two allied faces, delighted to find me asleep in the room they insisted on referring to as quote, mine.

They won't win. I refuse. They're not going to make me move into that crippled house and send me off to Sacred Sequel. Can't they imagine how embarrassing it would be to show up for school a week late? Everybody looking at you and asking, What's her problem? You'd be branded as a Problem from Day One. No one would have anything to do with you, brushing past you in the hallways as if you didn't exist. Either that or pointing out how you're eating alone in the cafeteria again, "but Jessie prefers superior company, which leaves her nothing but herself," so you're picking at your squashed muffin and totally knowing that you've done *nothing* to justify them saying that but still dying inside. They exchange glances when you know the answer to questions and cast their eyes upward when you pretend not to and snigger when you don't, conspiring with unpopular Teachers to like you and the popular ones to call your name when you've given up paying attention, making you hold your head up so high that your neck falls into spasms and your stomach hurts from clenching and moons of sweat stain the underarms of every T-shirt you own.

No! I won't go back. I'd rather die. I've got to come up with Plan C, figure out a way to play out the non-school thing so they'll *leave me alone.* I'm back at the deserted Works Yard this morning, putting my brain to work. I'll come up with something, I have to, especially since the good weather can't last forever. However, it's promising here when you think of it, so many trains passing by on the way to somewhere else. It's Hopeful. Except that you'd also think they'd do a better job of blocking access to the tracks in case somebody accidentally Suicided themselves by climbing up to take a curious look down the tracks at totally the Wrong Moment and

Saturday morning

I broke off writing when Matthew Cavanaugh appeared. I heard a rustle in the bushes and looked up to see a Male figure, but there wasn't enough time to get scared before I recognized Matthew. He's taller than most people and lanky, skinny, with that long skinny face, and he still had his hair dyed black even though it's black already. His clothes had become more normal and less Military though, just jeans and a T-shirt.

"Where did you come from?" I asked.

"Been following you," he said. "You're a naughty girl."

It would have creeped me out if anyone else had said that, but Matthew doesn't mean any harm. He isn't a judgmental person, he's just curious. You can accept people who take an interest in what you're doing without holding you up to any standards. Matthew doesn't hold to any of the standards yet devised, which he says have let too many people down already.

"I don't know how you got my address," I said.

"Cooper left this piece of paper on his counter."

"Cooper?"

"My old buddy Cooper. He's sure pissed at how your Mom said he couldn't see you."

"She did?"

"No phone calls, no visitation."

It had never occurred to me that he'd want to. "You're saying Cooper wants me to call him?"

"I guess that would depend on what you told him."

It was true that Cooper approved of schooling, like Dr. V. Maybe not the same degree of schooling, but Cooper approved of you not ending up a Loser like him.

He didn't think he was a Loser. He lived the way he wanted. But he was aware that other persons believed him to be a Loser. His ex-girlfriend, for instance.

"Who does she think she is, telling me I can't call him?"

"He says he agrees. A clean break is better. What's done is done. But he's sure pissed that she chose to come out and say it. Taking him for a doofus, that he couldn't figure it out for himself."

The Lord giveth and the Lord taketh away. "You phrase things so weirdly, Matthew. I don't know why you put things in such a misleading manner."

"I'm just telling you what he said. He misses the little chick. You never knew what she was going to come out with."

"How's he doing, anyway?"

Matthew had stretched out on the ground, propping himself up with his elbow. "He said to deliver a message if I ever ran into you. Hello. That's the message."

He went to all the trouble of stealing your address off the counter and following you around and this was all he came up with. That's Matthew Cavanaugh. Every time you saw him, it was as if he had to take revenge for something you didn't remember doing. Afterward he'd settle down. Not that I could always be bothered giving him a chance. Sometimes, back in Kingston, I discovered that I had other things to do. Wash the yard, walk the cat. But I didn't have anything else to do yesterday morning except tell Matthew Cavanaugh everything I was up to.

He already knew. I guess I'm pretty transparent, at least to people my own age. But after we'd moved to the Mall for lunch,

Matthew gave me some useful tips on studying for non-school, pointing out how it's egotistical to believe that anyone is paying attention to you, including the elderly janitor in the Food Court. If I watched the janitor, I would see that he swore at everyone in Chinese before whapping their tables with his folded grey cloth. I should also consider the fact that everyone craves attention, as shown by the lengths people go to achieve it, e.g. shooting Presidents, broadcasting their sex lives over the Internet etc. But if they have to go to these lengths to achieve attention, it proves they don't get it ordinarily. To be left alone, all I had to do was follow what amounts to Plan C:

a) Dress like everyone else, which I was already doing, i.e. The Gap,

b) Keep moving, choosing one Library branch one day, another the next,

c) Mind my own business, which would encourage people to mind theirs,

d) If anyone asked, say I went to an Alternative School. That would explain everything. And finally,

e) Avoid McDonald's. After my preceding experience, this seemed self-explanatory, although it turned out that Matthew had an additional opinion about the carcinogenic propensities of refried fat.

Then he gave me a present.

"Come on," he said.

"Where to?"

"You'll see."

Matthew knew the laneways even better than I did, leading me on a crooked pathway north of the railway tracks. I figured that he must have explored Toronto the previous summer, when he'd lived on the streets with those Homeless Persons before they shipped him back to Kingston. He was fifteen at the time and they could still do that. But he said he'd only come to know the neighbourhood since he'd been in town this time, a little more than three weeks. He hadn't run away again. He'd departed. He was sixteen now and he could legally drop out. He was living in a Homeless camp and no one could touch him, Matthew said, whacking sharply three times on the Dumpster behind the Italian Supermarket.

"Registration forms," he said, noticing the Dumpster.

"You fished them out? Matthew, that's gross. There was decayed eggplant in there."

"How are you going to get a report card?"

"That's months away," I answered, but he kept looking at me. "They're computer-generated. You could always mock one up."

He nodded, leading me ahead. "What I was thinking, maybe the whole world is full of people pretending. Maybe all sorts of people get up in the morning and pretend to go to work. They get on the GO Train and get off at some arbitrary station, then they drift around the Malls all day. Maybe that's who all those people in Malls are. Either that or they go into the office and pretend to work. Their arms are moving paper from one side of the desk to the other, but in their heads they're lying on a beach in Cuba. Then they go home and say to themselves, That's not really my wife. My real wife is the babe I fuck at night in my head, and my real kids are the ones on the computer developing new software. My real kids aren't those brainless Losers with their mouths hanging open in front of the TV. My real kids are going to make me rich. Here we are," Matthew said, opening a back gate.

"You're staying here?" I asked, following him up the walk.

"You don't recognize it?"

I did. We'd arrived at the back door of the house where I'd seen the black-and-white cat.

"You've got Paws?" I asked.

Matthew looked down at his hands in mocked perplexity.

"Stop it," I told him, then saw he had a key. "So you're really staying here?"

"People are lax about security," he said, opening the back door. "It's easy to jimmy your way into a place the first time, and everyone has duplicate keys. You usually find them in the cutlery drawer. So you boost a key and come back any time you want to." Seeing that I was about to freak, he added, "It's OK, they both work. They're both at work. You want to see if it's your cat? I only saw him a couple of times back home. I can't really tell."

It was true, Matthew wasn't allowed to come to the apartment back in Kingston. I followed him on tiptoes into the house, my heart beating like a big bass drum.

"You should whisper," I said. "We shouldn't be here."

"Why?" he asked. "You should tell your Mom to get a security alarm. You can manage to get past them, but it's not worth the effort to break into an alarmed house when other people don't bother installing."

"You haven't been inside their place too? When I wasn't there?"

"Cat usually hangs out in the bedroom upstairs."

"I don't understand how you knew about the cat."

"So you're hanging around outside going, 'Paws, Paws' through the window. It seriously disturbed me at first. I thought you were going, 'Pause, Pause,' like the Pause button on the VCR or something. Pause life. Put it on hold. Then I remembered. Here," Matthew said, opening a door.

He lay curled up on the bed in the sunshine. I couldn't believe it. "That's my cat," I said. "That's really him. It's absolutely the right cat. Paws," I said, and he stood up, arching his back, looking up at me with those yellow eyes. I'd found my cat. It wasn't a mistake or even wishful thinking. That black freckle on his nose. Those few white hairs in the middle of his back. I'd found Paws. It was the first nice thing that's ever happened to me in my life.

"Thank you," I told Matthew, and he closed the door to give me some privacy. Paws has never been a real lap cat. He deigns to sit on your lap sometimes, but it has to be his choice. So I went and sat on the bed beside him, letting him decide, and after sniffing the air, Paws stepped his front paws delicately onto my thigh. He let me pat him, arching his back each time, his black hair gleaming in the sunlight, feeling warm and showing undertones of red and brown. After a minute, he hunkered down, his front feet still on my thigh, and actually started purring. He knew me! Paws recognized me! That's when I had my happy cry.

I didn't take Paws with me, but I'm going back later today to visit. Matthew says the people go to their cottage every weekend. They come home from work early on Friday, pack up and drive to their cottage. That's why we had to leave fairly soon, but I can visit Paws later this afternoon. I won't take him, at least not yet. I was in kind of a daze, but it seemed like a comfortable Home. Paws looked well fed and his dandruff was brushed off cleanly. You want to think for a while about removing him from a place like that. Where would he live around here, anyway? Not in the tent, not inside. They weren't getting me to move inside, not even for Paws.

Even for Paws? You've got to think. I'm not used to this. Something nice finally happened. I can't imagine why.

TWENTY-FOUR

Florrie Brouwer—Her Book
January, 1944

I found this old diary hidden away. What is it? More than a year and a half later. Thank God no one else found the thing. I have to burn it. The soul cries out against burning books, but this is clearly an exception, and God knows, we can use the fuel.

Yet I have some time this morning and the stub of a pencil and it amuses me to bring it up to date. End the story it started, then deliver it into Granny's little war stove on top of the oven. We're all so far beyond that trip it's funny. Not funny. It's tragic. But you can't think about that—about anything. To get through the war, we've all learned to live in the moment, paying such close attention to the world around us that everything looms vast, clangs thunderous. We are like ants. A blade of grass is a tree, a footfall could be fatal. Every morning is a revelation. Each breath, a gift.

Elisabeth van Nostrand had few gifts. She was a niece of the Farmers Noort, a pudgy, friendly, bubbly girl from the Youth Storm whom I didn't even mention in that last ridiculous entry. Her parents were the ones who lined up our visit to the farm. I am sorry to record that she was killed five months later, hit by a tram turning into Central station. She'd been looking the wrong way. Literally and figuratively Elisabeth looked in the wrong direction. Not that you can hold it against her. She was young and her parents told her what to think. Given more time, Elisabeth might have started to think for herself, to look in a different direction, listen to what good Dutch people were saying all around her, hear some cry of common sense and come to a different conclusion.

I plan to burn this and still have trouble being as indiscreet as I once so effortlessly was. I feel all the pressure of a year and a half of keeping quiet, of obscuring my utter change of heart, my 180-degree change of sympathies and direction . . . a year, in short, of putting an end to my childish fantasies of revenge and starting to act against the great Evil now manifest in the world.

Still, let me mourn Elisabeth, who died young. Let me mourn Jannie Schippers, who is stubborn. No change in *her* direction. Jannie has become the veritable poster girl for Aryan Youth. They're training her up like a circus horse, the elite athlete, the Teutonic promise. Jannie knows she's being used and she agrees to it. Agrees *with* it. Why not be indiscreet and say it? Jannie knows very well why people turn 180 degrees against the Occupation but she still remains a convinced supporter. Well, at least she's useful. In dangerous moments, I find myself picturing Jannie, her eyes a reminder: *It would be a mistake to assume that all Fascists are stupid. Be careful, Florrie.*

I once admired Jannie for being easier on other people than she was on herself. I might not have been able to put it into words, but that's the feeling I got. And it's changed. That's what has changed about her. In all her recent training, I think she's submitted so gloriously to so much discipline—she's got used to exercising such enormous self-control—that she's lost all sympathy for people who just want to lead ordinary lives. I believe that ordinary people puzzle Jannie. She thinks: You could improve yourself if only you followed a program. Get up at such an hour as I do, run so many kilometres before breakfast, eat a nutritious meal (as if we wouldn't all kill for a nutritious meal), train for X hours and study for Y . . .

I think she still has great fellow feeling for those who submit themselves to a strict taskmaster—not just athletics, but mathematics, music, war—whether they reach the heights or not. The best are those who win, but she feels for anyone who tries. The rest? Expendable. I think Jannie truly believes that—and smile quietly to myself. If she only knew how I spend my days. She'd have to accept me as a peer, wouldn't she? One of those who lead dedicated lives, exercising the shrewd self-control I believe she admires.

Why do I know so much about the new Jannie? Because of the time I approached her after my disgrace. It was an impulsive decision. Usually I avoided the old Youth Storm crowd, right from the start.

"Want to fall off my bike, Florrie?" they called.

"You can rip my uniform if I can rip yours."

"Such an awful girl. A liar on top of everything else."

"On top of what, did you say?"

I spotted Jannie striding down the broad sidewalks of Apollolaan—Diana gracing Apollo's street, her hair catching a breeze, her shoulders broad, her arms swinging free. She looked as if she owned the place, which made me so furious that I walked straight up to her.

"You know, I saved you from the soldier," I said. "I think you might try to show more gratitude."

Jannie stopped and met my eyes. She didn't bother with any greeting, either. "You saved me from the soldier," she agreed. "What I don't understand, Florrie, is why you didn't save yourself."

"I fought him off with everything I had."

"I know. I don't mean that. I mean afterwards."

She meant that I didn't lie about what happened. The day Maaike van der Velde's *awful* father brought her to our house, I didn't look uncomprehending when she told my father how gaily I had climbed onto the bicycle and ridden off with the soldier, and how soiled was my uniform when I returned. Yes, I might have said, so what? Nor did I cry like a baby when I had to face her brutal father's lewd and prudish lip-smacking. I didn't wail: How can you imply such awful things? How dare you besmirch the honour of the *Wehrmacht?* The soldier took me on a bicycle ride and we had a fall. How could you claim otherwise? And more to the point, prove otherwise?

Instead, I told the truth. I took Jannie's place on the bicycle because I knew the soldier was drunk and I thought I could jolly him along better than my serious, beautiful friend. I even mentioned Jannie's period, not noticing at first how my father recoiled. Why did I let it pour out, insisting on describing the rape as Maaike turned white, then red? How did I know things like that, words like that? Your daughter went willingly, Maaike's father repeated. Such a dirty mind, it's no wonder.

You're the one with the dirty mind, I told him. Taking such interest . . .

Slap! My father's *slap*! Speak respectfully!

I didn't. I wouldn't. He hated what I said, what I knew, and soon he hated me. They all hated the way I kept on speaking, day after day, especially once they found the soldier and he told them, Ah, she wanted it. And his superior stared them down.

"I should probably have shut up," I told Jannnie. "But I was late, and I've always been on time before. I didn't think it was such a good idea to say that nothing happened, then turn up pregnant."

"And were you?" Jannie asked. "Pregnant?"

"I might have been until my father beat me."

"I see," she replied, giving me an intelligent look that bordered on approval.

"That's not the only reason I didn't shut up. He should have been punished. What I said was right."

"There's never only one reason for anything, is there?" Jannie replied. "You're my friend, Florrie. I'm grateful. We're just not supposed to visit you. Wait till after the war." Then, in faint exasperation, "You could have managed things so much better. We don't always have to be right, you know."

I do. And it worked out for the best, anyway. My father throwing me out, Granny taking me in. The work I've done for the Resistance since, that I've been able to do since because I'm trusted here, yet not precisely distrusted back in the NSB.

"Isn't that our friend Jan Brouwer's daughter? Florrie, wasn't it? Wasn't there something about her? I remember hearing something . . ."

"Stay away from that Florrie. Jan was a little harsh on her, maybe. She's a little unstable, maybe. A firecracker. Best to leave her alone."

I know what they say—and agree! Still, I mourn Jannie, seeing her from a distance, being chiselled into an Aryan symbol. Imagine the power of all that discipline channelled into the right cause, our cause. What a comrade she would have made! I mourn that lost possibility—and grasp whatever other chances come my way!

Elisabeth, Jannie, Maaike van der Velde. I should write more about Maaike van der Velde, rounding off that story, too. Not that I think it's really ended. Stupid girl. She's the sort of person who haunts you throughout your life. I'll be hobbling through the zoo in the year 2000 and Maaike will undoubtedly hobble past, sending me sprawling with her cane. She won't do it intentionally, of course. She never does. Even at the moment of my disgrace, I understood that Maaike didn't have a *clue* what she was telling my father. Of course she didn't—that made it even worse. Stupid, stupid girl. How could she be so hopelessly blind? Yet gradually my fury cooled into simple exasperation—which is to say, into one's familiar, age-old, time-worn reaction to Maaike. Exasperation, Maaike: they go together like bread and cheese.

What finally brought this home to me was running into Maaike shortly after my father kicked me out, coming face to face with her on Prinsengracht. She went red as a beetroot again and tried to step aside. My initial impulse was to slap her stupid face. But then, it's strange—I found that I wanted to tease her. She stepped to her left, I stepped to my right. Her right, my left—until she finally met my eyes. Her expression was both resentful and weak. Resentful mouth, weak pleading eyes. The virgin was facing the fallen woman. But guess what? She was still a virgin and I'd got back up! It made me laugh to see things that way. And you can't hold a grudge when you've started to laugh, can you? I can never hold a grudge. And I'll get my final revenge on them all by the glorious expedient of winning the war!

I ran into Maaike again just the other day. I see her quite frequently on my rounds, but this time I couldn't resist sneaking up on her. The Allies are about to land, the war will be over by Christmas—had she figured that out yet? She still has all of her eggs in the NSB basket. So many people these days are letting it be known that they "never" supported the NSB, leaving true believers like Maaike and her father to circle the wagons, their guns bristling out, still convinced of the Fascist cause. What a dreadful man her father is! Such a massive, thuggish, bitter man—with that squeaky little voice! Even the other Fascists can't stand him. He's spent *years* in the movement, fellow supporters are leaching away, and they still only ever give him joe jobs. Dirty jobs. They trust him but they don't respect him. Isn't that a strange combination? Aren't people *fascinating?* The way Maaike continues to adore such a miserable father utterly fascinates me. I don't know why she can't see through him the way everybody else does, as if he were a child's lie.

She was looking moodily into the canal near my Granny's house. When I touched her shoulder, she jumped and spun around, her lips white.

"Are you all right, Maaike?" I asked in genuine wonder.

"I'm fine," she answered, barely moving her lips. The eyes are supposed to be the window of the soul, but in Maaike's case her prissy mouth seems to give more away. "Of course I'm fine," she said, shaking herself and adding grudgingly, "And you?"

"I'm hungry, but what's new. Isn't everybody?" I watched her flinch. Extra rations for the NSB. She still seemed thin as the rest of us, though. "Aside from that, I'm healthy, thanks be to God."

She nodded, biting her lips nervously but straightening up as if she planned to shoulder her way past.

"Although worried," I added, touching her arm to detain her. "Axing Day. People say there's going to be such a bloodbath when the Allies land. They'll arm the Resistance. Give them a free hand with the NSB. They'll butcher my family—your family. They may not talk to me, but they're still my family. And they say they're going to tar and feather any women who went with the Germans. Cut off their hair." I pulled my hand off her coat, running it through my crowning glory.

"That's all nonsense," Maaike said, although she looked ghastly. It occurred to me that she wouldn't have lived this long without extra rations. Not to be sentimental. Many people haven't.

"So you think it won't end up being neighbour against neighbour," I said, pretending to sound relieved.

"The enemy won't land. The Reich will win. The Reich *is* winning. I don't know where you could possibly have heard otherwise." She glanced at me suspiciously. "Or why you keep wanting to make me feel guilty about what was clearly your mistake."

"Nothing was further from my mind," I cried.

"I'm sure."

Actually, she was wrong. I was just giving her a half-friendly warning, that's all. It's not too late to change. I've changed. Yet I wondered—could Maaike ever change? Even if her father found it expedient to do a 180-degree turn before the Allied landing? The funny thing was, I could see Maaike going against her father to stay true to her Fascist beliefs. Of course, he won't. Old man van der Velde won't change. He'll be the last living Fascist, you just watch. But it also struck me that Maaike is perfectly capable of turning against her father if something finally convinces her to change. I have no idea what that could be, yet I sensed in her a kernel of stubbornness so hard as to be almost magnificent. Unsprouted, of course. As yet.

"Maaike, you're impossible," I told her fondly. But for some reason, that made her mad.

"I want you to leave me alone," she cried. "I want you to stop following me around. You're following me. You're everywhere I look."

"As if I had time," I replied, honestly surprised. "Now *there's* a guilty conscience speaking."

"I don't have a guilty conscience," she said. "You're the one who should feel guilty. It wasn't my fault. You should have let me lead the group that day. If you'd let me lead the group, none of this would have happened. I was supposed to be leader, and now you're following me everywhere so I don't forget it. Why can't you just go away and leave me alone?"

I was too astonished to feel angry. How could I, when she was shaking? Her thin shoulders were shaking, her hands clutching the cool air. She looked greenish, pale, sickly. Christmas is still a long time away and the Allies won't be here before then. She probably won't last the war. No zoo in the year 2000, after all.

You become unsentimental, but I've known Maaike since before I can remember. Piet said later that he'd been watching from the attic window, and he saw me reach out to pat Maaike's shoulder. I don't remember doing that, but I can imagine how the impulse—or habit—might still have been there.

"I'll leave, then," I told her, calling over my shoulder, "Farewell, Maaike."

"Stop following me," Maaike hissed. "You've got to leave me alone."

And so I will leave her—feeling guilty, feeling important. To what end, who can tell?

Yes, that was Piet I mentioned. I'm running out of time. Granny is going to cook dinner soon. Cousin Johanna found some potatoes this morning that weren't too bad. I should hand over my contribution: twists of paper to start the fire, twists starting with this last daring page. Can I even write it? Pieter, my Piet. Breathlessly jotting . . .

That I didn't understand what I overheard when I caught Piet and Jannie's Uncle Bertus speaking to the man from the ss. That it wasn't any wonder. Neither Bertus nor the ss were supposed to understand, either. Piet was operating as a double agent, a secret agent working for our side—hidden now, it's far too dangerous for him to be outside—but colleague, comrade . . .

And mine.

Who hides him? Who feeds him? Who carries the ration books he counterfeits out into the aching wartorn world? Who loves him and cherishes him? Who's going to marry him after Christmas, after the war?

Me, me, me, me, me! We're engaged. We're a couple. Joined *body and soul* for the rest of our lives.

There. I've said it. No secret is left unrevealed. Except the unknown future, of course. Now I'll make my paper twists from this poor old book, moving from these last scribblings back through the impossibly immature writing that comes first. I don't recognize myself in any of the earlier pages—even in the effusions of a year and a half ago, that melodramatic girl on that agonizing trip. Was I really like that? I've changed so much, thank God.

In another time, another place, I'd save this funny old diary, opening it sometimes in future years to marvel anew at all the changes I've gone through. But the past doesn't matter now. Far better to use it up. Make paper twists of my scribbled youth, my adversaries and dearest friends—Piet, Johanna, Jannie, Maaike, poor Elisabeth—back through the fervent entries from school—Käthe, Anna, Maartje, Fraanje, Greta— twist them up, my youth, lost youth—Cornelia, Bep, Cor and Jan—the lost youth of Amsterdam . . .

Kindling.

TWENTY-FIVE

Friday, September 15

My life is filled with indignity, i.e. the way that people never leave you alone. I noticed this yesterday evening when I was forced to decamp from my tent, moving into the garage because of the weather. It was a miserable day, merely cloudy in the morning, but cold. Unseasonably cold, it seemed to me, more like late October than mid-September.

You can't help obsessing about the weather these days, it seems so upset. I read in the paper last week how the hole in the Ozone Layer is bigger this year than it's ever been. And in the afternoon, lashings of rain started to fall as if the sky was going to drain itself empty. Absolute flapping blankets of rain were blown against the library windows. I couldn't have left the library even if I'd wanted to, and when I couldn't delay it any longer, cycling back left me sloppy wet. I had to change before dinner, then found the weather pervading my tent afterward, the cold and wind and rain. I was forced to move into the garage, making a camp with my foamie and sleeping bag on the empty side of the concrete floor, meanwhile pulling out a lawn chair to read on. That's where Pudge and his so-called wife found me when they got home from work. In a lawn chair reading Nietzsche.

As Pudge likes to say, Who asked? Who asked them to walk in uninvited, shaking off the rain? Who asked them to pull out two more lawn chairs? Who asked for their second-hand shrink-wrapped interpolation of my actions? It's Pudge's father who's the shrink, not Pudge. I admit, I made a mistake. I left a non-school essay lying around in the kitchen. But they didn't have to come outside and blame me.

"This," the wife said, showing me the essay. *How I Spent My Summer Vacation*, final version.

> *Instead of vacationing this summer, I spent my time creating a Home. It wasn't any Home I was planning to inhabit. Instead, it was a Project I undertook on behalf of other persons. It was as if I was paid to create a full-sized Doll's House they could play in, i.e. a Playhouse, which is a word with many meanings, including Theatric.*

"Thank you for bringing it out," I said. "I have to hand it in tomorrow."

But instead of giving it back, she hugged the paper against her chest, her eyes looking big and black. Pudge stood up and hovered behind her like a shadow.

"You're right, of course," she said. "And I'm so sorry, Jessie. I suppose it's true, Murray and I have been caught up in our own little world. But Jess, it isn't as if we haven't agonized about how to help you deal with all this change. You know how badly I wanted you to take summer courses or camps. I badly wanted you to meet some kids your own age. But you wanted a job, and it seemed to go so well. Everything seemed to be going so well, except for that tent. I guess I should have seen that tent as a cry for help, shouldn't I?"

"Looks pretty much like a tent to me," I said.

"But Jessie . . ."

Blah blah blah. The rain driving on the windows conveniently drowned out her monotony. It drowned out Pudge, who insisted on saying that you sometimes acted with Subconscious deliberation. You couldn't bring yourself to express something straight up, so your Subconscious found another manner of relieving itself, i.e. leaving an essay on the counter. As if I'd never heard of Freudian slips. As if I wasn't totally familiar with the concept of Telling It Slant. What did he think I was, anyway? Some uneducated doofus? Some total Loser? You're already having a bad enough time for weather-related reasons when people come out to your refuge and insult you?

"Something else Freud said," I told them. "A cigar is sometimes just a cigar. I forgot the stupid essay on the counter, OK? I made a mistake. So why don't we just leave it alone? You can go back inside now."

"But Jessie . . ."

"You can please go back inside now."

Eventually, they did, looking at me reproachfully. I still don't know what their problem was, to be honest. It's a good essay, and you'd think they'd be proud of my abilities, or at least my spelling. Michelle has never been all that good a speller herself.

One day, if it is my luck to have a Home of my own, I plan to embrace the artful life. My walls will be colourfully painted as a backdrop for the photographs I plan to take, i.e. not for the fictitious, but for representations of Real Life, at least as far as I see it. Meanwhile, my furnishings will be Collectibles. They'll have a history reflecting back on itself like a Hall of Mirrors. In this manner, my real Home will have depth, not newness and superficiality. You'll be able to sink into it like an old shoe. For that reason, I'll be able to get my cat back from the people who have stolen him. Cats like shoes. They like to lie on them and purr. My home will feature a purring cat, Art, Collectibles, and a garden full of blooming roses.

I think that's worth an A, and plan to award myself one. In fact, I was taking a red pen out of my backpack to do my marking when the door blew open again. Pudge staggered back in, rain blowing behind him, wind blasting. They'd warmed up my eggplant casserole and Pudge was bringing out a plate. As if I hadn't eaten already. As if you didn't get hungry bicycling around half the day and have to eat the moment you got home.

As if anyone had invited Pudge to sit back down.

You couldn't get a moment's privacy in this overcrowded world. I was about to say so when another blast of wind made the garage shudder. It was such a cold slicing wind that it pierced the old board siding. It pierced your skull, chilling the thoughts from your head. The garage was cavernous, having been built for bulky Fifties cars. Pudge's little hatch-back left plenty of room for storage. For echoes, too, and frightening creaks. Sitting in my lawn chair, the lone light bulb swinging on its cord, rain lashing at the little pained window, I felt very frail and vulnerable to a Tornado raging in. You could picture it sucking open the door, sucking you up into the raging air like the innocent Child out in Alberta, the little red-headed minister's son. You could see it lifting and spinning the garage like Dorothy's house in *The Wizard of Oz*. It could take you at any moment. It was getting closer, raging just outside.

"It's counterintuitive," I told Pudge. "People don't know that unnaturally cold weather like this is another symptom of Global Warming." You could tell he'd never thought of that. He looked surprised, and didn't answer for a moment.

"Is it really?" he asked.

So I told him about Global Warming as I ate, how Amoebic Cities are spreading across the Globe, squeezing the Environment between them. How the Environment is fighting back in unpredictable fashion, i.e. ice storms, droughts and Tornadoes. How life has become a swirl of Events, swirling people around the globe until some poor Somali lady ends up as a parking-lot attendant in Toronto, subject to car-borne racism, while Homeless Persons camp between established neighbourhoods, falling into social cracks.

You can have a conversation with Pudge if you catch him at a good moment, i.e. without his wife. We discussed the confused nature of postmodern life. It turns out he feels that there's so much going on these days that you can start to feel overwhelmed. I never would have pictured Pudge as feeling overwhelmed, but I guess he must. He was acute on the subject of how things can start coming at you all at once. You want life to be predictable and known, but there's so much going on—not all of which you asked for—that you can feel crowded out by it, shoved into a corner and shunted aside. He was right. I agreed with him. I might even have felt that way sometimes myself. So Pudge talked for a long time about how people yearn for quick and easy solutions to the problem of feeling crowded out. But there are so many variables these days, he said, you seldom encounter the exact right thing to do, and usually have to fall back on the least wrong one.

"What you call Amoeba City, I think of as a great experiment. People from so many backgrounds and cultures living together, it's never really been tried to this extent before. Some of the people who lived here first can feel pretty resentful. It's as if they've discovered a new branch grafted onto the family tree. So you're saying that's my new sister and brother? My new stepfamily? Who asked? The big guys never asked your opinion. You were compelled into this step-relationship by events swirling, as you put it, beyond your control. And suddenly you're living with someone you don't really know.

"Your friend Matthew is right in saying that people aren't going to go back to where they came from. That's just not going to happen. We're all in this together now, those who wanted it and those who didn't, those who had some inkling of what they were getting into, however fatuous"—laughing—"and those crowded-out people who didn't have a clue. So what do you think we should do about it, kiddo?" he asked.

Why should I have an answer, being half his age? As a future photographer, my job was merely *seeing*. It annoyed me that Pudge should expect anything more.

"Kiddo?" I asked, and he chuck chuck chuckled.

"My grandfather's term. He was just a kid when they moved to Canada. Which put him in a bridging position between his immigrant parents and the new country. He was big on building bridges, my grandfather. He never believed in great solutions. Final solutions being something he fought against. He believed in incremental day-to-day decency. He believed in accommodation, in making coalitions. He believed in respect and compromise. I guess compromise isn't a very catchy catchphrase, but what's the alternative? I've never found any alternative, myself. Or am I wrong?"

"You're a lawyer, Pudge," I told him. "You make it all sound so simple. That's your job, to make it seem simple for people to give you what you want."

He chuckled unhappily. Does he think I'm stupid? I'm far from stupid, check my test scores. I felt a little annoyed at his backhanded way of talking about things, if also victorious in the way I'd defeated him, although my relatively benign mood ended when Pudge's wife burst through the door again, rain spattering in behind her.

"So," she said. "All sorted out? Who's ready for some lemon pound cake?"

Matthew Cavanaugh advises me to leave. I've boxed myself in with pretence, he says. Not only do I pretend to go to School, I work with counterfeit textbooks and do fake homework. He doesn't know why I think that I can reach the Truth through a welter of lies. Welter Shelter, he says. Better to step outside the box. Do a run. Join him outside, learning from the unbridled world spinning around us.

I agreed to an Experiment on Wednesday, skipping non-school to take off for the Beach. Matthew got a bike, another Kona. I guess panhandling must be as filthy lucrative as they protest in the newspapers. It was another one of those eerie fall days we've had recently, starting off sunny and cool but turning hot. I went from shivering on my morning run to sweating puddles on my bike, Matthew pedalling behind me. The sun felt fiercely piercing. I don't remember it burning so fiercely even a few years ago. It made my skin feel temporary and thin. But I tried not to think about Global Warming and especially not the Ozone Layer, leaving myself open to the happy chances of the day.

I still haven't figured out Toronto. "The Beach" refers to a neighbourhood of cottagey houses tricked up into real estate, but also to the sandy beach running for miles along the lake, separated from the houses by a park-like expanse of lawn and a Boardwalk. We rode down to the Boardwalk, dismounting to see a wide distance of sand sloping down to the lake, where wavelets splashed and sparkled in the sun. You didn't want to go swimming there, pollution aside. A Canadian cold front rolled in on each slap of water. But after we'd chained up our bikes,

Matthew produced the day's surprise. He'd got a kite in Chinatown, one of those fold-out kites he'd hidden in his pack, a butterfly with black-rimmed eyes staring from its scarlet wings.

When was the last time I'd flown a kite? Matthew jigged the balsa-wood frame out flat and we tied on the tail. Then we ran happily along the beach, Matthew holding the kite and me letting out string, both of us laughing like you laughed with Bradley Pigott chasing fireflies. The kite didn't want to go up at first, skittering along like a big red bumblebee above our heads before sheering into the sand. But when Matthew took charge, he managed to launch the kite into a high layer of wind, riding it up among the gulls screeching and gliding above us. He gave me the string, and we spent hours guiding the kite into spirals up and down the beach, scarlet spirals on a deep blue sky. Little kids ran beside us, a flock of toddlers, and we sometimes let one of them take a turn, running the kite back and forth while making little peanut footprints on the sand.

"Lovely day," a mother said, and I have to admit that it was.

Of course, there's only so much you can do with kites. There you are, tied to the sky by a slender string. It's not like in fairy tales. You can't climb the string to a giant's castle. So finally we grew bored, and Matthew handed the string to a nearby mother. "It's yours," he said. "It has your eyes."

I had to laugh. She was wearing eyeliner. At the beach?

"I can't do that," the mother said. But Matthew pointed out these kites weren't meant to last more than one evanescent day, doing the trick with his vocabulary, i.e. she could see that he didn't really need to be in School and so she had no excuse to refuse him. Afterward we ate hot dogs beneath a tree and Matthew wanted to neck, even though his tongue was as cold as an uncooked dog and tasted like mustard. I don't think I like necking, but guys seem to feel an affinity, and at least Matthew stopped when I told him to. I spent the rest of the afternoon reading while he napped against my shoulder. I'd given him Nietzsche, but I guess he needed to sleep. Having seen his Homeless camp, I knew why. Trusting yourself to sleep there must have been hard, i.e. trusting anyone else.

As to what I learned, it was mainly that you could skip School in plain sight and nobody cared. All those mothers must have known that we should have been in School. It didn't matter that Matthew was sixteen already, he should have had both a Home and a School. A Home and School Federation. Not that Matthew agreed. He felt the mothers knew approximately what we were up to. They just nostalgically remembered the times they'd skipped, or wanted to, and concluded that it wouldn't do us any harm.

I must be disputatious, however, given what happened the next evening with Pudge's wife and her lemon pound cake. I think there's a mean undertone to mothers. I think a big mean part of them wants you to fail so you'll never leave them. They're secret fans of failure. Of giving up. Of being a simpleminded member of the herd. Before his wife barged into the garage, Pudge and I had been engaged in a stimulating debate, and I don't say that merely because I was winning.

But she spoiled it, getting her own chair and serving out cake exactly like Gram, making me perceive exactly how weird it was for three people to sit on lawn chairs inside a garage, eating lemon pound cake under a lone dangling light bulb while a storm raged outside. It made me anxious. All I wanted to do was unroll my sleeping bag on top of my nearby foamie and get to sleep, my friendly CDs cranked up to maximum so they could mask what raged.

My hints in this regard were disrespected, however. In this respect disregarded. One of those.

"You don't want to sleep in the garage," the interloper said, sounding as if I'd made a bad joke. But when I insisted that I wanted to sleep out here, that I needed my sleep, that I had tons of work to do tomorrow, she turned all sharp and needling, almost as if she was going to cry. What did I do to deserve that tone of voice? I hadn't done anything to deserve it. The concept of deserving doesn't exist in the real world, i.e. you never deserve anything, especially this.

"I hoped you and Murray could work it all out. I thought there would be less pressure between the two of you. Less history. But nothing seems to work. Nothing we do seems to work, and I can't seem to figure any of this out on my own. Frankly, Jessie, I just don't understand what you want. What do you want from us? From me? Can you define for me precisely, please, what it is you want? Then maybe we can start to achieve it."

"I want you to leave me alone so I can get some fucking sleep."

"Can't you please learn to watch that mouth?"

"Watch your own fucking mouth."

She stood up, knocking over her chair. "You want to talk tough?" she cried, these awful tears appearing. "ok, we'll talk fucking tough. You fucking march yourself out of this fucking garage and upstairs to your own fucking room. You're living inside from now on. I've had precisely fucking enough."

Why did she need to make me? I hate it when she loses Control. It's distressing. I also hate that little white room, and now I have to sleep there all the time, at least for the predictable future. It's jail-like, a cellular room, this bland little square decorated with nothing but a nasty teal Accent Cushion. I don't want to sleep there. I refuse to sleep there. But where else can I go? I can't go to Matthew's camp, even though he says it's fine. He unsheathed his knife, saying anybody lays a hand on me, he'll kill them. But that sounds too much like a prediction. It makes me anxious. I need to come up with Plan D. I'm back in the library today, in the big Reference Library downtown, so I have access to the predominant ideas of historic civilization. I'll come up with something. I have to.

In the meantime, I'm cultivating two smaller plans to circumvent the weekend.

On Saturday, I'm planning to visit Paws. The people are away for a couple of weeks, so I have enough time for a good long visit.

On Sunday, I'll take Matthew to meet Dr. V.

I have that much left, at least. It's not much, but I guess it's what I have.

TWENTY-SIX

The girl is not alone. She has brought a boy! This is not part of the arrangement. She walks inside with a boy behind her and runs water into the kettle. I should not have let it become a habit, that the girl makes tea. It is presumptuous. I do not know what to do. What should I do, Father?

This is Matthew Cavanaugh from school, she says. I've told you about him, so I thought it would be okay.

Heil, he says quietly.

What do you say? I ask him sharply.

Hi, he replies. She's told me about you, too.

There is something disconnected about the boy. I do not like him. He is loose in the joints. He does not move like a person in control of himself. It is a mistake for Greta to make friends with this boy. She will lose control of herself also and grow uninteresting. She will grow ordinary.

It is true, however, that he is clean. Recently showered. A clever face, though not intelligent, I think. Not bookish. He sits down in the chair unasked.

She's told me all about you, he repeats. That is one lovely garden. A good place to sit and read Nietzsche.

What does he insinuate with that knowing voice? That he feels contempt for books? For thought? I dislike this boy on sight.

You must not make tea, I tell the girl. It is not necessary, I will leave soon. Do not rattle the canisters.

You're going out? she asks.

It is my concern.

I think my father shares your concerns, the boy says. From what she's told me. He gestures at the girl. She's told me the kind of things you say. *Arbeit Macht Frei.*

I have no idea what you're talking about, I say. In fact, I must leave immediately. Look at the time! You may turn off the kettle.

Matthew, shut up. Please excuse him, she tells me. He's kind of a changeling. You can't take him anywhere. He says weird things. Matthew, shut up.

All right, he says. I just thought it would make for an interesting discussion.

There is nothing to say. I must leave. Turn off the kettle.

Please sit down. Please don't leave. I wanted to have a nice visit. I have no idea what he's talking about. He does this, then he calms down later. He'll calm down later.

He lies, that one, I say.

I figure most people lie, the boy says, then nods at the girl. It's what we were talking about. How people live a different life in their heads than they do in front of the world. They go around pretending to be one thing, when inside their heads they're something else. It's the only way they can get through daily life.

That is a cynical philosophy, I tell him, if also correct. Now you may go. I must leave.

For instance, you don't have anywhere to go.

Get out of my house.

I mean, from what you told her, I figure you're an old Nazi preserved from the war. You've been hiding out here in a state of preservation, hanging onto your beliefs. Hitler didn't order the Jews killed, it was lower echelons. Six million weren't burned off, that was propaganda, Jewish propaganda for the creation of Israel. Goethe's *Volk* weren't really out there killing Jews. They were supporting the Fatherland for nationalistic reasons. My father believes all that shit, too. That you told her? He used to collect all these old Nazis hiding out here. You get to recognize them. The vocabulary. *Arbeit Macht Frei*.

He turns aside and tells the girl: That's the sign the Nazis put up in concentration camps. Work liberates. It mocked the Jews. She's been mocking you, the fact you don't know who she really is.

I sit down. I cannot breathe. Father, what have I done!

She's Dutch, the girl says. Her father was in the armed resistance.

They even dare to speak of you! What can they know about you, these spies? What do they know about me?

My dear Father, he was not in the armed resistance, I breathe. They were thugs. We were ordinary Dutch people. This is our only sin in the modern world. To be ordinary people when all wish for fame. I have never said one word about armed resistance. We are in this country honestly.

It's true, she never said a word, the girl answers. I got that from something Francie said, or Pudge said, I can't remember. What they said about Dutch immigrants after the war. I guess I made the rest of it up in my head. I'm sorry. I do that. I don't know why you're saying this, Matthew. I wish you'd stop. You're making everyone anxious.

The water boils, the kettle is singing.

Turn it off and go away. I am old and feel ill. I will go out another time.

It's OK, I'll make you a nice cup of tea. We'll have a cup of tea. Matthew's going to leave now.

She didn't deny the Nazi thing, he says. You noticed that?

You've upset her. You don't know what she went through. Gramps never talks about the war, it's too stressful. You're bringing it back. You're making her sick. I should never have invited you. Now leave.

He stands up. *Sieg Heil! Sieg Heil! Sieg Heil!*

Matthew, get out of here.

I just want to hear you deny it, he tells me. I know you won't, but I don't think you should be insidious to her, either. I don't like that. People should have the courage of their convictions. Now who said that? I think she told me some-body said that.

You will both leave. I do not wish to see you again.

Who said anything about being in the country dishonestly? That's in her conscience, he tells the girl. Not all of them possess a conscience, at least that I've noticed. Too bad. We might have had an interesting discussion.

I do not wish to see either of you again. You prosecute an old lady.

Persecute, he says. Another of your Freudian slips, he tells the girl. We'll go on the Web and I'll show you some neo-Nazi sites. You'll recognize the vocabulary.

He opens the door, but the girl hesitates.

Come on, Jess. Let's get out of here. I only wanted to see her and make sure.

Jess? I say, and she blushes. This deceiving girl. This spy!

I don't know what he's talking about, she answers. You've got to believe me!

How can I believe her? *I don't know what you're talking about.* This is exactly what I said myself.

That's her real name, the boy tells me, as if I had not under-stood this by now. Jessie Barfoot. We're all liars here. Sick, isn't it? Welcome to the modern world.

I'll come back later, the girl says, as he pulls her outside. He's this, he's this . . . I don't know how to explain.

I tell her: You will not set foot in my house again.

I slam the door and collapse against it. Father, what have I done?

From outside, the girl's cry, Go away and leave me alone! I hate you! I fucking hate you!

She says it too late. What a pity.

Sunday, September 17

Plan D:

First, Get Paws.

How am I supposed to get him without Matthew Cavanaugh?

Where am I supposed to put him?

Where am I supposed to take him?

What if Matthew's right?

He can't be.

Plan D, Revised:

First, Check for Websites under Neo-Nazi. That will clear things up.

Monday, September 18

Plan E:

Find Matthew.

Get Paws.

Where are we supposed to go?

Matthew will know.
I know shit, I'm a naive doofus Loser.
Matthew will know. Go find him.

––––––––––

I want to wake up. I do not want to have this dream.

It is not a dream. It is words spattering the ceiling like shrapnel. It is words repeating inside my head like records skipping, sharp needles digging in my brain. It pains me so very greatly, Father!

Ah yes, Maaike van der Velde. Miss Maaike, Miss Maaike van der Velde. My Gertrud speaks of you often. She speaks of you highly highly.

I don't want to have this dream. I must wake up. I want to wake up right now!

I am not asleep.

I want to wake up anyway.

I cannot. Look at the words on the ceiling. Listen to them skip. Skipping needles in my brain. His deep voice, my shrill squeaking. The repetition. The pain!

I'm glad to hear you, Sir, she squeaks.

No doubt. No doubt, Miss Maaike, Miss Maaike van der Velde. It is the wish of all good Dutch citizens to be of help to the Reich. *Heil!* Reich. *Heil!* I have noticed this. Yes. I have noticed noticed you. Yes, I have noticed. Yes.

But I have something to tell you, sir. Do you have time for me to tell you something important? Important. Or should we meet in person?

You have something to tell me? Tell me, Miss Maaike van der Velde.

I can't stand this any more. Why doesn't it stop? I want it to stop.

I have learned about activities, sir. If I make myself clear, there is something hidden, something hidden that must be brought to light. Brought to light. Brought to light! Will you see me, sir?

Miss Maaike, I am busy. If you have something to tell me, you tell me now. Tell me now, it's all right. What do you have, what do you have to tell me, Maaike van der Velde? Miss Maaike van der Velde. My Gertrud speaks of you often. She speaks of you highly! Such an example, an example, an example . . .

I am in hell. Will I never escape?

Dear so-called parent and guardian:

Here's something else for you to find on your counter. I wish to point out that it's not a Freudian slip. I'm merely slipping you a slip of paper.

In any case, all I mean to say is that I've had enough of everything. I'm out of here. I don't want to live around here any more. I want my own life, free of lies and ignorance.

I've left you the rest of the eggplant casserole in the fridge for dinner.

No, I haven't. I need dinner too, you know. You can always scramble some eggs.

TWENTY-SEVEN

Berlin
March, 1945

I'm so frightened. So hungry and so cold and so frightened. Although my dear Father provides for me and I must not complain. He has found us a good room in a sturdy building from which we may run to the Zoo station when the sirens sound. Three or four times a day. Although it is not just the sirens here, but cruel bombs raining down from the English and American pirate ships that kill so many people. The noise! The shattering! Brick, bone, glass, flesh.

I pick this up to write some news. I have not written here since we got into the van Ks' auto three? weeks ago and drove out of Amsterdam, the enemy fighting towards us, fighting in the south of our own dear country, fighting for the bridges at Arnhem. I thought their invasion of Europe would fail. Perhaps they had a beachhead after their D-Day, but I was sure that our *Wehrmacht* would push them back out. Instead, they're advancing. Arnhem is a battle zone. Where I bicycled as a carefree girl, enemy soldiers camp. The so-called *Wehrmacht* we encountered almost three years ago were enemy reconnaissance; I see that clearly now. What did I say to help them? I am such a foolish trusting girl. I make so many mistakes!

My news is that I saw Jannie in the Zoo station yesterday. She and her family, her parents and sister, have been living in Germany since last fall. It's been bad here, but they haven't

277

suffered the hunger of Amsterdam this winter. My dear Father did not let me go hungry, but many people back home turned to wraiths around me. They died in the streets. Skeletons shrouded in skin were laid out in doorways. It was their stubbornness, refusing to work for the Reich any longer. The railway workers refused to move any more cargo to the east. Why did they do that? And deprive themselves of wages and food? Deprive their children! How could they deprive their children? You would see children too listless to play. Listless children in a city without birds. Cats eaten too, dogs, precious trees cut down for firewood. This is what I left behind, starving people who claimed that the Allies were winning. How could they call that victory? All I could see was defeat.

I scarcely managed to talk to Jannie. War is so loud. Distant bombs rumbling, sharp explosions nearby. The screaming! A woman shouts, My children, my children in Meissen, I sent them to Meissen, how can I get to Meissen, where are the trains for Meissen? Pray for your children, a man says. The Red Army is approaching Meissen. Maybe they're already there. Reds swarming to the east of us, Americans marching in from the west, bombs raining down from above. Berlin crouches in between. And suddenly Jannie stands there, tall in the crouching crowd. She will rise like a phoenix from the ashes! Just as the Reich will rise again one day!

"Jannie!" I cry, battering towards her through bodies as thick as quicksand. "Jannie!"

"Maaike van der Velde," she says pleasantly. She has a dazed, pleasant expression on her beautiful face. She stands very close beside me. "We must not, of course, use these names again."

"They're all we've got," I say.

"It's best to start over completely. That way, nothing holds us back. Is your father alive?"

"Over there."

"Mine is at the hotel. He must talk to my father about papers. You need new papers. You are an old friend. I know that your father is resourceful."

"My father is good at getting food."

"We don't know who any of these people are. Many are from the Baltic states. They might be on any side. However, they don't know us, either. We don't really know each other," she says, slipping away.

My dear Father was very pleased with me. "New papers!" he said. "I will find Schippers."

S, I mean.

What does it matter?

"Don't leave me alone, Father!"

"My little Maaike will be brave. When the siren sounds, she will run like a rabbit to the station."

And I did. Evening siren singing its long one-note song, endless roar of airplanes overhead, bombs falling, fire flaring. The streets are never fully cleared of rubble. Bricks and glass lie everywhere, a piece of lampshade, a shred of curtain. I've seen a sleeve from someone's coat, a sleeve of good warm fabric, but as I bent to pick it up, I wondered what might be inside and drew my hand back sharply. Everything is shattered here. Buildings, windows. It smells chalky as a demolition site. Worse. Ashes, you breathe in chalky ashes and unspeakable fumes. This war is a Satanic Mill grinding the city to pieces.

Not that I've seen much of it. I see one route, from here to Zoo station. Sometimes I don't even see that, leaping up blindly when the sirens sound at midnight. We have to sleep fully clothed against the cold and air raids. It's so hard to make it down the unlit stairs. Harder still to run on the rubble, especially in the pitch of night with frozen blocks for feet. People fall; they cut their hands and knees. You see so many useless hands in the station, torn clothing wrapped around them. There is no circulation in their chilblained hands. Infection sets in. How will these people survive? I tell myself that I will not fall. I will run across the glassy rubble like an Indian fakir on a bed of burning coals, my feet so light they scarcely touch the ground. It *is* like coals, the glass burning with reflected fire. I will make it to the station. I make it to the station. What will I do if my Father isn't here, doesn't find me there? He always does.

Two weeks later? Hard to know.

My Father could not find Mr. Schippers. That is because all the Schippers except Jannie were dead, killed when their hotel was bombed. He found Jannie a few days later. She'd been talking at the protected back of the lobby while her family was upstairs. She was injured but helped dig out the bodies; I suppose she was strong from shock. They treated and released her. My Father brought her here.

"I've brought your friend," he told me.

"Your sister," said Jannie, who seemed pale and tired, sitting down on our one chair.

"That's true," my Father told me, as I hugged myself, upset by Jannie's condition. "Are you listening? No more Maaike, you're going to have to remember that. You're Martha van Tellingen, and this is your sister, Hendricke. Meet your old Father, Gerrit van Tellingen. Your old Father will take care of you both. That's how things work from now on. That's the agreement."

"That's the agreement," Jannie said, nodding. She told me, "You should remember our new story. Our new life. We van

Tellingens were working in factories in the east and fled in front of the Red Army. We were not particularly good people, I'm afraid. We only worked for the Reich because we were forced to. At least, that's what we will say when the Americans ask. My father looked into stories. He thought this one the best."

So we had the Schippers' papers now. I didn't want to think about that.

"I don't want to think about the Americans," I said. "Are you going to be all right, Jannie?"

"She's Hendricke," my father said. "You don't need to worry about Americans. You don't need to tell anything to anyone right now. Your job is to take care of your sister. She'll get better if you take care of her properly." He took back my old papers and gave me the new ones. "Hold onto these for dear life."

Jannie is asleep now. My Father is out searching for food. He seems to have some gold. I am left to guess that Jannie brought us some gold as well as the papers; her family was quite highly placed. I am not told about our old papers, either. Perhaps someone else bought them unsuspecting. I hope they were altered. I don't like to think that someone may have assumed my name, my identity, and I insist on keeping this diary, at least. Very secretly, of course. But I think I might be excused. I plan to show it to the *Führer* one day to demonstrate that under the worst of conditions, the least of his subjects remained true. I believe that he'll be interested to learn of one tiny soul who never wavered in her dedication. Two Dutch souls, for my dearest Father stands staunchly beside me. I believe that our *Führer* will be interested to learn what our lives were like. This is what happened on the ground—often underground at the Zoo station! This is how his followers survived.

I worry about Jannie, though. She isn't well. She got a concussion in the explosion and broke her left arm badly. Her back was cut by tiny pieces of flying glass; I'm still picking them out. I also think there's some infection, since she's started to run a low fever. I clean her wounds thoroughly and they don't look septic, but I'm afraid she might have some sort of blood poisoning. This morning she found it difficult to make it to the station when the air raid sounded. She had to hold onto the remaining buildings, she was so dizzy.

"Run ahead, Martha," she called, inching along the walls. Not that I would leave her, tugging her along by her good arm, trying to keep up her spirits with encouraging chatter. Truly she is my own dear sister! I've always felt a secret admiration for Jannie. Who didn't? But now she's my own sister and I get to take care of her!

She accepts this. That's the best way to put it. Jannie is as undemonstrative as ever, letting me bathe her this afternoon as if she were marble. One might use the word "stoic," except that she's more passive than that, only rousing herself when we have to run to the station. She sleeps often and never cries—in such great contrast to my nerves. I flutter about, suffering so badly from diarrhoea. All that good food gone to waste. And the smells! My dear father provided us with sausage yesterday and I couldn't hold it in for more than a few hours. I'm such a silly girl, my asthma rising to choke me whenever the sirens wail. I gasp and strain not to panic. Jannie scarcely blinks, and works her way slowly through her food, never gobbling, always thanking my—our—dear father politely, although she doesn't seem very enthusiastic. She doesn't seem interested in anything. Well, her parents and sister were killed; she was injured. It's probably best if she's a little numb, suffering as few of the nightmares as possible.

Nightmares. We're surrounded by nightmares, packed into a damaged building meant to hold half the people it does. A quarter. We hear crazy laughter through the walls and wails of despair. War is so noisy! Day and night, we're surrounded by heated arguments—the only heat we get around here—and hungry crying children. A madwoman upstairs plays a guitar at all hours, stopping abruptly in the middle of songs. The old man next door snores so loudly I can't get to sleep. I lie here wakeful as Jannie moans in her sleep, "Florrie! Florrie!" All the time, "Florrie!"

Yesterday, as I was cleaning her back, I finally told her, "You shouldn't worry about Florrie Brouwer. She isn't a good person. She's self-centred and wilful. Also a sneak and a liar."

"Poor Florrie. Speak no ill of the dead."

"She isn't dead, not to my knowledge. And if she is, one had best mourn worthier people."

"She was put on a train after they arrested her. One of the Jew trains out of Westerbork. When have you ever heard of anyone coming back from that?"

"If she was arrested, she deserved it."

"She ended up in the underground after her father threw her out. They were feeding *Onderduikers*. Jews. She and her cousins, all arrested. Even her grandmother was arrested, along with the Jews."

"Well, there you go."

"There's a chain of events, Maaike. If I hadn't let her take my place on the bicycle that day, if I had been braver—to be honest, less embarrassed—none of the rest would have followed. I've tried to push myself since then to be very brave and true. I've worked very hard to be good. But nothing can undo what happened. Don't hold my arm so tightly—I've always thought that it was my fault and not yours. I would have known how to handle it afterwards. I certainly wouldn't have got pregnant."

"She got pregnant?" I felt disgusted with Florrie, as loose as that. It certainly served her right. I shivered with disgust.

"I overheard some Dutch people whispering in the station not long ago," Jannie said. "Their train was bombed on the way east and they escaped. They were hoping to make it all the way home. Why, I don't know. Someone's mother had been killed in Rotterdam at the beginning of the war. Why go back to that? I'm going somewhere new as soon as I can get out of here. The last thing I want to do is stay in Berlin. It's all bad memories here. But going home is out of the question, too. You know that we can't go back, Maaike? You know what they'll do to us? I want to go forward. I've got to rest. I've got to get better and get out of here. That's my job. I have to train for it properly."

"It's not your job to upset yourself."

"It would have been Florrie's only hope of getting out. The train getting bombed. Though I don't know where she could have hidden all these months. They were arrested last August."

"She's probably been working in a factory in Poland. And now the Red Army is there, she'll be one of their heroines. You don't need to worry about her. They'll award her a Worker's Cross, or whatever it is they give them. You don't need to worry."

"I think it must have been Pieter Verhoef who turned them in. He was really one of ours, you know, pretending to be one of theirs. I heard that early on: a double agent. He worked closely with Uncle Bertus before the resistance shot him. That's why Piet was never a member of Youth Storm. It was all hush-hush, but I overheard people in the ss talking back in '42. Pieter was such a strange boy. He should have been born centuries ago and been a pirate, I think. I lost track of him for quite a while. But a couple of days after Florrie was arrested, they found Piet's body. Shot. Executed. The underground must have got him for turning in her family. No one could tell me the real story. But I think Piet got his own private Axing Day."

I shivered again and hugged myself. The diarrhoea threatened. "It's self-indulgent to talk like this," I told her.

"You're right," she said. "I shouldn't think about the past. It would be better if I were on my own. You remind me of things, Maaike, although it's not your fault. I look at you and keep thinking, It's not her fault. There's something about you that makes people say that. Maybe you're one of those people who hasn't really done anything yet. Not on your own."

"What does that mean?" I asked, feeling offended. "I've done a great many things in my life." I was tempted to tell her one salient thing, but Jannie was drifting off to sleep.

"I'm tired," she said.

Later

How much later? Air raids, air raids. When will it end? Jannie is very sick. I think it's turned into brain fever. Her ravings! I can see now that it was starting when I wrote here before. We took her to the hospital but what could they do? They can still amputate limbs or stitch people up, but they had no room for her, and said we should nurse her delirium at home. My father carried her all the way there and all the way back. It was raining; we got very wet and cold. I had wanted to see more of the city but hated to see it this way. Ruined. Half the buildings were blasted away, their facades left leaning, dirty curtains hanging through the windows. Everywhere I smelled dirt and ashes. I don't know how we can survive. How do people survive this? What do you have to do to survive?

Bathe her, try to reduce the fever. Her skin is so hot, it's like paper catching fire. Not long ago, my dear Father came back with some food. He heard her ragged breathing and grunted in surprise.

"You must be prepared," he told me.

"You said she'd get better if I took care of her properly."

"She seemed stronger than this. Maybe there was something more to do, little Maaike, but how do I know? I never got the benefit of an education. I don't have the education of damn doctors who learn how to turn people away. My little girl isn't a nurse, but I know she tried her best. I'll tell you this much: We kept our side of the agreement. Henk van der Velde is a man who keeps faith. Any fool can see that."

Jannie's breath was like wind rattling loose stone.

"How can I survive this, Father?" I cried.

"You let me take care of that. The Red Army is almost here. We're leaving soon."

"Jannie!"

"Well, well. So is she. To a better place, little Maaike. Don't cry."

Take her papers from her pocket, papers to sell. Replace them with a scrawled note my Father does not see. Here lies Maaike van der Velde. Find her perfect body and record her useless death.

Useless?

Gerrit and Martha van Tellingen are heading west.

TWENTY-EIGHT

Wednesday, September 27

I realized that what I was really upset about on Sunday, the preceding Sunday, wasn't the old witch next door. It was the way the people had left Paws alone in the house while they went off to Ireland. OK, so they hired a Service to come in and feed him. But only every other day? Poor Paws, he would have been so lonely. I was totally upset when I saw the information sheet on the counter. But Matthew had a good idea. We should phone and void the Service, saying there was Illness in the Family and the trip was postponed. Then we could move into the house and take care of Paws ourselves.

The Service didn't blink. Matthew did a Respectable voice and we had all the information. We just had to mail them a cancellation fee, which we did in cash. So now we're here for two weeks. It's up on the kitchen calendar, two clear weeks marked off by a two-headed arrow running over the boxed days and Dublin! Dublin! Dublin! written on top of it in red ink. They may be mean, but at least they're very methodical people, i.e. middle-aged.

Late-middle-aged. He's fifty-two and she turned fifty this year, for which they threw a big party with balloons, illustrated in both their photo albums and on the computer in terms of a saved invitation design. They have two grown-up children, a guy who works in Real Estate in Calgary and a younger daughter at Lakehead University up in Thunder Bay. The daughter's room is still in place, as if she might be screwed up enough to flunk out and land on them any instant, which makes me anxious. The son has a live-in. There's no wedding picture, but he must live with the dark-haired lady in all those albums, and they're not expecting him back. His room is now a genetic spare room, cloned straight out of Ikea. According to computer files, the family has owned this place for eighteen years and both parents work for the City. It felt a little uncanny living in their house at first, but now that I've got to know them better, it seems more normal.

It seems like our place. We're Mr. and Mrs. Bumstead, like the characters in some old comic strip, and this is our typical suburban house. Sub-urban, in terms of going underground. Putting it that way was Matthew's idea. I'd never heard of the strip in question. But Matthew is good at making a game of things, just like I'm good at working. The first few days we lived here, I preoccupied myself with work. That's what my crippled family does, and I'm going to have to get over it, but it was useful at first to proceed through my textbooks and do a multitude of homework. I've dropped German, however. You can drop courses throughout September, and I took full advantage.

The first day was awful. I felt so exposed. The house is exposed, the first house on the eastern side of this little street just up from the main drag. The southern exposure looks out on a laneway, behind which is the back side of a row of brick stores criss-crossed with metal fire escapes like broken spider-webs. I kept thinking of people looking down from the fire escapes, or across from the apartment block on the opposite side of the street, but Matthew says they're all Cheap Dives so no one pays attention to what their neighbours do. They can't afford to, in a manner of speaking. He also points out that the people in the house to the north speak almost no English, and the garage and gate cut off the backyard, behind which is another laneway. Matthew has never set eyes on neighbours on the far side of the lane, and he's been coming here for a while to take showers, so I guess he should know.

I guess you get used to it, this level of tension or attention, or maybe the lack of it. We keep the front curtains closed so we're not blatant, and we're prepared to say we're coming in to feed the cat while the Mahoods are away. But initially I felt restrained to stay down in the furnished basement, where they keep the computer and TV along with the most comfortable sofa and armchairs. I spent my first hours curled up there, leaving only to york up the few contents of my stomach, although I felt better after that. I got Matthew to bring Paws downstairs, then turned on the television and engaged in a mind-numbing marathon of Popular Culture, watching the Shopping Channel with its Hopeful life-altering products, and Judge Judy's domesticated court cases. Judge Judy in particular proved that many people are worse off than I am, i.e. the ones who watch daytime TV.

Eventually, my stomach calmed down enough to get hungry, and the casserole I'd brought didn't stretch far. But the thought of going out for pizza made me queasy again, so Matthew volunteered to do the shopping if I cooked. This struck me as a stereotyped decision of labour, especially since Matthew refused to take my money. I'd brought my Wad along from the Brick Bank in the basement, but he said he earned enough to support us and preferred to do so.

"The whole idea was to progress forward," I told him. "Not to retreat to some Mythical Past."

"Except it's kind of a game being here," Matthew replied. "We're the cartoon Bumsteads, when you think about it, living in cartoon sub-urbia. You can't take any of this too seriously. It wouldn't be healthy."

I had to agree, at least once he explained who the Bumsteads were. So Mrs. Bum gave Mr. Bum a shopping list and he went out for groceries. Once Mrs. Bum looked around, she could see that the Mahoods probably spent most of their time in the basement, too. The main floor, which had looked happy through the window, felt unwelcoming on closer acquaintance, with an overstuffed sofa and thin patterned carpet. But downstairs, they had portable TV tables you could pull up to the old plaid sofa and chairs and wall-to-wall shag. It was less portentous down there, even if the computer was outdated and the bookshelf held more photo albums than books, along with the usual board games.

Mr. Bum brought back some pizza with the groceries so Mrs. Bum wouldn't have to cook the first night. He also found some Basketball on TV and pulled out a doobie to smoke. I tried one of his doobies once in Kingston and it made me freak out, so Mrs. Bum declined for the moment, although the Second-hand Smoke relaxed her. I guess she just likes Second-hand. Being a piece of etc.

After Basketball, when Mr. Bum wanted to neck again, Mrs. Bum felt she owed. But she refused to have sex, feeling shocked by the safes he'd found in the upstairs bathroom. The Mahoods were too old for that. They should have acted their age. It was disgusting. Mr. Bum felt let down, but he was kind enough to sleep on the floor by the sofa when Mrs. Bum was too timid to sleep upstairs. Paws slept in an armchair. Paws prefers not to sit on laps, but if two people are interacting in the same room, he insists on being there. The one drawback is that Paws snores.

The Bum routine grew out of that day, exaggerated at first then calming down, much like Mr. Bum himself. He's usually out during the day, earning and spending, i.e. supporting his family and stocking up the house. Mrs. Bum suffers from a Female Complaint, I'm afraid. She's Agoraphobic and refuses to go out. But she's developed an internalized routine that keeps her busy, starting off with strenuous morning exercise in place of running, followed by showering, shaving, cooking breakfast, packing lunches and studying.

As I say, there was too much studying at first, but that has gradually declined into textbooks in the morning and recreational book use in the afternoon, after which she cooks dinner, inhales Second-hand doobie and either plays board games, watches videos or reads the children's literature that represents the bookshelf's only books. Mrs. Bum's goal is to learn how to stay calm without relying on overwork. She's making progress, especially after figuring out how to leave her pack and the cat cage from the furnace room beside the back door, meanwhile blocking the front entrance with a telltale chair. If the Mahoods return suddenly, Family Illness etc., she'll hear the chair fall down and be able to flee out the back door with Paws. Having a Plan always relaxes her considerably.

She/I. I/She.

Which was it that finally went to bed with Mr. Bum? After a couple of nights sleeping in the basement, Someone moved upstairs to the screwed-up daughter's bedroom, leaving the spare room to Mr. B. But he kept hanging around the screw-up's door, shuffling his feet and telling lame jokes, the deaf genie and twelve-inch pianist etc. It was both cute and pathetic in a guilt-inducing way. Eventually, you started to ask yourself why you were making such a big deal. It was supposed to hurt the first time and be a little bloody, but you did that every morning in the shower with your razor. Why not give him a chance?

Finally you said he could come to bed and he bounded across the room in comic-stripping fashion, making fun of his explicit Eagerness before launching himself on top of you. You were both laughing, but it was shocking how strong he was and maybe even scary as he fumbled off your T-shirt and panties, saying how beautiful you were and how long he'd waited to see you naked. Not that he really saw you because he couldn't hold it and had to rip open one of the queasy safes, his hands shaking, after which there was a sharp splitting pain that luckily didn't go on for long, nothing did. That was it?

"Sorry," he said.

"That's all right."

I guess it was, to get rid of some Virgin Airways baggage. It was also fine afterward to rest beside a person who didn't expect anything from you, at least for the time being. I did the thing like in the Movies of laying my head on his chest and had this funny mournful feeling all mixed up with understanding. He didn't say anything either, but touched my hair as if he'd never seen it before. I felt almost safe, like the times back in Kingston when you watched TV with your mother on the scratched old sofa, your legs intertwined. I couldn't remember feeling safe before in Toronto. Then I made the mistake of scratching my nose and Matthew saw my pits.

"What's that?" he asked, suddenly awake. I'd never meant anyone to see my shaving nicks and hid them away. But he was strong when we wrestled and the sheets pulled back so he saw Everything even before he pinned my arms wide, kneeling above me and dangling. I mean, you got an Eyeful, although I didn't mind it this time, educationally speaking. But I also had to look up at his face, where his deep brown eyes were disapproving, even disgusted, which I would never have suspected. "You're not going to do that," he said, sounding like a grown-up Male.

"I can do what I want," I said, sitting up and hugging myself shut.

"You do that where you sweat and you'll get an infection."

"I almost did this summer. It got all red and blistered. Then I got unlucky and it cleared up."

I heard myself sounding as Female as religious Melissa Duffy back in Kingston hair-tossing at her father. I enjoyed it, actually. It was another new game. Everything felt evolutionary, maybe half evolved, a Link that was still Missing but loping closer. I could almost see how you'd enjoy it.

"People accumulate enough scars without self-infliction," Matthew said. "Look at what my fucking father did." He rolled over to show me the stripes on his butt. "It's not like it's attractive. Several women have said."

"Who said? Your mother changing your diaper?" Honestly, quote, Women. Men are so Transparent. He'd obviously been flying Virgin, too. Before that, I'd assumed that he wasn't, but judging from his Male boast, he'd missed out getting any last summer on the streets. I also kind of liked the stripes, tracing them with my finger, then realized how sick that was. Doing it to yourself was different than someone imposing it on you.

"I'm sorry," I said, so he sat up.

"It's all right. It's finished. The last time he tried it, I got him back. It was kind of funny, seeing him down on all fours, shaking his head like a dog. I mean, this is someone who doesn't pay Support. I don't know how people can live with themselves. To go so far as quitting your job so they can't garnishee. I don't understand burdening yourself with that level of spite. It gets my Mom pretty irritated. I mean, she's back to working two jobs. I'm not exactly going to hang around and add to her burden, am I? They're coming at her from all angles. The teacher says my youngest brother is very musically gifted. He could use some proper lessons. Tyson? I'm going to send him the money. I don't know how the fucker can live with himself, not supporting those little kids. He never even visits. It wouldn't hurt him to visit. You're supposed to supervise your family. Also yourself, right? You look cute down there shaved, but don't cut yourself any more. Do me the favour."

I've always been sorry about Matthew's Family, but I didn't see that my personal hygiene was anyone else's business, especially to sound as if they were ordering. Matthew looked at me a long time when I said so.

"I should probably tell," he said, which gets me every time. After the shoplifting back in Kingston, he always said he was going to tell my mother. I don't know why. He wasn't trying to blackmail something out of me. He never told, either. But he always spent a moment mulling whether he would tell, and as I failed to figure out his reasons, I always felt out of breath.

"You wouldn't," I said, tugging on his arm. "You won't tell I'm here. You won't rat me out, Matthew. If you do, I'll tell them you're here, too. And you're sixteen, and they'll put you in jail."

"What makes you think I give a wet fuck about that?" he asked. I couldn't understand his removed expression and started to shake, also with cold. "Look," he said, moving closer. "If you have to cut yourself, you take a blade to the muscle of your upper arm. You can leave parallel scars that don't look too bad. They look tribal. Rub them with alcohol after." He draped the comforter over me until I stopped shaking. "You'd probably feel better if we did it again."

That's how the Bums developed a bedtime routine and sometimes in the morning shower, all soaped up, although I know one of the reasons he does that is to keep an eye on my personal hygiene. I still don't understand why he thinks it's any of his business, even if he did walk up the basement stairs on the way out yesterday going, "I love you."

Maybe he didn't. Matthew is prone to mumbling. I hope that isn't what he said. It would make you feel even more guilty, I mean about not relishing bedtime. If I was an actress instead of a mere pretender, I guess I'd try to fake it. But it makes me feel bad that he's noticed how bedtime leaves me cold. Frigid, in his Male dialectics. Not that he holds it against me. Some people just are, he says. It's not like they can help it.

Privately I suspect it would help if he wasn't Premature. A couple of times when he held it longer, I felt near-relish. But it's also true that I panicked on the verge of enjoyment and pulled back. You don't want to start moaning out some fetid vocabulary. You don't want anyone to gain that much Power over you. You want to retain Power over him, which is easy for a Female if she keeps her cool, i.e. remains Frigid, at least if he doesn't turn you in to your mother, which he could at any moment.

When you think about it, Mr. and Mrs. Bum have a crippled relationship. But I'm sure they're nothing out of the ordinary. She's Frigid, he's Premature, their association is an underhanded Power Struggle. Welcome to Modern Life. Not that I have any grounds for complaint, having failed to figure out an alternative, just like everybody else.

"Is there something you want?" Matthew asks. "Try to tell me what you want. I'll try to give you what you want."

I don't know why people keeping asking me what I want. How am I supposed to know what I want? I'm fifteen and three quarters years old. This Amoebic Globe is spilling over with choices. It's a fluid swamp of impossible choices, a maze of alleyways, and they don't print maps to help you get out of here. I've never seen one, anyway. I don't know how other people decide what they want. How can they find the confidence to say, I want this and not that? Especially when they know they won't get it anyway.

My only salvation lies in the fact that the Crucial will take me soon. I know it will. I can feel the wind at my back. In my mind I've become like the little red-headed minister's son riding the Tornado way up in the sky. I'm so far up there now I'm looking down on clouds. I'm way out there, riding high with no human net to catch me, nothing below but the unfor-giving ground. Or maybe I'm like Dorothy in *The Wizard of Oz*, who was carried aloft in a house where she shouldn't have stayed. I'm riding that house through the Eye of the Tornado, the I of the Tornado, and any moment it will drop me down in the Land of Oz. Then we'll face the Crucial question: How do I get Home?

I found *The Wizard of Oz* on the bookshelf here, and the book is notably distinct from the Movie. The book was written at the turn of the preceding century when life was apparently hard and rude, and Dorothy's adventures through the magical Land of Oz don't seem to bother her that much. She's also granted Silver Slippers when she kills the Wicked Witch, not Ruby ones, and when she clicks her heels together at the end, she orders the slippery magic around like a servant. "Take me home to Aunt Em!"

By the time they made the Movie, they were almost forty years closer to the anomalies of Modern Life. It seems to me that Movie Dorothy's adventures are more frightening and tearful, and they certainly give little children nightmares when they're shown on TV, especially the flying monkeys. But it also strikes me that her final spell has grown cryptic. "There's no place like Home," Dorothy says, clicking her heels together. "There's no place like Home. There's no place like Home."

On the one hand, you can interpret her as saying, "There's

no place as good as Home." But if you think about it, she could also mean, "There's no place in the world that feels like Home, because cousin, I've tried them all." I think you're doing Dorothy an injury to believe that after all her radical adventures, the only thing she can come up with is the first childlike alternative. You've got to believe that all the Trauma she's gone through, flying monkeys, sarcastic trees, enslavement etc., has rendered her more adult. When she clicks her blood-red heels together, returning to her stepparents in Kansas, it strikes me that Dorothy is yielding to Compromise. She understands that there's no first choice available, no true Home open to her, and she's making the best of a bad lot.

I've never wanted to do that. I've always wanted More than that. I want to know what More is like. Getting Paws back felt so fine, I've developed Greater Expectations. I want More. Please sir, More. I know I don't deserve it, but who does?

Jeez! Is that someone at the door?

TWENTY-NINE

A man is looking in the kitchen door. I am besieged. Also stupid to leave it open. Why didn't I lock the door? When did I grow so careless? Although they find me in the garden anyway. They trap me, these men.

I am busy, I say, scarcely turning my face.

I'm Jessie's grandfather, he says. If I could have a moment?

I said everything I know when her mother called the police.

I'm sure you did. But there's something I hoped to say to you.

This has nothing to do with me. Why can't anyone see that?

I'm sorry for the intrusion. If I could have a moment, I'd like to apologize for my granddaughter. From what I understand, the girl imposed on you, and I would like to apologize. I didn't bring my family up to be liars.

So. It would be suspicious not to hear him. I asked for none of this, I say, still making my tea.

And I'm very sorry you got caught up. My daughter should have supervised the girl. I've made this point. It should not fall to neighbours to supervise children.

They work all day and leave the girl running wild. Always in my garden.

It was an imposition. I should have taken the girl up home with me for the summer.

She should not have been left. However, it is the parents, I think, not the grandparents. At a certain point, one retires.

You've got a point there, he says. I glance at the man. He holds onto my door frame, clearly in pain. The hip, I think.

298

I appreciate this apology, I tell him. I have been treated like a criminal because I gave the girl some tea. It was weak tea with sugar and milk, as if it matters. I will not detain you further, but I appreciate this apology.

It was owed. My name is Henry Barfoot, and I'll be next door with my daughter and that. The girl contacts you, I would ask the favour of telling me. Police are likely to scare her off, but she'll come home if I say.

The police have made it clear that I am to contact them. I must do as they tell me. I wish no more trouble.

And yet, I think, if I sent the girl to this man, it might end without talk. I might be forgotten. But if the police truly scared her off so she didn't return? Would that not be better?

I remind myself that she will not contact me. My hope is that she loses herself in some other city and never comes back. What would I do if she came back? Living next door to that! I have made such a mistake, Father!

It is an upsetting subject, I say, to explain my shaking hands.

It is an upsetting subject, he agrees, and I would prefer it hadn't gone outside the family. I prefer not having the police involved, God bless 'em. All I ask is that you think about this. They would never have to know she contacted you. Girl thought the world of you. I heard nothing but Dr. V this and Dr. V that when I had her up home for the weekend. Should have kept her with me, but there you go. Now what we want is to get her back safe.

That is what we all want, yes. I hardly knew the girl, however. I gave her tea. If she thought the world of me, it was because she didn't know me at all. She made up some story that I am a retired professor from the university. I was a book-keeper. I kept house for my dear father. And the police treat me as if I am a criminal who tells lies.

Girl had some imagination, he says, shaking his head. It was a lack in her life, I believe. She never had a father.

At least that was not a lie, I say.

She told you about her father? He speaks keenly. The police also spoke keenly on this subject, but did not provide information. There is a mystery here, I think, but I do not wish to know it. I pour my tea and sit down in the chair, making a point of not inviting him in.

I told this to the police, I say. She merely remarked that her father had died before she was born. It was a family tragedy, she said, but did not specify. I was not concerned to ask her. This is none of my business.

I sip my tea. It is rude not to offer a chair and tea to this man, who is in pain. But I wish he would leave! Instead, he shakes his head.

That being the problem with the police, he says, God bless 'em. They're forced to poke their noses into everyone's business. I prefer to have less of that than more. If I could sit down, he says, taking a chair uninvited.

Excuse me, I cry, but I have far too many uninvited guests!

I apologize. Waiting in line for a hip replacement. Maybe another four months. Problem is, I rode a motorcycle in the service following the war. Courier. In your country, as a matter of fact. Cobbles down there in Nijmegen damn near did me in. Nijmegen, Arnhem. I was just a kid on a motorcycle, but it comes back to haunt you. She said you're from Amsterdam originally.

That much is true.

I was in Amsterdam. Fought through the winter down near Groesbeck. All those hills. Quite some fight to get Arnhem back from Jerry. I was just a kid, got in on the tag end of things. But I stayed on in the service after the war, like I say, and I had some leave there in Amsterdam. Yours is a beautiful city and country.

This is my country. I have lived here for more than fifty years.

I beg your pardon. I don't imagine your father fought in the armed resistance, either.

The girl made up stories. We were ordinary people. There is a mania these days for fame. Most of us have lived ordinary lives.

That is also true. We went along with what was coming along. When I hit eighteen back in '43, I signed up automatic the moment they'd take me. That was what you did back then, and you had no idea what you were in for. Few of us were heroes, no matter what they say. We were kids trying to stay alive, keep our buddies alive, and that's what your Jerry was doing, too. I hold no brief against your rank-and-file German soldier. He got sucked into the war same as I did. Now your Nazis, your officers, your Hitler, that's something else.

Clearly, an officer is something other than a soldier, I agree. But he is not mine. I was clearly not in the army. I am an ordinary person.

I am also an ordinary person. I will freely admit that I usually put two and two together long after I need to get four. Back in August, the girl's up visiting me and Mrs. Barfoot, being my wife. Girl natters on about the Dutch resistance, but it doesn't make much sense. She's also on about some German garbage. German books were not a popular item among the Dutch I met. I would say they hated Jerry. They were at great pains to assert their own history and identity. I heard about their Queen, not some King of the Elves. Girl didn't even know you had a queen. Have a queen, as a matter of fact. Takes some time, but it finally strikes me as a little off.

My queen is Queen Elizabeth of Canada.

I'm glad to hear you say that. She's a fine lady. And I believe it is possible to come to this country and assume a Canadian identity. You're very welcome. If I may say, I don't presume to judge what you might have done during the war, being a young girl then, and remembering what I had to do myself. I believe that I fought on the just side, but I was also lucky in my birth. If I'd been a young mutt in your Netherlands at the time, I can't presume what I would have been pressed to do, and what I would have done. I only hope that I would have grown to accept responsibility for my actions. I hope that I would not walk around this country wearing blinkers. And if I felt more comfortable in blinkers, which the Good Lord knows, many people do, I hope that I would at least have the sense to keep my opinions to myself. I don't take kindly to your filling my grand-daughter's head with Nazi crap, if I can make that much clear.

You said you wished to apologize to me, I say faintly. That is why you came here.

That also.

Liars in this family, I breathe.

I apologize for the fact you're drawn in. I would prefer this not to leave my family. If you hear from the girl, I would prefer that you told me, if I can make that clear, as well. I would also like to hear more about the boy you said she brought here.

I told the police. I told them she brought a boy, she said from school, but I was ill. I had no wish for company. They left. It was the last time I saw her, Sunday afternoon. She lied to me! She told me that she went to school. I had no idea that she was not registered in school, no matter what the police might claim. Nor can I remember seeing her during the day.

Neighbour on the other side, nice young lady, she saw my granddaughter with a boy on the street. I've got a description.

She also saw the girl talking with a bum outside the holy church. Panhandler. This youth admits to me there was a boy looking for my granddaughter. He can't remember a name, being a little loose in the head, but he doesn't like the boy. I put that to you as a marker.

I did not like this boy. I disliked him on sight. He was sly. But I saw him one minute. What can I tell you?

I would like to be sure of this boy's name. Her cousin has an idea, some runaway. I'm pretty sure I could find the kid. But I don't want to waste time looking if he's not the influence in question. I would prefer the certainty of a name. The police don't need to be involved if I find him.

And what is so certain about a name? I ask.

Matthew Cavanaugh, he says, watching my reaction. Already he can see the truth.

This is Matthew Cavanaugh from school, I say in the girl's quick voice. *I told you about him, so I thought it would be* OK.

He gets up, nodding. I wait to see if the hip is a lie, but he grimaces. One almost admires him. But when he pauses in the doorway, my breath fails.

Now you got me on this one, he says. I don't mind you didn't give the name to the police, but I can't say as I see why. You got it down pretty clear. Why say the boy was here if you're not going to give 'em the name?

And if someone has seen him at my door, does it not make more trouble for me not to say? All this makes so much trouble for me! I do not like this boy!

Still he watches from the doorway.

Whose father taught him something about the war. He also thinks he understands about some Dutch girl from long ago. Why does your granddaughter speak so much? She has no idea what she says.

You're right there, he replies. I may say in her favour that she didn't understand your meaning. If she had, she wouldn't have given you the time of day. Not the way I brought her up. The old man stops to think. But now she knows what you are, he says, I would guess that you don't expect to hear from her.

I do not expect to hear, I say.

Finally, he nods.

You may rest out your time on this earth as far as I'm concerned.

You don't know who I am, I tell him weakly. You and the boy, you cannot know.

I know who you are, he replies. Feel punished?

I meet his eyes.

There will be no peace, I say.

THIRTY

Friday, September 29

We left the house after lunch, the people's charter being due
back from Ireland at 4:45 p.m. Mrs. Bum was a painstaking
Housewife and had been keeping the place unsullied all
along, but in the final hours she made it especially nice for
the Mahoods, scrubbing and wiping it with rubber gloves,
which Mr. Bum approved on account of Fingerprints. She also
added Touches, i.e. turning down their sheets like the magazines did and putting After Eight mints on their pillows. Mr.
Bum had previously eaten all of the After Eights in doobie-
related hunger, but the Mrs. made him shop to refresh supplies,
and on his own he'd added a new cat cage to carry Paws away
in. He pointed out that removing the cage from the furnace
room would have constituted Theft, and it's true we're not
Thieves and shouldn't appear so, distressing the Mahoods with
intimidations that their house guests had not been respectable
people, even though we aren't.

Before leaving, I stopped to look at the plumped living-
room cushions and the chrysanthemums fresh from the
garden, feeling bad that they might miss Paws even though he
wasn't their cat. I ran back up to the bathroom, finding an old
lipstick in a colour Mrs. Mahood shouldn't have worn anyway
and writing on the mirror with my left hand, *I'll take care of
Kitty.* Then I realized they wouldn't see the message before
growing worried and ran back downstairs, writing the same

305

thing left-handedly on the mirror above the fireplace. I was going to throw out the lipstick, then realized that the only reason Mrs. Mahood would have retained such an inappropriate colour was for Sentimental Reasons, i.e. she'd worn it when she was young and improbably happy. So we wiped off the lipstick tube and left it on the mantel, Matthew having acquired a piece of cloth to wipe down everything I touched, following behind me like a paranoid puppy dog, which probably defines him.

Then we left, Matthew losing the key in a Dumpster because we can't go back, which makes me feel sad. We've had to come to a Homeless camp on the waterfront, where Persons have built shacks and fire circles on abandoned industrial ground. It wouldn't be my first choice, except that I can't think of a first choice. I can't think of any choices at all. I'm just following Matthew around to see what he'll come up with, which I hope ends up being better than this. Not to be impolite, but Paws doesn't like it here. Matthew bought him a red harness and leash so he doesn't have to stay in the cage, but the harness is an indignity that makes him crouch beside me with his ears lowered, looking up reproachfully. The Smells must assault his sensitive nose, all the soot and chemicals, diesel blasts from noisy trucks, garbage winds, gull shit and the decayed sewage odour of Persons who need showers, not that it's their fault.

I don't understand the vocabulary here. Everyone has a joke name, a Street name: Warrior, Boo, Starling, Mohawk, Elvis. I don't know whether you're supposed to take them seriously or not. I tried to assume the name Dorothy myself, but instantly Mohawk, who's this Mohawk guy, shortened it to Dottie. That's an expression Gramps uses so I know what it means. Poor woman, she's gone Dottie. I tried to take it back but they won't let me. Hey Dottie, Hi Dottie, Persons call, at least when they don't talk about quote, jailbait. Matthew walks differently here, which I don't like. Cock of the walk, one of them calls, crowing like a rooster. Entomologically speaking, the Persons use a great deal of animal imagery, and Warrior amuses himself by applying it ironically to Paws.

"Someone let the cat out of the bag," he said the first time he saw us, laughing so hard he doubled over, this skinny older guy in his twenties half hidden by greasy hair and tattoos.

"Is this a cat-and-mouse game?" he asked, wandering past.

"Here, Kitty, Kitty, Kitty."

"Hel-lo, Kitty," he greeted me, making Matthew leap up with a Look on his face that got me anxious. "All right, man," Warrior said, backing off.

We're supposed to share this shack with someone who isn't here yet, and I hate to think what he smells like. Matthew says that he and the guy are buddies from last summer. He uses a rougher tone of voice around here, and I've found myself listening to the tone as much as the words, wondering who this new semi-Matthew Person is. I don't know why he's got to change like this. I don't understand why people call him Score. I especially don't understand why Matthew's being so compliant to this tall flash man who just pulled up in his shiny red penis car, this little sporting car he could barely pull himself out of. Who knows what's in the package Flashman's handing Matthew?

I do. I'm not Stupid.

I'm vastly Stupid, having believed that Matthew earned all that money from Spare Change.

He makes me keep my Wad hidden in my panties. What if word gets out? That self-acclaimed Warrior makes me anxious. I don't know how I'm supposed to protect myself when Matthew goes to quote, work. I don't know what I'm supposed to do all day. Try to clean up the Homeless camp? Roll a boulder uphill and watch it roll back down? I'll have to go to work with Matthew, except the last thing I want to do is tie myself up in That.

You know what I really want? I want to go Home to Kingston and curl up on the sofa with my Mom, our legs all intertwined, something good on TV, Paws deigning to lie on my stomach. That's all I really want.

To look on the bright side, I got Paws back. But Paws used to take care of me, agreeing to sit on my lap when he sensed I was Blue, his warm coat gleaming in the sun. Now he's filthy and keeps trying to run away from loud noises so I have to tie his leash around my wrist. Sometimes he starts panting, looking up at me Hopelessly, his eyes rolling back. Poor Paws wants me to take care of him and I have no clue how.

I guess I'm probably immature. I'm just not ready to grow up yet. I don't know how you're supposed to take responsibility in this metastatic Mega-City, this Homeless Home, pocketed with Evil. It makes me so anxious that Evil is out there. Of course it is. Why wouldn't it be? The Amoeba is so formless and embracing that Evil is going to find a place inside it, just like everything else. It's going to multiply, just like everything else. And I have no clue how to stop it. I'm fifteen years old, and I don't have a single clue how to handle this whole huge Globalizing world.

Look, you can keep your Crucial. I just want this awful Tornado to whirl me back in time. I want to go back to a time when things were simple and unknown. I want to go back! And I especially refuse

Later

Matthew came and sat down beside me, interrupting my writing. I took the opportunity to tell him that I especially refuse to live off Traffic. He looked at me for a long time, smiling weirdly.

"What do you think you've been doing all this time?"

"I didn't understand that before. I'm Stupid, ok? But I'm going to pay you back half of everything, and all of Paws's cage and his leash."

"What do you think you were doing all those years, living with Cooper? My old buddy Cooper. All those trips to Mexico. His place out in the country. How does Cooper increase his income sufficient to his tastes?"

Matthew is a Liar. It came to me quite clearly that Matthew is a Liar. That simplifies everything, doesn't it? I put poor shivering Paws back in his cage and my Diary into my backpack.

"Where you think you're going?" Matthew asked.

Not that I deigned to answer. He walked along beside me as I left the camp, which wasn't really for Homeless Persons because it was their Home. As a truly Homeless Person, I didn't belong there. I had to leave, walking away from the waterfront. Paws was heavy, but I thought I could manage, even though it was hard not to bump his cage against my leg as I walked. I had to put him down quite often, sometimes standing beside him to rest and sometimes finding a bench. It was turning cold, getting dark. The street lamps blinked on with an electrical jitter as the orange sun set.

I ignored Matthew when he offered to carry Paws. I ignored him anyway, trudging north. I think it was ten o'clock when I finally reached this little park near Dr. V's house. Matthew is a Liar and he lied about her, too. It's too late to go there now, but I'll sleep on this bench tonight and see her first thing tomorrow. Dr. V will help me. She'll know what to do. She has to, since I don't.

"So you're giving in and going home," Matthew said, not that I deigned to correct him. "Life is a little rough out there for Miss Priss. Who do you think you are, Jess? Some cut above? You think everyone should lie down and roll over for you?"

He phrased it like Rhetorical questions. But Rhetorical implied you knew the answers and I did not.

"You know where to find me," Matthew said.

It's nighttime in the city. Orange lamps glow above. People shamble by. Dogs bark. It's cold. I'm anxious. What's new?

THIRTY-ONE

It is a relief to take the decision. One gains perspective, under-standing that nothing is important. I have said this frequently in life, but chiefly in an effort to convince myself. Now I know that it is true.

It does not really matter what happens to your house, Father. Understanding this has lifted a burden from my shoul-ders. I have felt crushed by the weight of this house and the question of inheritance. But to whom would I will your house if I held onto life as long and hard as you did? There will be nobody then as there is nobody now. I will allow the bureau-crats to dispose of the estate. They will no doubt hold many satisfactory committee meetings before they do so.

Of course I have tidied. One wishes them to find everything in order. The police will find it next time they return to ques-tion the suspicious old woman.

What will they find? Nothing. There is nothing left. No will left. I make a pun! It is quite amusing, actually. And the sunset, spectacular.

Now the night is quiet. The effect of these pills is not unpleas-ant. I will not mix them with alcohol as is suggested; it is unchar-acteristic. However, I believe I have broken the oven correctly. The combination of pills and gas should do the trick. I do not care if I have broken your oven, Father. It is not uncomfortable to kneel here. Foolish old woman, to think of physical comfort at a moment like this! The knees are numbed now, that is all.

What do you say, Father?

Ah yes, Maaike van der Velde. Miss Maaike van der Velde.

So. It is him. He has come. I have been expecting him, this ghost who haunts me. It is our old conversation which haunts me. I do not believe in ghosts. I do not believe I will see anyone again in some extra dimension. I believe in nothing.

Yet if I am wrong, I will see Jannie there. I will see you, Father. So, it might not be so bad, fire, brimstone and all.

Go on, old ghost.

Maaike van der Velde. Miss Maaike van der Velde. My Gertrud speaks of you often. She speaks of you highly! Such an example to the other girls. Such an example to the boys and girls!

I'm glad to hear you say so, sir. I always like to be of help.

I did, it is true. I only spoke the truth to this man. I have spoken the truth again recently and look where it has got me.

This is what it is like to be of help, it is true. One receives merely sarcasm and dislike. Listen to your heavy sarcasm, old ghost.

No doubt, no doubt. It is the wish of all good Dutch citizens to be of help to the Reich. I have noticed this. Yes.

But I have something to tell you, sir. Do you have time for me to tell you something important? Or should we meet in person?

You have something to tell me?

Yes, I did. Your sarcasm did not stop me. I had something to tell you, and I do not attempt to deny it.

That sermonizing grandfather the other day, telling me that he hoped he had grown to accept responsibility for his actions. He hoped he did not walk around wearing blinkers.

Where do you find these blinkers? Excuse me, I grew up in a time of rationing. We had few luxuries such as blinkers. We had to use what we had available.

God help us, we used our eyes.

I have learned about activities, sir. If I make myself clear, there is something hidden which must be brought to light. Will you see me, sir?

Miss Maaike, I am busy. If you have something to tell me, you tell me now. What do you have to tell me, Maaike van der Velde?

Do you remember Florrie Brouwer, sir?

Poor Florrie.

I remember the girl, yes.

She's awfully busy, sir. She goes all over town.

What of it, Maaike? People go all over town looking for food. That's the way things work these days.

But she has food, sir. She delivers it to a place where there aren't supposed to be people living. She delivers food to the building where her cousin Johanna works, I've watched her. Most of those offices are closed, sir. Yet the people next door admit they've heard movement at very odd hours. There must be someone hidden there, sir. I can give you the address, but that's not all.

What more, Miss van der Velde?

In the attic window, upstairs in Florrie's grandmother's house, I have most clearly seen the face of Pieter Verhoef. You remember Pieter Verhoef, sir. He's supposed to be working in a factory in Germany. He was called up. He shouldn't be in Amsterdam, sir.

This is what I said. Yes, this is what I said. Jannie believed that Pieter Verhoef turned in Florrie and her family and friends but he did not. No, he did not. I hated Florrie for being the walking proof of my naïveté, my weakness, my stupidity, my mistakes. Of my innocence, old ghost. So you see, I got rid of my innocence. Young people often wish to.

I presume the Gestapo shot Pieter when they broke into his attic, or soon after. They would have hated him for making fools of them. It is too bad, although it is also true that Pieter was a soldier and died in his cause. One must respect him for that.

As for the others, Poland. I have recently read a book by a scholar suggesting that many more prisoners survived the work camps in Poland than was previously believed. This is not a popular author. However, he has a doctorate, and it is my hope that one day his research will prove true. One wishes that these people had been allowed to live out their lives, after all.

Poor Florrie Brouwer; perhaps she lives out her dramatic life in Poland. It is a country with a dramatic history and culture. I hope that she and her cousins and their Jewish friends have lived happily there. I hope that you were not damned by being forced to act on my insistent information, old ghost. I understand, of course, that you might have been damned by many things you did before I called. In that case, it is possible I gave you something to sincerely repent. After all, you had a daughter.

Did you never repent, Father?

You are right. It would have done no good.

Would it?

THIRTY-TWO

Murray? What's that screaming? Someone's screaming outside. It sounds like Jess. It's not my Jess? Jessie?

Wait for me. Be careful on those stairs. We'll get there. We'll get there.

Jessie? Jessie?

What's that racket?

It's Jessie, Dad. She's out here. *Jessie!*

Somebody help me please!

Oh God, it's my baby. She's there. I can see her. She's just next door. Murray, she's there. Jessie! My baby!

Just let me open the gate. Be careful. Be careful. It's OK, there's no one else in here. There's no one in here but Jess.

Oh God, baby, she kept you here, didn't she? That old witch. She had you in here all along.

She's dead. The old lady's dead. She's all blue and cold and she's got her head in the oven.

You come with me, baby. Murray will fix it. Murray's going to call the police. Murray?

You OK, Jess?

I've got to get Paws. We can't forget Paws. He's right over there. I want to get Paws.

Oh my God, Murray, she's got the cat. That old witch even had the cat. Daddy? Daddy, that old witch had Jessie. She even had the cat. She was right next door all along.

She was not right next door. Jessie Barfoot, what you been up to? Been putting your mother to all this worry. Young lady,

you've got lots to answer for. Now you get back at the house.
Get back at the house and no more nonsense. I'll have no more
of this nonsense. You hear?

. . . Still, for a long moment, I stood in that garden. I stood in
that garden with one clear thought in my head.

Matthew is right. The world hands you enough scars that
you don't need to resort to self-infliction. It's a hard enough
place without making things harder for yourself. There are
no fairy tales out there any more. You can't hide behind
metaphor and illusion, no matter how hard you try. The
mean old world is going to sneak up and make you face it
right on.

So, face it right on. How bad can it possibly be? Aside from
the fact that you've just seen your first dead body. And your
mother is crying, which is embarrassing. She's crying and she's
wrong, which is worse.

And look, there's Pudge, staring in the old lady's doorway.
He's closing it quickly. Look, there's Gramps. He's old.

It's true, Gramps is old. That old man can't protect you any
more. They're not going to protect you, Jess. You have to grow
up. Matthew is right: You can't go backward, you don't have
any choice. Life surges forward, like Niagara Falls. That's just
the way it is.

And this Fall garden at dawn is the most beautiful thing I
have ever seen.

I've got to get that digital camera.

Of course you do, baby. We'll get you whatever you want. We're going to make a whole new start.

So many pictures everywhere. Look at the frost on that little red leaf. It's all white around the edges. It's just so internally luminous. I could take a picture of that.

You're so smart, you can do anything you want. Now come on home. Let's go home. Please come home, baby.

But you've got bare feet. Look at your bare feet. You shouldn't have come out here in bare feet.

She sounds so grown-up. Listen to her, Murray.

What's so funny, Jess?

I'm sorry, it's just . . . I want to leave now. I want to get out of this goddamned place. Come on, let's get out of this goddamned place.

What are you talking about, baby?

You don't want to catch your death out here, that's all.

EPILOGUE

Monday, September 3

Labour Day again, my second Labour Day in Toronto. It's a time of year that always brings out the melancholic in me. The warm kindness of the air begins to wane. At night you feel a crisp warning in the wind, while the trees start to drop their facade of freshness and make their amber demands upon your eyes. I've already seen a small tree assuming its fall colours down the block. They might try to call this autumn, but really, it's fall. The fall of openness, a drop in possibilities. You have to go back to school again tomorrow as if nothing ever changes, when it does.

Actually, I have to admit that it's not so bad to go to an alternative school. When I transferred in after Christmas, it didn't take me long to discover that the teachers let you get away with almost everything. Well, you don't have to admit *that*, but I sometimes let on to Michelle that I enjoy certain parts of school. It keeps her happy, and I've belatedly discovered that life is easier if you keep people happy. Their happiness builds a scaffolding around you, holding you up.

Think of the double meaning in quote, holding you up. Sustaining you, detaining you. They detain you because sustaining you takes time. In some ways, I guess it's probably not so bad to take it slow. It makes you want to claw the walls sometimes, but it's probably not a bad idea, at least until you finish high school next June and can legally get out.

318

Get out in a normal fashion, I mean, the way every graduate wants to. Art school at the other end of the country, etc. I don't think there's anything abnormal in staking your hopes on that.

Meanwhile, what can I say to sum up my second summer in Toronto? It was better than my first one, that's for sure. I'm starting to be able to think rationally about that first summer, although I still seem to see the mental pictures of roses, cages, alleyways etc. from a distance. Well, even at the time I talked about looking through the wrong end of a telescope, how it gave you a distanced perspective. *Perspective* might not be the right word for what I had, although it's a kind one. I don't think there's anything wrong with being kind, to yourself as well as others. That's probably what I've learned from having a baby in the house. They respond so unstintingly to human kindness—feeding, rocking etc.—gurgling like these little brooks. In fact, I'm sure we all feel the same way. We yearn for kindness like water. So why not give it out sometimes and hope that a portion flows back?

I'm glad Michelle had another girl, actually. Maybe this time she can get it right. It's too bad I've ended up being so quote, difficult. On the other hand, it will probably feed my Art. Photography being an art form, I don't care what anyone says. Artists all have shitty childhoods, so why should I be any different? It might have been nice to be the exception that proved the rule, but that's not how it worked out, and I'll be all right.

I don't want Baby Emma to have a shitty childhood, however. The world doesn't need to be filled with artists. Aside from anything else, somebody needs to buy your work. You can already tell that Baby is intelligent from her eyes, so I think she should be a lawyer. Judging from Pudge, lawyers are very well-adjusted people who can crank up their income when they need to, i.e. to buy a new house in a better neighbourhood far, far away from that abandoned place next door.

Abandoned or discarded? She shucked it off, she shucked off life like a butterfly shucking off her chrysalis. Shrink says I shouldn't think like that, how there's nothing attractive in what the old lady did. Nothing compelling or seductive. She said herself that there's not necessarily any improvement when a caterpillar becomes a butterfly. "Perhaps a butterfly is just a caterpillar in disguise." But I like to think she was freed by what happened. I'm responsible for her death, after all. Yes, I am, Dr. Shrink. I'm the one who let out her secret. I accept responsibility. Just let me try to shine the best light upon it.

It's sick, but in this new nightmare I've been having lately, I'm setting up lights around what I saw in the kitchen that morning, photographing the crime scene. I know that's sick, the slow-motion circling around her. As if I needed to make photographs. As if I'll ever forget what I saw.

I'm all right. I'm all right. I'm going to be all right.

I think I am, actually.

I like this new staid and leafy neighbourhood, even if my friends don't live nearby. There's something relaxing in the well-kept predictability of the houses, and the elementary school is supposed to be one of the best in the city, which is exactly what Baby deserves. The local Collegiate may not have worked for me, but it might eventually work for her. Meanwhile, Flatbread Alternative is only a short bike ride away, and I've got plans for my final year. Now that I've dropped math, I think I can probably get away with making photographs for nearly every assignment, writing those few crucial lines underneath to subvert the meaning of my images, asking you to question what you see.

Cutlines. That's the newspaper term. Lines cutting into the images, right? It was fun working on the newspaper this summer. OK, so it's only a giveaway from the local print shop and T.J. hardly paid me anything, but I was lucky to find it. Pudge was good enough to find it for me. Pudge is a good person, I admit, just like Michelle. Maybe they're a bit jejune in their tastes, but that's not surprising. Most people are. They want me to take the usual baby pictures of Emma, and I'll keep doing that. But I'm also planning to step up my own project, waiting until Baby's out of the picture before I take it, if that makes any sense.

This is how it works: Michelle lifts her out of the crib and I shoot the little hollow Baby leaves in her bedding. Michelle lifts her off her blanket where she's been wriggling and tossing toys, and I shoot the wrinkled blanket with its periphery of rattles. That strikes me as the most interesting thing about babies. Their personalities aren't developed yet, so they're fairly absent from the scene. You read into them. When I complete the project, my images are going to give you more to read into. They'll underline the process that you're already engaged in.

"That's a very interesting idea," says Michelle, looking at the first shots over my shoulder. "But I miss her little curls."

You can't have everything. I think I have to accept that it will take time to develop a discriminating audience for my work. You might even say that your audience is another artistic creation. At least, that's what Alex says, and he's pretty shrewd.

Better than shrewd. Alex is so talented and smart that I think he's even managed to get rid of Matthew Cavanaugh. Which is also best for Matthew, when you think about it, so the courts don't find him. Matthew would probably get far worse than parental custody. The Mahoods seem unnaturally hyped on punishment, if you ask me. I understand their diminished sense of security and I'm really sorry. But they might think of it this way: Sometimes you struggle to understand what happened, and then you let go. You try to, anyway.

Michelle is wrong to call Alex a tough, however. He should be welcomed more enthusiastically into the house. Michelle and Pudge don't get the fact that he's an exceptional visual artist despite his rough background. Also because of it, just like me. And the fact we're going to Art School in Vancouver next year is entirely my idea, thank you very much. You should be happy, Michelle. We'll be getting a new start.

By the way, if you're reading this diary to find out about my sex life, you're wasting your time. It's none of your business. How's your sex life after Baby, by the way? What was that you said to Francie on the phone the other day? How it's a dim but pleasant memory?

"Jessie's always going to be a handful," you told her. "She always has been. But I think she's learning to handle herself a little better, anyway. Dr. Ripkin is optimistic."

He makes your teeth hurt, he's so optimistic. But he's right, they're right. I have myself in hand. I open my hand and there I am, a seed.

That's what happens at the end of summer. Plants go to seed. A more promising view of the fall.

I like the double meaning of quote, promise, too. I promise I'll live up to my promise.

Alex says the world is such a bugger that most artists don't succeed. But maybe I'll be one of the exceptions, you never know.

ACKNOWLEDGEMENTS

Many people in Canada and the Netherlands were kind enough to offer support, encouragement and help with research during the writing of this book. I'd like to extend special thanks to Herman Divendal in Amsterdam, who proved wonderfully kind and adept at bringing people together. Mies Bouhuys was particularly gracious in sharing her experiences of life in the Resistance as well as her perceptions of the role of collaborators during the Second World War. A.C. Haak, historian with Friends of the Park, offered timely information about the accessibility of the De Hoge Veluwe National Park in 1942.

I'd also like to thank both the Toronto Arts Council and the Ontario Arts Council for grants that helped free the time I needed to write this book.

For their work in bringing it to publication, I owe an enormous debt to my agent, Jackie Kaiser, and editor, Diane Turbide, both of whom laughed in all the right places and offered shrewd advice throughout. Copy editor Cheryl Cohen was particularly good-humoured about tackling the grammatical oddities of my characters' diaries. Gabe Knox helped greatly with the vocabulary, collecting malapropisms and correcting slang. As always, my husband, Paul Knox, offered unstinting support, and I am deeply grateful.

This book is dedicated to my friend Sharon Stevenson, a poet who was greatly concerned with questions of responsibility and guilt.